DAYTIME AFFAIR

Joshua Lorne

D0332932

AVON
PUBLISHERS OF BARD, CAMELOT, DISCUS, EQUINOX AND FLARE BOOKS

DAYTIME AFFAIR is an original publication of Avon Books.
This work has never before appeared in any form.

DAYTIME AFFAIR is a work of fiction. The details, the names,
and the characters are not intended to, and do not, relate to
any real persons living or dead.

AVON BOOKS
A division of
The Hearst Corporation
959 Eighth Avenue
New York, New York 10019

ISBN: 0-380-00150-0

First Avon Printing, November, 1974.

AVON TRADEMARK REG. U.S. PAT. OFF. AND
FOREIGN COUNTRIES, REGISTERED TRADEMARK—
MARCA REGISTRADA, HECHO EN CHICAGO, U.S.A.

Printed in the U.S.A.

"COMPULSIVELY READABLE . . . RIGHT UP THERE WITH THE BIG ONES!"

Publishers Weekly

Sweeping across the sound stage, into the dressing-rooms, and up through the very corridors of power at United Broadcasting's soaring skyscraper——DAYTIME AFFAIR reveals the turbulent saga of **Phillip Searing**, producer of AFFAIR OF THE HEART——whose skill at corporate in-fighting is equalled by his raw sensual urges, and whose one dark secret could destroy him . . . **Vanessa Langley,** who must choose between a starring role and her unborn child . . . **Elliot Chamberfield**, who uses every trick in the book to get to the top, and would drag his own mother through the muck to stay there . . . **Gaye Vulkner**, the network president's daughter, whose enormous sensual appetite. and exotic tastes propel her to new highs, on camera and off . . . **Brian Hocholtz,** scandal sheet reporter whose taste for dirt brings him to Gaye . . .

THESE ARE THE PRINCIPAL ACTORS IN THIS NOVEL OF DUSKY PASSION AND EARTHY HUMAN DRIVES . . . THE BOLD, BRAZEN WORLD OF THE

DAYTIME AFFAIR

For Claude Judith
and for her . . . love

1.

He watched impassively as the tears coursed down her cheeks. A golden late-afternoon light beamed through the hospital window. She leaned down and brushed back a lock of the child's hair fallen onto the tiny dead face. The nurse, teary-eyed, slipped out of the door; the lock clicked softly and the woman was alone. Trailing a weighted hand carelessly behind her, she crossed to the window and stared out into her sorrow.

He was on the far side of the window, in the shadows, but she gave no indication of having seen him; nothing to show he even existed in her world—until she winked. He glanced instinctively up at the monitor. Camera one had the closing shot—across the bed, the motionless little girl, and the brave right profile of Gwen's tear-stained face. It was a left-eye wink. The camera wouldn't catch it. The organ music built its pathos, milking the hearts of 7.8 percent of all the housewives in America. The crescendo, the hold; the monitor faded to black. Phillip checked the studio clock. On the nose—twenty-eight minutes thirty-five seconds after the hour. Not a bad show. He made a note to compliment the director. Poor guy had been through the mill the past few weeks. He was due for a boost of the spirit.

The commercial blared out the jarring jingle and the studio dimmed from Klieg to worklights. Assistant set decorators moved in and started clearing the set. The dead child bounded out of bed. Her mother was ready with her street clothes. Half an hour to make it to an audition at Paramount. "We've got to hustle, darling, you've just been killed out of a job."

The three cameramen rolled the big color cameras back against the wall. They capped them and went up to scheduling. Phillip finished his notes and handed the whole legal pad to the girl next to him. She had been assigned for the three days he was in town. "These are for the art director and Fogarty down in the scenic shop. Make sure I get a carbon, dear, and ask them to give me estimates as fast as possible."

"Yes, sir. Will you have anything for the actors?"

"No. Just what I told them this afternoon. I have no complaints. I wish all our shows were doing this well."

She hurried out.

"Mr. Searing?" The resonant tones of a theater-trained voice sounded behind him. It was a young studio page with a note in his hand. "Mr. Chamberfield's office phoned from New York. They'd like you to call back right away."

"Thank you."

"It's the second time they called today."

"No, it isn't. It's the fourth." Phillip ducked under a low microphone boom and walked over to the rapidly vanishing hospital set. Gwen was still there, wiping the teary glycerine from her cheeks with a tissue. She released her hair from the little blue ribbon that gathered it at the neck and looked up and smiled when he approached. "That ought to hold the ladies of the afternoon."

"If I ever catch you winking off-camera again I'll can you."

"You would have to plant yourself right outside the damn window."

Phillip thought of the first time they met. He had been the sponsor's representative for a show on which she had a bit part. She played a nun who brought a food package to the house of a destitute invalid . . . a one-shot deal.

8

Phillip was new on the show and spent most of his day wandering about the converted movie stage with his hands stuffed into his pockets. Later in the afternoon Gwen managed to place herself near him just after she came off-camera. "You're with the sponsor, aren't you?" she asked.

"Yes," he said pleasantly.

"Goodhart Soap Company?"

"Yes."

"I like your soaps very much."

Dressed as she was in the flowing black habit, her fingers entwined in rosary beads, Gwen was the picture of purity. She wore no lipstick, and a beatific smile crinkled her good pink cheeks. The young advertising man couldn't tell whether she was serious or putting him on. Nobody said things like that. It just wasn't done, but he answered "I'm glad to hear it."

"Oh, yes," she said sweetly, "Goodhart Soaps. I use them all the time—for dishes, and for my dainty things, and for fucking in the shower. The lather feels so much nicer than trombone oil." And with that she raised her eyes to heaven and floated off humming "Nearer My God to Thee."

That was a few years ago. Now he was with the network, not the sponsor, and he had moved up to vice president of daytime programing with eight shows under his executive command; he had precious little time to walk around with his hands stuffed in his pockets.

A couple of stagehands rolled off two walls of the three-walled set. Gwen turned her back, wiggled out of her bra, and twisted into a tight red jersey. The loudspeaker spoke. "Is Phillip Searing out there?"

"Yes, Roger, I'm here."

"Oh, Mr. Searing, Mr. Chamberfield's office in New York called twice while we were on the air. The girl said it was urgent they reach you."

The formality of the director, twenty years older than he, made the young executive smile. A good man, Roger. Refreshing to work with someone with manners. "Thank you. You gave us a good show today. *Main Street*'s getting tighter every week."

"I'm glad you liked it, Mr. Searing."

"Oh, and by the way, Roger."

"Yes, Mr. Searing?"

"You're fired."

There was a momentary freeze in all studio life. Heads turned, ears cocked, feet stopped shuffling. Phillip allowed the pause to play out its full curve before adding: "Unless you learn to address me by my first name."

"Yes, sir," said the director of the show. The relief was audible. "Would you like us to get New York for you?"

"No, that's all right. Give me a call, though, at the hotel tonight, would you please? I'd like to talk a little, but basically the show has no problems at all."

"That's good to hear."

The actress scooped up her handbag and the two of them moved toward the exit. "I'll only have time for lunch," she said. "We have a read-through of tomorrow's script at four."

"I have some calls to make myself."

The steward of the Stagehands Union came up the stairs. He offered a mock half bow and stepped out of their way. "Mr. Searing!"

"Bob, I've got to give you credit. The sets are down and the props are struck. You've even got the cigarette butts off the floor already. I'm astonished. You fellows really know how to haul ass when there's no chance of milking us out of some overtime."

"You know us, boss-boss. Salt of the studio. Always trying to save the company money." He put a match to the pipe he had packed. He was a soft-spoken man whose sense of humor shone through twinkling brown eyes.

"I know that, Bob, and don't think we don't appreciate that offer you made to take a voluntary across-the-board cut in salary. I'm going back to New York on Tuesday and I'm going to see if we muck-a-mucks can't work it out for you."

"Please do, Phillip. Our consciences have been bothering us since the last contract talks we had. We'd like to give a little of that money back."

"Right. I know just how you feel. I'll see what I can do to help you. So long, Bob."

"Good-bye, Mr. Searing. Give my regards to Broadway." He grinned at Phillip and flashed a quick wink at Gwen.

"I didn't think union and management were speaking to each other," she said as they moved toward the exit.

"Bob's a good man. A very good man."

"Aren't you going to call your boss?"

"When I get around to figuring out what he wants."

"He said it was urgent."

"I've already spoken to him twice today. Anything really urgent would have been discussed then. He's got something up and I'd like to guess what before I speak to him."

"You two are still feuding, are you?"

"Don't you ever tell anybody you know about that." Phillip shouldered open the massive door that led to the Los Angeles sunshine. They stepped into a wall of summertime heat. "If the Lord had only been as clever as our air-conditioning department!"

They walked down the narrow alley between the sound stages to where he had parked the car in the morning. It was a rented white Thunderbird that would rack up very little mileage, except for the one daily round trip from the Bel Air hotel to one or another studio. Phillip unlocked the passenger door and the actress slipped in. She jumped from the burn on the black-leather upholstery, then reached over and unlocked the driver's door. She took a plastic raincoat from her bag and put it under her legs. "Phillip, I've got an hour and a quarter before I have to be back."

"So?"

"We could go over to my place, couldn't we?"

"Let's just stick to lunch," he said, and patted her knee. "We'll spend the weekend together."

The sun glared brilliantly, even through the sulphuric haze that was called the Los Angeles sky. Phillip swung the car out. As they approached the main gate, the guard on duty stepped out of his air-conditioned cubbyhole and waved them down. He was dressed in the network's blue and white with the logo of Republic Broadcasting International stitched to his breast pocket. A gleaming silver, twenty-five-year company clip held a pre-tied tie in place. "Mr. Searing, Mr. Chamberfield has been trying to reach you from New York." He spoke with the halting quality of one who has served others for many years.

"Yes, thank you, I know about the calls."

"You can talk to him on the phone in my booth, if you like."

"No, I'll take care of it later."

11

The old man pressed his gray mustache outward along the sides of his mouth. He was ill at ease. "Sir, I have instructions not to open the gate for you until you talk to Mr. Chamberfield's office."

"You have what!" The voice level didn't change, but the tone was furious.

"I'm sorry, sir. Yes, sir, I was told to have you call him right away when you got here."

Phillip stared at him in amazement. "And just what happens if I don't?"

Gwen touched his arm for calm. "It's not this man's fault, Phillip, but it could cost him his job."

Searing turned to her, but spoke more to himself. "Chamberfield has been on my back ever since I stepped into his old job. And since last week the pressure's been incredible. There's something up and I can't figure out what it is." He opened the car door and climbed out, leaving the motor running for Gwen's air-conditioned comfort. "All right, Officer. Will you get him on the line for me, please?"

"Yes, sir. Right this way, sir." The little man practically bounced to his booth. He held the door ajar, but Searing placed his hand on the man's shoulder and guided him in first.

The connection was made. "Searing here, for Elliot Chamberfield."

A female voice piped up three thousand miles away. "We've finally got you. Mr. Chamberfield has been trying all morning." Her tone was dressed in the annoyance of her boss. How unpleasant she's become, he thought. Why is it secretaries have a tendency to assume the uglier qualities of their employers? "Is he there now, Rosalynann?"

Some clicks, a hum, a longish pause, and "Where the hell have you been?" Phillip recoiled from the blast. He should have known better than to keep the phone too close to his ear. Chamberfield never spoke when he could shout, and rarely shouted when he could scream. "You've been avoiding me, goddammit! I know you've been on that set all day. When I call, you answer! I've got better things to do than sit around waiting for you to return my calls, you understand, Searing? Searing, are you there?"

After a moment or so of silence, Phillip brought the

receiver back to his ear. He spoke pleasantly. "What is it you want, Elliot? We talked twice this morning."

"I don't give a damn if you have to keep the fucking thing taped to your head. When I call I expect a response."

Phillip held his temper and kept his answers cool, because he knew how that, more than anything, bugged the hell out of his boss. "Did you have a reason for calling, Elliot, or was it just to chat?"

"I want you back here first thing tomorrow morning."

"Tomorrow? I wasn't planning on coming back until Tuesday."

"I need you here for a meeting."

He had counted on the long Memorial Day weekend for a much-deserved unwinding with Gwen in her cabin at Tahoe. "Elliot, is it really that important that I be there?"

"Do you think I would have called you if it weren't important? I want you in this office at ten o'clock tomorrow morning. And Searing, don't be late!" The phone was slammed down with a deafening crash.

He returned to the Thunderbird and steered it through the gate. "It's off, sweetie, I've got to go."

"Tonight?"

"Yeah. I'll have to finish up quickly and grab the Red Eye Express back this evening."

"How about the weekend on the lake?"

"I'm sorry, I don't have any choice."

"You really do wreak havoc on one's social calendar."

He took her hand and pressed it to his lips. The car was moving down Highland Avenue toward the Boulevard. "I'll have to take care of some things before I go. Where shall I drop you off?"

"Hamburger Heaven, I guess, on Sunset. I'll grab a cab back to the studio later." They rode in silence for a block or two. She stared at his near-perfect features . . . high brow, iron-gray eyes, with crow's feet deep enough to show he knew how to laugh. He always reminded her of a Kennedy with his tall, elegant good looks, his unflappability. "Will you be back soon, Phillip?"

"Hard to tell. I can only justify it when I'm needed and the shows on this coast are doing pretty well. It's the New York group that's giving us the headache."

"What's with your boss, anyway?"

"Elliot? He just likes to play power games, that's all.

13

He knows he can't get me on the big things, so he enjoys sticking pins in when he can." Phillip laughed. "To each his own." He stopped the car in front of the restaurant. Gwen leaned over and pressed her cheek against his. She kissed his temples and then his lips, and she got out. "Boy am I glad I'm not married to you. In a marriage I'd really get screwed. Come back soon."

"I'll try."

After takeoff Phillip spent some time organizing his thoughts on the shows he had covered. Two soaps and three game programs. He was pleased that he had ended his stay with *Main Street*. It was the best show under his leadership, thanks to the professionalism with which it was produced, directed, and written. He used it as a model when he attempted to reshape the daytime serials that were in weaker condition. He jotted a reminder to himself to buy a new color TV set for the producer of *Main Street* to reward his continued good work.

Phillip downed two Scotches and the underheated meal and tried to sleep. Impossible! Even after the lights in the cabin were extinguished, it was impossible . . . so he sat there and let his mind bounce back through the months.

It had been a tiring year, but a successful one, professionally, that is. Well, what year had not been successful for him? Phillip Searing was success. In college as a tennis champion, then in the world of advertising, and now in television. It was a steady and predictable climb up every ladder he chose.

Success . . . except for his marriage to Jacqueline Goodhart and even that was successful in all aspects but one, the relationship between man and wife. And his part in that failure was probably due to his insatiable drive. "Why, Phillip?" She had asked when they were still trying to talk out their differences. "What the hell do you push so hard for?"

In a moment of unusual candor he had admitted that it was probably due to his father. "I was always very angry that my father never tried to make it. He could have been a great tennis player, you know. But he didn't put himself into court competition long enough to prove it. He lasted about a year and a half, and then gave up . . .

14

accepted a job at a lawn club in Seattle and collected his paycheck steadily at the end of every week. He sat around the clubhouse talking about what he could have been instead."

"So what does that have to do with you?"

"Well, it's probably just oversimplified cheapo psychoanalysis, but I figure his inability to lay it on the line created my absolute necessity to. That's also, by the way, one of the reasons why I love your old man. He laid it on the line when he started out. He gambled on an idea, stuck with it, and succeeded. I respect him mightily for that."

And the feeling was mutual. Jacqueline's mother and father adored him and still considered him a son, even though the divorce was final and he'd left the Goodhart Soap empire. And that respect dated back to his own "laying it on the line," when he'd left the empire a year and a half after he'd joined it.

It was the first time he had flown in the new family plane. Papa Goodhart had been in New York for the annual company Christmas dinner and brought the newlyweds back with him to Grosse Point for the holidays.

There were fur-lined lap robes and hot toddies waiting in the limousine that carried them through the snow-covered hills to the baronial mansion. The dinner was formal as customary. This time Phillip didn't have to borrow a tux, and he'd learned how to cope with the array of table silver. After dinner Papa invited him into the library for brandy and Cuban cigars to discuss his blossoming career with the company's advertising division. Phillip had wanted to tell him of his decision then, but felt that the moment was not quite right. He owed a lot to this distinguished gentleman and he didn't choose to insult him.

Later the whole family bundled up against the briskness of that December eve, trooped across the freshly fallen snow, and plowed down the back expanse of white lawn to the large duck pond. The groundskeepers had swept the powder from its frozen surface and built a large bonfire for them near the little gazebo, where the family donned their skates. Hand in hand, he and Jacqueline skated far ahead of the others. Her younger brother, Gordie, and a high-school girlfriend, took off in their own private

15

direction. The sky had cleared and glittered with the same sparkling brightness as the ice-laced branches which surrounded the pond.

Later still, they drank hot apple cider with sticks of cinnamon from large china mugs. They sang Christmas carols and the younger ones threw each other into the soft snowbanks. But when it was time to leave, Phillip asked Papa G. if he'd mind taking one last turn around the pond with him. The two men skated in silence for a time, and then, "All right, Phillip. You can tell me now. Are you and Jacqueline having problems?"

"Oh, no, sir. It's not that at all." But he was curiously pleased that Papa could read him so readily.

"That's good. I was worried. I realize I've spoiled her and she has a lot of maturing to do, but if you two love each other, that's all that matters."

Phillip smiled, letting his glide ease him against the older man's shoulder. They passed between two miniature islands with birch trees whose branches hovered silently above the ice. "Papa, I do love her. We're very happy together. But you're right: I do want to talk with you about something."

"It has to do with your position in the company, is that it?"

Phillip dipped down and scooped up some snow as they passed a bank, but it was too powdery to stick into a ball. "I owe . . . I owe you an awful lot. You took me into your family, the job, the townhouse and all. But even more importantly for being my friend, my confidant, so to speak."

Without breaking stride, the old man took Phillip's elbow and squeezed it warmly. "Well, then if I'm your friend, you'd better tell me what's on your mind."

Phillip took a deep breath and plunged in. "Sir . . . I've reached a decision. I wish to leave the company."

Franklin Goodhart raised his eyebrows in surprise. "Can you tell me why? I had lunch yesterday with Fitzsimmons and he tells me you've got the makings of a first-rate advertising executive."

"I like him and I'm pleased that he thinks that. But you see . . . I've been the account exec on one of the afternoon serials we produce, and that's given me the opportunity over the last year and a half to understand the

16

workings of television a little bit. What goes into making a good show, that sort of thing. Well, sir, the truth is I'm fascinated with the medium. I can't get it out of my mind. I knew from the first that the whole business excited me, but I thought it was just the newness of it, the excitement of watching a new show put on every day. But over the year I began to realize it's more than that. I'm not a star-struck kid, Papa."

"I never said you were. Come on. Let's get our cold bones to that fire and see if we can rev it up a bit." They turned back, hunching their shoulders into a wind which was now against them.

"I've been offered a position with an NBC soap opera and I'm going to accept it."

A spray of snow whipped across Franklin's face. Phillip glanced sideways to see if he could read it. It was almost expressionless. "What sort of position?"

"A minor one, associate producer. But it's a chance to really try the industry. To see if it'll last, this feeling I have for it, as I think it will. But I want you to understand why I made the decision. I think the potential of the medium is unlimited. The role it can play in society is extraordinary. It's the most powerful medium of communication ever invented and I want to be a part of it. You see, sir, I come from people who watch television. It's as much a part of their lives as brushing their teeth. My own family spent more time in front of the set than in almost any other activity. Now granted, I couldn't wait to get out of that environment and get away from those kinds of people, but this last year I've seen what goes into making a television show work and I've come to understand better the people who watch it. I want to be a part of helping to shape the programs that reach the people of America. I want to help those people who watch it."

"A little idealistic, don't you think?" They reached the gazebo. Franklin leaned over to stir the fire embers with a long stick. They flared and the light gilded his face.

"No, sir, not idealistic at all. I don't want to change television in a drastic way. I don't think that's possible without losing the audience and that's self-defeating. What I want to do is entertain them . . . to help them take their minds off their problems, but also to give them something worthwhile to do it with. Not in an educational way, but

17

in a commercial, entertaining way. I want to give them the best that television has to offer, but make it more, make it special. I want to enrich their lives." He paused, somewhat embarrassed by his enthusiasm.

Franklin sat on a fallen log. His gloves were off and he held his hands out to the warmth. He looked tired, Phillip thought. Then Goodhart looked across the fire at him. "You realize you're throwing away a fine career?"

Phillip leaned forward from the stump he was perched on. "Sir, I remember one of the first conversations we had in the library that first Easter Jacqueline invited me here from Stanford. You told me how you started your whole business, gambled your life savings on an unproven formula for a new detergent by some unknown chemist, whom everyone else thought was a quack. But you had faith in his product and yourself. And you took the risk. You sold your business, mortgaged your house. And you stuck it out. Well, I've reached that point in my life. I've found something that excites me, challenges me. I love television, Papa, just as much as you loved the idea of your new company. I realize I am giving up a solid career in advertising for a short-term contract with NBC, but if I don't make the jump now, I may never. I've got to prove to myself that I can be good at it . . . no, *better* at it than those people already involved. I am willing to take that gamble."

"And if you fail? What then? I won't be able to pull any more strings to get you back to G and L. I let my men run their own departments, and I can't tell them more than once who I'd like to see hired. You've risen on your own, but if you leave and fail somewhere else . . . so? Of course, I won't let you starve. I wouldn't want my daughter to be put through that. You'll get another job, all right. But that's not the point, is it? You're taking an enormous risk."

"I realize that, sir. And I appreciate your concern . . . not only for your daughter but for *my* future and welfare."

Franklin looked up at the sky. "It's clouding over again. We're in for some more snow tonight." The thick slice of moon disappeared behind a bank of dark clouds. The older man shifted his gaze to Phillip and studied him for a long moment before asking: "What does Jacqueline think of all this?"

"She thinks it's silly, but she knows I want to do it and she's given me, somewhat grudgingly I admit, her approval."

Goodhart grunted. "Abby felt pretty much the same when I told her my idea. But she gave me full backing and support. I hope her daughter will show the same courage and determination to stick by you."

"I think she will, sir. She's a good woman."

"I'm glad to hear that."

"And I want to be worthy of your admiration."

Franklin rose and pulled on his gloves, kicking snow on the bed of coals. "Phillip, I admire your guts. I personally think you're making a mistake, but I won't try to change your mind for all my competitor's market. It's your life and Jacqueline's. And if you think it is the right move then do it—and God speed on your journey."

Phillip felt a tightening in his throat as he shook his father-in-law's hand. "Thank you, sir. I won't disappoint you."

"All I ask is that you don't disappoint yourself."

And Phillip didn't. Within eight months of becoming associate producer, he was elevated to full producership. The afternoon serial under his guidance became one of the strongest on all four networks. Within two years, he was rehired by Goodhart Productions to be executive producer of two of their house-produced soap operas.

Within four years, he had all four Goodhart serials under his wing and he was considered the brightest, most effective young producer in the world of daytime.

But just as fast as the career flourished, the marriage dissolved. It couldn't really be blamed on either of them. But whatever it was, they continued the charade for several years until Phillip made the move to RBI. The same month he accepted Chamberfield's offer to head the network side of the daytime schedule, he moved out of the Sniffen Court townhouse Papa G. had purchased as a wedding gift for them.

Nine months now at RBI, he thought. Nine months as vice president and already he was looking ahead to the next plateau. It was an industrial malaise, he guessed, lack of satisfaction in one's present position.

He stretched his legs out in front of him and rested his head back on the wide first-class seat. Phillip Searing always traveled first class, even after the edict that all RBI executives were to fly economy. He just made up the difference out of his own pocket. Phillip didn't like to travel second class . . . didn't like to do anything second class. He played life as he used to play tennis: to win. He let the philosophy that had succeeded for him on the Stanford courts be carried over into his business career. And his rise in the world of television was testimonial to his effectiveness.

He lit another cigarette and stared out of the small oval porthole at the constellation-dotted blackness. He felt secure . . . he felt equipped . . . he felt prepared for anything Elliot Chamberfield might throw at him.

2.

If the forty-third, -fourth and -fifth stories of the Republic Broadcasting International corporations's Sixth Avenue monument to itself were ever sliced off by the wing of a low-flying jet, the network (or web as *Variety* liked to call it) would find itself in the same pickle as this nation if the White House and Congress suddenly dissolved. It would be headless, directionless, impotent. There are those who would argue that in both instances such a condition might be for the good of all, but the newly appointed chief of programing, who was elbowing his way out of the executive men's room, was hardly one of them. Elliot Chamberfield, thirty-nine years old, was now one of the most powerful men in television. There were only three other comparable positions. He had achieved the level of Silverman at CBS, of Diller at ABC, and although these titans had reached their plateaus at much earlier ages, Chamberfield was proud to be in their class.

Elliot relished television. He relished very little else. To him those three floors, electric with the crackling of power, were America, his dream, the focal point of his life. He strode down the blue-carpeted hall and turned right into his new office.

Rosalynann looked up when he passed her desk and pouted. "He didn't even nod." She turned to the secretary across from her. "I don't know what's gotten into him. I've been working my tail off all week long, lugging up files and ledgers from downstairs, and cleaning out his old office. And since he got this job last week, he's been worse than ever."

"It happens to all of them." The older secretary nodded knowingly. "Once they get up to this floor they think their brother-in-law's Jesus."

"I've got half a mind to let him go out to the island alone this weekend." Her hand flew to her mouth. "Oh, hell! That secret's out." The pretty blonde giggled and turned back to her electric IBM.

The new king entered and surveyed his throne room. The design was functionally modern, the decor spare. He had instructed that every trace of the former occupant be removed, and the office redecorated in company-bland. The prime position remained that of the wood-veneer cabinet, with sliding doors covering the four television sets. He had insisted on a color monitor for each network. Nothing in the room or on top of the massive oak slab which served as the standard desk for all vice presidents offered a clue as to the nature of the person who occupied the space. Elliot Chamberfield was an eminently practical man.

He extracted a bottle of Canoe from the center drawer of the desk and shifted over to the floor-length windows. He smacked a palmful onto his cleanly shaven face. Elliot liked to shave before leaving the office. He liked a change of shirt, too. He had read somewhere that Richard Nixon had a shave and a change of shirt every afternoon, and it was Elliot's custom to emulate powerful men. Not that there was normally any call for it. His post-office activities rarely consisted of anything more notable than downing perfect Manhattans with the sales force and chatting about business in the Plaza Hotel Bar. But he enjoyed the ritual. It was one of the very few attentions he paid to himself.

Today, of course, he had a special desire for doing a bit of primping. Not only was he celebrating the completion of his first week at the new plateau, but he was about to offer himself the long-sought indulgence of squeezing out his closest rival within the programing department.

Five-twenty-five. Just about right. Searing would be furious at being kept waiting all day. That'll teach him not to return phone calls. He recapped the cologne, replaced it in the drawer containing his personal bank statements and a few letters from his parents in St. Louis, and sat down. He leaned over to the phone and buzzed Rosalynann.

She responded with a gay, irreverent, end-of-the-day "yes, Mr. Chamberfield?" Her tone belied their professional relationship.

"Get Phillip Searing up here now!" Then more humanly he added, "After that, why don't you call the garage and have Walter bring the car around?" Not only did his new post mean a healthy raise in pay, but it was also accompanied by a chauffered limousine to transport him to and from the office. His apartment was no more than a short ride away, but the car was a status symbol.

"Yes, sir."

He dropped the receiver and waited. As he straightened some copies of the *Hollywood Reporter*, he anticipated the confrontation.

Searing was a problem. He was the next logical choice to replace Chamberfield should the board have the whim. Elliot was aware of Searing's strength. He recognized the same toughness and abilities he liked to attribute to himself, and when he had needed to place an equal in his former position as head of daytime programing, in order to free himself for his next move up the ladder, he chose Searing. But now things were different. Elliot was where he wished to be, and he had no need to have a man as young and ambitious as Searing in the wings.

But the situation was delicate. He couldn't afford to have his superiors know he was disgruntled with a man he himself had hired. That would be bad politics. Nevertheless, his first week had gone well. He had impressed his superiors and now Elliot could make his move. It was a gamble, but he held the trump card.

The intercom startled him. "Searing will be up in five minutes." Elliot erupted with a vengeance as frightening as it was expected.

"I don't want him in five minutes! I want the son of a bitch in here now!"

"I told him that, Elliot, but he said he was in a meeting," Rosalynann whined, long used to his tirades. "I'll try again," she said soothingly.

"Never mind, goddammit. I'll get him myself!" Elliot stubbed the button reserved for executives, nearly knocking the phone off the desk. He dialed his old number, muttering to himself, "You miserable son of a bitch. I'll show you who waits for who."

Phillip was nearly finished when Rosalynann's call came in. He and his assistant were discussing the long-term story projections on two of the soap operas that had dropped slightly in the latest ratings reports. He had arranged the meeting for the end of the afternoon, so as not to let the entire day go to waste, having been forced to wait since 10:00 A.M. for the "urgent" conference with Elliot.

Phillip had taken the elevator one floor up to the forty-fourth floor at the appointed hour, only to find that the meeting had been postponed until eleven-thirty. At eleven-thirty it was delayed until 3:00 P.M. and from then until some undefined hour convenient to the new VP of programing's active calendar.

Phillip had known Elliot would buzz him back immediately after he told Rosalynann that he was in a meeting. He grinned at Barry. "He'll probably stomp on the floor now that his office is directly above." He took his suit jacket from the door hanger. "Come on, walk me down the hall."

Barry Friedman, a kinky-haired bespectacled kid, gathered together the papers they'd been working on and crushed a smoking cigarette dead. They were at the door when the buzzing started on Phillip's executive line. Phillip closed the door and shot a soft *"sieg heil"* to the ceiling fixture. They ambled down the hall as Phillip spoke.

"The rest seem to be holding fine, Barry, but *Affair* still needs a stronger maternal pull. *Surgery* won't be a problem either, if we can clean up the relationship between Candice and Fleming's son. I sent a memo to the writers on each show that Tuesday morning is deadline. I want to see some solid structure in those areas, even if

24

they have to put the whole three-day weekend in on it."

"*Affair* is the bitch. I've been working on something m-m-myself." Barry stuttered when under pressure. "I'll discuss it with Caroline tonight."

"No, save it for me when you're ready. I don't want you discussing story ideas with the writers until you've cleared them all with me. Those poor people are confused enough as it is." He stopped at the open door of a smaller office and looked in at his other assistant, a mod-dressed, young man behind the desk. "Greg, did you get Vern Tuttle on the phone?"

He shook his head.

"Keep trying, okay?"

"I don't know why we're having so much trouble with *Affair*. No matter what we do, we don't seem to be able to click in." He smoothed the ends of his bushy mustache.

"Well, we're going to have to, my friends. It's Elliot's baby. He created it and he's been on my back about the low ratings since I stepped into his job."

Barry leaned against the door jamb. "It's not your fault the ratings are low."

"What difference do you think that makes to him?" He stepped back into the hall. "You two have a pleasant weekend. Don't work too hard, but I also need a summary of the other six projections on my desk first thing Tuesday morning."

The two young men groaned audibly. "There goes the beach," Greg said, sighing.

Phillip smiled. "My babies. My babies want to play in the sand. Okay, make it Wednesday, but first thing, yes? You understand?"

He washed his hands in the gleaming white-tiled washroom on his floor and then went upstairs. Rosalynann was brushing her hair. Phillip gave her a quick inspection. "You've got lipstick on your teeth." She picked up a small compact and started to look before realizing that she hadn't worn lipstick for six months. He pushed open the inner office door and entered without being announced.

Elliot was seated behind his desk, his shoulders hunched slightly forward, like a used-car salesman making his hook.

The difference between the two was striking. Phillip, several years younger than his boss, was by far the more youthful. He was well groomed, tanned, and stood with

25

an easy erectness. His suit was a tailor-made modishly conservative English cut, and his shoes also English imports. Despite the fact that he had put in a full day of work after a night of flying, he seemed fresh and rested.

Chamberfield, on the other hand, looked rumpled. His readymade suit was baggy and its stripes were too pronounced for his squat figure.

But they had one quality in common: ambition. There was rumor in the secretarial pool that if Julius Caesar, were President of RBI, he would have reason to trust either of these men even less than Cassius.

Phillip smiled with disarming cordiality. "Hello, Elliot, have a busy day?"

The man behind the desk said nothing.

Phillip drew out his gold cigarette case and offered one graciously. Elliot dismissed it with a pass of his hand. After a silent pause which would have been unnerving to one less used to power politics, the man in command lifted a Xeroxed page and let it float in the direction of his conversant.

"The Seventy-Market Nielsens are in and *Affair* has dropped again."

"I saw the sheets."

"You saw the sheets." Phillip caught the contemptuousness in Elliot's voice. "That show is losing the time period so bad it's affecting the whole afternoon schedule."

"That was just the Seventy–Markets. The Nationals should be better."

"Seven tenths of a point to CBS."

"I was working on it in the meeting you just pulled me out of."

"Oh, you were?"

"It's only one show, Elliot. I've got seven others to keep going as well." Despite the lack of invitation, Phillip decided to sit. He crossed to the couch on the far side of the room. It provided a stronger position than the guest chair next to the desk.

Elliot drew a cigar from a carved wooden case. He worked it carefully, snipping off the end with a smoking tool and moistening it slowly with saliva. When some of the thick blue smoke had been extracted, he cleared a sliver of tobacco fron his tongue. "That show's built solid, Searing. Why's it being fucked up?"

26

Phillip tightened the Tissot band on his watch and reminded himself that he had to pick up another one. They were attractive, but didn't last more than six months. "We've been through this a dozen times."

"Well, let's go through it once again."

Phillip studied his boss. He must have changed his shirt recently, since it was only mildly disheveled. Even his shoes were scuffed and he knew Elliot would have had them polished before lunch. "You want to know why *Affair*'s not working." It was a statement, not a question.

"That's what I asked you."

"It's constructed all wrong, that's why. The characters are wrong, and there's little in the format that works."

"That's my format, you know. I devised it."

"Yes."

"So you're saying the format I devised is all wrong." Phillip found no reason to respond.

"Searing, you really think you know more about television than I do." He shook his head theatrically as if he were saddened over the lack of understanding of a child.

"Did you bring me back from the coast for this, Elliot?"

"I want to know what's wrong with my show."

"All right. I'll tell you again. Ever since I took over daytime, you insisted I leave that one show alone. You wanted it to get better. You wanted the Nielsens to improve, but you wouldn't let me touch it except to stop the bleeding when it was cut too deep. That show's got cancer, Elliot. It needs major surgery. First of all, it shouldn't be a live show. It ought to be taped, so we'd have time to correct any serious faults. As for the show itself, you've got two main themes running through it that are so tangled and confused they'll never straighten themselves out. You've got a lead girl with a fake Italian accent, and no housewife out in Des Moines or Wichita gives a goddamn about a foreigner. You've made a hero out of a soldier and that doesn't work, not after Vietnam. You've got a politician in there who's supposed to be the pillar of society, and you know what the Nixon regime did to that idea. You have neither a maternal figure for the older ladies nor a heroine in serious trouble. Nothing matters in the show. Nothing is life and death, black and white, good or bad. Caroline's written a collection of bad Broadway-

27

musical curtain lines and even most of *them* are intellectually over the heads of the audience."

Phillip was surprised he hadn't been cut off. If Elliot had been using anything like his normal game plan he should have been shrieking invective by now. But the little fat man just leaned back, puffing calmly on his smuggled-in Havana, and peered out toward Central Park. "And what do you intend to do about all that?"

"That's the point. There's nothing I can do if you're not open to change."

"And I bought you for RBI because you were supposed to be so clever."

Phillip let the insult pass. He paused for a second and then let drop the one suggestion he knew Elliot would not go for. "If I were in your shoes and it were the weakest show on my schedule, I'd yank *Affair* off the air."

Elliot hardly reacted. And that, thought Phillip, was very peculiar. The tension in the air could be cut with a letter opener, but neither raised a voice. "No, I'm not going to do that. I'm not going to do that at all."

"I didn't think you would," Phillip said. "It wouldn't make a very good impression on the board, having to admit that a show you created and fought so hard for was the weakest link of the afternoon."

"That's right. That's right, it wouldn't. But it could be done." An ugly sneer played around the left corner of his mouth.

Phillip sat patiently in the middle of the couch, his arms folded, waiting.

"Interesting. You were such a golden boy at Goodhart Productions. Everybody kept telling me what a genius you were. Phillip Searing, the bright young star. Fix any show you give him and save you money on the budget, too. I didn't have any trouble at all convincing Russell or the board to bring you in. You had quite a reputation. Excellent man. Watch out, Elliot, they told me. He might give you some competition." He paused a moment and looked at him. "Tell me something, Phillip. How come you can't do as good a job for us as you did when you were working for your ex-father-in-law? It is 'ex,' now, isn't it?"

Phillip was growing weary of the game. "What do you want, Elliot? What's on your mind? Why don't you just lay it out straight?"

Chamberfield leaned far back in his chair. He put his feet up on his desk and locked his hands behind his head. "I've been thinking of giving you that show."

Phillip cocked his head.

"Yeah," Elliot continued, "I've been thinking of giving you *Affair*. I don't think you've been putting enough of your attention to it and I'm sure you could do better if you tried."

"Don't put down my work, Elliot. I've had eight shows to whip into shape in the last nine months and seven of them are doing just fine. I'd planned to start logging in more hours on *Affair* next week." It wasn't an apology; it was a hold for time to figure out the game plan.

Elliot leaned back in his chair. "Yeah." He was inwardly amused at a private joke. "Yeah, that's about what I had in mind for you to do. As of Tuesday I want you to start logging in more time. In fact, as of Tuesday, you can devote all of your energies to the show."

"Now what the hell is that supposed to mean?"

"Not so difficult to understand, Phil. I think *Affair Of The Heart* needs your complete and undivided attention, like my principal used to say in high school."

"I can't spend all my time on one show, no matter whose favorite creation it is."

Elliot's voice became menacing. "Well, you're going to have to, because that's the only show you've got." His feet dropped to the floor and he lurched forward far across the desk. "*Affair Of The Heart*, that's it!"

Phillip was stunned. He felt a blazing heat between his temples.

Elliot dragged another puff from his cigar and let out a thin controlled stream of smoke. "I think Vern Tuttle's a lousy producer. You're going to take over on Tuesday."

"You're telling me you want me to produce *Affair?*"

"That's right."

"I'm no longer a line producer, Elliot. I'm a vice president."

"Well, I guess you'll have to give that title up, won't you? We can't have a vice president producing a single soap."

There was a long moment. "Is this some kind of a joke?"

"No joke, Phil. Russell and I talked things over yesterday morning and we both agreed you're the only one around who can dive in and pull our baby out. You see, I've come to the conclusion you're right. It does need drastic surgery. Keel was skeptical, but I assured him you were a solid member of the team and wouldn't dream of letting us down. Now you won't refuse the chance to bail your company out, will you?"

Phillip rapidly calculated the turn of events. If the president of the network were involved in the decision, there was little he could do to reverse matters. It was unprecedented to replace a producer with a vice president, but Elliot must have sold Keel on the premise that team spirit should prevail over personal ambition. Son of a bitch! Phillip knew that if he allowed himself to be wedged off the forty-third floor, getting back on would be no picnic. He pretended to examine a blotchy red-and-black ultra-modern lithograph. His jaw muscles tensed and he cleared his throat. Other than that, he gave no indication of the fury that was bottled up inside. After a moment he turned back to the flabby-skinned face and the little porcine eyes regarding him. "I suppose you told Keel the move was mandatory in order to save the show from extinction."

"And it was the unvarnished truth. If *Affair* doesn't pick up by the end of the summer we may have to cancel it."

"Which would make you look like a bloody fool since you were the one who forced it on the air in the first place."

"It's a good show, Searing."

"It's a piece of crap, Elliot."

Phillip had touched a nerve. Elliot snapped forward suddenly and slammed his hand down on the desk. "All right, Searing, the sparring match is over. You start Tuesday morning across town, and I want those ratings raised by the end of the summer or your ass is in a sling."

"I suppose that will go for you too, if I fail?"

Elliot paused before answering, then smiled caustically. "Okay. We're riding tandem on this one. And you're right. You're right. I don't want it to fail." He paused. "So I'm going to give you free rein to do anything you have to to fix it up. Carte blanche, Searing, so it's all

30

yours. But you do it, you understand? You fix up my show."

"And what happens if I don't want to become a producer?"

"You may think it's hot, but it can be cold as hell out on the street."

"And if I go to Russell myself?"

"You can, if you like. *If* you want to show him you put your own personal ambition ahead of the company." He smiled broadly. "Besides I didn't say anything about cutting your salary. You'll still draw your same fifty."

"Mighty decent of you, friend."

"Forget it." He pushed his chair back and swaggered to the half-open door. The conversation was over. "Is the car downstairs yet, Rosalynann?"

"Yeah. He rang a few minutes ago."

"All right. Let's go, huh? It's getting late. Don't wanna be too late for the ferry, do we?" He turned back to Phillip. "Think it over."

"What's there to think over? Do I have a choice?"

"You could quit."

"You'd like that, wouldn't you?" They regarded each other like primed vipers. "No, Elliot, I'm not going to make it easy for you."

"Have a nice weekend, Searing."

Philip left. He passed the girl and walked straight on toward the front. His rage multiplied geometrically with the stomp of each heel into the carpet.

3.

By the time he reached the reception area, paneled in rosewood and decorated by a sloe-eyed, slack-mouthed creature in a copy of a Pucci original, Phillip realized he had no choice but to accept. It was either that or pound the pavements and there were precious few television networks around to knock on. An out-of-work orchestra conductor would have fatter pickings for himself. And damned, he thought, if I'm going back to Goodhart!

He stalked past the receptionist, who was assembling her personals for the afternoon escape.

"Have a nice holiday, Mr. Searing." The girl spoke with a nasal whine probably cultivated at a small college near Boston.

"Thank you, you too," he clipped. Christ! Holiday! Memorial day. That's right. His eyes flicked up to the clock on the wall. It was fifteen minutes to six. Typical of Chamberfield. He had to choose the very eve of what should have been a long, pleasurable weekend for his goddamn bombshell dropping. Diabolical bastard! Phillip could really have used that vacation.

He hit the down button with his fist. An elevator appeared, the soft bell pinged, and the red down light brightened. He stepped on. The steel door hummed shut. He touched the plastic button for forty-three and reached instinctively for a cigarette.

In a few moments he made it to his own metal box of an office. His throat was parched and his pulse beat rapidly. Fortunately he'd given his secretary the afternoon off. He would be spared the necessity of explaining his mood. The floor seemed empty. Believing everyone had split early to get a jump on the holiday traffic, he permitted himself a show of his fury. He shoved the office door open, flinging it hard, causing the knob to smash resoundingly against the inside wall. A startled form spun around and looked up from the couch.

"My god! Are you trying to give me a heart attack?" She placed her hand under her left breast to check the tempo.

Phillip clicked the door closed softly and muttered what could be construed as an apology. "I didn't know anybody was here."

She leaned back again, retucked her feet under her skirt, and resumed her telephone conversation. After a moment, she covered the mouthpiece and gestured for his attention. "I'm using the tie line. It's my kid sister in Oregon."

He peeled off his jacket and threw it across the room. He dropped into the swivel chair and swung his legs up onto the large slab of wood and stainless steel. He pulled a drag from the remainder of his cigarette, then crushed it brutally in the free-form ashtray which was also standard VP equipment. Katina looked up from the phone. He swirled around in his high-backed chair. He didn't want her to see his face. His mind continued to whirl. He'd have to get a grip on it. He ought to approach the matter with at least a modicum of detachment.

Phillip was used to sudden attack from hostile quarters, but this swindle caught him off guard. He had known Elliot might move against him, but it was impossible to imagine he would take so drastic a step so early. Two months from now, Phillip's own position within the organization would have been secure enough to demand almost anything he could have wished. But then that was precisely

33

why Elliot acted as quickly as he did, wasn't it? He's got you by the balls, old buddy.

Phillip swiveled the chair back and studied Katina. She was still talking in her long-distance voice. She went well against the long, beige couch by the windows. Katina Wrens was one of those rare women who possessed the remarkable combination of executive decisiveness and feminine charm. She carried herself with the style of an English queen before all but a select few, with whom she let her hair down. She was gracious and warm, but maintained a distinct sense of independence. Still in her thirties, she had accomplished the near-impossible at RBI. She had forced the male chauvinists of the network to grant her executive status and a windowed office on the forty-third floor. Precedent had been established for female promotion, but not much. RBI tolerated very few women executives on either coast, and she had had to fight fiercely for every raise. There were perhaps only seven or eight steps between the corridor cubicle and the office, but the move from receptionist-secretary-"smile-at-the-pigs"-gal Friday took her over ten years to manage. Then she held her job only for about eleven months. Once she had made it, proved she could handle the myriad details involved in the four-hour Saturday-morning schedule of children's cartoons, proved she could deal with Federal Communications Commission's demands, concerned parents' groups demands, board of directors' demands, and, most importantly, proved she could keep her eight kiddy movies bringing in the highest gross profit of the entire network for the least amount of cost, she quit. She quit to write poetry. It was astounding.

"What the hell do you mean she wants to write poetry?" Keith Burke had screamed when Phillip informed him. Burke had held the Elliot Chamberfield position for ten years before he was ousted in a power play with the new president.

"She's quitting to write poetry," Phillip repeated calmly.

"She can't quit to write poetry. We need her here. Why can't she write poetry at home in the evening?"

"She can, but it would be difficult for her to get here in the morning. She's moving to Ibiza."

"Where?"

34

"Ibiza. It's a little island off the coast of Spain. Big drug-culture place."

Burke was flabbergasted. "Not our Katina—is she into that stuff?"

"I don't think so."

"No!" He shook his head disbelievingly.

"There are a lot of writers around there. That's the island Clifford Irving lived on, the guy who promoted the Howard Hughes hoax."

"Another crackpot," Keith muttered. "Did you offer her any more money?"

"Yes."

"How much?"

"Two thousand a year."

"What's she making now?"

"Fifteen."

"You think she'd stay if we offered her twenty? It's going to be a bitch finding somebody to fill her slot."

"No, I don't think she'd stay. She's set to go."

"Unbelievable." Burke wagged his head. "Poetry," he said. "Poetry! Who the hell's going to read it?"

Katina glanced up from the phone and caught Phillip staring at her. She smiled and charaded that she'd be off in just a second. Phillip remarked to himself how much lovelier she looked, now that she had been free of job pressures for three weeks. Her honey-blonde hair, usually swept back so that she could hold telephone receivers more easily, now fell softly around the curves of her face, presenting its heart shape like a jewel in a Valentine box. There was a luster to her skin, a delicate glow that emanated from the same warm core that caused her eyes to sparkle with humor. She was free. She had ended her indentureship to the world of business and she was heading for Spain, where communication would be conducted only with her muse and a small, select group of friends chosen for their personal rather than sales appeal.

They had met in October. Both worked late one evening after most everyone else had gone. Phillip had been in as VP for about a week, and the rigors of the transition between managing four soap operas for the sponsor to heading all eight for the network was taking its toll. He had wanted to Xerox some memos which needed to be dispersed to his individual producers the following morning, but his secretary was gone and the duplicating machine was on the fritz. He was in the process of kicking it verbally when Katina popped her head in the open doorway. "Can I be of any help?"

"Yes!"

With the expertise of a seasoned professional she fixed the machine, ran off the memos, collated them, stuffed them into inner-office envelopes, and was on her way out before Phillip even got to ask her name. When he found out the next morning that not only was she an executive and not somebody's secretary, but an executive who worked under his area, he asked her out to lunch.

They ordered fish at Twenty-One and got the "What do you do's" out of the way fairly fast. By salad time they could leave their elbows on the table if they wanted.

"Poetry. Yes, I write poetry. And not roses are red, violets fuschia. Real confusing, double-entendrish poetry that nobody can understand."

"Are you any good?"

"I don't know."

"Has anybody read it?"

"No, just me."

"How do you know it's worth continuing?"

She looked at him strangely, cocked her head to one side, and chewed on the inside of her lower lip. "Funny, you seem sensitive enough to know the answer to that. In fact, you seem sensitive enough not to ask a question like that. Just goes to show, you can't tell a book by its cover."

Phillip grinned and wiped his lips with the linen napkin. "I'm a product of my environment, Miss Wrens. Just a salesman of high-priced shoes. Nothing is worth anything until somebody puts a price on it, isn't that right?"

"No, that's not right. And neither are you a salesman. There's more to you than that. But I don't think you have the foggiest idea where it's at."

"Do you?"

"No, but I try to find it. Not here at the office, certainly. But with my poetry."

"You mean when you read your poetry you discover something in what you've written?"

"No, not at all. It's not in reading it I find anything.
36

It's in writing it. It's while I'm writing that sometimes I feel a little freer, a little closer."

"Closer? To what?"

She shrugged her shoulders. "I don't know." She thought a second and then repeated her answer. "I don't know. Anyway, what I mean is it has nothing to do with whether I'm any good or not or whether anybody reads it. Even if somebody were to read it, and get something out of what I wrote, it would be theirs. It would be for them, not me. You know? I write to write; they read to read. One has nothing to do with the other. Why should that surprise you?"

He toyed with the silver creamer the waiter had brought with the coffee. "The only thing that surprises me is that the girl who's expounding this theory of noncommunication has spent eleven years with Republic Broadcasting International, one of the largest communication networks in the world."

"First of all, I didn't say noncommunication. I said communication with myself and, yes, that's true. I've put my time in, and in other ways too. Second, I'm not a girl. I'm a woman. I've been married and divorced. I've had my lonelies and my fats, but I'm learning very slowly. It takes time." She paused. "And you? What state of chaos are you in now? I understand your marriage is no picnic."

Phillip poured them each a cup of coffee from the carafe. "People do chatter, don't they? I'll tell you sometime. If I get to know you better."

It was then that he started knowing Katina better.

They settled into an easy office-type affair. Phillip found it comfortable to spend many of his nights with her on West Eighty-Eighth Street, rather than returning to the elegant but empty suite he had rented while his divorce went through. Neither of them claimed that classic love had touched them, but their brief affair served to soften the pangs of separation and loneliness for both. They demanded nothing of each other save respect for privacy and solitude, but when one wished to talk, the other usually spared time to listen. Perhaps it was love, but it was of a nature Phillip had never before encountered.

Katina responded both to his need to be alone and to the sexual forays he threw himself into in search of escape. It was during this time that he discovered how serious she actually was about poetry. Hour after hour she worked and reworked a single line, a turn of phrase, a word, an expression, a cadence, a rhyme. Her diligence and dedication impressed him enormously.

"You know I'm jealous of you," he said one night.

"Why?"

"You sit there and work with the patience of Job. You lose yourself so completely in those few words and you never ask anything of them. I'd give a great deal to lose myself like that."

"Have you ever?"

"I don't know. Maybe. I think so. When I played the piano I think, not since."

Katina looked up in surprise. "I never knew you played the piano. You never told me that."

"Didn't I?"

"No."

"I gave it up before I left Stanford. It's not important."

"Yes, I think it is. Why don't you play again?"

"Now? Don't be silly. It's been too long, and who's got a piano?"

"Rent one. There's room for it here."

"I don't live here; you do, remember? I'm just a bedroom guest sometimes."

"As you like."

He kissed her on the back of the neck, and cupped his hand under her breast. "Let's keep it dirty, Tina. It'll be easier for both of us."

But that was in the winter. As Phillip's responsibilities grew heavier, he came to the apartment less and less. In March his duplex was ready for him. And then for a while Katina found a friend of her own. . . .

She finally cradled the receiver and turned back to greet him. "I've come for you to kiss me good-bye."

Phillip looked away. He found it difficult to match her cheeriness. "When are you leaving?"

"Tonight."

"What happened to the boyfriend?"

"Gone." She rummaged around in her bag for cigarettes, but came up with only a crumpled empty package. "Do you have one? Today's the last day. I promised myself when I get on that plane, I'll kiss them good-bye for good, filthy weeds!"

He drew his case out of his pocket and pushed it across the oaken wood. Katina uncrossed her legs and padded barefoot across the thick, dark carpet. She took a light from a silver lighter, originally an office-warming gift, held a long drag and exhaled slowly. "You're the only person I know who keeps a table lighter that actually works."

"I never keep anything unless it works."

"Is that why you don't want me?" Her expression was a come on, but Phillip was in no mood to respond. He turned away to stare out of the window. She sat down lightly on the edge of the desk and turned her own attention to the window, as if the reason for his quietness were to be found in the skyline of New York. "What's up?"

He said nothing for a moment, then suddenly, as if shocked by a series of electrodes, he charged out of his chair, paced angrily across the room and slammed closed the sliding door of the color monitor. He drew a lungful of air. "You're looking at the new producer of *Affair Of The Heart*."

"What?"

"I've been stripped of my vice president's bars and shuttled off back to the studio."

"Who did—?"

"Who do you think? And he hasn't even been upstairs for five full days!"

"But why?" Katina was incredulous.

"Bastard!"

"Why, Phillip? He's there. He's gotten where he wanted to be!"

"I'm a threat. His only threat. He's hungered after that job for years. I'm the only one in the company who could match him for it and he knows it. If Keith had stayed for another couple of months, it might have been me up there. I'm as strong as he is and he knows it. He can't afford to have me around."

"But you're not in a position to just take it away from him."

"He's being careful. If he plays his cards right, that job'll give him more power than the president of the network and he doesn't want a threat from anywhere. I know what he's doing. I know exactly what he's doing. This was the first move. The next one means I'm out. It'll take a couple of months to see any ratings jump on that show, even if I put Henry Kissinger on in drag. Chamberfield knows that. He's going to fabricate some way of getting me out before the figures climb. But I'll get back on this floor—don't worry about that. I'm going to make that show better than his atrophied imagination ever dreamed it could be, and he's going to pay for it, son of a bitch. That budget's going to skyrocket, but that show's going to have class. Okay, he wins the round, but there are fourteen more to go!"

Phillip paced up and down the room, rhythmically building up pressure. Katina stepped in his way. She grabbed his arm and they froze. She pressed her body hard against his. He reached down and took a handful of her hair, pulling it down toward her neck. His face plunged forward and their mouths crushed.

"You're a fool, Phillip!" Her jaw tightened with excitement. "Get out. Get out while you can, while you're still able to think like a human being. You're going to turn yourself into a carbon copy of him, and he's no different from any of the others. They're all animals." She held his head strongly against her own. "Phillip, you've got to see that. You'll become like that, too."

"I'm going to kick his ass one of these days from the home side of that desk up there."

"For what?" She studied his steely resolve. "What's so important? I started in this place at seventy-eight dollars a week making coffee and bright eyes for these guys and I worked myself up to be the only woman executive in the department. But what did it mean? I spent eight hours a day looking at kiddy cartoons. I slaved for ten years taking all the shit that rolled down to me, because shit rolls downhill, you know. And in bucketfuls when you're a woman. And for what? So that I would have an executive title? An expense account and the privilege of watching Bugs Bunny all day!"

She paused. He backed away.

"Don't give me any lectures." He let a slight smile cross his face. Katina smiled, too, then reached behind her and tugged at the bowstrings of her halter-top dress. It fell, exposing two perfectly shaped, May-tanned breasts with a thin separation over the nipples where a bathing top had lain. Phillip bent down and kissed them, cupping them in the palms of his hands, rolling the wrinkled tips between his teeth. He moved toward her belly. Katina's fingers spread rapidly through his hair. Phillip knelt on one knee and rested his cheek against the upper softness of her thighs. Holding her tightly, he suddenly stood up. He hoisted Katina into the air and she came down horizontally on the desk. She heard the pencils and paper scatter noisily. She felt his grip reach under her arms, pulling and squeezing in one long motion. Then the heels of his hands pressed deeply into the soft fullness of her breasts, distorting their shape, stretching the skin to a bruising sensual immediacy. Down they clawed, down to her hips.

She arched her back and drew her body up to meet him, holding the collar of his shirt for support. She kissed him again, biting his mouth and his neck and his ears. He twisted her arms outward, forcing her chest forward. She broke loose and tugged at the leather belt he wore.

Katina slid to the floor, dragging his pants as she went. Her hands cupped his genitals. Phillip reached down and drew her up to him. He sat her once again on the edge of the desk, the cold altar of bureaucracy, and pushed her backward. Her thighs spread open of their own accord. She gripped the sides of the wood. Her head twisted and her hair fell over the edge.

And she waited. It seemed an eternity passed before he touched her again, but then it was there. She felt the soft nudging of his swollen piece. Her knees stretched further and further apart opening themselves for him. Deeper and deeper it sank, slowly and fluidly, as if there was no end to it.

They remained like that, buried to the hilt but straining still to meld even closer. They remained like that until they exploded.

Later they slid to the floor and puffed cigarettes. They lay nude and relaxed, studying the underside of the desk. Katina's sphere of vision encompassed the window and it suddenly dawned on her that they were completely exposed to the view of anybody on a higher floor in the building across the street.

"Hey, Phillip, anyone standing in that top office over there can see right in here."

41

"So they can." He craned his neck to see if anybody was doing so.

Katina pinched him playfully on the stomach. "You louse! What do you mean putting me on display like that?"

"Relax, they'll just think I'm casting for a new series."

"Oh, Phillip, we could have such a beautiful life, you and I. Scampering over the world, doing nothing but what pleases us for the rest of our lives."

He lay on his back, his fingers pushing deeply through the soft pile of the carpet. "What pleases me is to make it to the top of this mountain."

"I know, I know, I know." She sighed, sitting up, slipping on her dress.

"I'm going to miss you," he said genuinely. "Very much."

"Oh, not so much. You'll be so busy playing God on that soap you'll have forgotten me by the next Nielsen report."

"Will you write?" He stood to dress.

"Of course. Might even send you a poem or two." She laughed and ran a comb through her hair.

"I probably won't write back. I'm a disgusting correspondent."

"I can imagine."

"Shall I take you to the airport?"

"No. If I see you there I might change my mind and stay to trap you."

Phillip laughed, buttoning his shirt. "You couldn't live with a man for more than a few months. You're too independent."

She gathered the few things she had strewn over the couch, stuffed them back into her shoulder bag, and jammed her feet into her clogs. She looked at him. He sat on the edge of the couch. She moved over and softly brushed his hair back from his forehead. "What is it, Phillip? What's happening to you? I've never seen you so depressed."

Phillip sat still. "I don't know. I'm on some kind of a down streak for the first time in my life. Maybe it's cumulative. The whole business with Jacqueline and the separation and now this. I'm not used to not winning. I've never not won before. There's an attitude involved in winning, you know. If you know you're going to win, believe it totally, nine out of ten times you will. But if you let the thought

42

enter your mind you might lose, then you haven't got a snowball's chance in hell."

"Maybe you've started taking it all too seriously."

"Maybe, but I'm not used to getting kicked out of places. I don't like the feeling."

"Do you like the game?"

"No. But this character upstairs is not going to throw me out of it. If he thinks I'm going to jump on his losing horse and ride it out to pasture with my name on it, he's going to be sadly mistaken. I'm going to turn that nag around and win with it."

She took his head between her hands and kissed him. She kissed his eyes, mouth and chin, and pressed her nose up close so she could breath in the aroma of his body. Then she held him back and spoke. "Phillip, I mean it. If you ever get fed up enough with this rat race, you'll know where I'll be. You can start a whole new life anytime you want."

"Doing what?"

"Just being you."

It was a long slow kiss, full of tenderness and mutual respect.

"Take care of yourself, Tina. Think of me."

"Oh, I will that," she said. "Don't worry." She left him sitting on the couch.

It was a clear, early evening. A wind had blown the week's pollution away. He could almost see the thousands of cars honking each other across the George Washington Bridge, hastily making their escape from the oppressiveness of the late spring heat wave. Manhattan was evacuating like a multi-drained sewer.

Phillip reached for another Dunhill. He smoked too much. He would have to cut down, too. Life would be thinner without Katina.

But there was too much to do between now and Tuesday to float in emotionalism. He snapped open his briefcase and began collecting the few personal objects with which he warmed the various offices he had inhabited the last few years. A few framed color snapshots, the silver table lighter, and a small golden statuette of a race horse over which he dwelt for an instant before moving on.

4.

Fire Island stretches for over twenty-five miles, an elongated sliver of sand dunes off the coast of Long Island. Dotted with small vacation communities which are reached from the mainland by ferryboat, it is a perfect retreat from the summer heat and tempo of the city. Because no automobiles are permitted, the major threat to pedestrians comes from children racing tricycles or bicycles along narrow footpaths through brush-covered dunes.

Fair Harbor, one of the communities closest to the city, is populated predominantly by wives and children. They are plunked down by commuting fathers who join their families on the weekends. The houses are wooden and close together, but the absence of cars and panhandlers makes the place seem like a village in the early 1800s. The inhabitants walk to and from "town," dragging children's wagons filled with grocery bags and stopping to chat with passers-by in a distinctly nonurban way. The big event of the week is the gathering at the end of the bayside dock for the arrival of the husbands and weekend guests.

It was late Saturday afternoon of the Memorial Day weekend, the first big weekend on Fire Island. Vanessa and Joe Langley were in the spacious, old-fashioned kitchen of one of the two-story beach houses farther out from the hub. They were scaling and gutting the twelve fish they had caught that morning. It had been gloriously hot for a week, and they were taking advantage of it. They were house guests of Vern Tuttle, the producer of RBI's *Affair Of The Heart,* a serial on which Vanessa played a minor role. She was a beautiful young lady of twenty-four with the musical voice of a trained singer. Her features were delicate: deep, soft, hazel eyes, and a small fine nose which was worrying her. "My nose isn't as red as yours, is it, Joe?" She swept the plastic cleaning utensil across the top side of the fish, sending a spray of translucent scales flying in all directions.

"Hey, watch it, you'll get it in your eye."

"I can't control this thing. It keeps slipping out of my hand."

"Wrap a towel around the fin so you can get purchase."

"Purchase? Ha!" joked Vanessa. "Listen to him with his purchase." She was happy with her day and the prospect of two more like it. They had separated from the rest of the guests and their hosts to spend some time alone. But what pleased Vanessa most was that Joe had emerged from the funk he had been in for a week. "You really are rather clever, aren't you, Joe?"

"What's that supposed to mean?"

"Who would have ever thought after four years that you'd come up with the surprise of teaching me how to clean fish? I'm really quite impressed."

"You'll be more impressed with the way one of these dead slimys can swim under your shirt down your back."

"Don't you dare!"

He shot her a look reminiscent of John Wayne refusing to be pushed off a Colorado cattle ranch, and sliced through the belly of the creature he was holding.

"Is my nose red, Joe? You didn't answer me before."

"You look like W. C. Fields after two fifths of gin."

"No?"

"Yeah."

"Vern'll be furious. Valerie would never go out in the sun."

"Fuck Valerie."

"I've got to be careful, that's all. Valerie's an indoor girl. She'd spend most of her time in libraries and museums."

"Maybe she got her nose burned staring down a dinosaur."

"Hey, that's not bad. You should talk to the writers about that."

Suddenly Joe dropped the banter and answered with a savagery that was startling compared to the light-hearted quality of the rest of the conversation. "No, you talk to them, goddammit! It's your fuckin' job, not mine!"

"Hey, what's the matter?"

"I'm sick of talking about that goddamn show, that's all. Valerie this, Valerie that. I'm not married to you. I'm married to a goddamn character in a soap opera."

"I'm sorry, Joe."

"It's all you ever talk about. On the ferry yesterday afternoon, at dinner last night, breakfast today. I'm goin' bananas. It's enough to blow my mind."

"I'm sorry, Joe. We're all involved with the show. It's . . . it's natural."

"Well, I'm not on the show and it's not natural for me." He slammed another fish down on the chopping board and lopped off the head with a hatchet.

"I'm sorry."

"And that's another thing, goddammit! Stop saying you're sorry. Shit!"

"All right, Joe, my lord!" Vanessa stared at her husband. Joe was tall, thin, and quite attractive in a Jesus hippy sort of way. He had a bushy head of curly brown hair which flowed over his ears and down to his shoulders. His high, rounded cheekbones gave him a devilish quality when he smiled, but it was pleasant, almost childlike. "With that angelic look, you should certainly be easier to live with," she said cheerfully.

"I'm not so bad. Just lay off that show for a while and I won't get so bugged. Between you and that faggoty little associate producer of yours, I don't think I could sit through another meal."

Vanessa leaned past him and washed her hands in the sink. "I thought you liked Colin."

"Oh, he's all right. Once he realized I was yours."

"I'll cut his gizzard out if he ever lays hands on you." She picked up a fish and brandished it for emphasis. "I love you, baby," she said in a typical Bogart fashion, "but Colin is only after your emaciated body." She finished washing and started slicing tomatoes for a salad.

"My emaciated body! You dare talk about my emaciated body! You're so skinny if somebody painted a red stripe down your front you'd look like a thermometer."

"I'm not skinny," she protested. "I'm voluptuously thin."

"No you're not—you're skinny. But don't worry, I've got a remedy for that." He pivoted mischievously around. A diabolical gleam flickered in his eye. His hand was oozing with fish innards.

"Joe, no!"

"We'll fatten you up with fish guts. Slimy, revolting fish guts." He crept toward her slowly, Bela Lugosi playing Count Dracula.

"No!" Vanessa squealed with a terrified giggly, high-pitched scream.

"Fish guts on the neck, fish guts in the nose, fish guts over the eyes and down the throat and under the arms. I'm gonna wash you in fish guts, my dear." He grabbed her with one arm and brought the intestines closer and closer to her face with the other.

"No, no, please, Joe!"

"Who has an emaciated body?" he asked.

"I do, I do. Yours is fat as King Henry the Eighth's. Round and roly-poly. Not the fish guts, Joe."

Just then, the screen door opened and in strolled a slightly effeminate young man in brief bathing trunks and a see-through shirt. He was toting a beach bag over his shoulder which he dropped off in the pantry. "Is this a private orgy, or can any old fish join in?"

Vanessa broke away from Joe and ran to the side of the kitchen. "Colin, you're a lifesaver!"

"I'm known for my timing." He plopped himself down in a straight-backed chair and eyed Joe. "I just saw Vern and Lucile lugging some boat stuff down by the dock. Why don't you give 'em a hand? I'd offer, but I'm exhausted. Been chasing life guards around their chairs all day."

"Go on, Joey," said Vanessa, "I'll make some snacks so we can have drinks as soon as they get back."

Joe grinned and washed off the gook in the sink. "Sure you don't want to come along, Colin? Put a couple of muscles on the old bod. You're getting kind of flabby there, my boy."

"Well, I'll be damned, you've noticed."

"I take an interest in all of Vanessa's friends."

"Umm, I see."

"And if I ever decide to switch, you'll be first." Joe dried his hands on a dish towel.

"Big thanks for small favors. We'll see who's in the market for what at the time."

"You two are disgusting." Vanessa turned to her husband. "Go on, Joe, another couple of minutes and they won't need any help."

Joe ducked out of the door and jogged down the path leading to the dock. The screen door slammed with summer familiarity.

"Watch out for the boys in the Pines!" sang Colin and then he sighed. "Between you and your husband, I don't know who to go for first."

She cocked her head and gave him a long, slow look out of the corner of her eye. "Whom. And you leave my husband alone. He's got enough problems without having to worry about which sex to be chased by."

"Well, then, I guess I'll just have to turn my attentions to you." He walked around to embrace her from behind. He circled his arms around her waist and rested his cheek against hers.

"You're impossible. Go on over there and peel me some onions."

He popped a section of tomato into his mouth and drew a blade through an electric sharpener. "I've a sneaky feeling there's something I want to tell you, but the sight of your delicious hubby just blew it out of my mind."

"Why don't you do that here near the faucet." She pointed to the onion he was about to slice into. She turned on the spigot. "It won't make your eyes tear so much."

Colin brought the vegetables over to the sink and worked under the stream of cold water. They performed

48

the chores in silence for a time. When they spoke again it was with the relaxed air of close friends. "Joe seems to be enjoying himself."

"I think so, yes."

"It must be difficult for you at times."

She found a small bowl and spooned some Dijon mustard into it. "It could be a lot worse, I suppose. He's trying, he really is; he's been very good. It's been more than a year since he's had anything."

"Still. . . ." Colin cleared the drain of some accumulated onion skins and plopped them into a plastic-lined garbage pail.

"I know he's moody, but so what? I'd rather him be moody than back on the needle."

"Is he still with the psychiatrist?"

"Four times a week."

"Oh, Mary! That must be eating up your whole salary!"

She laughed. "There's sure not much left after the rent is paid."

"Criminal! Criminal! You know what I think? I think the government should pay for that."

"Oh, yes, right away."

"I mean it, lookit, it's because of the crappy society we live in he got hooked in the first place, right? And if he were still hooked, it would cost society all the people he'd be mugging or whose apartments he'd be ripping off to support his habit. Not to mention the hospital bills of the people he might hurt or even those he might kill, God forbid! Not too long ago, a friend of mine got it on Riverside Drive. He was out walking his dog at about two in the morning and two guys jumped him, took his money, and then beat him so bad he'll probably have to be hospitalized for six months. I think we owe it to the ex-addict to help pay for his rehabilitation. I think we owe it to ourselves. The goddamn politicians! All they care about is protecting their fucking districts and getting elected again. Christ! It was their fault he got hooked."

Vanessa cut him off gently. "Let's forget about it for now, okay? It's not my favorite subject. Fortunately I've got a good salary and we can afford to pay the doctor ourselves."

"It really pisses me off." Tears started to roll down his cheeks and he began to sniffle from the onions.

49

"You see, you jabber so much you forget to keep your onions under the water." She took a tissue from a box and held it to his nose. "Here, blow," she said and he did. "Now I even have to wipe your nose for you. Oh, Colin," she sighed theatrically. "Whatever are we going to do with you?"

"Hey!" He shrieked suddenly. "I know what it was I wanted to tell you. Guess who I saw roasting on the beach this afternoon?"

"Liberace?"

"Rosalynann Patachoutz!"

"Who?"

"Rosalynann Patachoutz. Elliot Chamberfield's secretary. And you know what she told me? Catch this! We're in for some surprises on Tuesday, my dear. Vern's been replaced as producer."

"No. . . ." Vanessa dropped her salad preparations and stared at him. "No," she repeated. "Poor man."

"That's only half of it, love." Colin sucked in the sides of his cheeks and peered at her over the tops of his large, thin-framed sunglasses. "Guess who's replacing him? Phillip Searing!"

"The man from Goodhart Productions?"

"My dear, he's been daytime VP with RBI for about nine months. Where have you been?"

"I haven't seen him for a long time."

"No, he rarely comes to the studio. He watches the shows from his office and gives notes out to Vern by memo . . . but he'll be around now, so watch your bottom. He's supposed to have gone through most of the actresses on his shows at least once."

Vanessa bristled. "Don't be funny. You know I wouldn't do anything like that."

"Sorry. No offense intended."

There were a few moments of silence. "Are you sure, Colin?"

"That's what Lady Rosalynann said, right from the horse's ass, so to speak. But from what she told me, I don't think anybody knows except Chamberfield and Phillip Searing. Not even Vern."

"But how can people be so cruel? My God! Vern's got a wife to support and a son in college. And they've just put a down payment on a new co-op. How can they just cut him off like that?"

Colin waved his hand in a gesture of half-hearted resignation. "That's TV." His attention dropped to the onion he was peeling.

"Do you think we should tell Vern, Colin?"

"What good would it do? The decision's already been made. There's nothing Vern could do about it now. He wouldn't be able to persuade them to change their minds. They don't work like that. The only thing we'd accomplish is to ruin the weekend for all of us. Besides, there's still the outside chance that Rosalynann's screwed up her facts."

Vanessa picked up on the ray of hope. "Do you think so?"

"No. But there is the chance."

"It seems so unfair."

Colin put his arm around her and hugged her close. People don't react that way any more, he thought. But that was precisely what set her apart from the loud-mouthed, pushy, ladder-climbing actresses who glided with such syrupy sincerity through the weekday afternoons of bored housewives. "Hold on, darlin'," he counseled, "our time may come yet. Save your tears. You might need them for yourself."

"You don't think there'll be any cast changes, do you? If I lost this job. . . ."

"I wouldn't place any bets on anything. It's anybody's guess what Searing will do. But one thing is certain: there'll be some action. If they canceled out the producer that means they want some serious changes. Between you and me, I like Vern but he's no producer. I think the show will be much better off with Searing. He's got the decisiveness to do whatever is needed to lift the ratings."

Vanessa spotted Vern, Joe, and Lucile from the window. They were pushing a homemade wheelbarrow filled with fishing poles and boating gear toward the house. Not wishing to be present when the threesome clattered up the back steps, she took a handful of dishes from a breakfront and carried them into the dining room. She spread them on the round captain's table near a bay window that opened onto the water. Then when she heard Vern's soft voice, she stopped what she was doing and rushed upstairs to compose her thoughts.

The dinner conversation, thanks to Colin, was spirited. Even Joe was relieved that each time Vern brought the subject around to the afternoon serials it suddenly shifted to something else. He figured Vanessa had clued Colin into the promise to avoid shoptalk. He did notice, however, that she was unusually solemn.

After dinner Vanessa offered to help with the dishes, but Lucile shooed her out of the kitchen. Vern settled in with a new bestseller and Colin prepared to take the sand taxi over to Cherry Grove. Joe took Vanessa by the hand. "Come on out. Let's get some air."

Vern dropped his glasses down on his nose and looked up from his book. "If you want to be alone, walk over to the bay side. Everybody and his mother'll be on the beach."

They stepped out into the darkness. Vanessa felt a surge of relief.

The summer evening was balmy and the stars were out in force. A sweetness was in the air from some overgrown honeysuckle nearby. Nothing was spoken for a long while as they wound their way through the low trees toward the bay. Joe was drinking in the night. Vanessa was absorbed in her own thoughts. The quiet moments were the ones that kept the fabric of their marriage from shredding. Verbally, Joe had so many defenses it was rarely possible to reach him.

Vern was right. The little port was practically deserted. They walked out to the end of the dock and sat down, facing the water and the twinkling lights in the distance called Long Island. Beyond the lights, of course, was Manhattan. The distance from both was reassuring.

"Why were you so quiet at dinner?"

She allowed the glittering ripples of the water to hypnotize her for a long moment.

Joe bent over and nestled his face against her throat. He toyed with the rich thickness of hair that covered the nape of her neck and absorbed the scent that skimmed the texture of her skin. "Why were you so quiet, hmm?"

"You asked me not to talk about the soap."

"Ah, hah! So that's it." He let his lips play along the edge of her ear.

"Something serious has happened. Colin told me while you were down at the dock."

"What can possibly happen that's serious about a soap opera?"

"Vern's been replaced as producer."

"No shit?"

She turned to look at his reaction. The single light burning at the far end of the dock caused his profile to appear in silhouette. "He's been replaced by a guy named Phillip Searing."

"Do you know him?"

"No. I've seen him, that's all. It could mean a shake-up for all of us."

"What's Vern goin' to do?"

"I don't know. He hasn't even been told yet."

"They don't screw around, do they?"

"Joe, what would we do if I were fired?"

"Maybe find a different dinner conversation."

"I'm serious. What would we do?"

"What do ya think? You're the only one of us bringing in bread? I'm workin' too, ya know? Don't forget about that. Maybe I'm not pullin' down three or four bills a week, but I'm workin'. Right? We lived on that kind of money before you were an afternoon prima donna and we can do it again." He always seemed to be offended by any thought of financial dependence on her, yet his part-time job as dishwasher in a village vegetarian restaurant hardly brought in enough to pay the phone bill.

"You know I didn't mean it like that. We can live on your salary if you can get it full-time. But what about the doctor? Who's going to pay for the doctor?"

"Fuck 'em. I'll quit."

"No . . . no, you can't. It's important for you."

"What'sa matter? You afraid I'm gonna start shootin' up again?"

"No, but—"

"Sure you are." He looked at her sadly. "Sure you are. Okay, I know. I've never been any Rock of Gibraltar for you."

She twisted around and took his head in her hands. "It's not that, Joe. I know you won't go back to . . . I just want it to be as easy as possible for you to hold out, get rid of some of the reasons you started in the first place. I never want either of us to have to go through a repeat of last year. That's why I'm worried about my job."

He kissed her on the temple. "Well," he said slowly, "there's sure as shit no sense worryin' about it now. Anyway what have you got to be concerned about? You're terrific in the part."

"You just never know. It's only a small part and there could be a million reasons I could be written out of the script."

"So you're goin' to start worryin' about that now? Before you even talk to the guy. You're bananas. Vanessa Bananas." He laughed. Then he broke off and looked in the direction of a small cluster of boats moored about twenty-five yards out from the dock. "Hey 'Ness, let's row out to that cabin cruiser. The big dark one out there." He indicated a twin-screw Chris Craft about forty-five feet long.

"We can't do that." Vanessa climbed to her feet.

"Why not? Look, there's an old dinghy. We can borrow it and paddle out. The water's calm."

"Suppose we're caught?"

"Who's gonna catch us? What nut would take a dinghy out in the dark like that?"

"Suppose somebody's sleeping on board?"

"Nah. I heard a guy on the dock say today that it belongs to some Wall Street executive who's gone to Maine for the month." Without waiting for a response, he clambered down into the little boat, untied it, and was pushing it along the dock, hand over hand to where Vanessa stood. "Come on, 'Ness. Nobody'll know."

She hesitated for a moment, glanced around at the deserted dock, and then accepted his outstretched arm. "All right, but just a trip around it."

He pushed off. "Here, take this." He handed her a broken piece of orange crate she could use for a paddle. She placed herself starboard at the bow and Joe balanced at stern and port. They dipped deeply into the spooky still water.

Joe uttered a low, rumbling guttural growl.

"What was that?" Vanessa whipped around.

"What was what?"

"That noise."

"What noise?"

"It sounded like an animal. Did you do that?"

"I don't know what your're talkin' about. *RRRRRAGH!*"

54

"Damn you. I thought it was you! Stop trying to scare me."

"Oh, *that* noise."

Suddenly there was a loud clunk and they lurched forward in the dinghy. Vanessa screamed. "What was that?"

"We hit the boat. Remember the boat we're goin' to? We just hit it. If you was lookin' where you was goin', and not worryin' about bogeymen, you'd know that." He paddled his end around, getting him closer to a rope ladder that extended from the open deck of the cruiser. "Let's go up and look around."

"We shouldn't do that. That's somebody's private property."

"Anybody who has enough bread to afford a yacht like this has probably stolen so much from the government in tax dodges and other tricky tricks that his property ought to be considered public."

"Tell that to the judge."

"I'm goin' up. Consider it a proletarian revolt. I'm a member of the great unwashed and I'm revolting."

"You certainly are."

He made it to the rail and climbed over. Vanessa scanned the shore. They were too far out for anybody to recognize what they were doing. She stood up, holding tightly to the rope ladder, and climbed aboard.

"It's bloody wild up here, isn't it?"

Vanessa poked her head over the top. They were on the sun deck behind and below a gigantic flying bridge. White director's chairs were lined up in front of a long, cushioned bench.

"You wanna go to the Bahamas?"

"I wouldn't mind getting accustomed to a life on this."

"Come on up." He took her hand and led her up the ladder to the captain's bridge.

"Fantastic!"

"A-vast there y'ole maties! Top the mains'l n' gib the whoogie."

"What are you talking about?"

"I'm a talkin' sea talk, m' lady. Fibber the whatsits and up yerass!"

"That's pretty salty."

Vanessa sat down on the lookout chair. It was protected by a fitted plastic cover. She pulled Joe onto her knees and

55

ran her hands up under his shirt feeling the tight, lean flesh of his chest.

"Hold it there, wench, the captain's got no time for whorin', now. Them's might be pirates I might be a-spyin'" He leapt from the bridge to the lower deck with a blood-curdling yell. "On guard!" Grabbing one of the bench cushions in an armlock, he wrestled it to the deck, muttering and cursing in a loud voice. "Ya think ye can grab me gold 'n woman, huh? Take that, ya spineless jellyfish! And that! And that! And that! Uh, got me, ya yellow-livered bastard. But me ghost'll haunt ya all the days of yer miserable life and ye shall dwell in a house of barnacles forever!" He rolled over and played dead.

Vanessa rose from the chair and looked down at him, down the length of the steep flight of ladder steps to where he lay on his back. She stepped to the rail. Joe remained motionless, his arms sprawled out. Her hand moved to the top button of her blouse. She undid it. She undid the second, then the third. She shifted her shoulders and the blouse slid off. Then she reached behind and unfastened the hook of her brassiere. It too slid off and she guided it so that it floated all the way down to the lower deck and fell across his face. He opened his eyes and looked up. Vanessa's fingers went to her Levis. She unsnapped the top clasp and, taking the sides of the fly between the thumb and forefinger of each hand, teasingly drew them apart, undoing the zipper. Her hands worked in between the loosened pants and her skin and she slid them down the length of her thighs. After a little kick she watched them sail down and land on one of the chairs. Joe stared up at the figure between the step railings. She was still. The moon, behind and slightly to the side, cast a luminous glow across her left side, touching her cheek, her breast. All the rest was in darkness. She swayed with the faint rocking of the boat, but aside from that remained still.

Slowly Joe eased himself up. The wood of the ladder creaked as he stepped on the first rung, then the second, and the third. Vanessa remained immobile, a lone figurehead surrounded by sky. Joe pressed forward slightly when his head reached the level of her knees. Instinctively his mouth opened and he tasted the sweet flesh just above and inside the caps. He nibbled gently with his lips. He moved another step up. His cheek brushed the silkiness of her

56

panties. He pressed against it, feeling the warmth of her belly against his forehead. He let go of the ladder and cupped his hands around the smallness of her waist. He drew them down and with them the panties.

Vanessa kneeled, searching for his lips with hers, his hands with hers. She lay back, pulling Joe over her like a winter blanket. They kissed long and sensuously. Together they fumbled for the buttons of his clothing. She bit his ears, his neck, rubbed the length of her nudity against his. They tried to absorb each other. With his tongue Joe traced the soft curve of her shoulders, her breasts, fuller and heavier than one would imagine from such a slender girl. His tongue licked at her nipples, causing them to tighten. He raised himself into position and she wrapped her arms around his sweating back. Their breath quickened.

His hip movements slowed and then stopped. He took a deep breath and let it out gradually. "It's no use, 'Ness. I can't."

Their bodies froze in common antipathy. Joe let his head drop.

"It's all right," she said, trying to conceal her disappointment. "It's all right, Joe."

"Oh, Christ."

"Shhh." She kissed him maternally on the top of his head. "It'll come back. Don't worry. It's not your fault. We can wait." But tears formed in the corners of her eyes.

Joe's mouth crept down her body, kissing her and pressing her close as he descended. She felt the soft flesh of his lips and the brush of his hair across her breasts.

"It's all right, Joe. Really, it's all right."

"No, it's not all right." He moved down to her hips and along the hill of her inner thighs, tanned by the spring sun. His cheek toyed across the delicate forest of hair and his fingers played up and down her calves.

Hesitantly, uncertainly, her knees parted. Her thighs opened slightly, then more and Joe moved in to please her as best he could.

"It's all right Joe, it's all right . . . oh, God . . . it's been so long."

5.

Phillip Searing's weekend was unglorious. He cloistered himself in his duplex and let the service take all calls. When he felt hungry he called Goldberg's Pizza on Third Avenue, but the only diversion he had was an unwinding every couple of hours into the kitchen to brew a fresh pot of coffee.

He was familiarizing himself with the entire history of *Affair*. By the time he was finished he had read the story projections of the past three years, the character analyses for over twenty-five people, half of all the previous season's scripts, and reams of notes and rejected ideas.

He left the apartment only once: at 3:00 A.M. Monday morning. He went to the company broadcast facilities on Second Avenue, pulled several tapes of the more recent episodes from the library, and found a sleepy night shift technician to run them. He propped himself up on a couch in a viewing room normally used by agency brass and scanned five hours of representative shows. Fortunately there was a twenty-four-hour delicatessen around the corner, a veritable cornucopia of roast-beef sandwiches and Russian dressing. He took notes on the performers, production, character development, plot lines, sets, and costumes. At nine he hopped a cab back to the apartment.

After a quick shower he offered himself three hours of sorely needed sleep. Then he spent the day digesting all the material on which he'd gorged himself.

On Tuesday he was ready. Eight A.M. found him paying a taxidriver in front of RBI's Studio 23 at Fifty-fourth Street and Ninth Avenue. He slammed the door and walked briskly into the foyer of the three-story building.

The duty guard looked up from his daydream. "Morning, sir, surprised to see you here today."

"Morning, Pete!" The elevator doors opened and a mailboy dragged his cart out. Phillip let him pass and stepped in. "Don't bother to ring up, Pete, I'm expected." He pushed the third-floor button.

He walked the long narrow corridor to *Affair*'s production suite, his mind already churning out the day's schedule. A plain, freckled girl with an astonishingly flat chest perked up in surprise when he entered. Phillip made a note to shift her out of view; the first thing the show would have to take on was some class. "Mr. Searing, I didn't know you were coming."

Just like Vern to keep the news from his staff. She buzzed the inner office and announced him.

"Who's in there?" asked Phillip. He glanced quickly around to see what changes he might want to make immediately.

"Just Mr. Tuttle and Mr. Rosetti. You can go right—"

"Tuttle? What's he doing here?" he exploded. The girl was startled. But before she had a chance to respond, Vern himself opened the door. He extended his hand and smiled warmly.

What a pro, thought Phillip. Not a sign of bitterness. He was probably about to say good-bye to the staff. Phillip was gracious. "I'll step out for a few minutes if you like."

The man didn't bat an eyelash. "What do you mean you'll step out? Come on in. We don't have anything to hide." He laughed.

"Hi, Phil."

"Hello Pat." The show's chief director came out to the door.

59

"I'm glad you feel that way, Vern," Phillip said. "I don't like the situation myself."

The frail graying producer looked puzzled. "What are you talking about? Oh, the ratings drop! Right, well, I think we have that solved. Wait till you read the new story projections. Phillip, they're dynamite!"

Searing was shocked. That son-of-a-bitch Chamberfield hadn't told him. Of all the unthinking, inconsiderate! "Vern, excuse me, I'll be right back."

Leaving a chorus of gaping mouths behind he broke away from the lingering handshake and stormed out of the office. He double-stepped down the four flights of stairs and exited behind the guard.

There was a small grocery store at the end of the block. He found a pay phone in a dark corner in the rear and dialed Chamberfield's private line.

"I'm sorry, Mr. Searing, Mr. Chamberfield's tied up at the moment. May I take a message?"

"You tell him I want to speak to him now."

"I'm sorry, Mr.—"

"NOW!"

A click, silence, and then the big man's nasal voice. "What do you want, Searing? Make it snappy."

"You insensitive bastard! How dare you not tell Tuttle he was being replaced!"

"I didn't want to spoil his weekend, Phillip."

"Bullshit! That didn't stop you from spoiling mine."

"So did you tell him?"

"No, I didn't tell him! When I fire somebody I have the courtesy to tell him personally. I don't humiliate him by making him face his replacement." He lowered his tone. "I'm going to walk around the block two times, Elliot, and by the time I get back if I don't have a clear office, you can get yourself another sucker."

"Ah, Phillip, you've got such powers of persuasion! Go ahead. A walk is a good idea, cool you down. . . ."

By the time he got back to the production suite the flat-chested secretary was ashen-faced and Vern had disappeared. Phillip walked into the inner office, shut the door, and went to work.

He stubbed the intercom button. "What's your name?"

"Gloria, Mr. Searing."

"Come in a minute, Gloria, please."

The door opened and the secretary took a hesitant step into the room. She was uncertain what level of sadness she'd be permitted to show.

Phillip decided not to waste time making explanations. "There is a lot to do, Gloria, and precious little time to do it in. I'm going to have a series of meetings with the staff, starting with Pat Rosetti. I'll give you a list in about five minutes of the order in which I want you to send people in." He glanced around. "But not here. I'll work out of the conference room next door for today. Vern hasn't had time to clear his personal things out yet. Were you close to him?"

"I guess so."

"Then you can get them together for him during the afternoon, or call him and see if he wants to do it himself tonight. I'll have to come in here tomorrow."

She nodded her head.

"Now get yourself together and ask Rosetti to come up."

She slipped out and closed the door.

Phillip scrutinized the office. Drab browns, tans, and maroons; a cheap, common print of one of the French Impressionists, probably chosen more for its size and color relationship to the room than for any personal value. The carpet was worn and frayed. It was a dark-green, institutional style, and had been lying dead on the floor long before *Affair Of The Heart* moved in. Vern either never noticed it or was too afraid to spend any budget money to buy a new one. Three-quarter-length red curtains hung from the single window beside the desk. They were threaded through with white, green, and black, and looked like a moldy spaghetti sauce with peppers and onions floating on top. It reflected the tastes of a drab producer. Sweet man, though, thought Phillip. An anomaly in an industry like television.

He took a yellow legal pad off of the coffee table in the far corner of the room, sat down on the couch, and compiled his list. After a few minutes, the intercom buzzed. "Pat Rosetti's here, Mr. Searing."

"Thank you, Gloria."

He added and subtracted a few names, then went through the door to the adjoining viewing-conference room. He greeted the director and studied his face for signs of any loyalties. "Good morning again, Pat."

"Phillip. . . ."

They had known each other ever since Pat had returned from the army and tried unsuccessfully to re-establish his career as an actor. Before he was drafted in 1961, Pat had received excellent notices in a handful of plays and was well on his way to becoming a star. But three years later, when he returned from the army, he found himself still the physical image of a fumbling adolescent, but too old to play such roles. He drifted from bit parts to walk-ons and soon found that his need to support his new family was stronger than his desire to act. He made the transition to television and gradually became one of the best younger directors in the business. Phillip liked him and respected his work.

"Frankly, Pat, I need you. The cast and the crew respect you and I do too."

"That's nice to hear."

"I can't say you've flourished, but you've been operating under fairly impossible conditions. The fact that your episodes of the show are even semi-believable is an enormous credit to you. Now this is what's happening. Sit down." Phillip sat on the couch and Pat across the table on a brown-leather Eames-type chair.

"I figure we have a solid sixteen weeks more of the show, come what may. Three weeks more before the next thirteen-week block begins. But the decision from Sixth Avenue on keeping it or killing it won't wait for sixteen; it'll be done in about thirteen weeks from now. If Russell Keel or Chamberfield can't smile over their morning Nielsens by then, we can kiss all our jobs good-bye."

"You, too?"

"Me, too. I'm not down here as a fix-it VP. I'm in as producer—full-time and nothing else."

"Whew! I didn't know."

"Now look: in the next couple of weeks we're going to have to start making some drastic changes in the format. I mean sets, costumes, characters, plot, everything. We're going to have to do it as fast as possible, but with a minimum of audience shock. We can't destroy their reality for them. We've got to be very careful of that." He paused. "I'm going to fire the second relief director."

"Hoddy?"

"I saw his work and it's sadly inferior. This'll mean a heavy lot of work for you, doing all five shows, but I promise as soon as we're on the right track, we'll get a director to spell you. It means a bitch of an amount of work for you though," he warned.

"I can handle it."

"Good. I've more ideas I want to go over with you. What about meeting me for dinner tonight? I know you've got to get back to rehearsal now."

"That'll be fine, of course."

"Good. I'm glad to have you with me, Pat."

"Thank you." He started for the door. Phillip stopped him.

"You usually break the cast for notes at eleven, don't you?"

"Yes."

"Hold them there for me for a few minutes today, would you? That's all I'll need. Just the cast and your people from the control room."

"No problem. . . . Phillip?"

"Yes."

"I should be more diplomatic than this, in view of Vern I mean, but we've known each other a long time, you and I, long enough for you to know I'm not bullshitting." He paused. "I'm glad about the changes. You must not be, but I am. We'll have a show now. Vern's a nice guy, but he's no producer. If anybody can keep this thing floating, you can."

Phillip put his hand on his shoulder and walked him to the door. "Thanks. Well, you'd better get back to rehearsal."

After Pat left, Phillip tore the top sheet off of his yellow pad and handed it to Gloria. On second glance she wasn't so bad-looking, after all. She had a rather sweet face and a pert little nose set between two wondering brown eyes. Phillip decided to try and win her over. "What's your last name, Gloria?"

"Rupert."

"Gloria Rupert," he said. "Why don't you wear any makeup, Gloria Rupert?"

"Do you think I need it?" It was the sort of question

that most girls would have asked coquettishly, but it came out as a direct, if youthful, desire to know.

"No." He cocked his head and studied her with expertise. "No, I guess you don't need it."

"Then why do you want me to wear it?"

"I didn't say I wanted you to wear it. I asked you why you didn't. With all the actresses flitting around here pancaked and rouged like plastic flowers, I wondered why you didn't feel the need to brighten up to their color level."

"I'm not an actress. I'm a secretary."

"Good point." Phillip was impressed by the girl's forthrightness.

"I guess there's no reason at all for you to wear make-up." He grinned at her. She took visual refuge behind her typewriter.

He watched her, wondering what she was thinking. Then he said, very softly, "Gloria."

"Yes." She didn't look up.

"Will you ask Caroline Jackers to come up."

"Yes, sir."

"Thank you." His voice became quieter with each word. She was more and more tense.

"And Gloria?"

"Sir?"

"Are you afraid of me?"

"Yes."

"Good." But he smiled in such a childlike way she blushed for having admitted it. "I'm not as vicious as I appear, Gloria." He walked back into the conference room, but before closing the door he poked his head out and said, "I'm diabolical."

A few minutes later the head writer was announced, and a once-stunning woman of about forty-five slunk in.

"Hello, Caroline, please sit down."

She slid her tailored body onto the far side of the couch and crossed a pair of beautifully shaped legs. Her skirt hitched up. Phillip wondered how accidental it was. She'd been around. From the early fifties as a production assistant on the *Show of Shows*, through Gleason and Meadows, to soaps which she had always considered beneath her capabilities as a writer. She began a test of strength. "You can save the openers, I've heard."

"I see. And what do you think of all that?"

She folded her arms and slumped back in her seat, eying him with a little too much severity. She was the kind of tough lady who went to women's lib meetings in the evening after using her sexual attributes as advantageously as possible during the day. "What do I think of all that?" She calculated her position. "Well, I'll tell you. Hard, cold, and direct—I don't like it. Vern Tuttle has been good to me and I don't like to see him lynched. He hired me for this job, and together we shaped what I think is the most intelligent, subtle, continuing story on the air. I don't like the way he was fired. I think it was gauche and unnecessary, and I have a natural resentment toward anyone who replaced him."

"Does that mean you'd prefer not to work with me?"

"That means I'll have to get used to the idea."

"I see." She was tough. Not just honest. Maybe it had to do with Vern; maybe it didn't. If it did it was commendable. It was rare to find anyone in this business who would stick his neck out, even verbally, for a loser. But then maybe it just had to do with her. She'd spent a lot of years sliding around the studios. People got calloused and sore from that. She was a good writer. An intelligent writer, but cynical. That was partly what was wrong with the show. But . . . he should give her at least a chance. "Caroline, I want to talk to you at length about the show. I know what it's like now, as a collaborative effort, but I want to see what you'd do on your own."

"What does that mean?"

"Just what I said. *Affair Of The Heart* as it is now has a lot of problems, and the responsibility for those problems is spread among several people. Vern is out. I have a feeling that, left alone, you might incline more toward my vision than his. I'm interested to find out. Are you free tonight?"

"For dinner?"

"No, after dinner at my apartment. I'm meeting Pat Rosetti earlier."

She breathed a heavy theatrical sigh as if to suggest that putting off whatever she'd planned would be a hassle, but she'd do it for the benefit of the show.

65

"I won't keep you long."

"What time do you want me?"

"Nine o'clock will be fine. I should be finished by then. I'm at 102 Irving Place, 14th floor."

"Okay." She drew herself up to her full height of martyrdom.

"And by the way, what are you working on at the moment?"

"The script for the third week in July."

"Then you're ahead. Good. I'd like you to drop it for the day and put on paper your thoughts about everything you think is wrong with the show, and how you think each can be solved. In other words, if you were in sole charge how would you develop the story, the characters. Everything. I want to know it all."

"Jesus."

"It's a chance to come up with something unique."

She walked slowly over to the door and let her hand revolve sensually around the bulbous steel handle. "I don't really know that I'd change much, Mr. Searing." She looked up to see how he'd react.

"No?"

"I'm not sure."

Phillip was getting tired of the game. "Well, you put it on paper and I'll read it. I'd like to have it here by three."

"Three!"

"We'll discuss it when we meet tonight."

"You don't give a girl much time, Mr. Searing."

"I'm not talking to a girl, Caroline. I'm talking to a writer."

She twisted herself out the door.

Phillip went downstairs at 11:05. He could see through the observation window that everyone had already assembled. Some of the actors were rehearsing lines. Pat was going over some timings with the assistant director. Colin Dawes, the associate producer, was sitting on the piano, trying to impress a young male extra. The rest of the people were gathered in tight little folding-chair circles in hushed and animated conversation.

Phillip pushed the door open and entered. He stood there for a moment, scanning the roomful of faces. Everyone seemed to stop talking at once.

66

Pat came over to Phillip. "Why don't you let me open the meeting? It might soften things up a bit for you."

"Thank you." He moved over to the side and took a chair.

Pat took the center of the floor. He cleared his throat and pushed his hand across his thick sandy hair. The AD spilled some coffee. "Shit!" Colin tossed him a roll of paper towels.

"You all pretty much know what the situation is." He had a pleasant voice. His diction, from his stage work, was impeccable. "A decision was made on the forty-fourth floor to replace Vern as producer with Phillip Searing."

There was a soft "what!" from someone who had come in late. Pat continued.

"Phillip hasn't been here very much, but most of you know he's been in executive control of the show for about nine months. I think, though, since he will now be working with us exclusively, I should say a few words about him." A slight pause. He examined a distant nothingness. "I've known Phillip Searing for many years. I just want to say that this move was not his doing. He respects Vern as we all do, and if the decision had been his it would not have been handled in this way.

"Second, and without detracting from Vern at all, I want to say Phillip is just about the best damn producer in this business. I for one am very pleased that he's returned to roll his sleeves up with us. We need help. We all know that and I can tell you Phillip is just the man to do it."

Pat turned to the new producer and extended his hand. Phillip stood and shook it. There was modest and restrained applause. Phillip took the floor and began.

"The forty-fourth floor, like God, moves in mysterious ways."

A few people giggled.

"It's true. I had less warning of this change than you. But it's happened and we're going to make the best of it. We've got a show to do. A lot of things are going to change. We're going to develop a new look, a new energy, a new excitement. It can be fun. It *will* be work, mostly of course for the staff. There will be quick decisions, last-minute alterations in scripts, set changes, costume changes —all. The one break you'll have is that as of tomorrow

67

we'll be videotaping the show and not having to do it live any more. As you may have noticed from your new schedule, it means an earlier start to your day, but hopefully that'll be compensated for by the fact that some of the pressure will be taken off you. For a while, the tape will air the same day that we shoot, so it won't make much difference to you. But as soon as we can get a backlog of scripts, we'll be able to tape a few days in advance and give both you and us a breather. That's not a promise, though."

He found himself speaking to a girl in the corner, Vanessa Langley, who played a minor continuing character. She had huge black eyes that looked out at him with a kind of sympathy, and yet fear. She liked him, he felt, and with all that had happened he needed one of them to like him.

"There's no sense in deluding you. This industry thrives and dies on ratings reports. Nielsens, Arbitron, there are a few of them. They have very little to do with quality. They're simply a guide to audience taste, and for some reason the ladies have not been responding well enough to *Affair*. And when the ratings dip, our sponsors pay less for their time slots, and as RBI has no aspirations toward altruism the board of directors gets worried. I'll lay it on the line: if the ratings on *Affair Of The Heart* don't pick up considerably by the first National Nielsens for the fall season, the show will be dropped from the daytime schedule."

Phillip paused, giving them the time to examine their shoes while pondering their individual fates. He noticed that Vanessa looked particularly distraught. Her head was bowed and her long black hair, the blackest he'd ever seen, fell forward, hiding her face. She had been knitting during Pat's introduction but now her hands were still.

"The point is this. We're not going to allow the show to be canceled. We're going to work our asses off to keep it going, and if we all do that it *will* keep going. We're going to start now. It's up to each and every one of you to do your utmost to keep the energy up, keep the spirit up, and adapt as quickly as possible to every change.

"I'm fortunate to have inherited from Vern one of the best ensemble acting groups on television today. I say this not in an attempt to flatter you, but because I know your

68

talents. I've watched you all—not only on camera, but in theater productions as well. I know how good you are. You go on doing your part, I'll do mine. What else can I tell you?"

There was a shifting of weight and a few soft murmurs. A young man wearing a Snoopy sweatshirt raised his hand. He was the lead actor.

"Yes, Bill."

"I think we're all concerned about the same thing. Will you be making any changes in the cast?"

He scanned their faces. Such frail people, these actors. They wear their emotions on their jaws and stick them out to be punched. He'd soften it as best he could. "Yes, Bill, there'll be changes in the cast. We're going to be tinkering with the plot line and that'll necessitate giving more weight to some and less weight to others. Whatever happens, you should know it's not because we don't want you. It'll happen only when we've decided on a different direction for the show. But don't start to worry yet, please. Let's all wait to see what happens."

At twelve-thirty there was a corned-beef-sandwich-and-pickle meeting with the production staff. He gave them a version of the pep talk. "I'm interested in people who will break ass, not just take this as another job." They all assured him they would, but that remained to be seen.

The afternoon was spent working with the day's show and in ten-minute grabbed sessions with whomever was free. He scheduled some time with the set designer the following morning, since the guy was up at another studio solving problems. By three-thirty, at the end of the air show, Caroline's notes had been given to the secretary. Phillip glanced over them quickly, but reserved judgment for later.

The dinner with Pat Rosetti was productive. They had a simple meal at the Fleur de Lys, *escargots*, *noisettes d'agneau*, and a salad. The director's ideas corresponded very well with Phillip's thinking, and a good initial rapport was established. They spoke longer than he'd planned; Phillip didn't make it back to the apartment until ten minutes before Caroline was due to arrive.

He was exhausted.

He let himself into the foyer and draped his jacket over the back of a chair.

The place was hot. He switched the air conditioner on high, went over to the liquor cabinet, tugging at his shirt, and poured himself a stiff double Scotch. He drained it standing at the bar. He poured another one and went into the kitchen for ice. Then he slumped into a black-leather lounger to sip it. He drew a chestful of air, held it, and let it out. "Don't start with me tonight, Caroline," he said to the empty room. "I'm too bushed to go through any shit." He leaned his head back and closed his eyes.

A shower. A shower, my kingdom for a shower! He checked his watch. Maybe there was time. It would be another long night. The fifth in a row. Tomorrow was the set designer, the costume coordinator, the scenic people, and an ad representative for the show's largest sponsor. What the hell could he tell them before solidifying the direction of the story line?

The doorbell rang. It jarred him out of his thoughts.

Under her arm was the Gucci portfolio, Caroline's shopping bag of story projections and scripts in progress. "You look like you've fought the battle of New Orleans all by yourself."

"The end of the siege is coming, but it's the beginning of an ugly dawn. What will you have to drink?"

He closed the door behind her and moved himself to the bar.

"Another gin and tonic would be fine."

She plunked herself down into the plush beige sofa and stretched her arms out along its back. Her blouse tightened interestingly across her breasts. "So this is how a rich executive lives. Impressive. You've got good taste."

He brought over the drink and took his third double Scotch to his chair.

"I've lived in New York over twenty years and damned if I can find a place like this. I'm always just missing them."

"It's a problem, I know." Philip smiled politely. "Caroline, you'll excuse me if I seem anxious to get down to business. Did you read my notes on the story projections?"

"You wrote almost as much as I did." She laughed

70

softly, and it was only then that her smooth face, usually so carefully composed, gave away her age.

But she had style, he noted, and damn good legs. "So what do you think?"

"Most of it is a pile of crap." She smiled sweetly and took another sip. She peered at him over the rim of her glass. "Seems to me you want to turn *Affair* into a carbon copy of any other soap."

"On the contrary. But we're dealing with a specific audience. We still have definite guidelines to remain within."

"Phillip, you look tired. When was the last time you got a good night's sleep?"

"Let's stick to the problem, hmm?"

She rose and came around behind him. She set her drink down on an antique, marble-top chest that served the room as an end table. "Come on, I'm going to give you a massage and then you're going to bed. We can discuss all the rest tomorrow morning."

"I have a staff meeting at eight-thirty and a meeting with the designer at eleven. And I don't want a massage, thanks; sit down."

But she had kicked off her shoes and was removing her suit jacket. She threw it over the back of a Voltaire chair. "I never knew a man yet who didn't like a massage." She began to work his shoulders and the back of his neck. "Loosen up."

"Caroline, there are problems with *Affair*."

"Screw *Affair*. It can wait a half hour. And what good are you when you're so pooped out you can't even hold a drink up."

She took the glass out of his hand and pulled him slowly to his feet. "Come on, don't be such an old maid. Shoes off, shirt and tie! On the rug."

"Caroline, you're too much."

She fumbled with the buttons on his shirt. "Men are such egoists. You think we want to fuck you all the time. This will be legitimate, honey-chile, and you'll thank me in the morning after you've had a delicious night's sleep." She peeled his shirt off and took a quick survey of his lean, muscular frame. "Well, I can see you're not glued to your desk." She ran her fingers over the sheen of his tan.

71

"What a nice, lovely change from your average flabby executive."

"You moonlight as a masseuse often?"

She laughed, as she was reaching for his belt, but he pushed her hand away, yanking the belt out of the loops and throwing it over the chair behind him. Caroline dragged back the end table and made room on the deep, pile carpet. "If you knew how old I was, you'd die. I just eat right, drink right, exercise a lot, and sleep right."

"Ever have any fun?"

He stretched out prone on the floor. She hiked up her skirt and straddled his back. "You have any talcum or oil in the house?"

"Let's not make it a big production. I think it would be better to talk about a few things."

Her hands kneaded the bulges in his back, working over the satiny brown skin with the sureness of an expert. "Jesus, you're tense as a rock. No wonder you're such a grouch."

He took a deep breath and tried to sponge the rigidity out of his shoulders. "I don't want to sleep. We've got some things to talk about. It would be too easy to fall asleep."

"No hair on your back. I like that. I've never been attracted to gorillas. What do you do for exercise?" She pressed her palms up along the sides of his spinal column and then trailed her fingers downward in a feathery pattern.

"Delicious," he mumbled into the crook of his arm.

"I know. I asked you how you exercised."

"I go to the gym a couple of times a week. Tennis in the summer. Swimming."

She changed her attack. She started rhythmically pressing all of her weight into the area on either side of the spinal column, just underneath the rib cage.

He tried to speak, but the words came out as single, air-hammer blows. "Diving . . . football . . . croquet . . . mountain climbing . . . soft . . . ball . . . hard . . . ball . . . chess . . . and . . . checkers."

"Must be the chess and checkers that do it. You sure are built beautiful." She stopped for a moment to catch her breath. She allowed her nails to scrape along the rib cage, barely touching.

72

Phillip didn't move. He stayed stretched out and melted into the carpet. "Talk to me about *Affair*, before it's too late."

"That goddamned show. Okay. Take those pants off first." She climbed off his seat which she had been straddling. "You've got something in your pockets; it's cutting the hell out of the inside of my thighs." She reached underneath him, opened the top hook and zipper, and slid them down his legs.

"Caroline." There was a warning tone in his voice, but she paid no attention to it.

"I don't know why you're so worried about that show. We've got all the time in the world to patch it up. I know it's a piece of shit. But you know something? That's what they want out there in America-land. Shit."

Phillip kept his eyes closed and listened.

Caroline slipped off her own panties. She tugged her skirt up again and sat on his skin. Her hands squeezed hard into the flesh of his thighs. "You want to know what *Affair* is? It's a farce, honey. Nobody takes it seriously. You think I take it seriously? All that shit? Come on. I don't take it seriously and neither do you. Neither does anybody. Sometimes it can be fun. I managed to get in a few knocks here and there against the average Mr. Shmuck out there in blue-box land and they don't even know it. I do it for the money, and so do you. And you know it. We all do. So let's not get overly dramatic about quality." She pressed her thumbs into the soft muscles on either side of the coccyx. Then in one motion drew his French Rasurel briefs down and off his ankles.

"Caroline . . ."

"Screw you. Lie still and enjoy it." She reached over and flipped off the light, leaving only the small lamp glowing at the far end of the room. She pushed the heels of her hands along his back, stretching herself out on top of his nude body. Then she slid herself up so that one knee was between his parted legs. She sat.

With an effort he twisted himself over on his back and stared up at her in the darkness. He felt her dampness on the muscles of his thigh. She smiled down at him. "You're sure you don't have any baby oil?"

"Caroline, you're not going to like yourself tomorrow."

73

"You let me worry about that. What do you think I am, some papa-fearing teen ager?"

He wondered if she used the same methods of persuasion on Vern at their biweekly story conferences. No wonder the show never got anywhere.

She bent forward and let her hair fall gently over his slowly swelling piece. She slipped it into her mouth, sucked hard, and let it out again. Then she sat up.

Phillip watched her unbutton her blouse, watched the yellow silk slip off her shoulders, watched in silence as she reached behind and unclasped the straps of her brassiere. She wiggled her shoulders and it slipped from her arms. Her breasts were not small, but they still held most of their shape despite her age. She moved forward again, and let their weight lean gently on top of his privates.

"You're a pro," said Phillip, watching with a weird sense of detachment. It was as though he were watching someone else. "You're really a pro!"

"Never seriously, just for kicks."

The single table lamp, behind, silhouetted her body, giving the effect of a horseback rider in the night. She perched high on his stiff member.

"Caroline, you're in the wrong profession."

She sat hard and thrust him all the way in.

6.

She had been right. He did sleep like a baby and arrived at his new office bright and refreshed, eager to tackle the second day of the challenge. Caroline had slipped out sometime during the night. He tried not to think how she would react when she checked her office mail slot that morning.

There was a quick staff meeting at eight-thirty, some phone calls to make, and a list of instructions for the secretary.

"The important thing, Gloria, is to get in touch with Maude O'Keefe, as fast as you can. Try the Writers Guild."

At ten, he met with an advertising representative, who relayed the sponsor's concern over the downward slide of the ratings. The sponsor was making threatening noises about dropping the show, an important factor which Chamberfield had failed to mention. Phillip spoke enthusiastically about the changes he was instigating, the probable direction of the new story line, and finally placated the Madison Avenue rep into withholding any sponsor action until the results of the changes could be evaluated. It was eleven and he was in the middle of a meeting with the set designer, an elegantly dressed, albeit conservatively, gentleman, when he heard Caroline outside with the secretary.

"I don't give a royal fuck what he's in—I'm going in that room."

He smiled at the man across the desk. "Warren, would you mind very much taking a quick break? Run down to your office and bring up those designs you did for *Beekman Place* at Westbury last year. I hear they were quite good."

The door burst open and Caroline flew into the room. She stood at the entrance and glared at him. Blood surged through the veins of her neck. One hand was still on the knob, the other brandished a little pink slip. "You shit!"

Warren got up tactfully. "I'll just go get those designs." He steered a wide berth around her in getting to the door.

"You knew all along you'd canned me."

"That's not completely true. I hadn't finalized my decision till last night."

"What's the matter? Wasn't I good enough?"

"You were terrific, but with the kind of attitude you have I can't afford to keep you on." He looked at her appraisingly. "I told you you'd hate yourself in the morning."

"Very funny, you bastard. I could take you to the Writers Guild."

"You can, but I'm not firing you cold. Your contract will be bought up. Everything is above board. You're a good writer, Caroline."

"Splendid."

"But not for *Affair*. You're too sophisticated for our audience, you don't like them, and you should like whom you write for. You should be writing for *Harper's*."

"You made me make an ass of myself last night."

"I didn't make you do anything last night."

"I wouldn't work for you now if you tripled my salary. Vern was right. You have absolutely no human values of any kind."

She held up the pink slip. "When was this put into the box?"

"This morning."

"Swear?"

"Yes."

76

"Swear it wasn't in yesterday afternoon?"

"It wasn't in yesterday afternoon. I made my decision more on the basis of your attitude than anything else. Now come on, honey, take your paychecks and my thanks. I'm not in the mood to fight with you. I had a good time last night and I'd like to keep it as a delicious memory."

She crumpled the thin slip of paper in her hand. "Good luck, you shit. I hope *Affair* turns out to be the most maudlin, conventional, soapy piece of crap on TV." And she was already out of the door. He recoiled from the shock of the slam.

The intercom buzzed. "Mr. Searing, Maude O'Keefe is on line two."

He lifted the phone. "Maude, this is Phillip Searing. Are you under contract right now?" A pause. "Good. I'd like to talk to you about doing a show."

He signed her. She was perfect. She had a strong background in confessions-type writing and stories for pulp magazines, but there was a certain honesty about her style that was appealing. She had never been a head writer on a soap before, but she had subwritten a lot, sometimes as many as three episodes a week. She was a plain, older woman with a no-nonsense manner, three sons, and a strong journalistic nose for human-interest pieces. She took the job gratefully after Phillip promised to work with her until she felt confident enough to tackle it on her own.

Warren returned later with the stage-production designs. Phillip approved the style. "I can't give you specifics until Maude works up the new boards, but you can begin on a new living room, kitchen, dining alcove, and a plush doctor's office—the desk room not the examining room. I want elegance, Warren. Not more shlock. I want it done with the same taste you did for *Beekman Place*."

"You want me to start on all this now?"

"Just ideas. Start on the doctor's place. Rich bookshelves, antiques. He is a man of taste, a man of elegance. You can't start everywhere at once, of course, but begin. We'll be making a total, sweeping change."

"It will cost a fortune, Phillip. And we'll never get them constructed in time to get them on the air when you want them."

"You let me worry about that. Just give me beauty—and give it to me fast. Something the average housewife doesn't have around her. Something to contrast with the dreariness of her own life."

"You're going to be the Ross Hunter of television."

"Exactly. Beautiful people in beautiful clothes and beautiful surroundings leading the most mundane, drab, soap-opera lives. He's rarely lost money at the box office."

"It's fine with me. I've been dying to do something with a little style. I was going crazy with chintz." He collected his designs and stuffed them into his portfolio.

Phillip looked around the office. "What do you think you could do with a place like this, Warren?"

"This office?"

"Yes, depressing as hell."

"Well, we could—"

Phillip cut him off. "Just think up something for me, will you? Show me when you've got it down on paper."

"How much would you like to spend?"

"Whatever it costs. We'll charge the set budget with it."

"A pleasure. I've got some fabric swatches in my office now. I'll have them sent up."

Phillip rose. "No. Come back with me to my apartment after tomorrow's taping. You'll have your first sketches, and you can see my personal tastes and furniture. That's what I'd like you to follow."

Wednesday, the news hit the trades. *Variety* came out with a story captioned:

"SEARING SLIDES DOWN TO SAVE SLIPPING SOAP." That made it look as though Phillip had taken the decision on his own. Strange for Chamberfield to have had it slanted that way. But then he was probably just covering his tactics from Russ Keel.

"Jacqueline Searing on line two from the coast."

"Tell her I'm not here."

"I just told her you were here, Mr. Searing."

"Then tell her you made a mistake, I don't want to talk to her. And Gloria, don't ever do that again, do you hear? Never tell anybody I'm in, until after you've cleared it with me."

"Yes, sir."

78

"That's a good girl."

"What do I tell her?"

"Anything you like. You stuck your foot into it, so you pull it out." He hung up. "Now. . . ."

"You're a very patient teacher, Mr. S." Maude O'Keefe, the new head writer was stretched out full on the couch, two pillows jammed under her head and her glasses on the tip of her nose. She was a stocky woman, with a shock of iron-gray hair that a sense of pride prohibited her from dyeing. Phillip was sprawled out on a worn easy chair, his feet propped up on the desk. Maude had just finished when Gloria buzzed.

"Like it?"

"Yes, I do," he said.

"It's rough, of course, and we may hit some snags when we go to script."

"Rough? You've done the whole damn thing in five days. It's lovely, Maude. It's perfect. You've taken what we have and threaded it theme by theme into a whole new ball game. You've incorporated every idea we discussed last week. And except for one they all seem to work."

"Which one?"

"The vamp's affair with Charles."

"That'll work too, I think. Give me a little time to expand it."

He walked to the window and looked out on the next building's fire escape. "Maude, that's the best continuing story line I've heard in years. That whole cataract business with Valerie is superb. Once we start moving toward that eye operation with her, the ratings will skyrocket, and the fact she doesn't tell her boyfriend, because she doesn't want him to confuse pity with love . . . it's trash, it's garbage, it's soapy. I love it."

"It does mean phasing out Sally Gunderson," she said, "and concentrating on Valerie. I took you at your word. I didn't worry about who would be canned."

"That's exactly what I wanted. To me Vanessa Langley is the only sympathetic actress on the show."

"She does look vulnerable, even for an old *kvetch* like me."

"Now what about this vamp? How do you see her?"

"Young Liz Taylor, young Rita Hayworth. Everything

79

every woman's always wanted to be—rich, beautiful, sensuous, without a moral in her body."

"She'll be hard to cast."

"That's your department, Mr. Searing."

"Beautiful job, Maude."

"Well, I've had three weeks to put it together."

"Three weeks? What are you talking about? I just gave it to you five days ago."

"I worked twenty-four hours a day."

"You poor thing. You must be beat, but look: there's one more thing before I take you home. I'd like to go over some mechanics with you. I don't know how you've worked before, but I want to show you how I handle things." He tapped his copy of the outline. "Divide the story into thirteen equal segments, one for each week of the time period. Don't forget to put a major cliff-hanger in on Fridays to make sure there's always a serious dramatic question to tease the audience and keep them with us over the weekend. Then divide each of your segments into five separate divisions, one for each day. Every Monday you'll have to start to solve the question you left the audience hanging with over the weekend. Then each day after that you'll add new information to build up to the coming Friday's cliff-hanger."

Maude took notes furiously.

"Next," Phillip continued, "divide each day's action into a teaser and four separate acts. Let each act run about five minutes. And try to make each act one continuous scene. Sometimes you won't be able to, of course, but I'd like you to try."

"Okay." Maude flexed her fingers.

"We are contractually obligated to put each performer on the air a specified number of times a week. As the head writer you'll have to bear that in mind. Before you start writing every day, look at that cast breakdown. That's important."

Maude's gray head bobbed up and down.

Phillip handed a sheet of paper across to her. "Here's a list of sets already in use. We'll be adding more later, but try not to use more than four on any given day. Break it down to one for each scene. In fact, if it's a small scene maybe we can get away with a two-wall angle set rather than a complete one. But I'm not saying be stingy. I want the show to have class. Just don't be wasteful."

She stopped writing and dropped her pencil. "Wait a second. I'm doing shorthand, but you talk fast."

"Sorry." Phillip laughed.

"Okay."

"That's pretty much it. Keep special effects and exteriors down to a minimum. Moving automobiles, rain, snow, beach scenes. . . . They're always more money, so make sure they're worth it before you give them to us." He smiled at her. "Don't worry. It's not as bad as all that. I'm going to put up a big cork board in here with all the subdivisions, so we can juggle and switch things around as we go along."

"You run a military operation."

"There's a lot to keep track of. Since you're new at it, I'll try to keep you as free as I can from many of the details, but as we go on you'll have to learn to deal with it. Now, why don't we get out of here?" Phillip rolled his sleeves down and fastened them with a pair of gold cuff links. "Let's have a drink together and then you can go home and get to work."

"Okay, boss, whatever you say."

"As soon as we get the first couple of weeks blocked out, we'll get you a subwriter to do a couple of episodes a week. Start thinking of some writer you'd like working with. I've a few ideas of my own. But first let's lock in that breakdown." Phillip hugged the little lady as she wiggled her toes into a pair of loafers. "You're going to do a terrific job, Maude. It's about the only thing I'm absolutely sure of right now."

"Come in, Jerry, sit down."

The gangling man sauntered into the office with a portfolio of papers. He pulled out a tobacco pouch and looked around awkwardly. Carpets and draperies were not his style. He preferred his cubbyhole in the basement, filled as it was with the smells of wood and sizing, and decorated with a scarred desk, a wooden swivel chair, and metal file cabinet.

"What do you mean he doesn't want to wear it?" Phillip shouted into the telephone receiver. "Since when do actors have the final say about wardrobe?" He pressed a button on the control panel on his desk. Across the room, an automatic cabinet door slid open, revealing a television monitor. The monitor started heating up.

"Listen, Pat, neither of us has time to argue about this sort of thing. You tell that dumb son of a bitch he wears what we tell him to wear! I don't give a damn what leeway Vern gave him. If he doesn't like it, he can bloody well quit the show." He looked up at the screen, which now revealed a wide shot of the studio on it. Actors were walking around with scripts and plastic coffee cups in their hands. "Tell your cameraman to go into a medium shot on him, so I can see."

After a moment the camera zoomed in fast and established a young man in a vertically striped shirt arguing with someone off-camera.

"Look at him," said Phillip. "Against that wallpaper you couldn't tell him from a barber pole." He slammed down the phone and looked at the middle-aged man in front of him. "Jerry Dennis! What's up?"

"Can't do it, Phil."

"Never start a conversation with me like that, Jerry. What can't you do that we'll find a way to do."

Jerry Dennis pushed a stack of designs across Phillip's desk. "Can't have these ready by the time you want them. I spent all morning looking them over. They're too complicated. Too many little trimmings. It'll take three months to get them ready for you."

"Why?"

"Why? Yours aren't the only sets I've got to do. All the sets for every one of RBI's East Coast shows come out of my shop. You know that. You were responsible for them all."

"Well, I'm responsible for one show now. That's all, Jerry. And I want it done properly."

"What can I do? Stop production on everything else?"

"If you have to," Phillip said calmly.

"Come on, Phil. You know that's not possible."

Phillip studied the man carefully. Of course he couldn't do it; there wasn't enough manpower. There wasn't enough time during the day. But he wanted to throw him off balance a little. "All right, Jerry, I'll tell you what. Your union has contract negotiations coming up in the fall. Doesn't it?"

82

He nodded.

"Any chance you'll take it to a strike?"

"Depends on you fellows." He grinned sheepishly. "Our demands are always reasonable."

Phillip acknowledged the grin. "I know that, Jerry. I know that. Now I'll make you a deal. If you guys go on strike, I can tell you this. It's going to be a long strike. It's going to last a good four to five weeks, if not a lot more. Keel and Vulkner are prepared to sit it out for a long time. I can't tell you how I know that, but I happen to know it."

The man sat.

"Now with your summer schedule as slow as it is, unless there is a pilot to be shot here in New York, none of you fellows are going to get much of a chance next fall—you're going to lose out not only on the overtime but the regular time. Am I right?"

"Probably."

Phillip leaned back in his chair and steepled together his fingers. He held them in front of his pursed lips and spoke quietly. "Jerry, if you personally guarantee me that those sets will be finished according to my schedule, if you are willing to whip asses every day and every night, I'll approve all the overtime you need to do it."

"It will triple the set budget."

"I'm aware of that."

"Triple, Phil. That's an awful lot of money."

"But I mean work," Phillip continued. "No coffee breaks, no bull sessions. You've got to ride herd on your crew so hard they'll be ready to nail you to a crossbeam."

The intercom buzzed. He reached for the phone. "I want you to promise that if I ever catch anybody fucking off in your shop, and I'll be watching, you'll let me replace him without giving me any union problems." He spoke into the phone. "Yes, Gloria?"

"Claire asked if she could bring an actress by for you to look at. She's also got another stack of photos."

He checked his watch. "Yes, but now! Tell her to get up here right away, because I don't want to be disturbed during the camera rehearsal."

He hung up and turned back to Jerry. "So?"

"You're sure you can authorize all that overtime?"

83

Phillip glared at him. "Jerry, when was the last time you had trouble with my authorization?"

He shrugged. "You're in a different position now, Phil. I just want to be sure, that's all." He rose and took his designs.

"Go on, Jerry, don't play games. Get going on those things—I've marked them in the order I want them done."

He punched the intercom button. "Gloria, is Claire there?"

"Here she comes."

"Send her in." He nodded to Jerry, who waved and ambled out.

Claire Pappas entered. She was a short woman with a close-cropped haircut and a large man's tie hanging down the front of her tailored shirt. She had a small stack of eight-by-ten photographs in her hand. "Here's another load. As far as I'm concerned these are all possibles. You can pull out the ones you want me to call in for you."

"Drop them over there."

She put them down on the marble coffee table, the one piece Phillip had thought nice enough to keep. The rest of the office had been totally redone. The change was extraordinary. The room had blossomed from bland, drab, early Salvation Army to graciousness and elegance.

"Who's this girl you've got me to look at?"

"She was sent by a friend. I don't know if she's right, but. . . ."

He didn't give her a chance to finish. "So what are you wasting our time for?"

An edge of toughness crept into her voice. "Frankly, Phillip, I don't know what you want. I've gone through hundreds of pictures in the past two weeks. I've shown you over fifty, and you've seen a good thirty or forty in the flesh. I still can't seem to put my finger on what you want."

"I didn't say it was easy."

"I've tried every agency in town. Agencies I've never even heard of until this week."

"Did you try the Coast?"

"Of course."

"Chicago?"

"Yes."

"Houston, Dallas?"

84

"No."

"Atlanta?"

"No."

"You want me to do your job for you, Claire?"

She fumed. "This is a Cinderella hunt. You want the most fantastic sexpot on earth and she's got to be unknown."

Phillip calmly took a cigarette out of his desk box and lit it. "That's right, Claire. So you know what I want. You just have to find her for me, that's all."

"Christ." She gritted her teeth and started charging out of the office.

"Bring your girl in now and I'll take a look at her."

"Forget it. You'll never go for her. Too plain. Like Catherine Deneuve."

Phillip smiled, but he caught her before she was out of the room. "Claire?"

"Yes?"

"I'm not joking. That part is being written now. It's got to be filled in the next couple of weeks. I don't want any ordinary beauty. I want somebody spectacular. Go anywhere you have to. Get all the help you need. But I want that girl found."

* * *

It was Friday afternoon by the time Phillip relaxed enough to take a look at his mail. A late delivery had come in and Gloria had propped it up against the small metal horse before she had gone. He had given her the afternoon off in order to get a beat on the weekending mobs. He found the usuals: bills from American Express, Diners Club, and the Avis bill for the car in L.A. It reminded him of Gwen and he made a note to call her.

He felt drained. He had been so psyched up all week that it was only now, alone in the office with two relatively free days ahead, that he realized how tired he was.

Two days. An entire weekend. Bliss. He felt relieved, but knew it was only transitory. Monday morning would come soon enough.

He folded the bills back into their envelopes, and was stuffing them into his pocket when he noticed a personal postcard. The picture on the front showed an old man dressed in rough clothes, bent over, milking the udders of

85

a goat. He turned it and glanced at the signature. It was from Katina, and sent from Ibiza four days earlier.

"Dearest Phillip, Roses are red, violets are fuschia. Arrived in Ibiza, not Libya or Rooshia." He felt a tinge of loneliness. He had been so busy that he had hardly thought about Katina. Now he missed her.

He stuffed the card into his suit jacket and headed out of the office.

The halls were deserted. Their black-and-white checkerboard tiles were scuffed and waiting for the clean-up ladies. He walked down to the basement and up the wide sloping ramp which led to the construction shop and shoved open the huge steel door. The noise blasted out at him like a mechanical orchestra warming up. The whining of the electric saws, the hurried hammering, the compressor hiss. There was the aroma of freshly cut wood, sizing glue and shellac. Jerry Dennis was involved in a heated argument with a carpenter. Phillip waved to him when he looked up. The lanky foreman ambled over, shaking his head from side to side. He had to shout over the noise. "Jesus, these loggerheads can be dumb sometimes. That son of a bitch just nailed a bracing joint on bass-akwards."

"Don't let me distract you. I'm glad to see you got started fast."

Jerry looked over at the man who was nailing. "We get our help out of trees. See that one over there. Top limb."

Phillip smiled as Jerry pointed to a wooden skeleton frame of the doctor's office.

"I'm working 'em through the weekend on your stuff alone. Then we'll see where we are on Monday and I'll schedule the week."

"That's fine. Stay on regular overtime. Don't go into golden. That kind of money I don't want to start spending yet."

"I don't think you'll have to. I may be able to stuff a little time on *Surgery's* budget. They've been kind of pushing me kind of hard, too."

"No, don't do that. Mike McPhee is a friend and it's the first show he's produced for us. I don't want Chamberfield to come down on his back. Don't worry. I'll absorb the costs. Just keep it under control." He indicated the noise. "How do you stand it?" He yelled.

"I can't hear you. I've got a banana in my ear."

86

They laughed and Phillip strode out. The steel door cut off the sounds of the shop behind him. The studio upstairs was deserted. Only the work lights burned. He crossed slowly through the old living-room set already in place for Monday's taping. The schedule called for the lighting director to come in Sunday afternoon. He passed the vacant rehearsal room and walked down the corridor leading to the street. It was then he heard it, muffled but distinct, the crying of a woman behind one of the dressing-room doors. He listened for a moment. It was coming from Vanessa Langley's door, the second from the end. He knocked softly. The crying ceased and shortly there was a soft, "Come in." He opened the door.

She was sitting at her makeup counter in jeans and a thin tee shirt, her carry-all bag open with a box of tissues on top. Her eyes were red.

"I thought I heard a maiden in distress." He said softly. "You save your tears for the weekends?"

"When I have any control over them, yes."

"Is there anything I can do to help?"

She shook her head.

His voice was soft and gentle. "I've got an extra shoulder, if you'd like to use it."

Again she shook her head. "Thank you."

Phillip rose. "Rather be left alone?"

"Do you mind?"

"Not at all. I hope it's better for you this weekend."

She smiled and nodded.

The door clicked softly closed. He stood outside in the corridor for a moment. Then he went back to the rehearsal room, switched on the light and the amplifier next to the grand piano. It was connected to the small microphone used for paging people from their dressing rooms and there would be a speaker above Vanessa. He sat down at the keyboard as the equipment warmed up. The red light on the amplifier brightened. He flipped a switch and pointed a small microphone at the piano. Casually, effortlessly, he fell into a melancholy rendition of "Somewhere Over the Rainbow."

He played well, richly, if with a bit of rust. He played with soul, as they say.

He permitted the last tones to drift away, before reaching up to switch off the amplifier.

Vanessa was leaning against the doorjamb behind him. "All I need now is my faithful dog, Toto, and a Tinman to watch over me."

Phillip looked back and smiled. "Feel better?"

"Thank you. That was nice."

He started to rise from the stool and reached up to close the piano top.

"Play something else."

He sat down and flipped up the tails of an imaginary formal jacket. He stretched his hands in front of him, clasped them together, palms outward and cracked the knuckles. He began with a familiar étude of Chopin. He worked it through, halting every so often to repeat a stumbled series of notes or to gain some momentum in order for his fingers to remember a passage his head had forgotten. He stopped hamming and lost himself in the effort. Phillip played the étude through to the end, forgetting himself and his audience. When he finished he turned, but the doorway was empty. She was gone. Strange girl, he thought to himself.

7.

Gloria called in through the door. "Barry Friedman on line two, Phillip. Do you want to talk to him now?"

"Yes, Gloria, I'll take it." With an eye glued to the office monitor and one hand taking notes, Phillip reached for the phone. "Hello, Barry, want a job?"

The voice on the far end was young and insecure. "Well, actually. . . ."

Phillip cut him off. "Hold it a second, will you." He stopped to make a note for Pat to open the show with an extreme closeup rather than a general view. "Okay, go on. Sorry. I'm watching a camera rehearsal."

"Would you like me to call back later?"

"No, it's all right. What's up? You sound depressed."

"Well," said his former assistant, unable to stop the slight stutter in his speech. "I g-g-g-got some news over the weekend that . . . well, since we're friends, I wanted to let you know myself. Elliot promoted me to your old job. I'm the new director of daytime."

Barry paused for a minute to allow the news to sink in. "I didn't try for it or anything, Phil. You know that. I wasn't after cutting you out or anything." He wasn't sure what to expect. As Phillip's assistant for nine months he had learned the mechanics of running eight network shows; in fact he owed that knowledge mostly to Phillip. The last thing he wished to do was hurt his friend.

"So why are you so down? Congratulations! It's a big step."

Phillip knew why Elliot gave Barry the job. Because Barry was professional but didn't rock boats. Elliot wasn't about to replace Phillip with someone he'd have to start having power fights with again. Besides, this way Elliot himself could make all decisions for scheduling.

"Phillip, you know Elliot and I get along pretty well. I know you don't like him very much but, well, I like him and I guess that's why he's brought me along with him. The thing is I don't know that I can handle it."

"What are you talking about? Of course you can handle it. Just concentrate on the problems. Think them out. If you run into any real jams, call me. I'll give you whatever help I can."

"Yes?"

"What do you think, dummy? I'm going to let you sink just because you stole my job?"

"Thanks, Phillip. I won't forget that."

"But let's not kid ourselves. When this stint here is over I'm coming out fighting—if I have anything left to fight with. The thing is. . . ." Then he stopped. Something on the monitor screen was peculiar. Bill Peters suddenly grabbed his stomach and doubled over in pain. At first Phillip thought he might be kidding around, but the shot widened and he saw Sally Gunderson drop down to help the boy. The expression on her face was fearful. He raised the sound volume with the remote-control device. Other voices were asking what had happened. The stage manager ran into the shot, flung off his earphones, and knelt beside the writhing actor. "Somebody call an ambulance," a frightened female voice called out.

"Barry, I've got to go. One of the actor's just been taken ill." He dropped the receiver and raced out of the office, startling the secretary who was on the other line.

"Mr. Searing, there's a—"

"Gloria, call the shop. Have somebody get the station-wagon around to the loading ramp immediately! Then jump down to the set yourself. I may need you."

He plunged down the spiral staircase and charged into the studio. "Let me through!"

A circle had formed around the collapsed boy and everyone was talking at once. "Call an ambulance! Somebody call an ambulance!"

"I think it's a rupture."

"It's got to be appendicitis. Look at the way he's holding his belly."

Pat kneeled at Bill's side. Vanessa stuffed a pillow under his head for support. He was moaning and in what looked to be intense pain.

Phillip shoved the crowd aside and moved to the center of the circle. He took one look at the boy and knew he wouldn't be able to answer questions. He spun around to the associate producer, who was leaning over his shoulder. "Colin, isn't there a stretcher in this place?"

"No. They have one over at the main studio, but not here. You're not going to move him, are you?"

One of the set decorators stuck his head in. "We've got a stretcher in the prop room, Phillip. We used to use it on *Surgery* when it was taped here."

"Get it fast, will you please, Luke?"

"Sure thing." He ran out.

Colin squatted down and whispered into Phillip's ear. "Phillip, we ought to be careful. We've been told specifically not to do anything if there's an accident. If anything goes wrong he could come back and sue you and the company."

"This is not an accident. This guy's sick."

"He's not so wrong, Phillip," Pat broke in. "Bill collapsed. Judy's on the phone now to Roosevelt Hospital and that's just up the street. Shouldn't we wait until they can get an ambulance over here?"

"This is New York City. Even if they're up the street it could take till next Tuesday. He needs help now."

Luke came back with the stretcher and he and the AD unfolded it beside the boy. They laid it out parallel to him and tried to edge it under his body.

"Gently, gently, take it easy with him."

Vanessa soaked a makeup sponge in water and wiped the perspiration on Bill's brow. He was still moaning.

Gloria ran in. "Where's Mr. Searing?"

"I'm here, Gloria. Did you get the wagon?"

91

"No, it's out on a pickup."

"Dammit!"

Judy's voice came over the loudspeaker from the control room. "Pat, the ambulance will be here immediately. I told them who it was for."

Phillip stood up. They had managed to get the boy onto the stretcher. Luke and the other men were ready to lift him. "What do you want us to do, Phillip?"

He stared down at the horizontal form. "I guess if the ambulance is on the way, we might as well leave it to them."

Gloria came over to him, ashen-faced. "Strange," she said. "It happened so suddenly."

"Gloria, get on the phone to Maude. Tell her what's happened and that Bill will be out of commission for at least—what? A week, I imagine. Maybe longer. Tell her to start thinking and get right over here. No, Gloria, just get her on the line. I'd better talk to her. We won't have much time."

"Yes, sir." She rushed off.

"Colin?"

"Right here."

"Go out front and guide the ambulance men in here, so they won't waste any time. Then I want you to ride over to the hospital with them and wait until they tell you what it is. And call me as soon as you know. You hear?"

"Right."

"We're supposed to start taping in thirty-five minutes."

"Well that's out, isn't it?" said the AD, who was standing nearby.

"The hell it is," said Phillip. He turned to the bearded young man. "Charley, call the head of videotape and tell him there's been an emergency and we must tape—absolutely must tape—one hour later. That means we want two to two-thirty for taping; that gives them an hour to set it up on the machines for broadcast at three-thirty. Okay? Pat, let's you and I go inside."

They walked into the control room. Gloria put the phone down. "She's not there. No answer."

"Gotta be," Phillip said calmly. "Dial again."

Camera two had a wide shot and on the monitor they could see two uniformed men enter with Colin. They went over to where Bill was lying and one took out a pen and pad of paper.

Pat handed the producer a sheaf of papers. "Here's to-day's script, Phillip." They sat down next to the switcher's panel at the control board.

"Bill comes in only at the end scene and has just a few lines of dialogue. It shouldn't be too hard to work around him."

"Hello, Maude? Oh, good, just a minute. It's Gloria." The secretary handed the phone to Phillip and breathed a sigh of relief.

Phillip grabbed it. "Maude? Phillip. Listen, darling, we've got a problem. Bill Peters, the guy who plays Charles, collapsed on the set during dress rehearsal. We tape in an hour and half. Now, look"—there was a pause —"all right." Phillip turned to Pat. "She is getting her script."

Pat stood up, his eyes on the camera-two monitor. "What the hell are they writing out there? Why don't they just take him out, for Christ's sake?" He bolted out of the door.

"Yes, okay." Maude was back on the line and Phillip listened, then spoke quietly. "Right. Not much at all. We should be able to cover this info with someone else, no?"

Pat re-entered the room.

"Stupid sons of bitches. They were worried about who's going to pay for him. Blue Cross or Republic Broadcasting. Stupid shits. Poor guy could be dying for all we know."

"Wait a minute." Phillip turned to Pat. "Who's the fastest study on the show?"

"Ummm. Probably Vanessa."

"No good. She's in the scene."

"Then Wilma."

"Perfect." Phillip turned back to the phone. "The moth-er, Maude. The woman who plays the mother. Okay. . . . Okay. And I will too."

He replaced the receiver on the hook. "Let's go back up to the office, Gloria. She's going to call back in ten minutes. She doesn't think there will be a problem."

The AD entered from the VIP lounge where he had been using the phone. "The taping change is okay, but

Jesus, those guys are finicky. They insisted on getting clearance from Sixth Avenue."

"That means Chamberfield will be on the horn any minute," said Phillip. "Gloria, if he calls, explain the situation to him, but don't find me. Do you understand? Tell him that I'm racing around, but everything is under control."

Pat looked over. "Where's Colin?"

"I sent him over to the hospital with the ambulance. Why?"

"I wanted to break the cast and keep them from getting too flustered. I'll do it myself. It might be better."

"Yeah. Then come up to my office, will you?"

Five minutes later they had assembled in the office. Phillip was back on the phone again. "Okay, Maude. Fine. And after that there are only two more points made in the scene. Right?" Phillip was looking at his notes. He put the phone receiver on the amplifying box, so he wouldn't have to use his hands. "First, Valerie is covering up why she won't type this report. She's still hiding the eye problem from everyone. And second, that she may go to Chicago to visit her aunt for a while. Right?"

"Right."

"Let's rework the scene along these lines. Charles drops off the term report to Wilma, off-camera. Put it in past tense, asking her to get Valerie to type it. He has to go check on footnotes at the library, or something. Anything. It's not important. Have the whole thing play between Valerie and her mother. But in one long shot, have the mother get suspicious of Valerie's eye problem. We can eliminate the chatter and it will play very effectively."

The voice again. "We weren't going to play that until Friday."

"We'll move it up to today. So what?"

"What do we do about the rest of the week? I think we can write Bill's character out of tomorrow's episode easily. But he and Valerie have a confrontation on Wednesday that will be difficult to get around. What if he's not back by then?"

Pat was designing new camera moves in his script.

"Don't know, Maude. Don't know. Let's concentrate on today. Let's worry about that tomorrow after we hear about Bill."

Two hours later, it was all over. The show had gone well and no one who wasn't privy to inside information would ever know there had been the slightest problem.

When Elliot Chamberfield returned to Sixth Avenue from his three-bourbon lunch, he found a disturbing message and instantly grabbed the phone.

Phillip took the call, but the pressure was off by that time.

"What the fuck is going on over there, Searing? Barry called and said the whole show is in chaos."

"There's no chaos, Elliot. Everything went beautifully. It's on the air now."

"I know it's on the air. I just turned it on. What's he got, the kid?"

"Strangulated inguinal hernia. I got a call—they finished the operation ten minutes ago."

"Operation? Christ, that means you'll have to replace him. You'll lose him for weeks. You'll have to replace him."

"One way or the other."

"You got anybody in mind?"

"No, Elliot. I just finished today's show. Now I'm going to start thinking about tomorrow."

"Don't forget, friend, you're more than three weeks in already and I don't see those Nielsens going in any upward direction."

"Are you finished?"

Elliot hung up loudly.

Phillip mulled the problem over on his way home and halfway through a solitary dinner. To replace the actor permanently would be easier than giving him a four-day substitute. Shaking the audience's belief in a character by giving them a new face to look at once is bad enough, but twice within a short period of time would be disastrous. With the ratings as low as they were Phillip couldn't afford to disenchant them now.

He had just plugged the coffee percolator in when the phone rang. He reached for the kitchen extension.

"This is the RBI switchboard, Mr. Searing. We have a call from Hollywood for you. A Mr. Justin Teague. Can I switch him through to you?"

"Justin Teague? . . . Who? . . . ? I suppose so."

95

She cut herself off. There was a hum, a click, and she was back on. "Go ahead, please."

The new voice was vaguely familiar with its rich, rolling tones and cultivated delivery. "Mr. Searing?"

"Yes. . . ."

"We've never had the pleasure of meeting. I'm Justin Teague, Bill Peters's father."

And then it dawned. Justin Teague was not only Bill Peters's father; he was also a former matinee idol of millions of women during the early forties.

"My son just got in touch with me. Poor kid, he'll be out for a week or two, it seems."

"Yes, but he'll be all right. I spoke to the hospital late this afternoon. The operation is over and he'll recover quickly."

"I'm sure he will," said the father. "The thing is I know how concerned he is about his part. And you must be pulling your hair out now trying to replace him. You haven't yet, have you?"

"No, does he have a twin brother?"

The man laughed. "That would be nice. No, I'm afraid Bill's an only child, by that marriage at any rate."

"Don't let him worry about the replacement. The important thing is for him to get well."

"That's considerate of you, Mr. Searing, but let me come to the point. You see, mine is a very old theatrical family. My mother and father were performers of no small fame in their day, and Bill's the third-generation Teague to carry on the family tradition, even though he has chosen to change his name to Peters."

Phillip cradled the receiver between his shoulder and ear and lit a cigarette.

"I remember once when I had just started in the theater, long before Hollywood called me. I had let myself get caught in a rainstorm and picked up a case of the flu. I was in my first Broadway production at the time and I was heartbroken. I couldn't go on. Well, what do you think happened? My father stepped in, though he was far too famous at the time for the insignificant part I was playing. He went on for me for two nights before I was strong enough to return."

He paused dramatically and cleared his throat.

96

"What I'm saying is that I myself am available to you until my son is well enough to perform."

Phillip almost choked. The man couldn't be serious. How was he going to play a twenty-five-year-old boy? He must be at least sixty.

"Mr. Searing, I know what you are thinking. I'm too old for the part, of course. I wouldn't pretend to try to pull it off in reality. But since it's only for a few days, you might find it to your advantage to draw on my name and reputation. After all, if you substituted anyone else for the part, you'd certainly have some of the same problems."

The idea was ludicrous, yet. . . . Teague wasn't so far wrong. The publicity value of his name and the "Father Takes over Son's Role" aspect of the situation would be a coup. He felt instinctively it would mean extra rating points. Older women who remembered him from the movies would tune in to see their old flame. Their daughters would tune in, if only out of curiosity.

"Fortunately, I'm between engagements and free to help both you and my son. I appreciate how potentially troublesome this problem could be for you."

The gall of the son of a bitch, thought Phillip. Teague hadn't made a film in years. Yet intuitively he felt the move was the right one. "Mr. Teague, I would be honored to have you on my show." He thought he detected a sigh of relief on the far end of the line.

"I thought you would agree. You won't regret this decision."

"Have your agent contact our West Coast business-affairs department. Let them finalize the contract. I'll notify them he'll be calling."

"I'm very expensive, Mr. Searing." And he laughed in what he imagined was a good-natured way.

Pompous ass, thought Phillip. "Mr. Teague, you'll earn every penny of it."

"Thank you. Should I fly to New York immediately?"

"Yes, please. I'll need you here tomorrow morning." He glanced at his watch. "It's eight-thirty-five here in New York. There should be someone still in the business-affairs office out there now. I'll arrange for your tickets through them. Your agent will call immediately, won't he?"

"Yes."

"We'll book you a room here. Where do you like to stay in New York?"

"The St. Regis. Just tell them who it's for and they'll arrange to have my suite available for me."

A suite, thought Phillip. Jesus. "I'm delighted you called, Mr. Teague, I'm looking forward to meeting you tomorrow."

He placed the story with the publicity department on both coasts. They would break it the following day.

* * *

JUSTIN TEAGUE TO SUB FOR AILING SON. Both UPI and AP gave the story space. The *Times* carried a blurb, so did the *Post*. If they used it, the less sophisticated papers out in the sticks would have a field day. Human interest drama on soap opera. Terrific! *TV Guide* phoned earlier and wanted to send a reporter out. What more could be asked, thought Searing. Only Justin Teague, that's all.

"The son of a bitch is half a day late! Gloria, call the St. Regis and see if he's checked in yet. If he has, give him a polite reminder of the meeting and tell Pat to go ahead with the rehearsal. I'll come down with Teague when he shows."

And by the time he did show it was two-thirty-five. The actor made his entrance in the outer office dressed in gray flannels and a double-breasted blazer. Gloria looked up when she smelled the faint aroma of tobacco and gin mixed with a very American cologne. Phillip spotted him through the open door. He tightened his tie and went out to greet him. "Mr. Teague, I'm Phillip Searing."

"I'm pleased to meet you, Mr. Searing. Awfully sorry to be late, but I was giving an interview to a charming young lady from one of the TV weeklies and I let the hours just idle away. I did feel the publicity value for your show would be compensatory, though."

"It probably will be, Mr. Teague. Shall we get to work?"

The rehearsal went smoothly enough. Justin was charming to the cast and attentive to the director's wishes. Phillip tried to visualize what he'd look like on the tube. He was an extremely handsome man. His hair was silver gray and his build lithe. It was the eyes that gave away his age. They were blank, watery, and red. Phillip hoped the

98

redness was a reaction to the night flight from L.A., but he slipped a note to Pat suggesting that he be checked out before blocking him into any close shots.

The producer hung around while the actor struggled with the reading, rendering the lines with antique theatricality. "I hope I haven't made a deadly mistake," he whispered to the director. "He reads like Falstaff playing Romeo."

"He'll be all right. I think he's just playing with it for the moment. I'm leery of giving him any coaching yet. I don't want him to get the impression I'm jumping on him."

Phillip whispered again. "For what we had to pay to get him on the show, don't worry about jumping—stomp!" The producer shook his head in disbelief.

"What's he getting? I'm curious."

"Can't tell you, Patrick. You'll vomit."

"Ten grand for the three days?"

"I wish."

"More than ten grand? More than ten thousand dollars?"

The reading broke. Pat took Justin by the arm and led him off to the side. Phillip calculated the overtime he would have to pay the rest of the cast and crew because of Teague's lateness.

The next reading was better. Teague toned down his delivery and became almost believable. The age, of course, would never match, but that had been decided already.

The producer started to slip out quietly. Charley was leaning against the wall watching the actors. "Leaving?"

"I'm not needed," said Phillip. "Pat'll get a performance out of him."

"What odds are you giving?"

Wilma Brewley, the woman who played Vanessa's mother, came over. She turned so only Phillip and Charley could see the face she was making. "You had to do this to us. You had to stick us with him! He'll be the laughingstock of the daytime schedule."

"Don't offer faint praise, Wilma," joked Phillip. "I may let him sub for your part next."

"Do you know where that expression came from?" asked Charley, totally out of context. Charley was a tall lanky man with a reddish gold beard and sad eyes. He had been graduated from St. John's college in Annapolis,

Maryland, a school based on the one hundred great books course, and he had acquired a collection of totally useless information which he dropped from time to time like dandelion seeds.

"What expression?"

"Laughingstock."

"No, Charley." She smiled brightly. She folded her hands and waited to hear. "Where does the expression laughingstock come from?"

"It comes from the early days."

"Really," she interrupted.

"Astonishing," said Phillip.

"I'm not finished."

"Sorry."

"When people were put into wooden stocks set up in the town square, they had to stick their necks and wrists and feet through holes in planks of woods, and other people, the citizenry of the town, came along and tickled them. Hence, 'Laughingstock.' " He cleared his throat and raised his eyebrows.

Wilma looked to Phillip, who looked to Charley.

"Well!" said the lady, releasing a huge sigh. "That certainly was instructional. What other tidbits can you offer us today?"

Phillip said, "I'm afraid I'll have trouble digesting that one. You'll excuse me, both of you? I'm going off to mull."

Justin missed his 7:00 A.M. call the following morning.

At eight-fifteen, Phillip's phone rang. "It's Colin, Phillip. Pat told me to call you. Teague just staggered in."

"Staggered?"

"He's falling down sloppy drunk."

Phillip's stomach churned. "Thank you." He made for the studio.

* * *

"Justin, I didn't know I couldn't depend on you."

"What the hell are you talking about? I never failed to deliver a performance in my life. I don't intend to change that record today, even if this is just a shitty little melodrama." He swayed huffily back to the set.

Pat whispered to Phillip. "He doesn't know his lines, either."

100

"Do you want teleprompters?"

"I don't think we have a choice."

"All right, don't stop your rehearsal. I'll have a coffee urn set up in his dressing room and pour coffee down his throat every break you give him. You'd better block him so that he's as immobile as possible, though."

Phillip called upstairs and had Gloria send down the latest scripts. He looked them over in Teague's dressing room while he waited. Vanessa passed at one point. She seemed distraught.

A door opened somewhere down the hall and Justin bellowed sloppily around the corner. Vanessa sped off in the opposite direction.

"What's your name again?" roared Justin as they approached the dressing room.

"Colin Dawes."

"Well, Colin Dawes, you can take your fucking hands off me. I can manage perfectly well myself."

"I'm trying to help, Mr. Teague."

"Mr. Teague doesn't need your help, do you hear?"

Phillip went out to them. "All right, Colin, I've got him."

"I don't need you, either."

The producer took the actor under the elbow and guided him into the room. "Colin, pour us a container of coffee, will you, please? We need sugar; get some. Sit down here, Justin."

"Who the hell do you think you are? I don't need a babysitter."

"I'm going to get a performance out of you, if it kills both of us."

"I was acting before you were conceived and I was drinking before you were conceived. Don't worry about my performance."

"Let me explain something to you, Justin. We're not making a movie. This is as close to a live show as we can get. It's on tape, but we start the tape and play the show through to the end. We don't have time to stop and retake. Do you understand that? We go on the air two hours after taping. Good or lousy. Do you understand?"

"If you'll excuse me, I'll run over my lines."

"I'll cue you."

"I work better alone."

Phillip glanced at his watch. It was ten-fifteen. Three and a half hours for Justin to learn his lines and be in place for the opening scene. "All right, you work on your own, but I'll be back in a half hour to check you out."

"You really are very annoying."

"This may be nothing to you. But it's a livelihood for a lot of people." He lowered his voice menacingly. "And if you mess it up for them, Teague, I'll destroy you." He became more theatrical when he saw the actor's eyes widen. "I personally will make sure that you never work for anyone I know again! And I know a lot of people in this industry. I'll cut your theatrical balls off." He stood abruptly, and walked out of the room, bumping into Colin who was hurrying back with the sugar. "Stay with him and make sure he learns the part, Colin. I want it letter-perfect. If he starts anything, get to me fast. But try to soften the impact I just had. He looked like he dropped a load in his pants."

"I'll regale him with my wit, charm, and humor."

"Just sober him up." Phillip went up to his office, called Maude, and they discussed the changes on the new script. He also rejected four girls, through Gloria, for the part of Daphne. Periodically Colin reported on Teague.

11:10. "He's sitting quietly going over his lines as if they were the closet scene from *Hamlet*. Three coffees."

12:04. "He's on the set. Weaving is down to a minimum. Speech is still slurred. Had to force the last coffee in."

12:20. "Teague actually learned the lines for the scenes he's in and vomited, a positive sign, but a nasty stench!"

Phillip came downstairs, twenty-five minutes before taping. Vanessa was on her way to makeup. "How's the *Titanic?*" He asked.

"Listing, but possible."

"I watched the last run-through, and I think you'll come off fine."

"Do you mean that?"

"I'm not worried about you in the least."

"Thank you, I needed that."

Ten minutes before taping, Colin burst into the control booth. "He's gone, Phillip. He's disappeared."

Phillip charged out of his seat. "Where the hell were you? I thought you were keeping an eye on him."

"I was," the young man panted. "But he asked me to go to the makeup room and send down Tara. He said he didn't want to take time from his lines. When I got back he wasn't in his room."

"Check upstairs and all the men's rooms. I'm going outside. Get some help."

Phillip bolted out of the booth and across the studio. He pushed through the doors and outside. He looked up and down the street. Nowhere. Then he caught sight of a dingy bar sign at the corner. He sprinted toward it. Justin was there all right. He sat on a stool, slouched over a glass. Beside him was a half-empty bottle of gin.

"Come on, Justin. We have five minutes to taping." The old man looked up and grinned.

Phillip propelled him off the stool and shoved a five-dollar bill at the bartender. He half-carried, half-steered him back.

"I won't let you down. I haven't let down a producer yet."

He dropped the aging actor into his position on the set and called the makeup assistant over. She wiped the perspiration off the sallow face and applied a thin layer of pancake. She was an attractive girl with very ample breasts that Justin had difficulty taking his eyes from.

"What's your name, darling?"

"Tara."

"You're on the wrong side of the cameras, my dear. You're much too pretty to be a makeup girl." He was blinking through the Klieg lights, having just removed his sunglasses.

Pat's voice boomed over the loudspeakers. "One minute to air show. Places, everyone."

Tara and Phillip left the set. The stage manager, a young black with a bushy Afro, leaned forward from his station between cameras one and two. "Remember, Mr. Teague, keep your eyes on me. I'll give you the cue to start."

The stage manager pressed the headset close to his ear, listening for orders from the control room. "Thirty seconds! Tape's rolling. They'd like you to sit up, please, Mr. Teague." He raised his arm to the stand-by position.

Justin pulled himself up and threw back his shoulders.

In the control booth the TV monitors were lit up and humming. Each contained a separate picture that would be fitted into one twenty-nine-minute thirty-five-second television program, glowing pieces of an electronic jigsaw puzzle that a line of technicians would put together. A monitor showed what each of the three studio cameras was seeing, two monitors with prefilmed outdoor segments ready to roll, monitors racked up with pretaped commercials, a pretaped credit roll and slide insertions. Finally there was the big color unit in the middle showing what would go over the air.

Phillip leaned over the director's shoulder and pushed the mike button to the set. Camera one was on Teague and he looked tense. "Relax, Justin, it's going to go just fine." It was too late to start regretting decisions. But it didn't take any weight off the sickening lump that pressed into his stomach.

Pat looked up at the big control-booth clock, its second hand closing into 1:00 P.M.

"Bars and tone in."

"Bars and tone out. Beeps in . . . take 'em out. Stand by ten-second roll."

"Nine, eight, seven, six, five."

The AD talked into his own headset. "Stand by on the set. Stand by camera one. Stand by organ music, stand by announce."

"Camera two tighten up your shot a hair," said the director.

"Ready organ music, ready camera one. Ready announce."

"Stand by set."

"Ready, titles? Roll titles."

"Cue the music. Cue announce."

"Titles rolling."

"Ready on the set."

"Three seconds, titles ending."

"Camera one."

"And fade in camera one. Cue Justin. Go!"

The opening went well enough. Justin looked slightly out of things, but as the scene progressed he warmed up. The lines seemed to flow naturally, although he did a bit of paraphrasing. Vanessa's face was a good mixture of concern and evasion, an honest reaction to the drunken actor.

Then Justin had to rise. That's when it struck. He lumbered out of the chair a little too forcefully and knocked it over. He turned to look at what had happened and in his confusion knocked over a small teleprompter unit placed behind the sofa. The clatter was very loud, but no one stopped, except Justin. He fell apart. His hands shook so badly that, as he picked the chair up, he brushed the table and hit the lamp on top of it. The lamp tumbled off onto the floor. "Shit, what the fuck's happening here?"

There was a stunned silence in the studio. Phillip glanced at the clock. Five and a half minutes into the act. Another thirty seconds and a commercial break would have permitted them to isolate the first segment and keep it intact.

Pat pushed the studio button. "Mr. Teague, we will now have to start over again from the top of the act. Please, regardless of what happens, just cover and continue. Let me be the judge of whether or not to stop. We'll never make air time at this rate."

"Roger. Understood." Teague was good-sportsmanly definite. "Can we get rid of this lamp over here? It's in my way."

"Stagehand, remove the lamp. Tape is rolling. Thirty seconds."

Phillip came out to the set. He led Justin back to his chair and the stagehand snatched the lamp off of the table. Phillip spoke soothingly. "You were doing beautifully, Justin. I'm sorry you stopped. It was a lovely segment up to that point. You must let us control it from inside. You can do a lot of things, but you can't stop like that. You see, we could have kept the scene. The camera was off you."

"What do you mean it was off me? The fucking thing was covering the whole set."

"The only camera you have to worry about is the one whose red light is on. Really, it wouldn't have looked bad at all."

Some sparkle returned to the actor's eyes.

"Just watch Hal here, Justin. He's the stage manager and the director is in constant communication with him

105

from the booth. Pat'll have him signal you if anything really goes wrong."

The tape had to be stopped twice more. Once for Justin's skipping five minutes of dialogue and then for calling the character of Valerie by the actress's name. That slip could have passed, but he pulled a comedy bit to joke it aside that might have worked with Phil Silvers in the theater, but not Justin Teague on a TV soap.

"Vanessa? Vanessa?" he said. "Why am I calling you Vanessa? You're supposed to be Valerie." He turned directly to camera and said in a nasal voice, "That's not Valerie, friends, that's an imposter. What are you doing in my living room, imposter?" And he broke himself up with gales of laughter.

Phillip called editing facilities and ordered their fastest man to stand by with two machines.

The taping broke with forty-five minutes to air time. Phillip, Pat, Charley, and Colin hopped into a cab and raced over to broadcast facilities.

The show had been piped there via closed circuit and put on tape. In the minutes remaining they made three electronic edits, picking the usable portions from the three tapings they had done. Phillip took the timing notes from Charley and Pat gave the instructions to the editor. Two minutes before air time, they personally delivered the tape to the appropriate broadcast machine.

They caught the show in a VIP lounge and surprisingly it was not too devastating. In relief, they celebrated with drinks in Phillip's office.

When they were through toasting the end of the crisis, Phillip looked at Pat. "You gave him this afternoon off, didn't you?"

"I thought it would be better if he got some sleep."

"Just as well. You and I'll meet Maude at five and see about paring down his part in tomorrow's script."

8.

"Mr. Chamberfield called twice."

"Thank you, Gloria. Would you mind ordering me some coffee? I overslept this morning." He went into the room and hung his coat on the hanger. The phone rang again. He answered it himself. "Searing, here."

"Mr. Chamberfield wants to talk to you."

Phillip loosened his tie and straightened the reproduction of Warhol's Marilyn Monroe he had recently hung behind the desk.

Elliot's voice came through with a blast. "You didn't tell me you were hiring that old fart."

"Didn't have time, Elliot. Besides, it hit all the papers. I figured you'd read them."

"I was in a meeting all day. Jesus Christ, he looked like he was plastered."

"He was."

"Is that your way of improving my show? You're making it the laughingstock of the industry."

"Do you know where that expression comes from, Elliot?"

"I don't know what you're talking about."

Phillip smiled to himself. "It wasn't that bad and the publicity should boost the ratings. Take a look at the afternoon papers. *TV Guide* wanted to come in and do a picture story, but I put them off until Friday."

"Yeah? *TV Guide?*" Elliot quieted for a moment. But then he whined, "Well, I still don't like it. I just hope he's cheap."

"He's not."

"What do you mean? He's a fucking has-been. How much are you paying him?"

"Business affairs on the Coast closed the deal this morning for thirty-five thousand dollars for three days, unlimited use of name and image for—"

The explosion must have knocked secretaries off their forty-fourth-floor stools.

"THIRTY-FIVE THOUSAND DOLLARS! HAVE YOU LOST YOUR MIND? THAT'S MORE THAN YOUR TOTAL TALENT BUDGET FOR A MONTH!"

"It'll be worth it," he said. "Wait till the ratings come in."

"Fuck the ratings. You're making the show look like shit. And thirty-five thousand dollars."

"We'll see. You gave me carte blanche. Are you going back on that now?"

"From now on, any unusual moves on that show I want reported, you hear? And you'd better be right. If those ratings don't pick up because of this stunt you start packing." He hung up with his usual good-natured style.

Pat entered the office in a cloud of disbelief. "Thirty-five thousand dollars?"

"I didn't have the heart to tell him about the overages we're going to have for the tape and editing facilities."

The day was a modified version of the previous one. Instead of ginning in a bar, Justin had the foresight to bring his own supply. Colin managed to steal the flasks away from him, but not until the third run-through and by that time the actor had finished three quarters of one bottle. The show was botched and more money had to be spent on editing, but it got on the air.

The decision was made to slice every word possible from Teague's final performance the next day. Maude would do the polish work at home, but before she left she also came up with the one bright piece of news for the week. She had spoken to an aunt of hers in Des Moines, who had told her that her entire bridge club was watching Justin Teague. "They think he's marvelous, Phillip. Can you imagine? They want to know why I don't write him in more often."

"Unbelievable!"

"Do you want me to start working on some new scripts especially for him?"

"You do and you'll produce them too."

"You poor thing. You must be having a rough time."

"I'm glad to hear about your aunt's reaction."

"Phillip, she was crying. She remembers him from the forties. Thinks he hasn't changed a bit."

Dinner was a thick porterhouse steak. Phillip made himself a tomato salad with onions, a sauce of oil and vinegar and Dijon mustard, shook up a Beefeater Gibson to work him through the preparations, and moved into a nice rich Mouton Rothschild during the meal. He set himself a place on the terrace.

Phillip found it pleasant to eat alone. There was a certain freedom in solitary dining, in restaurants where no one knew him, or in the comfort of his own apartment.

He was about to carry dessert out from the kitchen, when the phone rang. "Phillip, this is Bill Peters. Am I disturbing you?"

"Bill, how are you feeling?"

"Better, thanks. I should be up and around by Sunday."

"I can't tell you how happy that makes me."

Bill hesitated a moment and then said, "I want to thank you, Phillip. I haven't had a chance . . . for having Colin look after me that day."

"Don't think of it."

"The flowers were lovely and I understand you came over yourself."

"Just once, but you were sleeping, so I didn't disturb you."

"That's very nice." Bill paused again. "Am I interrupting anything?"

"Not at all. Just finished dinner." He scooped up a spoonful of dessert and waited.

Bill cleared his throat. "Well," he said, "about my father. I just wanted to say I had no idea he would offer to take over that part, Phillip. I want you to know I had nothing to do with it. I haven't spoken to the old man in quite a while."

Phillip put the spoon aside. "He told me you called him the night it happened."

"No. It was my mother. They've been separated about fifteen years, but she felt he ought to know about what happened to me. I hope he hasn't caused you any trouble."

"Trouble? Why would you say that?" He tried to cover the irony in his tone.

"He's a lush. I doubt he's been any joy to work with the past two days."

"Nothing we couldn't handle."

"You're tactful."

"I'm just glad you'll be coming back soon." And as an afterthought added, "You don't mind his taking over the part, do you?"

"Frankly, yes. I was upset when my wife told me about it, but I've cooled now. I really feel sort of sorry for him. He was good, you know."

"I remember."

"Look, I just wanted to apologize for him." He laughed uncomfortably.

"It's not necessary. Just get well, and get your ass back here fast. We need you."

The following morning Pat was rehearsing the new scenes that Maude sent over, when Colin brought Justin in half an hour late. The older actor took one look at the revisions and went through the roof. "What is this? Why do I have only one scene left?"

Phillip was almost polite. "Those are the new scenes the writer and I have been working on. They are an improvement over the sections you were given earlier."

"I spent all the fucking night learning three damned scenes and now I come in here and you tell me I'm in only one."

"No, you're in two, but you speak in only one. I'm sorry for the inconvenience."

"The earlier version will be reinstalled immediately. I will be in three scenes." He turned away to his folding chair as if the matter were closed.

"The new scenes will be taped as written. No actor dictates terms to this show."

Justin stared at the producer through the sunglasses. "I'm not accustomed to a secondary role. This is not what I contracted for."

"Teague, you contracted to arrive and appear in *Affair Of The Heart*. To be a replacement for our leading actor. If our leading actor were here today, he would accept the revisions without batting an eyelash."

"That, my dear Searing, is why my son will be nothing more than a soap actor all of his life."

The cast stopped their rehearsal. Phillip realized Justin was playing to them and that his anger was as theatrical as his voice. "I don't want this rehearsal disturbed any longer, Justin. If we have to go on, I suggest we do it in my office."

But the actor continued grandly. "I will not leave this room until the matter is settled."

"Very well, it's settled." Phillip turned to the cast. "Today's episode will play five minutes short. We will tape the four scenes without Mr. Teague and I'll fill the remainder of the time with public-service announcements." He turned and strode out of the room.

Justin ran after him screaming, "You can't do this. I have a contract!"

"You certainly do and I'm going to sue your ass off for breaking it. Every actor in there is a witness that you refused to perform a script."

"It's unacceptable. Unacceptable!" His voice was shrill, almost hysterical. He caught Phillip by the shoulder just as he reached the door and screamed in his face. "Do you hear me? You can't treat me like this!"

"I won't put up with your histrionics any more. We are not running a farm for over-the-hill actors. I have a show to produce and you are in my way. Now, either get out there and do a proper rehearsal or I'll see you in court." Phillip brushed past and walked up to the office. He grabbed the phone and was in the process of informing the head of studio operations that there would be a short show that day when Colin Dawes burst into the office.

"I don't know what you said to him, but he walked back to the rehearsal hall, picked up his script, and told Pat he'd do the abridged version."

111

"Keep an eye on him and report to me periodically."

Colin slipped out of the office. Phillip glanced down at his desk. There were the overtime and editing manpower costs for the previous two days of taping. Nineteen thousand, four hundred eighty dollars and thirty-five cents. Elliot was going to have a heart attack if the ratings didn't pan gold by Friday.

Phillip watched the rehearsal on the office monitor with Gloria beside him taking notes. The actor had been nipping, that was obvious, but his one scene played acceptably well despite the liquor.

The producer grabbed a bite to eat with Pat at a restaurant nearby and hurried back to the studio for the taping. Fearing that his presence would upset Justin, Phillip kept himself out of sight. He spoke to the director on an open line and didn't slip into the control booth until the last possible minute.

The show taped beautifully. Justin was letter-perfect. He hit every blocking position on the nose and was as close to the character of the younger man as he conceivably could have gotten. Phillip figured it was probably due to the presence in the studio of the people from *TV Guide*, who had interviewed him between tapings and stayed to watch. Whatever the reason, Phillip was relieved.

The announcer passed him on his way out the door and in his best announcer voice said, "And so ends another tragic episode in the lives of the livers of *Affair*."

Three quarters of an hour later when the building was almost empty, Phillip heard what sounded like a female voice calling for help. He leapt up from his desk and went into the outer office. Gloria was listening, too. It came again.

Phillip raced down the spiral staircase to the second floor. No one.

He descended further. It sounded like the noise was coming from Justin's dressing room. A girl's voice called out, "Somebody, help!"

At that moment Vanessa came flying toward him. "Phillip! Phillip, come quickly!"

As he rounded the corner he spotted Mary, the plumpish senior makeup woman, frantically banging her fists at Teague's door. "What's wrong, Mary?"

"Mr. Searing, that old man has Tara in there and he won't open the door."

"No, no, please," sounded the voice from within.

Phillip looked around for something to use as a battering ram. Muffled sounds, scuffling, and a girl's sobs. Phillip pounded on the door. "Justin, open up!"

Tara cried out again from inside.

"Open this door, Justin!" He banged his shoulder against the locked door. It wouldn't budge. He stood back from it, leaned against the wall, and kicked at it with the full undersole of his foot. It broke and slammed against the jamb.

Tara was thrown back in Justin's makeup chair. Her blouse was open and her bra pulled up. He had her arms pinned back to the sides of the chair and her legs forced into a wide spread. Her skirt was pushed up around her waist. Her panties had been torn off and were lying on the floor. Justin stood between her legs, his trousers down, pressing himself into her.

Mary covered her eyes and shrieked.

Phillip grabbed Justin by the shoulders and shoved him back against the counter. The old man's head hit the mirror, but not hard enough so it stopped him from raising his own fist. Phillip parried and caught him with a hook, which slammed Justin against the mirror again, this time shattering it and spewing slivers of glass all over the counter. Tara leapt from the chair and rushed out into the corridor.

Phillip heaved the actor to his feet.

"She asked for it. She's a prick tease. She led me on!"

Phillip kneed him in the groin. The actor crumpled.

Outside in the corridor, Mary and Vanessa tried to comfort the hysterical girl. She shivered, pressed up against the wall. "It's going to be all right, dear," Phillip said as convincingly as he could. "I think we stopped him in time." Mary and Vanessa looked at him with incredulity, but Phillip refused to be contradicted. "I think you're all right." Maybe if he planted a seed of doubt in her mind now, the incident would have less impact later.

The two ladies hustled Tara down the corridor and up to the makeup room. Phillip returned to the actor. The corner of his mouth bled and he tried to raise himself.

"I'd like to have a drink."

Phillip heaved the old man to his feet. He snatched up his briefcase and shoved him out of the room.

The limousine was waiting at the studio door. Phillip let the star crawl inside.

He slammed the door and told the chauffeur to take his cargo back to the hotel. "But wait there until he's packed and get him to the airport. And, Teague, if I ever see you in New York again, you son of a bitch, I'll have you thrown in jail for years."

The car eased out into the Ninth Avenue traffic. Phillip watched it disappear and tried to collect his emotions before reentering the building. Mary came out with a shaken Tara. He found them a cab and sent them off to Tara's mother's house in Queens. Later he would arrange a leave of absence for her if she wanted it, maybe a long vacation. If RBI wouldn't pay for it, he would. He blamed himself for the incident.

Phillip watched that car leave, also. Then he walked wearily inside. Emil, one of the studio electricians, stood in the doorway.

Phillip was still burning. "Where was everybody? I don't understand."

"Who?" asked Emil. "Everybody split after the taping. Nobody was here."

"Where were you? Didn't you hear yelling?"

"You can't hear nothing when the big studio door closes. You know that, Mr. Searing. It's soundproofed between the studio and the dressing room."

He passed the man and walked across the stage. No one else was in sight. Emil followed after him. He walked with a slight limp.

"That's . . . that's why you was the only one to hear, Mr. Searing. 'Cause the noise will come up the stair shaft to the office before it'll ever get out here. See?"

"Yeah!"

Emil was not able to keep up with Phillip and dropped off halfway across the stage, but when Phillip reached the far side he called out. "Mr. Searing!"

Phillip turned around.

"He got her, didn't he? He got the kid."

Phillip looked at him impassively. "No," he said. "No, he didn't get her."

Emil smiled ever so slightly. "That ain't what I heard."

114

"Well, you heard wrong. And I don't want any stories going around." He spun around and walked out. The halls were vacant.

Gloria sat inside his office, finishing a slug of Scotch she had poured for herself. "I didn't think you'd mind."

"Are you all right?"

"Yes. Just a little shaken, that's all."

"Good girl." He touched her hair as he passed. "Do you have much more to do today?"

"Just that list of calls you wanted me to make for you. And that letter to Mr. Teague's agency."

"Forget it and go on home. I'll make the calls myself, and now I want to think about that letter." He handed her a twenty-dollar bill from his wallet. "Take your boyfriend out for dinner tonight."

"Oh, Mr. Searing, you don't have—!"

"Go on, you deserve it."

She left and he stretched out on the couch. All was quiet except for the air-conditioned whirl, a radio tuned to a Puerto Rican music station somewhere outside, and the sirens and the horns. One thing he hadn't done to his office was to have it soundproofed. That might have been pushing things. It's a pleasant room now, he thought as he let his eyes wander over the decor. The teak desk and high-backed leather chair, a brother of the black-and-chrome couch he was lying on, a few paintings, a few silver objects, marble coffee table, chocolate-brown suede chairs, and proper carpet and draperies. Style didn't require excess, just taste, he thought, and wondered why so few people had any.

He had almost lost touch with the ugly stain of Tara's rape, when he heard footsteps approaching. Vanessa Langley. He had forgotten she was there.

She gave a quick, awkward smile and swallowed.

"I . . . have your jacket. You left it on the floor downstairs."

Phillip sat up and cleared his throat.

"How do you feel?" she asked.

"Me? Oh, I'm all right. And you?"

She nodded and set the jacket on the coffee table.

Phillip rubbed his eyes. "Rough couple of days. Poor kid. She's a sweet thing, Tara. I hope it doesn't affect her too badly."

115

"It probably won't," Vanessa said. "Nobody wears skirts or blouses as sexy as she does, unless she's looking for a little excitement."

"You think so?"

"Um-hmm."

"Still, what makes a man do something like that?"

"What makes a man do anything?" she asked. She leaned against the desk, her big leather bag slung over her shoulder. She had taken the time to tissue her makeup off and brush her hair out full. Long, straight black hair that fell cleanly from a bright-pink headband to thin shoulders. There was something vulnerable about her, like a blown glass bird, but also something enduring. It was as though she had no protection of any kind, but that did not stop her from entering fire.

"What makes a man do anything," he mused. "That's an interesting question, Vanessa. They're peculiar animals, aren't they?"

"Yes," she said, *"you* are."

Phillip pulled himself up and went out to the cooler in the outer area. He took a long swallow, then dipped his head letting the cold stream of water splash across his eyes. He rubbed it over his face. Vanessa was about to leave, but he stopped her. "Wait, I'll walk you out."

"I didn't think people like you ever stopped working."

"On days like this we do."

They walked down Ninth Avenue. It was steamy and heavy. A swollen day.

"Feels like an electrical storm coming up."

"I don't think anything could get through that smog soup."

"Con Edison's gift to Manhattan."

They stood there for a time, glued to the sticky asphalt. They seemed tied together by the weight of their strangely shared day. Phillip had no particular desire to go back to his apartment and couldn't think of anybody who was in town he'd especially like to see. It was a Katina sort of evening. But she was gone. He'd write her a long, long letter, but not now. Now he needed to get some feedback. "I was thinking of going over to the Brittany. They make a fairly good drink and have a nice cheese dip at the bar. Would you like to join me or do you have to get home?"

There was something about the way he asked that made

116

her want to say yes. There was a kind of loneliness in him she had never seen before, not that she had been looking. She liked him well enough and found him kind, perhaps more so since she had started by being afraid of him.

"I guess I can join you for a while. This heat is too much to take and our apartment is breeze-controlled."

They walked the block to Fifty-Third Street and entered the Breton-styled restaurant. There was a TV-commercial director at the bar, trying to impress an ivy-suited client from somewhere in the Midwest with a lot of "so I told him's." They found a table on the opposite side of the partition.

"I like this place," Vanessa said, looking around at the French royal crests that lined the walls.

"The food's not bad, but they don't accept credit cards so it makes it a hassle for me. I don't like to carry much cash on me these days. Just a little bit of street tax in case I get mugged."

He ordered a double Scotch and soda and she a Virgin Mary.

"What's a Virgin Mary?"

"Tomato juice and sauce without vodka."

"You don't drink?"

"Not in the afternoons."

Phillip played for a while with the salt and pepper shakers, circling one around the other. The costumed waitress brought their glasses and a plate of Port Salut and crackers, courtesy of the bar.

"Are you from the city, Vanessa? I don't know anything about you, I'm afraid, except that you've been doing a lovely job in that tiny little part of yours."

"Not so tiny this week. With Bill's being out, I've been on three shows."

"That's true, isn't it? You're going to be rich."

She laughed. "Don't think I won't know how to spend it."

"You'll be cut back next week, though. We'll have to build him up again."

She shrugged. "Whatever. I'm very happy to be working."

"It shows. Where are you from?"

"Bal-mer."

"Where?"

"Bal-mer, Merlin, Nighted Stayes—Mercka."

"Where the hell is that?" asked the producer.

"That's the way they say it there. Baltimore, Maryland, United States of America."

"For the love of Mike! What a revolting accent."

"One time when I was in school, the *Baltimore Sun* ran a series of articles on the inimitable Baltimorian accent. It was horrendous. It was at that point I decided to lose mine. I went to a speech-therapy clinic that the University of Maryland was offering and they gave me some corrective voice tapes. I worked at it."

"Do you go back there much?"

"Not very much. My family isn't fond of my husband."

"Why?"

"It's a long story." She bowed her head and studied her drink.

"Are they right to dislike him?"

"You can't like everybody." She sipped. "They don't dislike him, not for himself, anyway. Just for me."

"What does he do, your husband?"

"You mean for work?"

"Of course."

"He's a musician, a singer. Plays a lot of folk and rock stuff. He used to have a special little following in the Village."

"Doesn't he any more?"

"He doesn't play much any more. He had an album contract with Atlantic that fell through at the last minute and it hit him rather hard. He really counted on that album—it was so close. Everybody liked him. He used to play down at a place called Anybody's on West Fourth Street, near MacDougal. You know it?"

"I've passed by."

"Well, one night a man came in to watch and then he came back the following night. Then once again, before he introduced himself to Joey and said he was from Atlantic and that they'd like to talk to him about cutting an LP for them."

"I see."

"You know how those record people talk. Before they finish shaking your hand, you're a millionaire, your name's up in lights, and the limousine's on its way to pick you up for your opening night concert at Carnegie Hall."

118

"They're ambitious thinkers."

"They wanted Joey to write a batch of new songs. They would need about seven or eight more to fill out the album, so he got excited and sat down to do it. He worked very hard and they talked contract, and everything was beautiful and meanwhile he was still playing for handouts on Fourth Street. But he told everybody about it, all his friends, family, everybody. It was very exciting for him. It was in the bag, set, finished, done." She stopped and looked down at the table. "It was in the bag," she mused.

"What happened?"

"Fell through." She gave a little nod, then shook her head. "It just fell through."

"Didn't they explain?"

"A guy named Alan, who was handling the deal for the record company, just said it was off one day. He didn't even call Joey. Joey called him after he hadn't heard from him in a week or two. Just said the company was full up on singers of his type and didn't want to take on any more. That was it." Vanessa's voice cracked a little.

"I think I'd hate to be a performer," said Phillip. "Somehow having a show rejected, or a proposal rejected doesn't compare with being turned down for a part . . . a record. It's all so much more personal. I watch so many actors scrounging for parts. They're willing to do almost anything to get them. Sometimes I'd like to reach out and say, 'Look here, it's only a part. Don't take it all so seriously.'" He paused, then he asked, "Have you been at it long?"

"Three years," she said. "I've been very lucky, particularly with this show." She thought a moment and then said, "We've had a lot of medical bills to pay, Joey and I, and I would probably have had to get a job outside acting if I hadn't started playing Valerie."

"Is one of you sick?"

"It's a long story, as I said." She looked down at the table.

Phillip stretched and looked around at the bar which was gradually filling with more TV-commercial people. A group of technicians were jabbering about the Mets. Phillip took his last swig and noticed that Vanessa's glass was empty too. He sensed she would like to leave. "I've al-

119

most forgotten our actor friend. Thanks for coming with me. I needed company."

He pulled the small table out, so she could edge around it comfortably. He paid the check and they walked through the bar, crowded with men who glanced sideways at her. She seemed unaware of the ripple she created.

He placed her in a cab and hailed one for himself.

9.

Rosalynann Patachoutz seemed in a bouncy mood when she returned to her desk after lunch. She was sopping wet from the noonday heat, but bubbling cheerfully. "You go out, Grace?"

The older woman was wielding her Selectric like a machine gun across the narrow desk divider. "No." She shook her head. "Had to get these expense accounts typed."

"It must be a hundred out there." Rosalynann dabbed her pretty face with a scented Washease from her purse. She gave herself a quick lookover in her compact mirror and pushed up some blonde curls. "Got some divine Charles Jordan shoes." She came out of her chair and moved across the space between them, pulling back the tissue of the cardboard box. It contained a pair of six-inch platform wedgies in pale green, white, and violet. "They'll go with that little shift I got at Bonwit's last week. Aren't they divine? I love them."

Grace looked at the shoes and sucked a piece of her hastily grabbed company cafeteria lunch from her teeth. She had been a secretary for RBI for nineteen years and had seen the Rosalynanns come and go about as fast as their fashions. She nodded with little enthusiasm. Grace never wore anything but flats herself, always afraid of being taller than her boss, a short, scrawny man with complexes.

Rosalynann hurried back to her desk, stashed the shoebox under her feet, and slid down with a contented sigh. She hadn't seen her boss all morning. He was at a staff meeting with the president of the web. Mondays were a blessing because of those meetings. He took a long lunch with Keel in the executive dining room, which left her enough time to gobble and shop.

She heard the heavy plod of his heels on the floor behind her and knew that the meeting had not gone well. He charged past her desk, entered his office, and slammed his door without even a glance. So ends a beautiful cuddly weekend, she thought. He could be such a Teddy Bear when he wanted to and such a bastard when he didn't. She stabbed the letter opener into the top of a stack of unopened envelopes.

Elliot rarely took off his suit jacket in the office. He was too conscious of the gut hanging over his belt, but this afternoon he yanked it off and threw it onto the chair in front of his desk. He jabbed the intercom button.

"Yes, Elliot," she responded in her Monday-afternoon tone of voice.

"The goddamn air conditioner is still on the fritz, Rosalynann. I thought that guy was coming up to fix it. Call him, will you? And call Searing too and tell him I want to see him in here right after the show airs. Four-fifteen."

"Right away, Mr. Chamberfield." Her tone irritated him. It was too familiar for the office. Gotta tell her a thousand times! But he didn't say anything.

Half an hour after his meeting with a West Coast packager was over, Rosalynann closed the door and pouted to her boss. "You haven't spoken to me all day."

Elliot looked up. She was standing in front of his desk, a hurt expression on her pretty, round face and a sheaf of papers in her fist. "I have too, Rosalynann, come on!"

"Only as my boss. Not once as my Teddy Bear."

Elliot winced. "Cut it out, will you, Rosalynann. The office is no place for that stuff." He wiped his sweaty neck with a handkerchief. He hated more than anything to be teased. "Damned guy still hasn't come up to fix the air conditioner, you know?"

"It's not my fault. I called them three times today."

She came around behind the desk and leaned up against his chair. Her skimpy skirt revealed an uncomfortable amount of thigh for his public tastes. He avoided looking at it, but put his hand on her waist and let it slip down onto her hip. "I know it's not your fault. I didn't say it was, did I?" He patted her rear end and took the papers out of her hand. "We'll talk at dinner, okay? You want to eat at Sardi's?"

"Yes, okay." She brightened considerably. Elliot's concentration turned to the papers. "I'll call for reservations."

"Fine, do that," he mumbled, and made a note in the margin.

She opened the door, glanced back at him, and added haughtily, "Right away, Mr. Chamberfield."

Fifteen minutes later she announced Phillip Searing.

"Vulkner thinks Teague stunk," Elliot spat at him before he had a chance to sit.

"We all do, don't we?" he asked calmly. "But that won't make much difference on Friday."

"I was called on the carpet for you today. I don't like that. I won't ever defend you again. You can be sure of that."

"I didn't ask you to defend me. I'm perfectly capable of defending my own actions."

"After this Teague business, I'm not so sure, Searing. Vulkner doesn't like to see shit on his network and that's exactly what Teague made that show. Even Sue Cameron's column said he looked tight."

"No one but the industry will read what she said."

"Well, Vulkner cares what the industry thinks, even if you don't."

"The ratings come in Friday. They're the only thing that counts."

"I have in front of me the facilities and manpower cost sheets for last week. Your little stunt was not only an embarrassment to the network, but outrageously expensive. What the fuck do you think you were producing? A Buzby Berkeley musical?"

"Teague required special handling," Phillip said, main-

taining his cool. The old rules of the "game" were in play
again. He watched his opponent struggle. Phillip knew
Elliot was actually pleased to be called before Vulkner
and Keel. His defense would make it clear to them that he
was not out purposely to oust Searing. And Phillip also
knew if the ratings did not bear out his judgment, he
would be doing exactly what Chamberfield wanted: hanging himself. But he maintained the countenance of a winner. "See the show today?"

"No, I'm too busy to watch the goddamned thing every
day."

"Shame. It was our best to date. Bill Peters is back and
in top form. I think we're finally on the right track."

"I just finished looking at a presentation for a new game
show that I think'll work perfectly in your time slot."
Elliot dropped his little tidbit with courtly smugness.

Phillip rose and smiled affably. "Don't waste your time
looking for a replacement, Elliot. *Affair* is going to be
home solid by the end of the summer, and the show you
created will do you proud. Now, if you're finished, I'd
like to get back for some auditions."

Elliot chewed on the inside of his cheek, but couldn't
think of anything more to add. Somehow the meeting had
not gone as foreseen.

Phillip left the office and winked at Rosalynann. She
was behind the desk, trying on her new shoes. "Very, very
chic, my dear!" he said. He knew he didn't annoy her so
much as she pretended he did.

On Wednesday, Phillip received the following note from
Katina:

> Dearest Phillip,
>   Have met some wildly interesting people here
> in Ibiza, and am taking time off to fly to London on
> the 12th. There's going to be a party on Saturday,
> the 13th. Lots of fun people, including me. Why
> don't you give yourself a break for a weekend and
> come on over for it? I'll be staying at the Chelsea
> Arms.
>
>   Miss ya,
>   Love, Katina

His desk calendar indicated the thirteenth was in two weeks. He made a note to send a telegram offering excuses.

"It's curious," said Pat Rosetti as they left the studio for lunch. "Today is the most crucial day he's had since he got here and you'd hardly know it. Neat, pleasant, cordial, systematic. To look at him you wouldn't have a clue his entire career is hanging by a thread."

"Is it?" asked Maude.

"Oh, yeah," he said slowly, drawing out the words for emphasis, "oh, yeah, yeah—it sure is. I understand the Justin Teague week was hated a lot upstairs. Those ratings are the only things that can justify his decision to hire the old fart. If they don't come up roses today, he's had it . . . and so have we. They'll probably dump us all and go into fast production on a replacement show for the fall."

They walked in silence.

Phillip punched the button and the actors faded off the screen. He let it go black and then sat quietly. He hadn't wanted to go down to the control booth. He stayed in the office alone and watched the taping on the monitor. He hadn't even bothered to take notes. He touched another button. "Gloria, call Pat and tell him the show was okay. Then you go on to lunch."

He released the intercom and stared out the window. He picked up a felt tip pen and doodled in green on a yellow legal pad. He lit another cigarette, crushed the empty pack, dropped it into the loaded ashtray, and shifted back so he could empty all of it into the wastebasket.

He walked across the room and back. His attention hooked onto a loose thread hanging from his tie. He let the problem engulf his mind. He opened the desk drawer and removed a fingernail clipper, the spring kind with a curved mouth. The curve made it difficult to cut the thread cleanly. He played with it for a while until it finally snipped off. Then he replaced the clipper and sat there.

His internal alarm clock had awakened him that morning at six-forty-five, as usual. He'd done the pushups, the situps, the chinups on the bar. He'd fixed the cereal and fruit, the ham and eggs, the toast and coffee. He'd breezed through the *Times*, then showered, shaved, and dressed.

At seven-forty-five he was behind his desk. At nine-thirty, he chewed out Claire Pappas for not yet having found an actress to play the vamp, and by noon all the minor details of the day's show had been attended to. There was a quick meeting with the director and writer about a scene change for Sally Gunderson, the lead actress who had yet to find out she was being eased out of her starring role. Pat felt her phase-out would be too obvious, so the three of them sat there and softened it.

His palms sweated. He wiped them with a tissue and studied the dark stain of moisture. Why? What was it? Why all the tension, the stress?

He went over to the air conditoner and turned it up fuller. He stood for a moment in the draft. The cool flow of air hit his stomach. He tried to pinpoint the knot that had been with him since he had climbed out of bed that morning, but he couldn't. It was an overall tightness.

Three hours to four o'clock. Two hours and fifty-two minutes to four o'clock. Ratings at four—Justin Teague—Chamberfield—lose the show—lose all—lose—not win—win, what difference? What are the odds? What do they matter?

What strange thoughts! He wasn't used to this. Why? Why was he losing control? Why the doubt? Could it have been a wrong decision to hire Justin? Of course, but why think about it? He'd been in tight corners before. He had never worried about futures. Was that it? Was it now a question of futures?

The phone rang. He let it die. Nobody should be calling now. It was lunchtime. Probably a mistake.

He could always get another soap on another network. And if not, there were many other things he could do. Was it because Chamberfield would win and he lose? Maybe. That was certainly possible. Chamberfield survived by devouring others. But that wasn't the problem. Chamberfield wasn't causing his palms to sweat.

He tuned in the air show. Vanessa was on again. What a lovely girl—so fresh, so full, he thought. She's going to be happy when she finds out she's been upgraded. No problem with that decision.

When it was over, he turned off the set and ambled over to the bar. He poured a double Scotch over some ice and was about to add a dash of seltzer when he hesitated, thought for a moment, and then in a burst of sudden angry exasperation walked out into the outer office and pitched the contents into the water cooler. Fuck it! He wasn't going to follow the former occupant of the office down the drain. "Gloria, it's close to judgment hour."

"I was just ready to go."

"You have money for the cab?"

"I have a petty-cash voucher here."

He signed it and handed it back. "Ask for Frieda. She knows who you are, doesn't she?"

"Yes, we've spoken on the phone."

"All right. She'll give you the advance copy. No chit-chat. Don't let anyone else see those ratings. Just bring them back."

She took her purse and headed for the door. He was still standing there, vaguely watching her move off, when she turned back to look at him. "Mr. Searing . . . Phillip . . . regardless of how these numbers turn out, I want you to know you're the best boss I've ever worked for."

"If you don't wiggle your little tail over there quick as a bunny, you won't be working for me much longer."

Twenty minutes and he'd know where he stood. Twenty more minutes. An eternity.

He set the empty whiskey glass down on the steel-gray file cabinet; it made a water ring at the base. Female voices drifted out of cubbyholes at the end of the production offices, from girls who worked for the studio, not the show. No one else was around. He reached into his pocket and drew out the Dunhills. He poked one between his lips and fumbled for the lighter. A packet of matches lay open next to the typewriter. He took it instead. He struck a match and held it to the tip of the tobacco. His hand shook. "This is nonsense," he muttered to himself "What's going on, Phillip? What's happening to you? You've never been shaken like this before."

And then he did a strange thing. He left. He sat down at Gloria's IBM, typed a fast note, and left. "Gloria, Please find Pat and give him the ratings. He'll be anxious to know about the show. I have to leave." And he did.

It was six o'clock when he got back to his apartment. He had heard the phone ringing since stepping out of the elevator, but took his time opening the door and entering.

"Two and a half points! Two and a half points, Phillip! You showed those dum-dums. Congratulations!"

"Thank you, Colin. Nice of you to call." So it had worked. He had won. Once again he was right.

But something made him regret leaving the neutral sack he had permitted himself to float in for the past couple of hours.

"You must be ecstatic yourself? Are you going to party it up?" Colin was bubbling with good nature.

He didn't want to let him know that the call was the first notice he had had. "No, I'm alone, actually. I don't have anything particular planned."

"Nothing sways him, Tarzan of the TV jungle. I'd be flying so high if I were you right now that you'd never get me down."

"Well, maybe . . . if I had anything to get high on, I would. Who are you with?"

"Vanessa. We're over at Joe Allen's, trying to figure out a way to celebrate. Her husband's out of town for the weekend. You wouldn't like to join us, would you?"

Vanessa and Colin. Why not? he thought. There was no one else in town he particularly felt like being with. "Have you eaten?" he asked.

"No, not yet. We'll probably go Chinese later on."

"I'll tell you what. Why don't you two come over here in about an hour or so? I'll call up a place around the corner that'll deliver and we can eat out on the terrace."

"Terrific! Wait. Hey, Ness, we're invited up to the mansion for dinner."

"The mansion!" Phillip laughed. "What are you talking about?"

Colin turned back to the phone. "The lady says okay, if you're sure it won't be any trouble."

"Of course not. Just give me time to take a shower and change."

Colin took another hit, holding the roach daintily between his long, manicured fingers. He pulled hard, shoving the smoke deep down into his lungs, and then pressed it forward until his face turned cherry red.

"You look like you've got a stolen cookie caught in your windpipe," said Vanessa, as she gathered the card-

128

board cartons together and wiped up some black bean sauce that had dripped onto the coffee table.

He released the pent-up sweetness and it shot out in a rush. "Goddammit, Vanessa! You just made me blow fifty cents' worth of dynamite shit."

Phillip came down from the kitchen with the freshly brewed French coffee. He filled the cups. Colin passed him the joint.

"Two and a half points!" Colin exclaimed. "Justin Teague, I love you. Who would have ever thought? Who would have ever thought? The old fart pulled it through. Old fart, hell," he corrected himself. "*You* did it, Phillip. You gave us ratings faster than anybody could ever have imagined."

"Here, here!" called Vanessa.

Phillip smiled a bit self-consciously. "It's a fickle audience, don't forget. We'll lose part of that raise, maybe even half."

Vanessa piped up hopefully. "But even at half, that's very good, isn't it? The show won't be canceled now, will it?"

"You never know. If we keep building solidly, probably not."

"It's like being on death row and getting a stay of execution." Colin suddenly bolted up to a sitting position and his expression turned serious. "Jesus! I just had a terrible thought!"

"What?"

"What if that was our last meal?"

"Colin, don't scare me!" cried Vanessa.

Phillip took another pull on the joint and aimed it toward Vanessa. "Colin, it's more than a stay of execution. Don't worry about it."

Colin sat back and began to roll another. "You're really in a unique kind of position, aren't you? No other producer has your kind of freedom." He paused to lick the papers. "Is it because you're a VP?"

Phillip looked at him carefully. Was it possible he didn't know about the animosity between Elliot and himself? Well, if it were unknown, there was no reason to bring it out now. "Yes," he lied gently, "I suppose it is because I am a vice president. They agreed to let me run the show

129

my way. But, of course, if I fail to deliver"—he smiled at them—"we all go out together."

They were silent for a while. Colin got up and padded over to the table where he had left his little leather stash bag with the grass and papers. He picked out his roach clip.

Vanessa too stood up and walked over to the windows. "Do you mind if I make myself another drink?" she asked.

"No, no, of course not."

"I don't feel like smoking."

Colin enveloped himself in grass smoke and the wings of the black Voltaire chair; Phillip sat on the couch, and Vanessa leaned against the large picture window and stared out into the night. She sipped, they puffed. They all reflected and dreamed.

Later, Colin left. He jumped up suddenly, remembering that he had ten minutes to make a ten o'clock rendezvous at Uncle Charley's South, a gay bar on Third Avenue. Phillip offered to drive Vanessa home whenever she was ready, but she wasn't in any particular rush. Joe was in Woodstock for the weekend and she would have to enter an empty apartment. The week had been grueling, and for the moment she was comfortable. She could let her mind drift and think of nothing.

Phillip watched her for a long while, staring off toward the river. "If you'd prefer," he said, "we can sit out on the terrace upstairs. It won't be as cool, but it might be more pleasant than the air conditioning."

They took the tray of coffee things, a drink for him and another for her, and walked up the steps to the second level. The terrace was just off the kitchen. They deposited the soiled cups in the sink, and Phillip opened the glass door to the outside. He flipped on the spotlight on the gently running fountain.

"This is magnificent."

He motioned her to a chaise and stretched out in a second one himself. They looked off into the skyline.

"My God, if this were mine I'd sit out here for nights on end."

"I do sometimes," he said.

"It's a wonderland," she said, almost to herself. She looked at the lights, the forms, the shadowed shapes and said loosely, since the liquor had begun to dizzy her a little, "You could sit out here and redesign all of it."

They sat awhile, content just to be part of the calm. Phillip, sitting slightly behind, was conscious of the outline of her cheek. Such a lovely face, he thought, so perfectly chiseled and smoothed, like a marble face by Rodin. "Tell me something," he said quietly, so as not to destroy the mood. "Have you always wanted to be an actress?"

"Ever since I can remember." She fixed her stare dreamily on a distant light and spoke as though she were centuries away. "But it wasn't the razzle-dazzle of Broadway or Hollywood that intrigued me. I was always afraid to be a star, should the Lord ever will that on such as me," she joked. "It was always more personal than that. I guess I wanted to be an actress in order to get away from myself . . . that was the psychological part, anyway. I could take all my frustrations and anxieties, and fears, and happinesses, too, and stuff them all into whatever character I happened to be playing—like my briefcase." She laughed and glanced sideways at Phillip. "It's true," she continued. "And that's one of the great things about doing a soap. Because Valerie is a continuing character, I can really become her, change with her every day as she changes, move through her ups, her downs, her loves and disappointments. In the theater you play the same part every night, beginning to end. But in a soap there's the excitement of never knowing what's going to happen to you. I find myself worrying over Valerie's problems sometimes when I'm not even working. Funny, isn't it? She's my Mr. Hyde . . . or Dr. Jekyll, whichever one I'm not. My alternate self. I've even gotten to the point of being able to switch to one when the problems of the other plague me." She took a sip from her drink and swizzled the ice around with her finger. "Even my parents believe I'm more Valerie than Vanessa now, particularly since Valerie's kind of a goody-two-shoes . . . and Vanessa's married to a bum," she added softly. "Mother watches me every day I'm on the air with a group of her friends. They all live in one block-long, brick, row house with the same back yards and front yards and the same aluminum screen doors and postage-stamp porches, and every day they congregate at Mother's and watch me. Do you know that sometimes when I talk to my mother on the phone she slips and calls me Valerie? Isn't that funny? She calls me Valerie! That proves I've really succeeded. Even my own mother thinks of me as somebody else."

Vanessa drained her whiskey glass and made no move to stop Phillip from going back to the kitchen to replenish it. He returned and settled on the lounge.

Five minutes passed and neither spoke. Ten minutes. The only sounds were the noises of the city, and then a faint sniffle, like a suppressed sob. Phillip noticed the stain of a tear streaking down Vanessa's right cheek. She stared straight ahead, in a world of her own. A few more minutes went by. The tear stopped, but the expression remained unchanged. Her face was warmly haloed by the glow of the fountain lights. Then she spoke. "It's too bad you're not a total stranger. You're the sort of person I think I could talk to, but I don't want you to know me. And if I talked to you and told you all the things that were important to me. . . ." She paused and gave a little sigh. "Then you would know me and I wouldn't like that. It would make me afraid of you." She spoke softly, dragging out each word, each phrase. "I wish . . . I wish you were a man at a carnival, costumed, behind a black mask, and I, too, were costumed and had on a white mask and we met like that and walked for one mile . . . and I spoke to you and told you everything that I could think of about myself. I got it all out and put it in you, and then I never saw you again. It would be like writing one's innermost thoughts on paper and putting it into a corked bottle and pitching it out to sea. But better . . . more sure."

"What makes you think you can't talk to me now?"

"Because there's Monday morning and Tuesday morning and Wednesday morning, and I'd be presented with your knowledge of me every day I'm on the soap, and more. And you would know my husband's a junkie."

"*What?*" A shiver ran through his body, as though a freezing-cold ice tray had been suddenly pressed against the skin of his upper back.

"He's not any more. He's kicked the habit. I shouldn't say he is, I guess. I should say he was. I shouldn't say anything, actually. Normally, I don't. I don't discuss it. I don't know why I told you about it. I . . . suppose I'm drunk . . . or stoned . . . or both." The thought caused her

132

to look down into her glass. There was still a watery taste of whiskey left on the half-melted ice. She swiveled the glass, raised it, and swallowed the liquid.

"That's what you meant last week when you said you had medical bills?"

"For the psychiatrist. After he came out of the clinic, I pushed him to go to see an analyst to straighten himself out." She thought for a moment. "He's making progress. He's been awfully good about it all."

"What about you?"

"Oh, me? Life goes on, that's all. On the days I don't work, I take classes and my agent sends me around for auditions, but I'm afraid to do them because I'm afraid to be tempted away from doing the soap. You know, they're often for a lead in a Broadway show or a movie . . . but I won't do it. We need the money too badly to take a chance on anything else. That's why I'm so frightened that something will happen to it and it'll be canceled."

"It won't be."

She turned and stared at him. It was as though she were seeing him for the first time. "You're so secure," she said. "Nothing sways you. How can you be so sure of yourself?"

"Would you believe me if I told you I'm not?"

"No."

He smiled. "I'm not. I just behave as though I'm sure of myself."

And then they were in bed. It wasn't certain who had made the first move. It had just happened naturally, like the melting of the ice cubes in the whiskey glasses. They had stood and kissed, and Phillip had taken her hand and led her through the kitchen and into the hall to the bedroom. Their clothing was dropped onto the carpet, and they had stood before each other dressed in nothing but their loneliness.

He let his fingers spread into her hair and then down across her back and over her hips and to the front. He lay her back against the pillows and spread her knees open gently, climbed between them, and kissed her lips. They lay connected, hardly moving, and all at once as if responding to some foreign signal, an explosion racked them internally. It was like a release of all that had been

133

pent up for weeks and weeks. And it came out in a flood of exhaustion.

Afterward, Vanessa held to him like a drowner to a solitary log. He waited, but she made no sound, no motion.

When she relaxed her grip, he climbed out of bed and went into the bathroom. He took a quick, cold shower, slipped into a velour robe, and went back. She was gone.

10.

Why the hell did she have to go out to the damn pool again? he thought. Didn't she realize Sundays were difficult days? Why don't I come out to the pool, Rosalynann? Because I don't enjoy being out at the pool, Rosalynann. What am I going to talk about out there, Rosalynann? I don't know anybody . . . nobody knows me. At the Beverly Hills, okay. There I can talk to people, but here? The place is filled with lawyers and doctors and merchants . . . or whatever those other Archie Bunkers do for a living. What do I know to talk to them about?

Elliot stared out of the top of the double Dutch door. It was hot, but a breeze skimmed the tips of the pine trees from the ocean to the bay side. I'd love to have . . . people to talk to. People who didn't want anything from me, who weren't always pulling on me like a litter of puppies on a bitch's teats.

"Come here, Thumper. I know, I know. A few more weeks and you'll have your whole family." He knelt down and ran his hand along the dachshund's swollen underbelly. "You're my girl. But you're an ugly-looking little mutt. I feed you too much. I spoil you. We're going to put you on a diet. Pickles and ice cream till you have your litter, but then it's weight-watcher's time. Right? You and me. We'll do it together."

He let himself sink down onto the floor. The dog pushed her backside up against him and curled. People don't realize. His was a difficult position to be in. A man with a job like his couldn't trust anybody straight out. He'd always been in that kind of position, people getting close to him to get things from him, except in college, and he'd worked his ass off there, so there was no time for friends. University of Missouri, a local station in St. Louis, then into RBI in New York. He was a wheel from the beginning. Couldn't trust anybody enough to have them for friends. Except Barry. Barry he could trust.

The cabin was stuffy and smelled of creosoted wood. He'd read the pilot projects he brought with him and made his margin notes. Things were going nicely. He liked the script proposals.

There would be at least two good pilots to choose from for each of the shows he wanted to eliminate. There was no sweat for the fall. All he had to do was ride herd on Keith Burke's choices. It had been clever to switch around a few of the prime-time shows, helped demonstrate his independence, but basically he couldn't be held responsible for his predecessor's selections. It was next year that would count and he had until February 20 to develop all the ideas, go to script, into production, finish, test, make his decisions, and lock in his nighttime schedule. And what if the ad agencies didn't buy his choices? What if he failed . . . what if he failed?

If he failed, he would be one out-of-work network programing chief, with no future anywhere in the industry. A job? Sure, he could always get a job, but it wasn't the same thing.

He got up and turned on the set, stared at it absently until it warmed up, and then dialed through the channels—zero. Miserable Sunday afternoon. Next weekend he'd have to stretch out the paperwork to last a little longer. He needed something to occupy him on Sundays. Boring, goddamned Sundays.

"Come here, Thumper. Come here, girl." The dog wiggled her bottom and wagged her tail all the way over to her master. He gently felt her belly again. "It's getting closer, isn't it, girl?"

Maybe Barry would be home. He could talk to Barry. He picked up the phone. No, he had said he was going to Fire Island. He dropped the receiver.

He left the set on and wandered into the bedroom. He lay down on the textured spread. He was hungry. Nah, shouldn't eat. Too much bulk, already. He pulled up his polo shirt and examined his belly. Two months' pregnant, like the dog—maybe three. Why do some people gain weight and others don't? Some people are lucky, that's why. Phillip Searing doesn't have any weight problems. Of course, he's always going off to play tennis or handball or some other ridiculous game. Fucking jock. Just like the college bastards. Still it kept the weight off him.

Try a few situps. What the hell? It was a bore, but who knows—maybe it'll help tighten a little of the flab—tighten up the old pot.

With an effort he maneuvered himself up to a sitting position. His butt sank into the soft mattress and made the exercise that much more difficult. The strain on his back was incredible. How did anybody ever enjoy this sort of thing? He dropped down and tried once again. The hell with it. Too much trouble. Where was Rosalynann, anyway?

The dog came over and licked his hand that hung over the edge of the bed. Be nice to have a drink. No, too early. Besides it would only irritate the ulcer. He ought to have the damn thing operated on—get rid of the agony once and for all. Goddamn burning all the time, sour stomach, sleepless nights, morning sickness. Wonder if Searing's got an ulcer? Probably not. Probably beats it all out with his goddamn handball games.

Phillip Searing. What the hell to do about him? What if the agencies reject the new proposals and Phillip Searing pops his head from behind the curtain and Russell Keel plays musical vice presidents? Elliot Chamberfield would be out on his ass.

Affair was a sure failure. So what if the son of a bitch picked up a few lousy ratings points? It was still almost a dead horse and it should be ridden right out of the network. But he'd have to come up with a way to get rid of Phillip soon . . . a way without backlash. If only he had

137

some inside dope on the guy, a personal scandal of some sort. But he'd need someone on the inside, close to Searing, to dig it out. Maybe. . . . There should be someone on that show he could trust.

Of course, he could always have Barry write him a memo saying Searing should be fired because of the enormous overcharges on the Teague business and the fact that he decorated his personal office with show money, or some other bullshit reason. Russell wouldn't interfere. But then he'd have to find a replacement for him and if the replacement failed, which was more than likely, then the whole responsibility would fall back on him. His show, his choice to replace a good producer with a bad one. Bad scene.

No worry come February 20, if the sponsors bought his selections. He'd be in solid as a rock. But there was the outside chance they wouldn't, and then it would be a little late to start thinking about protecting the old rear.

No . . . he needed something now on Searing. Someone who could give him a little inside scoop. He made a mental note to check over the personnel roster first thing in the morning.

* * *

The slight young man in the Paul Stuart suit was all ears. This was the first story conference he had been invited to sit in on, and he was amazed at the different curves it took. As associate producer, Colin's responsibility was to handle the day-to-day running of the soap, freeing the producer from mundane details and allowing him to concentrate on the long-range prospectus.

The entire production staff had known for weeks that Phillip and Maude were completely overhauling the shape of the show, but no one had any idea which direction it would take; which of the stories they were producing each day would emerge as the lead one.

Now, Colin knew. He was among the select.

"Okay," Maude said finally, "then Valerie's visit to the doctor will take place this Friday, giving us a good cliffhanger for the weekend, and I don't think we'll have any trouble with next week's line at all." She turned to Colin. "So, young man, what do you think?"

"I'm astounded. It's a different show. I feel like we just

threw out our book in New Haven three days before we open on Broadway. No kidding. Pins and needles, darling. I was totally enthralled."

Maude laughed and winked at Phillip. "Let's hope he's an indication of general American tastes."

The slight young man giggled. "Me? I'm a walking Nielsen book. I even relax with Muzak."

Phillip closed his notebook and lit a cigarette. "You like the Valerie story?"

"Very, very much. Vanessa is the most identifiable actress on the show. She has such a special quality, you know, she'll carry it off."

Phillip accepted the comment politely. "Fine, well, that should do it for now. Colin, you'd better run down and see if Pat needs anything. Also check the special-effects man and see if he's perfected that rain device for Wednesday."

"Okay, and listen . . . I really mean it: I think the changes are fabulous."

"Good."

Colin fairly skipped down the hall. He passed the casting office, spied Claire sitting on the edge of June King's desk with an index card in her hand. She looked up as he stuck his head in the door. "Well, what do you look so cheery about? Mother just kick off?"

"Not that lucky, darling. Bye!"

Colin glanced around the busy set. He found Pat changing a piece of Sally's blocking, and judging to see whether camera three could pick it up without being caught by camera one. Colin waited until he was finished. "Pat, you need anything?"

"Oh, yeah. Check with wardrobe and see if I can get another tie for Bill. The one he's got shimmies on camera."

"Can't have shimmying ties." He waited around a few minutes, joked with the boom man, and took a few gaffs from Luke Gillens about his suit.

"That's snazzier than anything we got in our prop room, Dude."

But Colin had spotted Vanessa going over her lines on the kitchen set. "Hi, ya, toots."

"How's tricks?"

"Friday night's were divine, Saturday was a wipeout, but the baths on Sunday were really swinging."

"And you used to be so sweet and innocent."

"I haven't been innocent since the obstetrician whacked me on my tush. Whips and chains from there on in." He paused, glanced around, and whispered dramatically, "Wanna hear some poop?"

"Only if it's good."

"It's the best news you'll hear for quite a spell, dearie. But cross that palpitating heart of yours that you won't tell a soul. I mean it, not even a hint to anybody. They didn't say specifically, but I know that they don't want the news out."

"Well, what is it?"

"Umm, maybe I shouldn't tell."

"Colin, come on now. I've got to get these lines down."

"It's fantastic news. You, my dear, are in for a surprise."

"Why, because I have three days on this week?"

"No, dear thing, because from now on you're going to be guaranteed five days!"

"Five days?"

"Five days a week, every week. Your part is being expanded. Starting Friday, Valerie will be the lead character on *Affair Of The Heart*." He grinned at her as proudly as if she had been the beneficiary of his own generosity.

But Vanessa only stared.

"Vanessa, do you understand?" His voice was too loud and he quickly lowered it. "I just came out of the story conference on the new plot and you will be queen of *Affair*. Isn't that fantastic?"

Her face had gone white.

"Christ, you have a funny way of receiving good news. Listen, got to run to wardrobe. Remember—secret!" He kissed her lightly on the cheek and scurried out of the set. Pat's voice called for places on the loudspeaker.

Colin and Phillip watched the one o'clock taping in the producer's office. Colin sat primly on the couch, legs crossed tightly, chain-smoking a pack of Tareytons. His boss stayed behind the desk. They both stared in horror at the screen. Vanessa was stumbling like a rank amateur through a scene she had rehearsed without a flaw. She's a zombie, thought Colin. She's blowing cues. There's enough space between her lines to drive a truck through.

Except for a tightening of the jaw muscles, Phillip showed no emotion. Toward the end of the show, Vanessa blew a series of lines and became visibly flustered. Wilma covered for her and improvised. "Not even time for a retake," muttered the producer, "and the budget couldn't stand it if there were."

The closing scene faded out and went to the theme under the titles. Phillip switched it off and picked up the control-booth line. "Judy, give me Pat, please."

The director came on immediately. "I don't know what happened to her, Phillip. She was fine during rehearsal."

"Is she still on the set?"

"No, she ran off to her dressing room."

"All right, let her be. I'll go talk to her later."

"I'm sorry, Phillip."

"It's not your fault." He hung up and looked over at Colin. The young man shrugged nervously.

"I don't understand, Phillip. She was super during the run-through."

"Did you speak to her?"

"Yes. I stopped to chitchat just after the story conference."

"Did she give you any indication she was troubled?"

"No."

"What did she say?"

"Nothing special."

Phillip regarded him oddly. "Colin, did you mention anything to her about the expansion of her part?"

Guilt flashed across his face.

Phillip was calm. There was no severity in his tone. "Did you?"

"I didn't think it would hurt. We're very close friends and she promised not to tell anyone. I know you don't want anyone worried about losing their parts. That was the point of the secrecy, wasn't it? I didn't think it would hurt."

"You didn't think . . . you didn't think. That's the point, Colin." He suddenly became icy. "Do you realize what you've done? You not only betrayed my confidence, but you shook an actress before a taping. You're an associate

141

producer, Colin. Don't you know that no one talks to performers before a taping?"

"We always talk, Phillip, you know that."

"No one talks to performers before a taping, do you understand? That's a cardinal rule of this business, unless you're specifically told to by the director or me. There's no excuse for what you took upon yourself to do."

Colin shrank into the couch. The words were soft, but explosive. It was the first time he had experienced the sting of the man and it overwhelmed him.

"Colin, I don't give a fuck about your friendships or pals on the show. The only thing that concerns me is what goes on the air and that show today stunk. And it's completely your fault. We can't afford to have lousy episodes. If we lost one viewer today because of that incredible performance, it's your fault. Do you understand?" he asked softly. "Do you read me, Colin?"

"Yes, sir," he whispered meekly.

"Now, get out!"

He leapt up as if someone had threatened him with a knife. He wasn't sure whether the producer wanted him out of the office, or was kicking him out of his job as well. Either way he wanted to escape as quickly as possible.

Phillip stopped him at the door. "If I ever catch you betraying a confidence again or speaking to anyone before a taping, you will be out of a job."

Later Phillip went downstairs to find Vanessa. He caught her hurrying out of her dressing room. The sudden shock on her face when she saw him was like a deer frozen in the headlights of a car.

"Vanessa, don't worry about the show today. It happens to the best."

She seemed to want to say something, but all she did was shrink away from the man.

"Are you all right?" He put out his hand, but she pulled back. She scurried around past him and down the corridor. "Vanessa!" But she slipped out the door.

Colin went to bed early that night. He was still shaken by the day's events. He had tried to talk to Vanessa several times, but she wouldn't respond. He had no idea what could have produced her reaction.

The phone rang. He switched on the night lamp and glanced at the clock. Quarter to eleven. My God! Who the hell's calling me at quarter to eleven? he thought. "Hello."

"Colin Dawes?" said an unfamiliar male.

"Yes?"

"Colin, this is Elliot Chamberfield. I hope I'm not disturbing you."

"Disturbing me? Oh, no, no. I was just looking over tomorrow's script."

"Good, glad to hear somebody else works late." He paused. "Colin, there's something I'd like to talk to you about privately. We've never met, but I've heard awfully good things about you and think it's time we did, in any case."

"That's very nice to hear."

The VP of programing. Calling at ten-forty-five. What a strange, strange day. "Would you like me to come over tomorrow?"

"No," said the voice on the far end. "I think we should make it less formal. Why don't you meet me for lunch, let's say at Twenty-One around one-thirty. That should give you time to wrap up the taping and get out."

"Twenty-One, yes, fine, of course."

Elliot kept Vern Tuttle waiting in the rosewood-paneled reception area for a full twenty minutes before he was ready to see him. Rosalynann watched the thin man fidget with his tie, unbutton and button his jacket, and look apprehensively in the direction of the men's room. Poor weak bastard, she thought. None of them could match the power of her Elliot. A few minutes later, Chamberfield buzzed.

"Mr. Chamberfield will see you now, Mr. Tuttle."

"Thank you." He tugged his tie down, straightened his collar once again, and walked into the room. "'I appreciate your seeing me like this, Elliot. I wouldn't have called, but I felt I had to speak with you."

They shook hands across the desk. "What's up, Vern? Find a job yet?"

He shook his head. "That's why I'm here. I haven't had much luck."

Elliot stared blankly, which made Vern feel even more uncomfortable.

"I tried all the soaps, the three other networks, Fred Silverman says there's a possibility on a CBS show, but it's iffy and won't be determined until after the start of the new fall season. I can't wait that long. My contract-severance pay is up this week and . . . well, I hate to lay my problems on your doorstep, but I've got a lot of bills to meet. Heavy alimony checks for my first wife, and I bought a house for my parents in Tampa that I have to make payments on."

"In short," Elliot interrupted impatiently, "you're broke and blame me for losing your job."

"I didn't say that, Elliot."

"Well, you think it, don't you?"

"Elliot, I've been in this business long enough to know you don't blame other people for your troubles."

"So why are you here, Vern?"

"I . . . I just thought you might know of something I could plug into, so to speak. It's getting kind of tight. And I thought since we worked so closely on creating *Affair* and getting it started, you would have a pretty fair estimation of my abilities and, well, might be able to put in a good word for me somewhere." He paused and then stopped altogether. All his cards were on Elliot's side of the desk now; he realized how pitiful they must look.

Chamberfield leaned back in his chair. He felt no guilt about having removed Tuttle so suddenly, and didn't even remember that he never called personally to tell the guy he was through. But maybe the man could be useful. "You ever have any game-show experience, Vern?" he asked after a long silence.

Vern looked up. "Four years with Goodson and Todman."

"Doing what?"

"Well, I was just starting out in the business, so it wasn't anything big. Assistant to one of the producers on *I've Got A Secret* and later in the development office for new shows."

"Perfect!" The word burst forth, startling Vern. "I'll tell you what: we're trying to find a couple of game shows in case *Affair* folds. I don't have time to ride herd over all the presentations and it really isn't down the alley of

144

our program-development man. I'll try to think of something along those lines. No promises, huh? But I'll see what I can do."

"Elliot . . . Elliot, that would be beautiful. Really, I can't thank you—"

The VP stood brusquely. "I've got a luncheon appointment."

"Certainly, I understand. Thanks very much for your time."

"By the way. What's this Colin Dawes like?"

"Colin?" Vern was suddenly curious. "Oh, a funny guy, really."

"Funny?"

"Oh, you know. A real card. Lots of wit. I enjoyed working with him."

"Smart?"

"Quite bright. I found him when he was still stage-managing Broadway shows. Met him through friends. He's very organized. Good at details."

"Ambitious?"

"Aren't we all?" Vern laughed, then cleared his throat. "Yes, I think so."

Colin was waiting at Elliot's table in the back when the VP arrived. He stood to greet him. Elliot studied him hard. Jesus, he thought, he sure looks like a fuckin' fruit. "Colin, I'm Elliot Chamberfield."

They shook hands and sat down. Elliot ordered a Jack Daniels and Colin the same. Colin pretended to study the array of fantastic doodads hanging from the low, oak beams of the former speakeasy room. It helped to take up the slack of Elliot's silence before the drinks arrived. Small children's toys, ships, planes, and mockups of products of clients who frequented the bar.

The room was crowded and the waiters scurried around like crabs.

Chamberfield downed his drink quickly, ordered another, and smiled in what he hoped was his most engaging manner. "I suppose you're wondering why I called you. I had a meeting with Vern Tuttle, and he told me so much about you I was curious to meet you."

"Vern? I haven't seen him since . . . he left the show. How is he?"

145

"Fine. He may be soon back to work for RBI."

"Oh, that's good. I'm fond of Vern. He got me started in television."

"You like television?"

"Fantastic. It's like opening night on Broadway every day."

"You like all that tension, do you?"

Colin laughed lightly. "I thrive on it."

"Ever thought you might want to go on and produce a soap of your own?"

Colin stared at him in mock disbelief. "Are you kidding? Of course I have. I'd love it."

Jesus H. Christ, Chamberfield mused, he's queerer than a three-dollar bill. How can Searing work with these guys all day long?

They ordered their meals, a steak tartar for Elliot— "My girlfriend convinced me I should lose some weight" —and veal in white wine sauce for Colin. They chatted about *Affair,* the people on it, the way it was going.

"What do you think of Searing?"

"Fantastic producer."

"You think so?"

"Absolutely first-rate. Look at the whole Justin Teague thing. Who would have thought it would have paid off so well?"

Chamberfield cringed. He didn't need to hear that from this creep. He suddenly wondered if maybe the guy knew something about the tug of war he and Phillip were engaged in, but he crossed it off as impossible. No one else knew. "Listen, Colin. I think you can be helpful to me, to Phillip, to the show . . . to all of us. Vern told me you're possibly the only person on the show I could trust."

"That's very flattering."

"I want you to do a little spying."

"Spying?"

Chamberfield smiled. "All for the good of the show. You see, Phillip is a very proud and stubborn man. He is undoubtedly the best producer in the business. That's why I agreed to his dropping down to do the job. But sometimes even the best can be too proud for their own good. He has an enormous task to accomplish and he can't be allowed to fail at it."

"You think he will?"

"I want to help make sure it's easy for him not to."

"What can I do? I do everything he gives me, but Phillip likes to handle so many things himself I find I have to hunt for work sometimes."

"That's the problem. What you can do is continue just what you're doing now, but at the same time kind of let me know personally, from time to time, exactly what is happening over there. If there is a crisis of some kind, anything you think is important enough for Phillip to turn his attention to, I want to know about it. You see, he won't bother me with things like that. He'll do just as you say—go off and handle them himself. I'll give him the backing of the entire forty-fourth floor, but I have to know what's needed. Do you follow me?"

"I think so."

"You haven't been in television long. You're used to the theater, where the director is king and the producer God. Well, it's different here. Here we work more as a team—a very large team, certainly, and because of that, sometimes, we have to do strange things. You see, there might be times where I could lend a hand . . . put pressure on a union, clear away some of the bureaucratic underbrush of the web, help out with a stubborn affiliate who wants to cancel the show and put on a local show instead. That sort of thing. But I can't help unless I know about the problems. Do you follow?"

"That's really very generous. I'm sure Phillip will appreciate knowing that."

"Oh, but you see Phillip can't know—that's the one thing that would make him very uncomfortable."

"You want me to keep it a secret."

"I think it would be much better that way, don't you?"

"Oh, yes . . . yes, I think you're quite right."

"Good. I can count on you then?"

"Absolutely. I'm very flattered you even thought of me." And after the lesson he got from Phillip the day before on keeping things to himself, he wasn't about to break this confidence.

"Feel free to call me at the office anytime. In fact"— he jotted numbers down on a business card—"here's my private number. Use that, and you won't have to go through the switchboard. My home phone is here too."

"Right, right. Fine."

They stood up and shook hands. "I've got my eye on you, Colin. RBI needs people like you."

Colin floated back to the studio on a Republic Broadcasting cloud.

Immediately after lunch Elliot shot back to the office and had Rosalynann set up an appointment with Russell Keel, Jr., the president of the network. He was received into the spacious office with its immaculate teakwood desk thirty minutes later.

When Elliot looked at Keel, he pulled his jacket tighter around his middle, and berated himself inwardly for not having resisted the chocolate mousse with the fresh cream.

At fifty-nine, his boss was a lean, trim one hundred and sixty pounds, held in check by triweekly workouts at the Athletic Club. The little hair he had left around the ears and in the back of his head was neatly clipped and his nails were professionally manicured.

On the wall hung three ornately framed, antique paintings of early sailing ships in turbulent seas that Elliot found boring. Instead, he eyed the silver framed photos of Russell's family on the low counter behind the desk chair. One in particular Elliot liked rather well. It showed the whole Keel family—Russell, Georgette, three boys and two girls ranging in age from nine to twenty-three. They were standing on the deck of a modern sailing craft and looked like an ad for Crest toothpaste.

Russell leaned back in his chair. "So you think this Tuttle is the man to take over game development?"

"I do. He's had the experience. He's a hard worker and he's got good commercial sense."

"And *Affair* is going to fold now? I shouldn't think so."

"No, maybe not now. We'll have to see."

"That Teague ploy paid off, didn't it?"

"I was sure it would."

Keel shook his head in dubious astonishment. "Smart move on Searing's part. If he continues that way we won't need a replacement show at all."

Chamberfield shifted his weight and tugged at his jacket. "He's doing all right, yeah. But I feel we should always be prepared for the worst."

Keel stood up and walked around the desk, so he could

show the young executive out of the office. "A strong backup never hurt anybody; I'm a believer in insurance myself. If you want this Tuttle, let's hire him back."

"Thank you, Russ. I hoped you'd agree." Elliot left the office feeling better. He was going to get Searing one way or the other.

11.

Phillip watched the golden brown liquid rise in the glass. He swiveled it gently to mix it with the ice cubes, then moved over and sat down on the brown-suede couch. Nice couch, he thought. Comfortable. Interesting how one becomes accustomed to certain seats in one's own office and rarely uses the others. A whole different point of view than from behind the desk. Positions. It was curiously relaxing to be in a less dominant position in one's own office, as though all the responsibility were abruptly removed.

The monitor was dark; the taping for the day and the afternoon preliminary rehearsal for Monday's show were over; almost everyone had gone for the weekend. He sipped his Scotch. The late-afternoon sun threw a shaft of orange light on the carpet and tiny particles of dust played inside it like weightless nymphs. It was a time to be on a tropical island or in a mystical summer forest of Sweden. A soft knock sounded on the door.

"Come in."

Vanessa entered quietly. Her face was flushed, her dread

of the meeting printed in the tightness of the skin. "You wanted to see me?"

"Yes," he said gently. "Would you like something cold to drink?"

"No."

A long silence. Phillip pulled himself up and crossed to the chair next to the one she had chosen to sit on. He rolled the glass between his hands and studied it with undue attention. "I think you know what I want to talk to you about," he said quietly.

No response.

"Vanessa . . . Monday was a disaster. I've never seen a performer crumble like that. Tuesday was a little better. I went down to try to speak with you, but you obviously didn't want to speak with me. I figured it was personal and whatever it was you would clear up yourself. You had two days off in which to do it. But today wasn't much of an improvement, was it?"

There was still no word. She stared at him with a combination of so much unhappiness and fury that he was thrown.

"What is it, Vanessa? Is it something you can talk about?"

Her head shook with a very small violent movement, and her eyes widened like a cat's, a gorgeous animal, cornered and unpredictable.

Phillip watched her carefully. He was wary, but intrigued. There was something fascinating about her misery. His voice remained gentle, soft, coaxing. "Talk with me, Vanessa. What is it? Is it something to do with Joey?"

She stared.

"With me?"

She tightened even more. A pressure began to build inside her head.

"It does have to do with me, doesn't it?"

It was as though every muscle in her body strained to the tearing point. She shivered and caught a huge breath. She spoke slowly, deliberately, fighting to maintain control. "I'm sorry for my performances. I am . . . I'm trying my best to get over this. It's just taking longer than I thought."

There was a long pause, before Phillip asked, "Get over what? What is it you have to get over? It's important for us to communicate. You're hurting yourself as an

151

actress and you're hurting the show. I—we—can't afford that. Not now."

"Okay." She brushed away a tear that had formed in the corner of her eye. "I'll tell you what it is, Mr. Searing. I'll tell you what's bugging me. All of a sudden I'm a star. Isn't that right? All of a sudden the two-day-a-week player, Valerie, is turned into a regular five-day-a-week star of *Affair Of The Heart*. I was . . . deeply hurt by your sudden decision to make Valerie the leading character. That's all. It's as simple as that."

Phillip was astonished. "Hurt? Hurt? You were hurt that we made you the star of the show?"

"It's not clear to you?"

"No."

"It's not really clear to you?" She was furious.

"I haven't a clue as to what you're talking about. Anybody else would be ecstatic to have a part upped like yours was and here you're going to pieces. I don't understand that at all."

"Well, let me explain it to you!" she screamed. "I'm not used to getting my breaks by sleeping with producers. I've never done it and I never will. I know that's the way it's generally done, but not with me. How the hell do you think I felt when I realized I'd gotten that break because I'd slept with you? I'm not a whore, do you hear? I'm a married woman and I love my husband very much and what happened at your apartment last week has nothing to do with anything, except that I was weak and lonely and depressed and you were warm to me and suddenly. . . ." She shrugged her shoulders, and turned away sobbing, searching for a place to come to rest.

Phillip was speechless.

"Nothing, do you hear, nothing . . . I've never gotten a part like that before. I've had many chances. Every pig producer I've ever auditioned for on Broadway wanted to get me—those who didn't prefer boys—and I've missed a lot of parts because I wouldn't. How do you think I feel now?" she yelled at the top of her voice. "You've made me a whore and I didn't even know enough to be able to choose!"

"Vanessa! Vanessa, stop it." He stood up and tried to put his arm around the girl to calm her, but she shoved him off, and shrank back like a wounded animal. "Vanessa, I want you to listen to me."

"I'm not listening to anything." She swung around him, ran over to the chair, and grabbed her handbag. "I'm leaving. I'm getting out of here and if you don't like it, you can fire me. The hell with you!"

Phillip caught her by the upper arm, turned her around forcefully, and smacked her across the face hard. Then he pulled her over to the couch and pushed her down onto it. She stared at him wide-eyed and held her hand to her reddened cheek.

"Now I want you to listen to me," he said in a controlled, modulated voice. "I want you to hear this and I want you to understand it. The fact that we slept together last Friday night has nothing—not one blessed thing—to do with the fact that the part of Valerie was expanded. Not one solitary thing, do you hear me? Of all the stupid, idiotic notions! Do you think for one moment that I would put this whole show, forty-five jobs, my career, on the line just because I'd made it with one of the actresses and wanted to give her a present? What kind of a simpleton do you take me for? Your part was broadened because you're the best and most appealing actress on this show—because you're a goddamn good performer and up till this week you've been a total professional. Now I'm beginning to wonder. Where's your sense of logic? Where's your head, Vanessa?"

Phillip glared at the teary-eyed girl for a moment and then went over to the bar. He poured out two large glasses of whiskey, downed one, and brought the other over to her. "Here, drink this."

"No, I don't. . . ."

"Drink it!" He commanded.

She did and he took the glass back. He extracted a handkerchief from his pocket and wiped her eyes. "The decision to up your part was made the first week I came into this job. It was made by Maude and myself with the concurrence of Pat. The fact that you learned about it when you did was sheer coincidence." He paused, took her chin between his fingers, and turned her to face him directly. "But I'll tell you something else, Vanessa. Despite how I feel for you personally, and I do . . . you must believe that . . . if your performances don't return to their

153

normal level of excellence, I won't have any choice but to fire you. There's too much at stake to tolerate any more emotionalism on this show."

Then he rose, walked over to the desk, and dialed a telephone. He put the receiver on the speaker, so Vanessa could hear the other party. It rang and a woman's voice answered. "Hello."

"Maude?"

"Hi, Phillip, nice of you to call. I haven't heard your voice for at least an hour."

"Listen, dear, I've just got a second. Can you remember exactly when it was we decided to move Valerie up to female lead?"

"What do you want to know that for?"

"I'm, uh, doing some backlogging in a diary."

He heard some pages being rustled. "Wait a minute, I should have it here. Yeah, here it is, about a month, five weeks ago."

"Thanks, dear. That's all I wanted to hear."

"Bye." She rang off.

He hung up and lit a cigarette. Vanessa hunched against the back of the couch and looked ashamed. He crushed the pack in his palm and threw it at her. "You jerky girl!" It bounced off of her shoulder and landed on the carpet. She left it there.

The door closed quietly behind her and he was alone. He scooped up the crumpled pack and, with a deft hook shot, sunk it into the wastepaper basket.

He collected their empty glasses from the coffee table and walked them back to the open bar. Mechanically, he washed them in the small stainless steel sink.

Vanessa, he thought. What a strange and complex girl. . . . So soft and vulnerable; the slightest hostile word enough to register pain. Yet she had the ability to cope with the monumental problems of her husband.

What a constrast to Jacqueline. He recalled how graceful she was when they were first married . . . how open and hungry for life . . . how intelligent, how witty, how refreshing . . . how independent.

How independent they both were . . . she busied herself with the decorating and organizing of the new house, and he started his climb up the company. But then the house was done and Phillip had been promoted and more and more his time became occupied by affairs of the office. And more and more the cracks in that "independence" began to show. Phillip discovered that inside she was a soft, gutless, neurotic child, a child who had depended on her father for her strength, then switched that dependence onto Phillip.

Of course it was hardly all her fault. Phillip buried himself in his new profession with all the tenacity and concentration he'd shown at tennis, and had little time to spare for her. Escape weekends, carefully planned by the new bride, were canceled at the last moment as he brought home work that carried him far into the night. "You're married to your goddamn office, not to me!" she would complain. He would attempt to ease his schedule to accommodate her for a while, but then somehow after a few weeks they found themselves back at the beginning. And her complaints began anew. . . . They turned to nagging, nagging to bitching, and bitching finally to a search for escape. And since Phillip was rarely there, alcohol and pills became the new security.

Phillip wiped his hands on the bar towel and sank down into his desk chair. He tried for a while to concentrate on the budget breakdown for the previous week but the double image of Vanessa and Jacqueline kept drifting across the surface of his mind . . . she became so destructive. That's what destroyed it—she became so bitterly destructive.

12.

There was the soft ping of a bell, accompanied by the No Smoking and Fasten Your Seat Belt signs. The lights blinked on in the first-class section and sleepy heads moved groggily. Although it was 4:00 A.M., New York time, Phillip was wide awake. He shoved the two weeks' worth of scripts he had been working on into the slim attaché case and snapped the gold locks shut.

He looked out the window. Through the grayish mist he could see the Thames lazily curving through the small towns which were rapidly blending into one metropolis. He leaned back in his seat and rubbed his eyes. Four free days. What a godsend.

The plane banked steeply, dropped its airflaps and cut its speed. It steadied its course for the runway approach. Phillip sprung his seat to an upright position and re-folded his suit jacket. The stewardess came down the aisle. He buckled his belt before she could chastise him.

She was waiting just on the far side of the customs area and beaming from ear to ear. She was brown as a berry and her honey-gold hair was sun-streaked.

"You've never looked so gorgeous in your life."

"Phillip!"

He put down his bags and she ran into his arms. Her hair smelled of the freshness of summer sun and her body was a light clean sea. He stepped back to appraise her. "Katina," he said, "you're eighteen years old."

He lifted his bags and they swept off to the taxi area. She linked one tanned arm through his and took the attaché case in charge.

"Well," she said, "I must say you look a little haggard. A little nervous and tight around the eyes. But other than that, you're still the handsomest stud I've seen in two months."

"You trying to get a part in a television show, lady?"

She did a half skip and squeezed his arm. "God, it's good to see you, Phillip. You're never going to want to leave."

"I didn't know until an hour before I called you I'd be able to come. The show's going to be pre-empted by news coverage for a couple of days, so I'm free."

The cab took them to the Dorchester.

Phillip checked into the distinguished old hotel with its morning-suited clerks and was ushered into the suite Gloria had reserved. He and Katina locked their arms around each other in the living room and let the bellman hang the clothes and arrange the toilet articles on a neat, white towel in the bathroom. The sun had burnt the mist away and they stood looking out on a brilliant morning in Hyde Park.

"I've never been to London when it's sunny."

"Then you've never been to London at all."

He changed his clothes and they ran out into the park. They walked for hours, strolling by the Serpentine, passing the rows of canvas-backed sun chairs filled with tourists and Londoners lining the water's edge. They talked of nothing and themselves.

"And what else do you have to do here besides spend some time with me?"

"My secretary set up some auditions through the talent agencies for Monday. I've been looking for a particular type of actress. Want a job?"

"No, thank you, kind sir."

Later it was Kings Road in Chelsea, a walk through the

mod boutiques and the sidewalks full of the hip and
fashionably dressed young couples. Katina eyed the shop
windows enviously. "I know it's nothing more than the
residue from my bourgeois materialistic past, but when I
get around all this beautiful stuff I want to buy, buy, buy."

"What do you want?"

"Nothing."

"I'll buy it for you."

"No, thanks. I promised myself I'd live only on what I
saved. Good for the aesthetic soul. I don't want your
handouts, your charity, your woebegone castoffs."

"What the hell are you talking about?"

Funny, she thought, he seemed annoyed.

They strolled through Portobello Road and then taxied
back to her flat. It was a tiny one-room affair, with a
Pullman kitchen and a bath. There they made love, silently, gently exploring secrets they had known well before.
But there was something strange about Phillip. Something
distant and removed. She had seen him brood before, but
not with the severity of the moment.

When they were finished they lay still for a while,
munching crackers and drinking wine. Katina watched him
swill nearly a quarter of the bottle in one long series of
swallows. He lit a cigarette and drew it down into his
lungs.

"You really touch bottom with those things," she remarked.

He leaned back up against the flowery wallpaper and
stared out into space, chewing the inside of his cheek.
Katina observed his nervousness for a moment and then
said quietly, "Would you like to go?"

"Where?"

"Anywhere you like."

No response. He drew in another chestful of smoke and
took a swig from the bottle.

"Don't feel you have to stay with me . . . if you don't
want to. I know you're here only for a few days."

Phillip rose and walked to the window. He gazed out
for a second, then swiveled and went into the bathroom.
He turned on the sink tap. Water charged out. He stared
at it for a moment, then closed it off. He picked up an
extra hairpin and twisted it around his fingers. Then he
walked back· to the window. Katina pulled the sweaty

sheet up over her nudity and followed his movements with cautious interest.

"This place depresses the hell out of me," he muttered, doing his best to subdue the angry frustration that churned inside of him. His eyes skipped over the small, drably furnished flat. "I don't know how you can stand to live here. Look at this kitsch." He flicked on a standing lamp in the corner of the room. "Mousy brown brass, 1945 ornamental garbage. Christ! Look at that view. Back windows of a soot-covered, brick-walled, out-of-use shoe factory." He ran his fingers over the crack between the window and the sill. They came up charcoal.

Four or five minutes passed by. Eventually Katina broke the silence. "Can you talk about it?" she asked softly.

He dropped down onto the overstuffed sofa and propped his legs up on the coffee table. "I don't know what it is. I want to do something."

"What?"

"Something!" He slammed his fist into the side of the seat.

She wasn't sure whether it would be better to coax him into releasing the pent-up energy, help him fly with the conflict, or try to get his mind off of the subject. "The world is ours . . . or yours if you want to split alone."

That was one of the beautiful things about Katina. She never seemed to be offended by the independent desires of others.

"I've been building like this for weeks," he said. "I've been nervous as a cat and there's been something gnawing at the pit of my stomach."

"Since you've taken over the show?"

"I guess so. Or since the kinks started getting worked out of it." He was quiet for another moment and then he said, "You know, I did a funny thing about two weeks ago. The Seventy Market Nielsens were coming out with the first solid indication we'd have of the status of the show. I don't have to tell you how important they were . . . I was all geared up. Sent my secretary out for them. The whole cast was anxious, because there was serious talk that upstairs might kill the show if it didn't pick up radically. Well, the moment came and I decided I didn't want to see them. No, I didn't even decide that. I just left,

159

split, walked out. I wandered around Central Park for a couple of hours until I went home." He waited awhile and then added, "I've never put off ratings in my life, certainly not ratings as important as this batch."

"Were you so afraid they'd be bad?"

"Not even that, really. I'd played a surprise hand with a bit of a bluff and I expected to win . . . even though the forty-fourth floor nearly spun out of the building."

"Why?"

"It was a bizarre move and it was astronomically expensive."

"So you were scared?"

"Well, I'm not even sure if that's it, Katina. You know me. I've never been one to put off hearing bad news, either. I've always figured the faster you know it, the faster you can rectify it."

"So why didn't you want to look at them?"

"I don't know. I think because I was getting uptight. Win or lose, I've always maintained control and somehow I didn't feel I was in control. I couldn't shake it off. I still can't. Something's wrong and I don't know what it is."

"Is Elliot on your back?"

"No . . . well, yes. But no more than usual. He's been on my back ever since he first hired me for the network."

"It all shows. I've never seen you so fidgety."

He tapped another cigarette out of a package and lit it with a long wooden kitchen match. A piece of paper caught fire in the butt-filled ashtray. Phillip tamped it out before it cracked the glass.

"And you're probably working on your third pack of cigarettes since this morning."

"I want to *do* something."

She watched him drain the remainder of the wine. "There's a time to reap and a time to sow," she said solemnly. "A time to stay and a time to go."

"What's that supposed to mean?"

She closed her eyes and held them like that. Then she said, "It means . . . what it means."

The aroma of Mexican grass wafted vaguely through the huge Georgian house like ghostly vapors on an Allhallows eve. Close to two hundred people wandered about from room to room chatting spiritedly about Alan Bates on the West End, and the difficulties of getting a new picture financed independently of the majors, and the lack of privacy left in Ibiza and the advantages of making one's tax home in Ireland rather than in Her Majesty's own personal province.

The house was lit like a Mississippi riverboat and there was an agreeable roar of electronic music, laughter, point-making shouting, glass-clinking, and shrieking. A very drunk blonde-haired nymphet bumped by, carrying her shoes in her hand and telling the young man pursuing her to "leave me the fuck alone, Chester," in a sweet, pleasant, drifting tone of voice.

Katina found the woman who'd suggested they'd come —a jewelry-bedecked actress named Heather she had met in Spain. She had trouble recognizing Katina with her clothes on. "Stoned and nudists, we were. The entire month! Stoned and nudists, mister, what was your name?"

"Searing."

"Yes, and your lady friend here was the queen of the beehive. Staying in London, Mr. Searing?"

"No."

"Pity." And she jangled off. They watched her caftaned figure melt into the crowd.

"Is she the hostess?" asked Phillip when she had left overhearing distance.

"No, a friend of hers. The hostess is a beautiful woman named Mary. One of the most charming women you'd ever want to meet."

They maneuvered their way through some Asians and a man who looked as though he belonged to Parliament's upper house. All of them were having a heated argument about the immigration policies of the government. A stocky shaven-headed black man with a gold earring and a thick curled mustache moved into the circle and listened for an opening. He was wearing a tribal dashiki and carrying a gnarled stick.

"They look like they were rounded up by Central Casting," said Phillip. He took two drinks from a white-jacketed barman and handed one to Katina. He tapped himself out a cigarette and inadvertently pointed the pack at her.

"No, I'm off, remember?"

"Hey, that's right. I haven't seen you smoke all day."

"Crushed out the last one at Kennedy Airport and haven't taken a puff since then."

"Just like that?" He snapped his fingers.

"Just like that." She snapped hers too.

"I wish I could."

"You could." And she grinned a challenge.

"Ex-smokers are holier than reformed prostitutes."

"And they feel better, too."

Katina and Phillip allowed themselves to drift through the carnival of faces, stopping here and there to drag on an offered joint or chat with an acquaintance from Ibiza.

"Still restless?" she asked after half an hour or so.

He shrugged.

"You won't find what you're looking for here," she said, and stood up on her toes, kissing his cheek. "But why don't you wander off for a while by yourself and see if you can't rustle up some diversion? I just saw somebody I want to talk to alone."

"Alone?" he questioned in mock surprise.

"Yes, darling. You may be the love of my life, but you're not around enough to fill the day-to-day necessities. And I just saw a very interesting man I was once introduced to."

"Well, I'll be," he exclaimed. "Left at the bloody altar, I am, and here I've come all the way across the pond to see you."

"Me and your casting session at William Morris," she said, grinning.

"Good fishing." He winked and toasted her beauty.

"I'm not fishing, Phillip. I'm just scooping my pick out of a glass-sided tank."

"You're almost as conceited as I am."

She kissed him again and took off.

For some reason Phillip felt freer after she'd gone. He had thought she would be able to push the right button and release him from his tensions, but it hadn't worked. She was too much into her own thing and momentarily too secure with it. Maybe she knew him too well. That was possible. She was in the "profound and meaningful" stage of their relationship. He couldn't take that. Not right now. Not that she had ever gone into it in any way, but the subject had been lingered over before, and the inferences were clearly there.

He didn't want probing; he wanted action. He couldn't just whirl her around and delight her, amuse her, conquer her. They knew each other too well for that.

He fetched himself another drink and stood off to the side examining faces. How undifferent they were from those in New York or L.A. or Chicago or Vegas. How banal the ripples of conversation that found their ways into his present consciousness. Jobs and money and the "then I did" and the "then I said" and the "then I went" and the "then I bought." Some of the faces even seemed to have a distantly recognizable form, as if he'd seen them at another gallery somewhere else in time.

"Enjoying yourself?"

"Yes," he said.

"Lovely to have you."

"Thank you."

"Katina's spoken a great deal about you."

"Has she?"

"Often. I'm Peter Royal. This is my house."

"I didn't know. Thank you for having me. I'm Phillip Searing." They shook hands.

"You're in television, aren't you?"

"Yes."

"Quite different over there than over here, isn't it?"

"In what way?"

"Oh, you know. You're all . . . well, you know, you take it all so seriously over there. We have much more fun with it here, don't you think?"

"Possibly."

"Well, it doesn't matter anyway. Having a good time?"

"Yes."

"Good. Have another drink. Bar's over there. Anything you like."

"Thank you."

He patted Phillip on the arm and dashed away, probably to welcome another new face. Cheerful man. What a delight. So rare to find truly cheerful people any more—people who aren't constantly on the want for something or other.

Through the rear bay window Phillip caught a glimpse of Katina talking to a suave young Englishman with a handlebar mustache. He felt a twinge of jealousy, but quickly suppressed it. What right did he have, after all, to be jealous? What was he offering her these days? Not even pleasant company on this trip. He was behaving like a total bore. She had every right to go off in search of new vistas. Still, it made him angry. Male chauvinism, he thought, and walked away from the window.

"Pretty, your friend. Are you having a spat?"

The question attacked him as soon as he turned. It came out of the mouth of one of the most sensuously voluptuous females it had ever been his pleasure to view. She was tall, nearly six feet, though he couldn't tell whether she was wearing platforms or not. Her hair was a rich, reddish auburn that flowed in gypsy masses of ringlets to her shoulders. She had a glistening seductive mouth and sea-green eyes that regarded him with a twinkling air of mischievous amusement. "That's the way they say it here, you know," she said. "One never argues or fights or complains—one spats." She cocked her head to the side and let her tongue flick up to her upper lip. Phillip could see that her large breasts were fighting fiercely against the flimsy green poorboy sweater. The clear outline of two small nipples told him she wasn't wearing anything underneath. There was no panty outline under the tight-hipped floppy-bottomed 1940s pants, and that told him that she wasn't wearing anything under there, either. He caught the smell of a light musk oil on her body.

"No, we're not having a spat."

For some reason the girl found that very funny. She broke into high musical laughter, which forced a laugh out of Phillip as well.

And then she walked away.

Phillip watched the teardrop hips sway out of reach without making a move to stop her. He downed the dregs of his vodka collins and accepted a toothpicked hors d'oeuvre from a passing waiter. Then he decided to follow. She was out of sight, but he moved off in the same direction. It was an unhurried pursuit, but compelling. For Phillip had begun to experience the kind of raw, sexual pull he hadn't felt in a very long time. He headed for the grand staircase with the ornately carved balustrade.

It took about ten minutes, but he found her in another room at the rear of the long upstairs corridor. It was a heavy room with thick Oriental rugs and low-tuned lamps. She was standing in front of a wall of bookshelves filled to capacity, and she was with two long-haired young men, bizarrely chic. They were sniffing something white from a miniature silver spoon that the redhead had on a chain around her neck. They turned away when Phillip stopped outside the open door. They turned away, but not before all three had looked him over very carefully.

So we're going to play hide and seek, are we, my little coke sniffer? All right, he thought to himself, I found you. Now, you find me.

He walked slowly down the corridor. There was a darkened door on his left that looked like it might contain a sink and toilet. He opened it. It did. It had a high, old porcelain sink with gold-plated spigots and antique mirrors set opposite one another. It also contained the drunken blonde nymphet and her pursuer. She was leaning back against the sink with one leg perched on the side of the immense claw-footed tub. The skirt of her dress was draped around her haunches and she dreamily gazed at herself in the mirrors, while "leave me the fuck alone, Chester" was humping her steady as a piston.

Phillip excused himself and closed the door. He backtracked to the heavy room, wondering if they'd even noticed the intrusion. Redhead and sniffers were gone.

He decided to let the redhead go her way. He would return to Katina. But Katina was not to be found. He searched the house, out into the garden, even out front onto Abbey Road, but he couldn't find her. He walked around the side to check the garden once again, and a tall figure came out from behind a tree. It was the redhead. She must have been following him.

"Jacques is mad for you."

"What?"

"My friend Jacques is passionate about you. He's pining away over some American naval officer he just spent two weeks in torrid Tokyo with, but he said he'd make allowances *tout de suite* for a fling with you. His own true love had to go back to his aircraft carrier." She bit her lip and waited for his reply.

He looked at her for a long instant. "No, thank you," he muttered slowly. "Jacques is not my cup of tea."

"How do you know? You haven't met him."

"Is your name Jacques?"

She broke into a wide grin. "No," she purred.

165

"Then he's not my cup of tea."

She turned and walked over to a wooden lover's swing that hung from the bough of a large, old chestnut tree. Phillip followed.

"Are you an Americanized English girl or an Anglicized American? Your accent's about fifty-fifty."

She didn't answer. Instead she looked him over with a peculiar kind of scrutiny. It was as though she were going to place a bet on a race in which she knew neither the jockeys nor the horses. "Are you a gambler?" she asked.

"Depends on the game." The swing moved in an ever-lilting curve.

"You look to me like a very forward-moving young man," she said after a while. "I'll just bet you've never done anything that didn't have a purpose to it in all your days . . . I have a father like that. Cold, calculating, never made a move unless it's in the scheme of things, and he's very successful. He's not just climbing like you are."

"What tells you that I'm climbing?"

"It's written all over you . . . business, sales reports, money, worry, fret, dynamism! Are you a stockbroker?"

"Television producer!"

"You're not! A big TV mogul producer?" She burst out laughing.

"You find that funny?"

"I find everything funny and a little pathetic. So you're a television producer. Well, well, well. That's very interesting."

"And you? What are you?"

"What am I?" She laughed again. "How should I know what I am? And if I'd gone to the trouble of finding out who I was, why should I make it easy for you to know?"

"Do you always talk in riddles?"

"Only when I'm trying to be clear." She grinned again and he did too.

"Will you gamble with me the next few days?" she challenged.

"How many is a few?"

"Four."

"One."

"Okay, one. That's not much, though. Will you gamble the next twenty-four hours?"

"Who's calling the shots?"

"Me."

"Why should I trust you?"

"It'll be worth it."

"Maybe."

"Maybe?"

"Can I hedge my bet?"

"No."

"Okay."

The taxi let them out in Kensington. He followed her up the darkened steps and into the building. An old, gated, see-through elevator lifted them to the fourth floor. There was stained glass in the front of the apartment door. She unlocked it.

There was no light in the apartment, except for that beamed in from the full-mooned sky. Phillip could make out a roundish entrance hall with spokes of corridors leading off in several directions. Moneyed young lady, he thought.

She put her bag down next to two small suitcases by the entrance and walked through one of the doors. Phillip waited. Three minutes, four, five. There was no sound. Somewhere in the apartment a loud clock chimed the hour of one. Phillip went to the door. He opened it and moved through. He passed a powder room on the left, a large bedroom on the right, and then a living room. She stood in front of the living-room window, looking up at the moon. Phillip walked over to her.

She turned as he approached and smiled slightly. He was about to say something when suddenly she threw her hand back and slapped him hard, full across the face. He reeled back.

She laughed at his expression and raised her hand for another blow. He saw this one coming. He caught it and twisted it behind her back, pulling her close and squashing her breasts against his chest. With his free hand he forced her head up and kissed her hard on the mouth. Her teeth tried to clamp onto his lower lip, but he grabbed her hair and yanked it backward.

She was breathing hard through her nostrils. Her hand came up slowly and unbuttoned Phillip's shirt. It slid in and felt for his chest and stomach. The tips of her fingers circled until she formed a claw of fingernails and ripped it down across his front, shredding the skin and leaving a trail of blood. She wrenched free and raced out of the room. Phillip tore after her, catching her as she was about to hide in a walk-in closet. She drew back from him, stopping cautiously. Excitement was pasted over her face. Phillip peeled off his shirt.

The two top buttons of her sweater were undone. Phillip reached out and grabbed them. In one motion he tore the sweater open and left the shreds hanging from her naked shoulders. Her breasts were extraordinarily beautiful. He stepped forward, grabbed her by the waist, and squeezed her to his body, letting the blood of his chest stain the rich, full mounds.

She softened, kissed his neck, his chin, his mouth, and slowly bent down. She kissed the nipples and ran her tongue over the welts that had risen from the scratch. She took him by the hand and led him to a couch in the next room. "Do you want some soapers?" she asked softly, running her lips over his belly.

"What are soapers?"

"I don't know, really. Quaaludes, I think. They give you a beautiful high."

"Can't get much higher than I am."

"Yes, you can." And she sank her teeth into his knee until the pain through his pants was too much to bear.

"Hey!"

"Did that hurt?" She took his hand and rubbed it over her breasts. Then she bit him again. He placed one hand around her neck and squeezed. He pried her off, but then she seized his hand. The more she bit the more he squeezed until her eyes flashed wildly. He yanked the hand out of her mouth. A half circle of blood began forming.

"Oh, his'm's hurt," she pouted. She put her mouth over the abrasion and sucked the blood.

The mixture of pain and pleasure produced a strangely erotic sensation. He grabbed her by the mass of hair and forced her head up again. He held it tightly as they kissed.

The girl released herself and stood up before him. She unhooked her own pants and let them fall to the floor. She kicked them away. She was totally naked, except for the silver chain around her neck and her shoes.

Phillip stood up. She smiled at him. He slapped her across the face. She laughed. He grabbed her arm, but she swung free. Her heavy breasts rose and fell with tremulous excitement. She backed off from him slowly. They grinned at each other.

"So you're a television producer!" She stood still and then slowly backed across the room. "You remind me of a boy I once knew. He was a janitor at Wellesley. I got kicked out of there for balling him in a rowboat on the lake." She kicked off one of her shoes, aiming it directly at his groin. He jumped aside and it hit a lamp, which crashed it to the floor in front of him. He tried to corner her, but she eluded him. She ran into the bedroom, her breasts jiggling weightily in front of her. He followed.

The room appeared empty. He took a step forward and then with an instinct for survival threw up his hand just in time to catch the full force of the door being slammed in his face. He threw it back open with all his might. He heard it hit her.

There was a stunned silence. He went in, and closed the door, looking into the corner. She was leaning against the wall, her head and buttocks pushed back. Her face was white and her breasts heaved.

For a moment, he thought she was hurt, but as he went to her, she suddenly shrieked and leapt upon him, wrapping her legs around his waist. He whirled, aiming her for the bed, and threw himself on top of her with all his weight. She grabbed his hair and pulled his head down to her, bucking her hips up into the air like a bronco. But this time she was going for the payoff. She sought his mouth and her tongue snaked inside, exploring, reaching, prodding, searching. Her hands clawed his belt open and crabbed about for the zipper. She pushed his pants down as far as she could with her hands and let one bare foot kick them off the rest of the way.

Her hips undulated wildly. Her thighs were sopping wet. He plunged into her.

She gasped, throwing her head back against the pillow, and twisted her hips as if to throw him off. But he held on, plunging in again and again. Arching her back and thrusting her pelvis high into the air, she made one last desperate effort to dislodge him. But he was too deep inside. She heaved a long, loud, sexual groan, and gave up.

169

He awoke to the face of a blinding sun aiming directly at his eyes. It was high into the sky. At least noon. He must have been exhausted.

And he was alone, as he discovered after pulling on his pants and making a full tour of the place.

The redhead wasn't just not there; she was gone. Really gone. At first he thought she might be out at the grocery store or something like that, but when an hour had passed and he had taken a shower, and shaved with a razor he found, he poked around for clues. There was no note—no leavings of a breakfast—only the dregs of a cup of coffee and a crushed paper envelope for an El Al plane ticket: a flight to Rome, leaving at ten-forty-five that morning.

Then he remembered the two small suitcases he'd seen in the entrance hall when they'd arrived the night before. He found his way back through the maze of corridors. The suitcases were gone, too.

"You don't know who she is? I thought you did. That's Gaye Vulkner, sweetheart. That's your board chairman's little stepdaughter."

"Jesus! Why didn't you let me know?"

"I had my own interests to attend to last night." Katina looked in at him from her bathroom mirror. "She's a weird child, Phillip. And, from what I hear, hates her old man with a passion."

"Why's she off to Rome?"

"She's got the lead in a movie being produced there. That's what I hear from the grapevine, anyway."

13.

The office door opened and Gloria distributed the morning containers of coffee.

Phillip was on the phone. "You mean to tell me you have not one girl lined up for me today? What the hell have you been doing the past two days?" He switched the hand holding the receiver and took a sip of his coffee. "Friday! I need her here by Friday!"

Maude O'Keefe looked up from her papers and signaled for his attention. "I think we can stretch to Tuesday of next week, if we have to."

He ignored her. "No, Claire, no! I didn't find anybody in London. If I had, would I be so uptight now? I want to see at least five girls in here by tonight. Do you understand! Five girls here tonight, Claire. And not girls you're just trying to make it with in bed!" He hung up.

His gaze fixed momentarily on the small race-horse statuette that was holding some papers on his desk, then he turned his attention to the others. "So?"

"So," Maude repeated. "What do you think?"

"This week's not bad, but I don't like the material for next week at all. Valerie's supposed to see her aunt about getting some money for the operation, right? Okay, is it going to be cut and dried? Just like that? I think you're wasting the opportunity for some tension. Build up the aunt a little more. Stretch out the dialogue. Give us a reason why she might not want to give the money. You could stretch the audience for a week if you handle it right."

"I didn't think you'd want to keep the tension up on this part that long."

"I'd keep the tension going for a bloody year, if I could. What do you think keeps them the hell involved? Come on, Maude. You've been in this business too long for that."

"Okay, you're right," she said wearily. "I guess I'm just getting tired. It's been a long two months."

"We just started." He looked to the other side of the room. Pat and Colin were lounging on the couch. "What the hell is this? The fact we pulled in some ratings a couple of weeks ago doesn't mean a damn thing. We lost fifty percent of them in the next report. This show's not home yet. We've got a hard row to hoe before we're going to get another thirteen weeks out of management." An edge of fierceness crept into his tone. "I'm warning you, all of you; it's nobody's turn to rest now. You either break ass or you're out. And Pat, you can relay that message to the cast."

He scanned their faces to see if he was going to get any feedback. "Okay, is that it? Can we get on with the rest of our work?"

Maude peeled herself out of the chair. "So you want me to make the aunt a possible bad guy?"

"Yes, but don't lock her into any background stories we won't be able to get her out of. Daphne's the villainess, ultimately. That's if we find one. You'll have to put off the first appearance of the vamp."

"I'll try," she said with resignation.

"Colin, what are you doing this minute?"

"I was, uh . . . I was going to get the cast in place for rehearsal."

"Forget it. They know what time it is; if they don't, they don't have to show up at all. Go down and see Jerry Dennis in the set shop. Remind him we're running on the wire on the parlor set and the doctor's office. Monday's the deadline and that's cold."

172

He spent the remainder of the morning going through stack after stack of eight-by-ten photographs of actresses he had seen and rejected. "Nobody!"

Later he found a few minutes to go down to the set shop himself and look over the materials Jerry had collected. He made the shop foreman reiterate his promise to produce the scenery on time.

He watched the dress rehearsal in the control room and jolted everyone's nerves a little more.

Pat caught him alone after the run-through. "Phillip, what's happening? Why are you coming down so hard on everybody, old man?"

"Because you've all lost your adrenalin. I thought the long weekend would give you a rest and get you charging in here, but everybody acts like it's an effort to start working again. You're riding on laurels that haven't been thrown yet. I've seen too many shows fall apart once it looks like they were a hit. This show is still in trouble, Pat."

"Everybody's working the same as usual."

"Right, the same as you usually worked when Tuttle produced. Before you were afraid of losing your jobs. I'll fire somebody, Pat, just to set an example if I have to."

"You're telling me you can't remember a one-line sentence change?" Phillip glared at the actor.

"Mr. Searing," Bill Peters pleaded. "We've gone through four rehearsals today. I was set. We're ready to go into the taping. I can't just do a turn around like that!"

"You can't remember one line at the end of the show, when you've had nothing to do for five minutes before it?"

"Well. . . ."

"Here!" Phillip took a scrap of paper from the production assistant standing by. "Give me a pen." He wrote the line on the paper. Then he tore off the small section he'd written on. "Luke, give me some double face."

The set decorator handed him a piece of tape, sticky on both sides. Phillip adhered the sentence to the back of the cabinet the actor was standing behind. "There, can you read that?"

"Yes," Bill said sullenly.

"Okay, trauma's over. Next time don't waste my time

making me think for you." He stormed away, followed by the assistant.

Colin whispered to Vanessa in another area of the set: "And he ripped into me for disturbing an actor before a taping!"

Phillip saw another batch of girls that afternoon. Six were recalls and the other five were new faces. But something disturbed him about each of them. One was too eager, another had eyes set too far apart, a nose too aquiline, one was not sophisticated enough, another too coldly calculating. Each of them swore she could look any way he could possibly desire. They held their hair up, down, swooped over an eye. They held different colors to their skins and all wanted to read a few more lines for him. Hopeless.

In the middle of the session, he left Claire in the room to take a call from Barry Friedman.

"I guess you heard about Elliot's heart attack."

"What!" Phillip's explosion reverberated around the room.

"Yeah," Barry said calmly. "Last night, but it's okay—nothing to worry about."

"Come on, you're not serious. He's thirty-nine years old!"

"Well, there's really nothing to worry about. I'll tell you what happened. Elliot was one of the guests of honor at a national broadcaster's banquet at the Waldorf last night—he and the other three networks' programing heads. A big dinner, many speeches and drinks later, he had a pain in his chest. That scared the hell out of him. So he went down to the hotel's doctor and had an electrocardiagram. He never showed up again. So you know the people in this business. Incredible imaginations. All of a sudden everybody was saying that Elliot Chamberfield had a massive heart attack."

"And did he?"

"No, he probably just got bored with all the stuffy speeches and went home. Rosalynann told me the EKG was normal, but get this. The hotel's doctor did say there were a few flutters and that he should be careful. He advised him to go see his own doctor. I've got a feeling Elliot made up the chest pain to get away from the banquet. He hates that kind of atmosphere. You can say what you

174

want about him but he's not a phony and he doesn't like to hang around in a room full of people all trying to impress the people sitting next to them. Anyhow, what a way to find out you've got a heart condition!"

"That's a funny story."

"Yeah, I've gotten three calls about it from Hollywood in the last twenty minutes. Anyway, look, I called to see if you had time for us to get together. I've got something I'd like to talk with you about. It concerns the job."

"You sound depressed."

"Well, a little. I knew I wouldn't have the kind of freedom you had in it, but I didn't think Elliot would make me ask for permission to go to the potty."

"Not going very well, is it?"

"I'm the new director in charge of rubber stamping."

"Why don't you talk to him about it? You're his friend, the only one he's got."

"That's just it. He won't talk."

It was partly by virtue of his friendship with Chamberfield that Barry had the job. Phillip knew that. And he knew Elliot would never lift his thumb off him.

"I know it's strange to ask you to help me with a job that. . . ."

"Don't be silly," said Phillip. "When do you want to get together?"

* * *

Vanessa pushed away the shower curtain and stepped onto the small rug in front of the bathtub. She yanked the bathing cap off and her long, black hair tumbled over her shoulders. She shifted her position so she could see herself in the bathroom mirror, cracked undecoratively across the bottom. She rubbed the towel over her skin and tried to rationalize away the fear that grew inside.

She slipped on the short terry-cloth robe she had had since college days and padded quietly into the bedroom. Joey was sprawled on his back, snoring off the morning hours for those he had missed last night. His clothes lay in small lumps on the floor, in little blobs on the rug he had brought home once when he was doing a two-month stint as a moving man. He'd gotten a large piece of living-room carpet for ten dollars from a girl he was sure was a

175

high-class hooker who was getting married and moving from the West Side to the East.

She had no idea what time he'd gotten home. She'd gone to bed at eleven, and lain awake for an hour or so, but he still hadn't shown. Another evening of no dinner together, no note, nothing.

She opened the shade to let some air relieve the thickness of their night in a small, closeted room. The light attacked his eyes. "Jesus Christ! Ness! What the hell are you doing?" He turned over on his stomach and flopped a pillow on top of his head.

She finished dressing, taking less care than usual to keep from making noise. Let him wake up, so what? She was getting tired of working all day and coming home to find him either gone or having done absolutely nothing to help out. It was too much.

She slipped on her shoes, walked into the living room, and surveyed the scene: cigarette butts in every ashtray, two wine bottles with enough residue left for a morning's barroom stench. Stale, dead, tobacco awfulness. Leave it, she thought resentfully. He can clean it up himself.

The painting was still unfinished. The words *Joey's House* sloshed in day-glo green paint on the living-room wall. It had been amusing four months ago when he'd sloshed them there because the wall needed painting and she thought it was his way of starting the job. But now, after staring at the eyesore every day, she didn't find it so funny.

She took a blouse out of the living-room dresser and went into the kitchen, slipping it on. The calendar next to the refrigerator stopped her. It was the twentieth . . . already the twentieth.

She boiled some water and made coffee as she ran over her lines for the day, but concentration was hard to come by. She read the cues over and over, but nothing stayed in her head.

Why doesn't he do something? Sits home all day. Maddening! Doesn't make the bed, doesn't clean the room, doesn't even wash the dishes.

The twentieth. Already the twentieth. Ten days late and she was regular. Lord, why did it have to happen now? Two times in eighteen months Joey's potency returned to him. Two times before he lost it again and both times had to fall in that week she'd slept with Phillip. At least Joey would think the baby was his and would be spared the anguish.

But how would she know? How could she be sure whose it was? And even if she were sure it was Joey's, would she want it?

A couple of years ago it would have been wonderful to have Joey's baby. But now? Things were changing. Things were different now. The lumpy mattress and paper-lantern honeymoon had ended. She wanted better things. And why shouldn't she have them? She was earning money, lots of it. It was all going to the psychiatrist—and for what? Well . . . that wasn't fair. He's off drugs and that was the main thing. The rest will come. He'll start doing things again, start working, playing music, begin again to communicate. He needs a little more time, just a little more. But a child? To have a child now with him? Christ . . . and suppose it isn't his. Suppose it comes out with jet-black hair and iron-gray eyes?

She put down the script and stared through the window gates to the playground across the street. A park attendant had just turned on the children's sprinkler; a circle of water formed around it.

The door to the small spectators' booth, high on the rear wall of the court, opened hesitantly and a head of tightly curled, sandy hair stuck itself in. He entered, walked to the edge of the balcony, and peered down at the players in the court.

Phillip slammed the little black ball with enormous force into the marred front wall. His opponent, a shorter man with a basketball belly, whipped it back. Phillip dashed to the forecourt in time to catch the rebound with a strong backhand that bounced just above the foul line and shot high into the air. Paunchy peddled backward on his thick legs. He took a swipe with the leathered hand, but missed and fell onto the hardwood floor.

"Holy hell, are you hot today!" He pulled himself up, rubbing his elbow and walked to the corner. Phillip retrieved the ball and tossed it to him. He stood, grinning and panting in the center of the room. "Are you pissed off at your boss or something?"

Phillip peeled the soaked sweatband from his head and tossed it aside. "You going to play or chatter?"

"Ready."

Phillip tossed the ball into the air again and with a powerful downswing shot it into the wall. Paunchy raced to return it. Phillip drove hard against the back wall, jumping high and catching the spinning sphere with a perfectly timed backhand.

The observer in the spectators' booth shifted his weight and looked around for a cigarette machine. In a moment the game was over. "Phillip!"

He looked up with a quick smile of recognition. "Hi, Barry. Been here long?"

"Few minutes."

"I'll meet you at the pool. Third floor. To your right and up one flight."

The pungent smell of chlorine hit Barry's nose as he opened the door. The low-ceilinged room was filled with a large heated pool of water that splashed over the tiled edges onto the small deck area dotted with drains. Five or six men were swimming nude and Barry was relieved to note that most of them were in the same weak condition he was. He sat down on a low bench and unlaced his sneakers.

Phillip walked through the door with a towel around his waist. "Let me swim a few laps, then we can talk."

"Okay. I'll just sort of splash around in the kiddy pool."

"No kiddy pool, sorry." He laughed.

"Don't they even have a little plastic thing for me to play with?"

"No. But you can ask the attendant for a rubber duck." Phillip dove in. By the time Barry had stripped down, he was on his third lap. The skinny young man jumped into the less trafficked area and watched his former boss streak through the blue. After seventeen laps they moved through the steam room and into the sauna. Except for them, it was vacant. They spread towels out on the hot wooden slats of the lounge chairs and stretched out. Phillip closed his eyes. "So how's Elliot?"

"Well, his own doctor took a lot of tests and told him that at the present he didn't have a heart problem, but that if he didn't cut down on the eating and the drinking and the smoking, someday soon he would."

"So is he following doctor's orders?"

"I just left him at a Madison Avenue bar with a bourbon in one hand, a cigar in the other, and a half-eaten plate of those little hot dogs. He'll never change, I guess."

"Until he has a real one." Phillip watched the stream of sweat pouring off his arms. "You know," he said slowly, "when you hear of something like that happening to someone about your own age . . . it makes you sort of sit back and say, hey, wait a minute—am I heading for one too?"

"You? No way. You're not the kind. I mean, look at you. You're in top physical shape, you exercise a lot, you don't pop Gelucils like I do, which only proves you aren't holding it all inside you. But I'm really worried about Elliot. He must have gained thirty pounds in the last year. He never exercises. He drinks too much, smokes too much. He's a walking casebook for someone prone to heart attacks."

Phillip sat up and wiped his face on a towel. "As Willy Loman says, 'It comes with the territory.' "

"Makes you take a look at the territory you're in and ask if it's all worth it, doesn't it?"

Phillip smiled at him and lay back down, his head resting on the bunched-up towel. He let the dry heat slowly work the tenseness from his muscles. "So what's on your mind, Barry? You didn't meet me here to talk about Elliot's health. What's up?"

"Well . . . it's an idea I presented to Elliot and I wanted to get your opinion of it."

"All right."

"Well, it's sort of a repertory company of actors to do high-quality original dramas in the afternoon."

"A repertory company of actors?" he asked without opening his eyes.

"Yeah. Remember that show Richard Boone had on prime time a few seasons back? He had a stable of actors who played different roles each week. Well, I got to thinking of all the really good actors here in New York that aren't working because of the shitty state the theater is in. Real actors, you know. My idea was to get ten to fifteen of them and put them into quality ninety-minute dramas, once a week. I mean, after all, daytime is considered by most critics, and intelligent people, to be the dregs of TV,

179

right? Soaps, game shows, reruns of old evening series. Nothing to appeal to any woman with a grain of intelligence. So give them classy actors in classy roles." He paused and looked over to the still-prone Phillip.

"So you presented it to Elliot?"

"Right. And he laughed me out of the office."

"What did you expect?"

"Phillip, I think it's a dynamite idea, don't you?"

"You want me to lie to you?"

He swallowed uncomfortably. "No."

"I'm surprised at your naiveté, I really am. Barry, you're in television now. You're not playing theater games. You've got to appeal to a mass audience."

"I know. I know. But we don't appeal to anything *but* a mass audience. There are other people out there, too. Chewed and digested pap, we give them, without a semblance of intelligence. Look at British TV. At least they make an effort."

"British TV doesn't depend on sponsor advertising to get their shows on the air. It's subsidized. Here they won't buy the kind of programing you're talking about. It's been tried. It won't draw an audience."

A tall angular man, who looked like a stretched older version of Barry, entered and spread himself out on a bench along the far wall. Barry chewed his lip and watched Phillip, who continued quietly. "Barry, your shows, the eight shows that you're now responsible for in the afternoon, have got to reach the largest possible audience before they'll be attractive enough for an ad agency to buy their time. You know that ad budgets are based on cost per-thousand viewers. How much does it cost them to reach a thousand people? The higher the show draws, the cheaper it is for the sponsor to reach his thousand."

"Okay, okay. But I'm talking about something else."

"No, you're not. You're talking about commercial television. And there are few guys as sharp as Elliot when it comes to that.

"Right, but that doesn't mean we have to put only mass entertainment on, does it?"

"You bet your ass it does—but there are many definitions of what constitutes mass entertainment. You're talking about quality, high-class, dramatic programing on a commercial medium. Look what happened to CBS a few seasons back. They put on *A Midsummer Night's Dream* by the Royal Shakespeare Company. Great cast—Diana Rigg, David Warner, Ian Holmes. Directed on film by Peter Hall. Scheduled on a Sunday evening at nine, when the highest set use for the whole week is in effect. Mass promotion. Schoolteachers made homework assignments to watch it and what happened? It fell through the fucking floor. Something like a third rerun of *Bonanza* wiped them out. Seven, maybe eight million viewers. The *Beverly Hillbillies* would have drawn thirty. They lost money. Well, you're not hired to lose money in this business. You're hired to make it. And that comes through being smart enough to give the audience what they want. You first have to get that audience seated in front of the set to want to see something."

"So it really is a boob tube. Is that your philosophy?"

"Definitely not. It's a dream machine. A fantasy box. People tune in and dream. They forget their own lives. No one wants to be reminded that life is a pile of shit. They want to escape all that. So you give them that escape and they tune in." Phillip stood to let the collected sweat roll off. The towel at his waist had slipped. He reknotted it.

"You know something: I know those people. They used to terrify me and I couldn't wait until I escaped from that kind of life. But now I sympathize with them. They're trapped. Trapped in a self-contented mountain of prefabricated houses with their McDonald's hamburger outings and Carvel desserts and on and on. They're all striving for the American dream. Three cars in every garage and chicken laced with pot. Strive for the sailboat, strive for the Buick, strive for the new room with aluminum siding. How are you going to change all that for them?"

"It shouldn't be that way. It just shouldn't," Barry protested.

"Of course, it shouldn't, friend."

"Then it's our responsibility to raise them up."

"Yes. But not by force-feeding culture down their throats. The people we want to help wouldn't sit still one minute for it. So what do we do for them? We give them something they want. Entertainment. But not just any entertainment. We give them the best we can within the limitations of the medium. The best acting, writing, direction—the best in all those technical areas which separate the professional from the incompetent. But that is all secondary to what we should be trying to do—even in the soap operas: trying to give them a better understanding of themselves, of the world they live in, give them a glimpse of something better."

"So you agree somebody should raise the standards. Well, we're in a position to."

"No, Barry, we're not—neither of us is that powerful. Chamberfield is, but he's only interested in numbers . . . not the people. Secondly, why shouldn't those ladies have their soap operas every day? They were more important to them than the Watergate hearings, remember? They want to know what is happening in the lives of their heroines because that's all the family many of those people have. They are stuck, those people. They're besieged with taxes, inflation, periodic unemployment, or dull and endless, unrewarding, jobs. They don't trust their government any more; their elected representatives have been proven to be hypocrites and liars. Their kids are running away at age fourteen and coming back with needle marks in their arms. And who's helping these people? That's where television comes in. Not by programing over their heads, but by programing with the best you can give them, and by lifting their lives from within. So, in my own way, I'm making *Affair Of The Heart* entertain and explore at the same time. That's what TV is about, Barry. And that's why I, for one, still want to be a part of it."

Later they walked east on Fifty-Seventh Street for a few blocks and just before going their separate ways, Phillip stopped. "I agree with you, Barry. The industry does have to grow, try new people, new formats. But it has to grow with the audience. You can't change it suddenly by trying to instruct them, to help them give up their flagstone walks. I'll tell you something: even Wilson Vulkner couldn't do that. Even the chairman of the board has to be financially responsible to the stockholders. You're not fighting only the television industry. You're fighting the whole structure of society. But, and remember this, *if* you work within the confines of that structure and slip it all under the door of mass entertainment, help the people that way—that, my friend, Barry, is where it's at.

That's the rub, my friend." He grinned when he said goodbye. "Tell your friend, Elliot, next time I hope his heart attack is more successful. Then maybe you and I can change it from the inside."

Phillip had a bite to eat at the Russian Tea Room and then took a cab down to his apartment. He spent the next few hours shuffling through the stacks of photos and resumes of young women that had accumulated like dust in every corner of the apartment. Still undecided, he went to bed.

14.

It was past midnight, but he was still awake when it rang. "This is the RBI operator, Mr. Searing. I have a collect call from a Miss Gaye Vulkner in Rome, Italy. Will you accept the charges?"

Gaye Vulkner, he thought, Gaye Vulkner . . . and it suddenly dawned on him. Of course. Why didn't I think of it before? Maybe because when Katina told him the redhead was an actress she also dropped the bombshell of whose daughter she was—and that was enough to shatter any coherent thoughts.

But now here he was lying in bed surrounded by a sea of pictures and resumes, trying to select a face from a shattered kaleidoscope of swirling, multifaceted, black-and-white images. And there is Gaye Vulkner, by far the most striking, the most vibrant, the most sexually alive creature he had seen. "Yes, Operator, I'll accept the call." You bet your chaffed bottom I'll accept the call.

She's perfect. She's absolutely perfect. She's exactly the girl I've been looking for. The revelation was confirmed in about the same amount of time it took the operator to plug the call into the apartment from Sixth Avenue. Now, if she's only free. . . .

"Gaye!"

"So you found out who I am. Figured you would. You don't mind my phoning collect. Daddy's paying for it anyway, right?"

He laughed. "Right. How did you know I worked for his company?"

"You are an important man; it wasn't hard."

"How did you make out with your film?"

"You know about that too, hmm? Well, it fell through. The guy's whole deal isn't even set yet, and he wanted me to stick around and help him promote it. He says he's got some of the money, but not all, and thinks because of my father I can help him get the rest. I'm going to change my name, I swear. I'm sick and tired of professional leeches."

"Don't cut your throat yet, little girl. What are your plans?"

"Jacques came down to meet me. Remember Jacques from the party?"

"Sad eyes, with the boyfriend in Vietnam?"

"That's Jacques. Well, he and I thought we'd pop over to Rio for a couple of weeks, see a few friends who are slumming it this summer. And that means we'll be stopping in New York, hence the call."

"How locked into those plans are you?"

"You don't want to see me?"

"Don't be an idiot. I've got a reason for asking."

"Nothing is locked in," she said. "I'm just bored, that's all, and I want to get away from Europe for a while. Nothing's happening over here."

"How serious are you about acting?"

"Is this an inquisition?"

"Answer me."

"You mean about my wanting to?"

"Yes."

"Well, I would like to, but now most film production is set for the summer and fall."

"Okay, look, I've got a proposition for you."

"Whips and chains?" she asked hopefully.

"Listen, I have a part open on my show that you could fit perfectly. Physically you're absolutely right and you just have to act yourself."

"What's that supposed to mean?"

"It's the part of a gorgeously bitchy misfit, a vamp whose entire drive is toward self-satisfying sex." She'd like that.

"Jesus, has Daddy's little company gotten liberal! Are we going to show all that on the TV BeeBees?"

"Only the gorgeous bitchiness. The sex'll have to stay in your perverted mind."

"And you want me to play the part?"

"You'd be terrific in it."

She didn't try to disguise the cynicism. "Why? Do you think it'll earn you brownie points with my old man?"

He opted for truth. "No, in fact it's the one thing that worries me about making you the offer. He might be extremely displeased, and that could be a hassle I don't need. But you are an actress, you fit the part better than anyone I've seen so far, and my time is up. I have to make a decision. Will you accept it? I have to know immediately."

"Hey, wait a minute! You sure do rush a girl, don't you? That means I'll have to stay in New York."

"Contractually for thirteen weeks. But the part actually runs for only five. After that you'll probably be written out. Gaye, I can tell you this: it's a nice part and you could shine in it. If you're serious about acting, the exposure could be terrific for you."

"The money wouldn't be bad, either."

"Money! You've got a problem with money?"

"Why? Doesn't it pay very much?"

"It pays three hundred a day and you'll be on three to four times a week. I hadn't even thought to mention the money."

"Why? Because of my father? Where do you think I learned frugality? Okay. Now, what do I do with Jacques?"

"Sweetheart, you'll have to figure that one out yourself. Homosexuality has never been one of my perversions."

"Or pleasures. Jacques is wonderfully sweet."

Phillip took a pad and pen from the end table. "Who's your agent in New York, Gaye?"

"Bill Yatton, IFA."

"Wire him and I'll call in the morning to secure the deal. I'll need you here by Monday. Do you have a place to stay?"

She hesitated. "I prefer to live alone."

"I was offering to help you get a hotel."

"No, thanks. My mother's apartment on Fifth can be opened. I'll stay there."

"Gaye, I can't tell you how delighted I am to have you."

"Mr. Searing-Producer, it's a wonderful and happy and exalted pleasure for me, too, and I am most beholden to your highnessship. You sound so full of business shit I don't even want to come."

He laughed. "You've helped me out a lot."

They chatted for a few minutes more and then rang off.

In the darkness, before his eyes closed, he calculated the effect the hiring might have on Chamberfield. But what could he actually say? It was a legitimate production move. Phillip couldn't help it if Gaye Vulkner was the stepdaughter of the chairman of the board.

It took until Sunday afternoon, two days later, for the news to reach Elliot's ear.

In a rare exhibition of corporate camaraderie the network president invited Elliot to his home in Connecticut for the day, a large white colonial house on a very expensive peninsula of land that jutted out into a body of water called Candlewood Lake. "We Keels love the water," said Russell, stirring up another batch of martinis. "In fact we even have an eight-sleeper ketch I dock over in Westport for salt-water activities."

"Do you?"

"Oh, yeah, got a picture of her in my office. You might have seen it." He tapped a glass. "Straight up or on the rocks, Elliot?" He hitched up his blue yatching trousers and tucked in the polo shirt.

"Uh, on the rocks, Russ, please. Don't bother about the garbage."

"Hey, are you supposed to be drinking with that heart condition of yours?"

"Uh, well, it wasn't too serious, Russ. I keep the consumption pretty low nowadays."

He poured the gin mixture into the two crystal goblets. "We'll get a little head start on the girls. Then I want to take you out and show you the lake from the liquid point of view." He looked out over the lawn to where Rosalynann and his wife were sunbathing on folding lounges.

187

"Pretty girl, that secretary of yours, Elliot. You see much of her outside the office?"

"No, Russ. Just thought she might enjoy coming up here, that's all."

"Mind you, I don't have anything against a man going out with his secretary. Nothing wrong in that."

They finished the first round of martinis and sucked on the ice until they both decided they were childish to deprive themselves, "It is Sunday, you know." They had another. Russell stirred again and poured, and they took them in hand and walked across the expanse of grass to the little wooden landing where the speedboat was docked. "Going out for a ride, girls. Anybody want to come?"

Rosalynann took her cue from Georgette, who waved them off. She wanted to take a shower and get dressed for dinner.

They started up the twin engines and pulled out into the center of the lake. Russell cut across to the far side, behind a couple of water-skiers, and guided the craft at a leisurely glide along the edge.

They putt-putted up the channel, saying nothing or very little. The two men shared equally the obligation to spend a social Sunday together, but that seemed to be the only thing they did share equally. "Oh, by the way," said Keel, almost as an afterthought. "You didn't get back to me with your thoughts on the Billy Joe Walker special for the fall."

The sun had fallen below a cover of high mountaintops, which took the burn off Elliot's tender pinkish skin, but the heat had not yet lifted into the evening. He wiped the back of his neck with a pocket handkerchief. "Frankly, Russ," he said, "I've been thinking about it, but I feel strongly that it's a lousy show and it'll hurt the time slot."

"Well," he remarked thoughtfully, "I can't say I disagree with you. I can't say I disagree with you at all, but we have to consider all of the ramifications of the thing."

"What do you mean?"

"The thing is, the administration's behind it."

"The administration?" Elliot was surprised. "I can't see Vulkner or the board bothering themselves about something like this, can you?"

"I don't mean our administration; I mean Washington."

"Washington?"

"The White House."

"What the hell do they have to do with programing a Billy Joe Walker special?"

Keel glanced at him out of the corner of his eye. Was it conceivable this man didn't know that the ultra-right wing, flag-waving Walker was a solid supporter of the President of the United States?

"Elliot," he said condescendingly, "the President and Walker are very close friends. It would please him to have Walker on the air."

"Russ, with all due respect to the President, Walker is a broken-down country-and-western singer who wouldn't draw flies, let alone a decent rating. What do we need him for? Our nighttime schedule is strong. We don't want to weaken it."

"You don't seem to understand," he explained patiently. "It was a favor to us that he approached us. . . . RBI has been under a lot of pressure lately from the White House to broaden our scope and the so-called bias of our news presentations."

"They're full of crap—our news show are the fairest of any on the air. Too fair sometimes."

"You and I know that, Elliot, but Washington believes otherwise and we're already going to court in the fall to fight an FCC suit. A pro-administration special could help cool down the bad feelings quite a bit. It might just swing some weight."

Elliot let his hand trail along the top of the water, enjoying the liquid vibrations of the gentle waves. "You think so?"

"I'm sure of it. It would look good on a list of shows favoring administration policy, a good balance, and the board and Vulkner would be grateful. They're very image-conscious, you know."

"I suppose it won't hurt the ratings too much if we slip it in judiciously."

"Good, I'm glad you agree." He slapped him on the shoulder. "You're going to do a hell of a job for us, Elliot. I'm sure of that, but you'll discover that we have to throw a few bones out if we want to keep the wolves away. One of these days I want you to look over a list I have of all the legal wrangles we've fought since 1968. You'd be amazed."

"I'd like to see that."

"I'll leave the details to you on the scheduling. Just make it as soon as you can, all right?"

It was long after dinner, just as they were getting into the car to leave, that the subject came up. They opened the door of the bright-red Porsche that Elliot had bought for weekends as a promotion present, despite the fact that he was now entitled to a company limousine.

"Say," said Keel expansively, "I didn't congratulate you on your boy Searing, there. He's really moving, that fellow."

Elliot guarded himself. "Not like that first jump. He only gained three tenths of a point in Friday's Seventy Markets Report."

"Three tenths is three tenths and it's steady. But that wasn't what I was talking about. I mean the casting thing."

"What casting thing?"

"Didn't he tell you? He cast Vulkner's stepdaughter in a part on his soap opera."

"Vulkner's stepdaughter!" The explosion must have been internal, because Keel carried on without a stop.

"An extraordinarily beautiful young lady, I understand. I've never met her. She was studying acting in London and he went over to convince her to do the part. That's what I heard. Vulkner's assistant told me about it."

"No kidding," Elliot muttered quietly. What the hell would it mean? And why wasn't he told about it before it was accomplished? "I was out of the office all Friday afternoon. Probably why I didn't hear about it."

"Well, I think it's an interesting bit. The papers will release the story on Monday. Could mean a nice piece of publicity and another boost. Vulkner is actually rather pleased, too. Seems he's not as close to the girl as he'd like to be and he's hoping for some sort of reconciliation."

"Well, Phillip knows what he's doing," said Elliot, restraining his anger as best he could. "That's why I put him in the spot."

"Certainly looks like it. He might wind up saving that show singlehandedly and we can save the investment in replacing it."

Rosalynann found the drive home long and tedious.

When he wasn't muttering profanities to himself, Elliot was tomblike.

Gaye arrived at the studio on Monday at two as arranged on the phone the previous day. She went straight to the producer's office, leaving a trail of over-the-shoulder lookers in her wake. Phillip was in the outer office. He saw her as soon as she started up the corridor.

"You look ravishing."

"Ravish me." She grinned and they both looked down to the secretary, who was trying not to be in the way.

"Gloria, this is Gaye Vulkner. She'll be doing the new role of Daphne."

"How do you do?"

Gloria looked at the tall beauty and mumbled some semblance of a hello.

"You read the script I sent over?"

"Yes."

"Will it work for you?"

"I can play this part with my eyes closed."

"Don't. It'd be peculiar on TV." He handed her a Xeroxed sheet. "Here's the day's schedule. Read it over and see if you have any questions."

Affair Of The Heart
  Hall #2
    7:00–9:00 Rehearsal
    9:00–10:30: FAX
    10:30–11:00: Run-Through

  Hall #1
    11:00–11:30: Notes
    11:30–12:00: Lunch
    12:00–12:30: Dress Rehearsal
    12:30–1:00: Notes
    1:00–1:30: VTR
    1:30–2:00: Break

  Hall #2
    2:00–3:30: Preliminary Rehearsal

She glanced up at him. "Seven A.M.? You expect me to be here by then?"

"Absolutely on the dot of seven." He smiled.

"Jesus . . . that cuts into one's life, doesn't it? And what's this FAX?"

"Short for facilities. That's the camera blocking and technical rehearsal. VTR at 1:00 P.M. is the video taping itself."

"And a big half hour for lunch. How generous."

"You'll also have to be made up and have your hair done during that time, I'm afraid." He headed for the door. "Come on, I want to introduce you downstairs before the rehearsal."

She took his arm as they started out to the spiral staircase. "I think your secretary's got a crush on you."

He shook his head.

"Oh, such modesty. I saw fires of jealousy shooting at me from those cannons she calls eyes."

"I think she was just taken aback by your beauteous splendor."

"Oh, Mr. Producer-Searing. You do know how to make a girl feel at home." She ran her fingers up and down his spinal column.

"Look, Gaye," he said, slowing their pace a little, "I think it would be best if you weren't too open with, uh, me." He cocked his head to catch her reaction.

"Oh, dear me!" She pouted, with the grin of a woman who knew how to get what she wanted and dropped her arm.

The rehearsal was on when they entered. Introductions were made. Vanessa stood as Phillip eased the tall redhead over to her. They contrasted quite interestingly, he noticed. The eye went immediately to Gaye—her statuesque figure, her fiery hair, sea-green eyes set off by the green of her clothes. But then it picked up Vanessa—much frailer, smaller, though the frailty made her seem smaller than she actually was, and there the eye lingered, because there was a depth in her that was puzzling and remote. It encouraged one to penetrate it.

"Vanessa Langley, Gaye Vulkner. This is your rival for the attentions of Bill Peters."

"I lose," Vanessa joked pleasantly.

"So you're Valerie. I thought you'd be plainer. How could anyone bear to think of such gorgeous black eyes going blind." Gaye turned to Phillip. "She changes the whole concept I had of my role. It's going to take a hell of a lot to win a boyfriend away from her."

Charming viper, Vanessa thought. She picked up her script and watched Phillip lead the girl away. She noticed the way Gaye slipped her arm through his and the way she tried to lean on him.

Phillip stayed for the first reading. The scene took place in Valerie's aunt's drawing room in the city. It was the first meeting of the two future rivals for Charles's affections. The scene started with Valerie and Charles deep in an argument left over from the previous act.

VALERIE.

(*On couch, nervously*) I told you before, Charles. I'm trying to redefine my life.

CHARLES.

A definition that doesn't include me?

VALERIE.

(*Rising and crossing to window, her back to Charles*) You don't understand.

CHARLES.

(*Rising and crossing to her*) You're darn right I don't! Look, I came all the way up here to find out one thing and one thing only. Do you still love me?

VALERIE.

I . . . I just. . . .

(*The doorbell rings. Valerie starts toward the door. Charles grabs her arm.*)

CHARLES.

Answer me!

VALERIE.

(*Quietly*) There's someone at the door. (*She pulls away and opens the door. Daphne Conrad breezes in.*)

DAPHNE.

You must be Valerie. Darling! (*She hugs Valerie closely.*) I'm Daphne.

VALERIE.

Daphne?

DAPHNE.

Daphne Conrad. Didn't your aunt tell you about me?

193

(*Confused*) I . . . I guess so.

DAPHNE.

Your aunt is a friend of my mother's. I'm all alone in this big city without a single friend. So she thought you could show me the sights. (*She spots Charles and zaps in on him.*) Oh . . . excuse me. I didn't know you had company.

VALERIE.

Daphne Conrad, this is my friend from Livingston, Charles Gordon.

DAPHNE.

Pleased to meet you. I'm sure. (*She holds out her hand and they shake. She eyes him.*)

CHARLES.

The pleasure is mine.

(*Daphne turns and flashes a big warm smile at Charles, who is enchanted.*)

(*Valerie watches the two.*)

END OF ACT II.

Phillip slipped a note to Pat to join him in his office after the rehearsal. The director came up about two hours later. Chivas Regal was poured over ice in two glasses. "What do you think of her?" Phillip dropped into the lounge chair next to the couch where Pat had sprawled in.

"What's to think? You react to a female like that with your balls. Between those breasts every male over the age of six would cheerfully be smothered."

"Will she work?"

"She's no great shakes as an actress."

"I think the secret is not to let her act. Just edge her into being herself. Did you see the afternoon papers?"

"Yeah, nice coverage. You sure do pull interesting casting moves, my friend."

The next day Phillip brought his secretary in to watch the taping of the air show. He studied her reactions to the new girl. Vanessa, Bill, and Gaye struck a rather good balance. The jealousy, the fear, the suspicion all merged into a stunningly sympathetic performance on Vanessa's part. And the Vulkner girl allowed herself to have fun;

she toyed with Bill the way she had toyed with Phillip at the London party and Bill reacted beautifully. The addition would be fine.

The show ended. The picture went to black. Phillip swiveled his chair around, swinging his legs off the desk.

"Did you like her, Gloria?"

"I hated her."

"Good, that's what I wanted you to do. I'm going down. Which dressing room is she in?" He started out of the door.

"I think she's sharing with Vanessa Langley."

"Vanessa?" Christ, he thought. That wasn't too smart.

"Yes."

He should have mentioned something about not putting the two of them in together.

"This room looks like a funeral parlor," said Phillip as he opened the door. Bouquets and floral baskets were spread all over the place, the massiveness of one outdoing the massiveness of the other.

Gaye bounded out of her chair and planted a kiss on his cheek. "I did it, didn't I? I really did?" She certainly was a child.

He pushed her gently away to arm's length. "Fine job, Gaye. On the nose."

He caught Vanessa out of the corner of his eye. "Vanessa, that last scene of yours was the best we've ever done. The tension, the concern, was terrific."

"Thank you." She smeared off some pancake.

"You'd think this was Broadway," squealed Gaye. "What am I going to do with all these flowers?"

"Set up a stand outside, pick up a little loose change," muttered Vanessa. Phillip went to the largest arrangement and poked through it for the card.

"Jacques sent this one and that big one there is from the king of the mountain himself."

"Your stepfather?"

"Ostentatious, aren't they? His secretary probably remembered I was related." She slipped off her costume and started wiping her face with a tissue. Vanessa was not overly ecstatic about Gaye traipsing around in front of Phillip in panties and bra.

"Did you call him when you got in?"

"Who?"

195

"Your stepfather."

"No, what for? Say, I have an admirer." She brightened suddenly. "That one's from an Elliot somebody or other and I've never even heard of him."

"Chamberpot?"

"Something like that." She handed him a card that had been stuck in the corner of the mirror. "Yes, Elliot Chamberfield. Who is this mystery man?"

"Vice president of programing for the network."

"Ah, so it's not a secret admirer; it's just business."

Vanessa gathered her things together and gave a last touch to her hair. Gaye wriggled into a jumper. "Do you want to take any of these ghastly flowers home with you, Vanessa?"

"No, thank you."

"It's a shame. They'll go to waste." She took a deep breath and let it out. "Phillip, I'm starved. Come, buy me lunch."

"Already have. We're having sandwiches in the control booth. I've ordered the tape of the show rerun for you, since you'll be rehearsing when it's aired." He turned to Vanessa. "You're welcome to join us."

"No, I've got to go over my lines." She swept past Phillip without looking.

"It was a good show, Vanessa."

"That's what you said." She closed the door behind her.

Gaye cocked a sly eye to Phillip. "Another heart bites the dust over Phillip Searing. I seem to be wreaking havoc in your harem."

"She didn't look well today. Something's wrong with her."

Phillip led Gaye through the studio and into the control booth, a rectangular room with a line of swivel chairs that ran the length of a long counter. On the opposite side of the counter there was a narrow walk space in front of the complicated bank of TV monitors.

Charley Reeb, the assistant director, looked up when they walked in. "They're rolling it back for you now, Phil. We'll have the picture in about three more minutes. You can sit here if you like, Miss Vulkner."

"Thank you." Gaye took the chair next to him and

reached for a pastrami sandwich. "You can't even see the studio from here!"

"We don't have to," said Phillip, perching on the production assistant's stool behind her. "The only thing that matters is what's on those television monitors."

"You won't believe this," said Gaye, "but as much as I've been around this industry, I don't have a clue to what all of you people do."

"Really?" Phillip said.

"Because my name's Vulkner everybody always took for granted that I knew how things worked, so they never told me—so I never knew."

"Why don't you give the lady a lecture, Charley."

"Sure," said the AD. "Well, let's see. Right now you're sitting in the chair Pat, the director of the show, usually sits in. Okay. Pretend you're the director. You've prepared everything in advance in rehearsals and now your job is to give the final orders to all of us here—the technical director, announcer, sound technicians, and the stage manager, who is out on the studio floor."

"What do I order you to do?"

"Well, you keep your eye on those monitors, particularly the three camera monitors, and when you see the shot you've rehearsed you just say 'Take camera three,' or 'dissolve to camera two,' or 'fade to black' or whatever, and the shot you've ordered will come up on that big color monitor. As you see, the rest of the sets are smaller and black and white. I'll have set the shots up for you. As your assistant director I'm in communication with all of the cameramen, the sound boom man, and all of the engineers responsible for getting the precise shot you rehearsed and the proper film or pretaped sequence in place. I ready them seconds before you give the order to 'take it.' Everything goes very fast in here—a lot of people talking all at the same time and each of us trying like mad to keep his own line of communications straight."

"There aren't that many people in here."

"In this room? No. In addition to us there's Ralph, who's the technical director. He punches those buttons in front of him when you say 'take it!' Then there's an audio man to play records and sound tapes, an announcer in that glass booth over there, the lighting technician who

197

makes sure the color is perfectly in balance and behind us, where Phillip is sitting, a production assistant. She takes split-second timings on a stopwatch."

Phillip broke in: "There's generally a network production supervisor here too, who orders our technicians and facilities for us. And if we have a tricky scene, censorship-wise, the network continuity man may join us to make sure we don't offend any sensibilities."

"Christ, how do all of you think straight?"

Phillip leaned over and patted Charley on the head. He smiled. "Not all of us do."

Charley packed a pipe and looked at Gaye. "You see what we lower-echelon people have to put up with?"

"What are all the monitors connected to?"

"Well, as I said, the cameras, and then the slide and film and videotape machines that are over at broadcast facilities on Second Avenue."

"Why would you want to film a sequence when you could record it on videotape?"

"Usually for outside work. Suppose we have a sequence with you and Charles in a rowboat. We'd shoot it outside and it would be easier to film it rather than tape it, although with tape cameras getting smaller and more compact all the time even that'll probably change soon."

Gaye turned to the technical director sitting to her left. "What happens if when I say 'take camera one,' you hit the button for camera two?"

"Well, if camera two has a shot of an actor in the middle of a costume change, the audience might get a glimpse of a guy with his pants down."

"*If* you were doing a *live* show," said Phillip.

"Yeah," said the TD. "Most of the shows we do are taped nowadays, so we'd just have to do the segment over again. In the old days though, when everything was live, boy, did we have some screwups."

Charley smiled. "A couple of years ago some night technicians on one of the New York local stations were running a late movie, and instead of watching that they were running a porno flick on another closed circuit chain. You see we can run a lot of things at one time, but only one goes out over the air." He laughed. "You can figure what happened. In the middle of the show the technical director accidentally punched up the wrong button and switched Deanna Durbin to Linda Lovelace."

Gaye roared. "I would have loved it."

A light began to flash on a bank of built-in telephones in front of the AD's chair. Charley picked one up, listened, said "okay, roll it," and hung up. He turned back to Gaye. "That was videotape control. They're going to run the show for us now."

Gaye watched herself with a critical, if amused eye. It was hard for Phillip to tell if she was taking the whole thing seriously. The only concern she voiced when it was over was that she looked too heavy.

"The tube always puts ten or fifteen pounds on you," said Phillip as they walked into the studio after it was over. "If you could knock off about five you'd look fine."

"More concessions! My God, this job does take a toll."

"So now you know all the secrets of television."

"Absolutely everything," she sang. "Oh, there is something I want to know. What's a Nielsen?"

They passed a scenery bin and headed toward the corridor. A lighting man and his assistant were adjusting several five-thousand-watt Klieg lights on a grid. "Nielsens are an abbreviation for the numerical ratings put out by the National Nielsen Company. It's an organization that samples twelve hundred households with eighteen hundred television sets to find out which programs the family is watching at given times. They test each half-hour time slot and give each of the networks a percentage for the overall rating. Obviously the higher the rating a network gets the more an advertiser will want to purchase time for his commercials. So from the network standpoint, the higher the rating, the more we can charge the advertiser."

"You mean out of all the millions of sets in this country they judge the audience by twelve hundred families?"

"That's about all. It's a sample of the tastes of America and if a given program doesn't get its share of the market, it's dropped by orders from the forty-fourth floor."

"Well," said Gaye, fingering her Yemenite necklace, "thanks for the lecture and the cheapo lunch." She grinned slyly. "Wanna come back into my dressing room? Maybe I can figure out a way to pay you back."

"No, thanks. We're working now, remember."

"My, how compartmentalized we are!"

Phillip went upstairs to the office.

* * *

"There's a call for you, Gaye." He bent and whispered softly so as not to disturb the rehearsal.

"Thanks . . . Colin, isn't it?"

"Yes." He beamed, flattered she remembered. "You can take it on the house phone outside. I'll tell Pat you'll be right back."

She slipped out to the hall. "Hello."

"Gaye, this is Elliot Chamberfield. Did you get the roses?"

"Oh, *that* Elliot Chamberfield. Yes, I did. Thank you so much."

"I've seen your performances the past few days. Very, very nice."

"Very, very nice to tell me."

"What night would you like to go? I've expected you to call."

"What?"

"For dinner. I sent an invitation with the roses. Didn't you get the note?"

"Oh, the note! I was so excited, I didn't read the message, just the name."

"I'd like to take you to dinner. Welcome you officially to the RBI family."

"Isn't that sweet." She had not the least desire to go to dinner with a total stranger. "But would you mind terribly if we postponed it for a while? I'd like to get acclimated first, you know, to the job and all of it. Could I let you know in a few days?"

"That would be fine. Keep up the good work and let me know as early as you can."

"Yes. And thank you again for the flowers. Very sweet."

"Don't mention it. Good-bye."

She replaced the receiver and had started back to the rehearsal, when she spotted Phillip. He was about to get away, but she stopped him. "I've got a bone to pick with you."

"It'll have to wait, sweetie. I've got to get upstairs."

200

She grabbed his arm when he reached for the door. "Now, Phillip."

"If it's business, all right. But if it's personal, it'll have to wait."

She held tight. "It's personal and we'll talk now, if you please, or I'll walk right out on that rehearsal."

Annoyed, he led her to a quiet corner near the staircase. "What's up?"

"Why have you been avoiding me?" Her face softened considerably.

"Have I?"

"Since I've been in New York I have seen you socially only once. One dinner at Lutece. Sex, zero. Friendship? Plus two on a scale of a hundred. Why?"

"One, I'm not avoiding you, and two, I don't like to be threatened. You came here to do a job and anything beyond that was neither promised nor implied."

"What!"

"That doesn't mean we can't pick up where we left off when your run of the show is over with, but now, no."

Her jaw tightened and her lips pursed forward.

Phillip looked at his watch. "I don't mean to be rude, but I've got someone waiting for me upstairs and I've got a show on my mind."

"You made yourself perfectly clear, Mr. Producer. Fuck you, you son of a bitch!" She stormed off.

"What's this Elliot Chamberfield like, Claire?" Gaye's fury had carried through the performance and made it something quite special.

"Golden boy of RBI. Fought his way to the top and is still fighting." She sat on the edge of the counter, mesmerized by the beauty of the actress. Gaye put her arms back. Claire helped her off with her makeup smock and hooked it behind the door. She caught a short deep breath as the luscious breasts were raised to slide under a thin, silk blouse. "He can be boyish and charming one minute, and a tough bastard the next."

"Just like Phillip Searing."

"Oh, no. Chamberfield's a very special guy. He's like a little boy, really. Everything's out front with him. He's happy, he's angry, that's it. But you know where you stand. You're with him, you're against him, you please

201

him, you don't. I think he's easy to read." She put her hand to her mouth and looked up at the wall. "I should keep my trap shut. He's probably got this place bugged. I hear he's a great admirer of Richard Nixon. I'm only kidding . . . frankly, I sort of like the guy. Anyway, the two of them are locked into the battle of the century."

"Chamberfield and Nixon?" Her hairbrush stopped in mid-stroke.

"No, Chamberfield and Searing. It's survivalsville. They hate each other. Right now Elliot's on top, but I'll give odds that Phillip climbs back one of these days."

Gaye started the brush again, tilting her head sideways and drawing it through the underside of the thick red hair. "So it's personal as well as professional?"

"It's personal, all right. Here, let me do that." She took the brush from the young woman's hand and continued the job. Gaye closed her eyes and leaned back.

She made the dinner appointment the following day.

15.

The sun beat on her shoulders brutally as she crossed Sheridan Square, oblivious to the traffic and her fellow unfortunates forced to remain in the city for the weekend. Small globules of tar bubbled up in the asphalt. The air had been still for a few days, leaving a buildup of car exhaust, Con Edison chimney smoke, and cinders everywhere. The grime seeped into the cracks of the skin, bit into the crevices like mini-bugs, burning and tearing the eyes. A three-shower day.

She passed the Riviera Bar and casually scanned the tables, a habit prompted by four years of frequenting the place. She had no desire to speak to anyone, though. Not today. Not now.

The Fourth Street gutters were lined with the usual collection of dog turds. Vanessa plodded past them. She crossed and looked over a collection of bathing suits in a window, giving her mind a brief respite. Then she moved on, past the tomato heat of the pizza joint, the laundry, the Italian restaurant on the corner of West Tenth that never seemed to have any customers, but always seemed ready for them.

Nobody could be better suited to star in a soap opera. If she were ever fired as an actress she could always write out her life story. Melodrama. No one would ever believe it. But the problems existed and had to be dealt with. What could she do? Not tell him? Keep it from him? Blow up like a watermelon and pretend it was nothing?

She let herself into the apartment and threw the police bar into place. She moved down the narrow hall and into the living room, picking up a small chip of plaster which had broken off and crumbled to the floor. Joey was stretched out on the rug in a pair of faded jeans. He had the ear phones on and was dreaming. The silent revolutions of the turntable provided the only indication he was actively doing something. She dropped her bag and went into the kitchen, pouring herself a glass of apple juice from a bottle in the refrigerator. She came back and sat down on the couch.

A slight breeze blew feathery balls of dust under the chest in the far corner of the room. Tenement tumbleweeds. He hadn't dusted, hadn't painted the wall, nothing. He listens to his music and dreams away his life. How did she ever fall in love with this child? Why? What attracted her to this runaway son of a West Virginia policeman. She knew. It was the defenselessness. It was the running away—exactly that. The sad little boy who had to flee a father who put him, five years old, behind bars so he would mend his ways. A chronic alcoholic for a mother. The boy who would smile shyly and move away whenever a fight started, tuck his head with shame and move away. He moved away—from parents to New York, to the Village, to five o'clock mornings at the Night Owl, to the guitar, to sleep, to acid, to hard drugs, to nothingness. The sweetness was still there—the vulnerability, the smile, the boyish charm—but so was the loneliness. Some people kill themselves—stick their heads in gas ovens; with Joey, it was a slow release on life. And then the turnaround—the drying out, the sickness, the needfulness, the grabbing to pull himself up again. And he had almost succeeded. It was the last stage. She trusted that. They were into the last lap.

But the struggle had taken its toll on her. It had been too hard. His weight had been too much for her. There were scars. As for love? Who knew now? It wasn't the love of four years ago.

She told him about the baby. Not then, but later that night. Ecstasy.

He bolted up in bed, propped himself against the burlap-covered wall, and hugged his knees. "We're going to make it this time. No risks like before. You do everything that doctor says. And me, too. This time I'm looking after you night and day. No more housework; I do all that now. No more standin' over the cooking stove. I do that, too. I'll take the laundry to the corner and. . . ." His excitement flooded over in a wave. Vanessa found it difficult to keep from getting caught up in it herself. She would quit her job when she began to show and he wouldn't need therapy any more. Of that he was sure. The baby would give him all the impetus he would need to continue.

"It's a new lease on life, Ness. It's like taking a hit. Look at me. I'm high and I haven't touched the shit. I feel like I'm flying. I've created something. Me, Joe Langley. I've created something. Finally."

Tears welled up behind her eyes and bubbled out over her lashes. "You're such a child," she cried, kissing him.

"It's goin' to be all right this time. We'll make it this time."

Sunday they took a long walk through the empty meat district and over to the docks. They listened to some amateurish tripe from the poets' circle and looked at New Jersey. They didn't say very much to each other.

When Vanessa came home from the studio on Monday, she found the house cleaned, beds made, dishes done, and the paint things prepared. On Tuesday the living-room walls were finished. She marveled at his industry and was pleased. Nonetheless, the toll was starting to mount. She found it more and more difficult to concentrate on her part. She made it through the tapings each day, but with effort.

At first the loss of memory served the part well. Valerie could easily be distracted by fear of the impending eye operation and of losing her boyfriend to the redhead, but by the end of the week it was apparent to everyone on

205

the show that she wasn't acting—that the loss of concentration was Vanessa's and not Valerie's.

Phillip questioned Colin about it, but he didn't seem to be informed. Phillip didn't press. Their relationship had been strained and formal since the day of the chewing out. Vanessa avoided the producer as well. Or she had nothing to say. Phillip decided to let the situation ride for a while.

Elliot was drunk. Four bourbons before dinner, a bottle of wine, during, and Irish coffee afterward. Gaye took his arm as he pitched out of the rear of the limousine. "Easy, tiger." She guided him through the large glass doors, past the uniformed doorman, whom he saluted, and through the sterile foyer with the stiff, uncomfortable-looking chairs that nobody ever sat in. They stepped into the elevator.

Elliot cocked his eye at her with the clever scrutiny of an alcoholic. "How tall are you, anyway?"

"Five ten in my bare feet."

"That's pretty fucking big for a girl. Wouldn't you say? For a girl? That's pretty fucking big!" The doors closed and he continued to stare, bobbing his head in agreement with himself.

"Shall we go up or would you prefer to stand here for a while?"

"Twenty-two." He reached out and touched the wrong button. She corrected the mistake. He made a fumbling attempt to kiss her as they shot silently skyward, but he missed, hitting her chin instead of her lips. "You're no five ten. I'm five ten and you're taller than me."

She lifted the hem of her floor-length skirt. "Platform shoes."

They worked their way into the apartment and he switched on the light. A dog growled softly from another room. He found her in the kitchen. "How are you, Thumper girl? Did you miss me? She's gonna have pups in another week or so. I'm gonna be a grandfather. Didn't you eat your dinner, Thump? Oh, look at that. That nasty old maid just gave you a can of dog food—and not the kind you like, either." He managed to get another can of dog meat open for her, heated a little canned gravy to pour over it, and added a raw egg to the concoction.

"You need your strength for your pups, don't you, Thump?"

Gaye glanced around at the garish decor and realized that Claire had been right. The guy had no taste at all. Everything seemed quite expensive, but as if it had been ordered for a Castro convertible showroom. Vivid colors were repeated in a turquoise shag rug, purple pillows on a white couch, lots of heavy imitation-gold lamps, a particularly ostentatious one suspended from a massive chain that swooped across one and a half walls. She kicked off her shoes and headed for the couch.

Elliot emerged and weaved his way to the floor-length floral-patterned draperies—the same purple and turquoise. He drew them open. "How about that view, uh? That's what I pay for in this cardboard hole."

She crossed to the huge windows adjoining a small terrace. The Fifty-Ninth Street Bridge appeared as a long ribbon of lights glittering over the blackened East River. "Lovely."

"Should be. I pay a fortune for the place. Want another drink?" He was at the bar—imitation white-leather with matching stools, pouring from a bottle of Jack Daniels.

"I'll have a joint." She pulled two out of her bag and held one toward him.

"What the hell is that?"

"Shit. What did you think it was?"

"Shit?"

"Grass." She lit up and pulled a long drag.

"You're smoking marijuana in my apartment?" His disbelief was total. He went to the door, locked it, and fastened the chain across.

"Do you mind?"

"Mind?" He hesitated. "Christ . . . no. No, go ahead if you have to."

She giggled. They stared at each other for a moment, in wonder of about equal proportions. The telephone rang. It took a moment to register, so deep was Elliot's concentration on the illegal act that was being perpetrated on his property.

"I hear bells."

"What? Oh, yeah." He rose and went toward the bedroom, stealing a quick glance back at the voluptuous devil. The ringing seemed to sober him somewhat. He

207

checked his watch. "Who the hell can that be at this time?"

"Colin here, Elliot, with the weekly spy report." There was a soft giggle on the far end.

Oh, Christ! He was growing to dislike the little chats with this telephone fairy. He'd come to the conclusion that his ploy had not worked. But he let him rattle on about a few inconsequential bits of useless gossip until he heard something that nearly woke him up to morning freshness. "Say that again."

"Just that Vanessa's been awfully down in the dumps lately and I was surprised. I thought all expectant mothers were supposed to be blossoms of joy."

"She's PG?" His voice rang with the excitement of pertinent discovery.

"Of course she is."

"Did she tell you?"

"Yes."

"Does anyone else know?"

"Well, her husband."

"No, for Christ sake. I mean on the show."

"No. It's our secret, but I thought you might be interested."

He said something to indicate that he wasn't, not very much, and rang off. Then a rosy glow came over him. The liquor came back to work in a sweet, sweet way, and the news provided euphoria.

Dessert walked in the door. She stood there plucking the tiny end of the thing she had been holding in a kind of a tweezer-type affair. She rolled it into a ball and popped it into her mouth. "Good news?"

"Terrific!"

"That's nice. Now what are we going to do for the rest of the evening?"

"Does that stuff you're smoking there, does that make you horny?"

"Jesus, you are unschooled, aren't you?"

She made one circle around the red and black room, at the same time reaching behind her back to unzip the dress she was wearing. She let it slip to the floor. There was nothing underneath. She lifted a bare knee up onto the bed, and let herself sink down onto the fake-leopard fur covering. She stretched out lazily and let her hand rub across his fly. "Yes, it makes me horny, sugar, like a nympho in a nunnery."

Jesus Christ! The daughter of the fucking chairman of the board!

And the next morning she was gone. Only a lingering (or what he was afraid somebody else might discover to be lingering) of marijuana smoke offered witness to the presence of the sex dream that had at some unknown hour vanished into the night. He shaved and showered off any telltale signs of the nocturnal activity, puckishly smiling to himself—the hot shower water flowing over his meaty shoulders in matched temperature to the warm glow of masculine pride that welled up in foggy remembrance.

But that was that. He toasted four slices of diet-white, smeared them with margarine and low-calorie raspberry jam, and washed them down with saccharined instant. Then he checked the apartment for lipsticked cigarette ends, glasses, or anything else she might have dropped, and that the maid in her customary laziness might forget to clean up, and Rosalynann might not forget to notice— since she usually stayed overnight three times a week and Wednesdays were on the agenda. He convinced himself there was no reason for him to feel guilty. We're not married or anything, damnit! I don't have to be grateful to my secretary. I never promised her anything. But still, it would be easier if she didn't know. Why hurt the poor girl's feelings?

He scrambled an egg for Thumper and left the dishes in the sink. "You don't seem hungry." He tried to feel under her belly, but the dog drew away and huddled in her box near the bed. "Uh-uh, looks like it's going to be soon, little mother."

He could see her entrance reflected in the glass-covered picture framed on the wall. He jammed his thumb down on the intercom. She dropped her purse on the desk and plopped on the floor the formless green canvas bag in which she carted around her life. Rosalynann stepped over to the open doorway. "Good morning, dear."

"Where the hell have you been? I'm here fifteen minutes already."

"The subway got stuck between Fiftieth Street and the Seventh Avenue station and besides, Elliot, I'm only—"

"Okay, okay, look. Thumper's acting funny and I think maybe she's going to deliver really soon. Maybe you should go over and take a look at her."

"Why?"

"Well, shouldn't somebody be there to help her or something? I mean she's going to have puppies."

"Dogs have puppies every day, Elliot. They don't need any help."

"You're sure?"

"Of course I'm sure."

"Well, look, take off early this afternoon anyway. So you can be there in case. There could be complications, no?"

"Elliot Chamberfield . . . sometimes you're really cute, you know." She closed the inner door and moved around the desk. "Good morning, Teddy Bear. Did my Teddy Bear sleep okay without me last night?"

"Yeah, it was okay." And he allowed himself to be slapped and kissed.

"You're not supposed to answer like that."

"Listen, make sure everything's going all right with that Billy Joe Walker Special, will you? I promised Keel I'd work it through. Also, I'm supposed to see a first draft on the Thursday nine o'clock show I may send in as a replacement. If it doesn't get here by noon call the packager and tell him to move his ass. And, uh, oh, yeah, call Phillip Searing and tell him I want to see him in here after his show tapes."

When she reached her desk, Rosalynann checked her appointment book and hit the intercom. "Elliot, you've scheduled an appointment with Vern Tuttle for four-thirty and that's about when Searing would be getting here."

"Don't worry about it. Bring Searing in anyway and let him wait. Oh, and look, call Jorine at the apartment, will you. See if the dog's okay."

Phillip stood up and shook hands with his predecessor as the graying man left the big man's office, twenty minutes after the "vital" appointment should have begun. Chamberfield you're so bloody transparent! he thought.

"Well, Phillip Searing, as I live and breathe."

"Hello, Vern, how's everything?"

"Couldn't be better."

"Glad to hear it."

Rosalynann called over from her desk. "You can go in now, Mr. Searing. Mr. Chamberfield's ready to see you."

The present and former producers of *Affair* shook hands. Ten minutes later Phillip left the building, revolted at the message he would have to deliver.

"But why?" he had asked. "What sense does it make? Even if she is pregnant and we aren't certain of—"

"I'm certain."

"Why force her to get an abortion now when you don't even know if you're going to renew the show?"

"Her performances have been miserable lately and now that we know the cause we've got to remedy the situation. Besides, as far as the length of time we'll run the show, that's in your camp, isn't it?" He rocked backward in his chair. "You've been doing such a splendid job of getting *Affair* back into shape I couldn't dream of dropping it from the schedule. Of course if the ratings fall again, then you'd be right, it would be a waste for her. But that's a problem she'll have to deal with."

Phillip lit a new cigarette from the end of the old one. What am I doing? I never smoke like this. Cool it. There must be some logic that will penetrate the warp of this piranha's mind. "Look, let me talk to her. I agree her performances have been weak, but let me talk to her. Maybe she's just uptight and is afraid to tell anyone for fear of losing the part."

"Okay, you do that. Talk to her, but in any case I don't want our virginal heroine blowing up like a balloon in front of eight million viewers. It's her choice. Either she gets an abortion or we kill her off during that eye operation and redevelop the story line around somebody else. I'm sorry, I don't like to have to do this sort of thing anymore than you do."

"But why now? What's the necessity of forcing the decision right now?"

"Because if we run, then I don't want to change a lead actress when the show's hot."

"It's been done."

"It won't be now."

"You'll never have to see the stomach. When she gets bigger, I can shoot her in closeups."

"Four months of closeups? Come on, Searing, what are you defending? An actress or the show you're being paid to produce? We've got a natural time coming up in a couple of weeks where we can dump the character logically. In three or four months we'll have to replace the actress in a locked-in part, and the audience will have to get used to a new face in a part they're accustomed to. Forget it. You go talk to her anyway you like, but as far as I'm concerned either she gets an abortion or she's out."

He had been planning to stop downstairs and see Barry for a few minutes, but when he left forty-four he had no desire to see anybody. He shook a few hands on the way to the elevators and waved wanly to the conglomeration around the water fountain, then headed for the street.

How do you ask a woman to have an abortion? What words do you use to place her in a deadend street and show her that the only way out is by killing a life inside her? For a man it's simple. A man just squirts it out and walks away, but a woman assumes the changes in the entire composition of her body. Weight down, push out, swell up, blossom. From the first second of the knowledge she feels the truth of the promise of that ultimate creation. Once when they were first married, Jackie was two weeks late and they concluded she was pregnant, just for a couple of days, then they found out they'd been mistaken. Even though they hadn't wanted a child at the time, the idea that she was pregnant was enough to send her into a depression for several weeks, when she discovered she wasn't. And now he was the one who had to play God for real. What right did he have?

And the husband? What would it mean to him? This frail psyche she's talked about, so unable to deal with the realities of life he had to shoot himself stupid with dope. How would he react to such an intrusion into the question of his domain? Another decision arranged by "those above?" Yet Vanessa couldn't afford to lose her job, and keep paying for an analyst five times a week.

Strange how she tied herself down to that character. What a weight it must be for her. She must be beginning to breathe, though. With the new contract she must be starting to see some daylight. Cautious girl . . . probably still lives as though she might be on an unemployment line tomorrow.

There was another card in the mailbox from Katina, postmarked Ibiza. It was an aerial shot of a steep mountain at the bottom of which a curlicue series of coves and inlets provided entrance to a vast expanse of azure sea. What a demanding appeal it made, just to drop everything and fly there. Forget the show, forget the business, forget dreams of success, authority, redesigning the television industry, making people happy through the tube, power manipulations—just climb on a plane and dive into that deep blue. "Dearest P. Back in Spain. I'm writing like mad and enjoying it more. Sun is hot, sea is blue, I'm in the water. Why the hell aren't you? Love K." He speared it on the kitchen cork board and lay down on the couch to ponder how to hurt least a girl he was growing fond of.

"How did you know I was pregnant?" she asked in a manner that indicated the answer hardly mattered.

"I was told."

"Colin?"

So Dawes was Chamberfield's spy. Well, well. He shrugged.

They made their way through the crowds and crossed Fifth Avenue at Fifty-Third, turning into the tiny vest-pocket oasis known as Paley Park. They walked under the lacy green canopy of meticulously trimmed locust elms toward the sheer waterfall that dropped in a sheet from the top of the rocky wall to the bubbling pool below. The roar of the cascade blocked out the traffic and all the other tortured agonies of the mid-afternoon city.

"William S. Paley built this place," Phillip remarked softly, "as a memorial for his father. Did you know that?"

She shook her head vaguely. Phillip knew she wasn't interested, but continued anyway for lack of nerve. "He paid a million dollars for the property and another million to build this. He brought in special stone craftsmen from Mexico to lay the floor, but when they'd finished he saw it and didn't like it so he had it ripped up and done over again. The Stork Club used to be on this property." He watched a frustrated mother smack her little boy for jamming a runny chocolate ice-cream cone into his little sister's hair. "Lemonade?"

She was still in a state of soporific suspension.

"Would you like a lemonade?"

"All right."

She watched him cross to the front of the park, to the tiny booth that sold hot dogs, pastries, and cool drinks. It's good she didn't see him till today. Couldn't have handled the scene before this. An awful couple of weeks. It probably did show in performance. Should've covered it better, at least on camera. Of course every time a little control started to surface that redheaded nymphomaniac would come in wiggling her tail in front of another nose and . . . well, the old scummy feeling would come back. Lord if old Sister Marie-Louise knew anything about her life! She'd rise up so fast she'd topple the marble statue of the Blessed Virgin. Poor Sister Marie! She had tried so hard to teach them chastity in parochial school. Fitting all her girls out in those dreadful blue blouses and little blue skirts with those long ugly leggings. How shocked she was the time Wanda Sue Finnerty got herself knocked up. She was so funny, Wanda Sue. You had to laugh. "I swear—I swear, Sister! I wasn't . . . I didn't— never, no! It must have been—I don't know, divine . . . divine action, Sister, is the only thing I can think of. I swear. I SWEAR!" Sister Agnes and the Mother Superior were so furious, but poor Sister Marie-Louise! She was truly pained. She was a true believer. Took everything to heart. A good Catholic girl would never permit. . . . Keep your blouses buttoned to the tops, girls. We have nothing more cherishable than our virtues! Who was it said if you give him a child for the first six years, he'll make him a good Catholic for life?

And the hammer of guilt beat on her head with the weight of all the teachings of her youth.

She watched him return from the refreshment stand, moving around sitters and standers with his animal-like grace, concentrating casually on the liquid so as not to spill it. So assured, so unruffled, never out of control. He smiled briefly when he handed her the cup. "It's not very good."

They sipped and leaned against the trough, neither looking at anything in particular.

"Vanessa, it's important that you decide for yourself." He began deliberately looking over to Fifty-Third Street, where a screaming police car was trying to siren its way out of a traffic tieup. "I can't advise you. The other thing is I can't even be certain it's not a bluff on his part."

"What reason would he have to bluff?"

"Reasons that may have nothing to do with you. But that's not the important thing. You can only go on the assumption that he will actually carry through and fire you if you don't have the abortion."

"Do you realize I'm a Catholic?"

"Yes!"

"Does Mr. Chamberfield?"

"I don't think it matters to him."

And suddenly all the anxieties of the past few weeks forced through her body and up to the muscles of her face; a stream of tears welled over her lashes. Her voice was deep when it emerged as though she were speaking from a self yet buried. "I can't lose that job. Don't you see?" Phillip handed her a handkerchief, which she twisted in her fingers. "We need it now more than ever. Joey is so happy about the baby he's going to step up his visits to the doctor to be well faster. If I have the abortion I'll lose my husband. He would take it as a personal rejection. He was so happy. The baby means so much to him. What am I supposed to do?"

He circled his arm around her and drew her toward him. She dropped her head to his chest and sobbed.

Phillip noticed the fragrance of Vanessa's freshly washed hair. He spoke softly. "I wouldn't pretend to offer you any advice, Vanessa. You have to do what you believe is right, for yourself and your family. I think I know as well as any man can how important a child is for a woman. When I was married my wife and I tried to have one, but we couldn't. And my wife never got over it. It changed her."

Vanessa stopped crying and listened. Couldn't have a baby, she thought. If he was sterile, then the baby would have to be Joey's. Strange, he doesn't even seem aware of the possibility of its being his. Maybe that's why. Maybe he's sterile. That would be a little relief—at least the guilt would be eliminated. But the hope was short-lived.

Phillip continued. "I think she could have coped with the situation if the sterility had been mine, but after tests, rather extensive ones, we found that it was Jacqueline who was barren. And she just dried up as a person. She became bitter and selfish and she started letting it show in ugly ways. So I know. I know what the baby could mean to you. I wish I could help. If there were anything at all I could do—anything—I would. I'd hate to lose you on the show, but that's purely professional selfishness. Your happiness is more important than that. Think it over. Don't rush. Be sure whichever path you decide on you'll be able to walk down in the future."

She looked over the table, down the row of trees and past the gate to the street beyond. Phillip couldn't think of anything else to say. The smallness of the park became suddenly oppressive, and just as he was about to suggest they walk some more, Vanessa rose quickly. Without glancing back at him, she ran, very fast, away.

16.

The offices of *Inside-TV* magazine were anything but plush. In contrast to the glamorous TV world that the magazine gushily exposed, the rag's offices were on the eighth floor of a decaying building on Forty-Third Street just off Times Square. The quarters consisted of three large rooms subdivided into minIscule cubbyholes by movable metal screens and even after three years, it still smelled disagreeably of its former occupant, a rawhide purse manufacturer.

In one of the pigeonholes sat Brian Hocholtz, age twenty-six, a young man of unwavering journalistic ambitions. He wanted much, and he wanted it fast, and was not above cutting any corner he could to achieve his goals. After ten months of searching the upper echelons of the news media for openings, he had disdainfully accepted a reporting/writing position with *Inside-TV,* a monthly gossip sheet focusing on the behind-the-scenes life of daytime television. He hated the magazine, hated his job, and wrote his interviews of the reigning soap kings and queens under a pseudonym. But Brian never forgot his dreams. Network news was his goal and he religiously watched Cronkite, Rather, Mudd, Reasoner, Chancellor, took notes, and practiced speaking into a microphone in front of a mirror.

Brian was certain his break would come one day, and late Friday afternoon, he felt it was getting closer. "She'll do it, you say?" He was shouting into a phone because of the din of his fellow reporters and their typewriters.

"Sorry, Claire, I can hardly hear you." The phone receiver was sandwiched between his shoulder and masses of his black hair. One leg was on the desk, displaying an argyle sock under a pair of wide-cuffed "Great Gatsby" pants. "What time?"

He dropped the leg and reached for his jacket. "No problem! Don't let her disappear on me. Love ya, babe."

He slammed the receiver down, pushed the desk back against the screen, and squeezed past it into the hall. Fingering his long, Fu Manchu mustache, he poked his head into the largest pigeonhole at the end of the hall and flashed a triumphant smile at the baldheaded editor smoking a cigar. "It's all arranged, Gus. Five minutes, and I'll be interviewing Wilson Vulkner's stepdaughter!"

The thin man growled through the cigar. "Make it juicy and come straight back. I want a rewrite on the Captain Kangaroo story."

Gaye was late by a half hour. She breezed into Claire's office, tossed her mane of red hair over her shoulder, and held out her hand to the young reporter. "I'm so sorry I'm late. You must be Mr. Hocholtz."

"Please call me Brian. The only Mr. Hocholtz I know is my father."

She laughed with the radiance customary to the role she was playing and turned to Claire, who was perched on her desk. "Claire, would you mind if we stayed here for the interview?"

"Not at all, Gaye. Would you like me to leave?"

"No. You can play censor. Do you mind, Brian?" She flashed him a warm smile.

"Of course not." The young man slipped off his jacket and laid it on one end of the couch. He sat next to it with a small tape recorder in his lap. "Don't mind this. We'll just switch it on and forget it." He placed the small cassette machine on the couch between them and held the microphone up. "Shall we begin?"

"What kind of things can possibly interest your readers?"

"They're not *my* readers. They're *Inside-TV* readers. Let's get that straight. They watch the soaps and like to know about the intimate lives of the daytime stars."

"Am I a star?" she kidded in wide-eyed amazement. "Claire, am I a star? You didn't tell me I was a star."

"Anyone on TV more than once is a star," said the older woman dryly.

"Well, golly jeepers! Then I must be a star! Brian, do you think I'm a star?"

"I think you are the most dazzling star I've ever interviewed."

"Aren't you sweet. How old are you, anyway?"

"Twenty-six."

"And have you been a reporter for *Inside-TV* long?"

"About a year and a half—which is about eighteen months too long."

"Why? Don't you like to interview soap-opera stars?"

"I find most of them very dull!"

"What would you rather be doing?"

"Hey, I'm supposed to be interviewing you, remember?"

"I know. But I can't talk with someone I don't know anything about."

"Well, in that case . . . I want to be a news reporter. Real news, you know? Network news."

"I see. Well, look I'll try to make my interview positively scintillating for you, so maybe you can have a coup or whatever it is. What do you want to know about my sex life?"

"Hey, wait a minute." He laughed. "This is a ladies' magazine. We have to keep it clean."

"Oh, really? Ladies like to hear about sex, don't they, Claire?"

"All the ones I know do."

"Do you want to know if I've ever slept with my stepfather?"

Claire broke in. "Easy, Gaye."

Brian smirked. "Personally I'd love to, but I

couldn't publish it. Your father's very powerful, you know."

"Well, I haven't slept with him. I find him repulsive as a father and a man. There! That should grab a reader or two."

"That's off the record, Brian," Claire said.

"You know what happened to me the other day? Blew my mind! I was on my way to the studio, walking. Cut through the park because it was early and there weren't too many people out. I was into my own little fantasy world. And all of a sudden this old biddy, must have been about sixty-five, in a little pillbox hat and all, comes rushing up to me, and screams: 'Daphne! You should be ashamed of yourself! Going after Valerie's boyfriend like that! The poor girl is going blind and here you are making her more miserable by taking Charles away from her. You should be ashamed of yourself. You're nothing but a cheap hussy!' "

Brian roared with laughter. "What did you say?"

"She pestered me halfway through the park, so I finally told her, 'Fuck off you crazy old cunt!' "

Claire roared.

Gaye tossed her curls angrily. "Who the hell did she think she was?"

Claire said, "It happens to a lot of the people on the soaps."

Brian unbuttoned a few shirt buttons. "Don't you have an air conditioner in here?"

"Being repaired. Sorry. It *is* kind of drippy in here."

Gaye checked out the flash of chest that Brian was casually displaying. "I've got an idea. The studio is cool and it's empty now. Why don't we go down there to finish this silly thing? I've got a little dope if you'd like some, Brian."

He hit the series of buttons on his recorder, grinning at her. "I'll erase that last statement, luv. I never know who listens to these tapes once I take them back to the office."

Gaye jumped up playfully. "Do you really think Wilson Vulkner would allow his stepdaughter to be busted? Not on your sweet ass!" She swung her purse softly into his stomach and sashayed to the door.

The studio was delightfully cool, and as deserted as an

abandoned airplane hanger. Even the worklights were out. Gaye led the parade through the hall door. "Look! We have the entire place to ourselves."

Claire peered into the dimness. "Little dark, wouldn't you say?"

"I'll find a light switch." Brian started searching the wall near the door.

But the redhead stopped him. "Who needs light when you have a blazing star in your midst? Follow me."

Half-groping, hanging onto each other's sleeves, the trio headed for a series of dim shapes that loomed ahead of them. Brian felt an arm touch his waist, the fingers running lightly on the skin under his shirt. When he reached out to grab the figure closer, Gaye came into his arms, pushed him away and moved ahead.

"What's that?" Brian whispered in his Boris Karloff voice.

"That, my dear sir," said Gaye, "is the living room of Auntie's Chicago apartment. And beside it is her master bedroom. How thoughtful of the crew to have set it up for us."

"Jesus, it's darker than some dyke bars I've been in," groaned Claire good-naturedly.

"Voilà!" sang out Gaye, followed by a thud. "I've calculated correctly. I've just stumbled over the couch. Do you have a lighter, Brian?"

The flash of flame lit the immediate area of the elegantly furnished set. "Hey, there's a candelabra on the buffet."

"Don't think you should—?" Claire warned.

"Oh, props'll have more candles," Gaye said lightly.

One by one, Brian lit the candles until their half of the living-room area was bathed in the warm glow of flickering light. "That makes it halfway livable."

Claire plopped into an easy chair and threw her sturdy legs up onto an ottoman. "I could get accustomed to living in a place like this. Got to hand it to Searing. The son of a bitch has taste."

Gaye made for the couch. "That's not all he has, my dear."

"Sounds like I should start my recorder about now," joked Brian, as he switched it on and set it on the floor.

Gaye poked around her purse. "Look, I'm bored with interviews. Who gives a damn whether people know who I am? I know who I am. That's enough." She drew out a neatly rolled joint and lit up, inhaled, and passed it to Brian, who had settled himself next to her on the couch.

He pulled a toke and studied her eyes, sparkling in the candle light. "And who *are* you?"

"My mother named me Gaye. And I am."

Claire snorted. "Better explain, dearie. Those of us beneath you are a little dense."

"Gaye is gay. Simple as that. I'm just a simple little rich girl who likes to have fun."

"You and Catherine the Great." Claire sucked in the smoke from her joint.

"She knew how to have fun, all right." Gaye squirmed around and laid her head in the reporter's lap, looking up at him seductively as she took a lungful of smoke. She pressed the joint between his lips and held it as he inhaled. "They say, Brian, that Catherine the Great died while she was being humped by a horse. Do you believe that?"

He lowered his arm so it fell across her bare midriff. He held the joint out in Claire's direction. "If so, she must have been one hell of a woman." He was becoming aroused.

Claire observed the seduction with an interested half-smile. "Nice way to conduct an interview, eh, Brian?"

"I'm sure Brian can invent something more exciting about me than I could ever tell him. No?" Gaye ran her forefinger across his lower lip.

"I'm not so sure of that any more." He slid his hand up under her blouse.

She threw her arms over her head and arched her back. "It's so nice to meet a pleasant young man. I just don't know a soul in this dreadful city."

"Poor little rich girl." Claire came over with the last of the joint and sat at the end of the couch. She lifted Gaye's legs and placed them on her lap. "One could almost feel sorry for you if you weren't so gorgeous."

Gaye took a deep pull and held it in before she exhaled. She pulled Brian's head down for a long, lingering kiss. Claire stroked the actress's bare feet as she watched the kiss.

Gaye broke for air. "You know what I've wanted to do ever since I started on this damn soap opera? Fuck somebody on the set."

"With the cameras on?" Brian massaged her breasts underneath her light-striped tee shirt.

"Umm, yeah. But since we don't have any television around, let's do the next best thing—come on, I'll play director and you two have to do exactly what I say." She disentangled herself from them and shot off the couch. "All right, both of you, up on your feet! We have a show to do and damned little time!" She imitated Phillip perfectly.

They rose and stood before her, both fascinated to the cores of their libidos. She barked a command. "You, grab the lights!"

Brian marched to the candelabra and picked it up. He saluted smartly. Gaye whirled to Claire. "And you, get yourself into the bedroom set!" Claire turned toward the darkened portion of the studio. "Young man, lead the way."

With Brian holding the candles aloft, his cassette recorder humming under his arm, the three moved into the wood-paneled bedroom set, dwarfed by the massive sound stage that housed it. Half the room was taken up by a large, canopied bed in which the wealthy aunt was supposed to rest in the afternoon.

"Turn down the covers and put the lights on the bedstand." They followed her orders and stood at attention when their duties were done.

"Now, you miserable clowns. Strip!"

Claire and Brian looked at each other hesitantly.

The older woman broke the tense silence. "What if someone comes in?"

Gaye exploded. "I'm the director! You do exactly what I say or I'm leaving!" But then she added more softly, "No one's around. And if somebody comes in, we'll just blow out the candles." She barked again. "Now strip!"

Claire reached for the buttons on her blouse, staring directly into Gaye's eyes. Brian followed suit. He removed his shirt, stooped to pull off his shoes and socks. He glanced over at Claire, whose breasts had just come into view. They were small, and sagged a little, with large brown nipples. Brian unbuckled his belt as Claire unfastened her skirt. She dropped it to the floor, and stood awkwardly in just her panties. The reporter, proud of the tan he had acquired over the summer, skinned off his trousers and shorts with one quick movement. Then Claire slipped hers off too.

Gaye took the candelabra from the small table and sauntered measuredly around them, studying their nudity. She finished her circle. "Well, if you two aren't the sorriest excuse for actors I've ever seen." She sighed dramatically and put the candles back down. "Well, you'll have to do. This show has to get on." She held out her arms, forming a T with her body. "Now, disrobe your director!"

They didn't need a second command. With deft fingers, they attacked Gaye's clothing. Brian started at the top, peeling off the thin tee shirt, freeing the full breasts, while Claire knelt and unzipped the slacks, shucking them down over her hips and pulling down the French-style panties. They stood back to admire their handiwork. Gaye knew that her body was in superb form. She paraded in a wide arc before them. Her breasts swayed and the small triangle of dark-red hair between her legs glistened.

Claire spoke out of the side of her mouth. "Well, at least we know our director is a natural redhead."

Brian laughed softly, but the tumescence below his waist belied his attempt at nonchalance.

"Don't speak until spoken to! On your knees!" They hesitated again. "Do as I say!"

They dropped to their knees on the thick Persian rug which covered the concrete studio floor. Gaye glared down at them, grinning. "Now crawl, like the dogs you are!"

Brian started circling her feet in imitation of an excited Saint Bernard. Claire was more like a small, well-bred poodle. She followed the wiggling, bare tail of the young man.

"And now bark!" Gaye grabbed the recorder off the bed, where Brian had placed it, and using the long leather strap, started to whip them on their buttocks. They passed in front of her, barking and howling like two unhappy canines. But their howls turned to laughter.

Gaye giggled so hard she fell onto the bed. "This is idiotic." She rolled over and looked down at the two on the floor. She reached out and pulled Brian to a standing position by his rock-hard member. He stood at the edge of the bed, jutting out over her face. She teasingly licked the length of it and smiled over at Claire. "Come on up here and let's improvise."

Claire crawled on the bed and buried her face as Gaye wrapped her legs around the casting director's head. The redheaded actress draped her long hair over the end of Brian's projectile and raised her mouth to its head.

If an unsuspecting technician had at that moment taken a short cut to the outside street, he would have witnessed the most unusual performance ever played out in RBI's Studio 23. There in the dimness of the austere studio, a studio that had given birth to some of the finest soap operas RBI had ever offered, three nude and writhing bodies, glowing in their sweat from the light of a single candle, cavorted in acrobatic display.

The exhausted young reporter went home after dropping Gaye off in a cab at her Fifth Avenue apartment. The office of *Inside-TV* would have closed hours ago. Screw Captain Kangaroo! He showered and slipped on a silk kimono, then listened to a playback of the interview on his recorder. It was all there—five minutes or so of stupid repartee, then the beginning of their little sex games. Some of it was muffled and reverberated badly, but it was more than clear enough to comprehend. The tape had run out just as the two women were working him up for a second foray.

He listened to its entirety before he slipped the small cassette out of the recorder, labeled it, and hid it in the back of a desk drawer. He didn't know just what he might do with such a splendid piece of reportage. *Inside-TV* wouldn't get it; that was for sure. But he knew that somehow, someway, Gaye Vulkner was going to be his passport to the top.

Elliot let himself into his apartment door after a drinking-work session at the St. Regis Bar. He was delighted because he had finally managed to prove that schmuck VP of sales to be a budding ignoramus as far as programing was concerned. "He can stick to his department and leave the hell off of mine!" Elliot muttered. "From now on maybe the son of a bitch will know better than to

225

badmouth one of my shows just because he doesn't know how to sell it!" He weaved as he entered, but as soon as he reached the bedroom he sobered. He sobered and he panicked. The attaché case he was holding dropped from his fingers and thudded to the carpet. Then all of a sudden he made a stumbling dash for the phone. He dialed. It rang. . . . "Rosalyann?"

"No, but I'll get her. Is this Elliot?"

"Yes, Dorothy, would you put her on quick, please?"

An interminable amount of time passed before she got around to picking the goddamn thing up. "Jesus, Rosalynann!"

"I'm sorry, dear, I was washing my hair."

"Thumper's having puppies."

"Really! That's wonderful!"

"Yeah, all over the bed. She even pulled down the covers to make herself a cozy little place. But what the hell do I do?"

"Why, is she having trouble?"

"How do I know if she's having trouble? I can't converse with her."

"Is she squealing or anything?"

"I don't know, Rosalynann. All kinds of weird sounds are coming out of there. She won't die in childbirth or anything, will she?"

"Oh, Elliot!"

"Look, you'd better come over right away."

"My hair's full of shampoo."

"Rosalynann, for Christ's sake! Thumper's having puppies! Don't you care? She's our dog. I don't know what to do if she has trouble."

"You're such a baby. All right, I'll come."

"Hurry up, will you? My heart's pounding like a tom-tom."

Forty-five minutes later Rosalynann let herself in with her own key. Her head was wrapped in a Turkish towel and she carried a portable hairdryer. "Elliot?"

"In the bedroom!"

She went on back. "Poor little Thumper. Poor little Mama Thumper." Elliot grinned sheepishly as though he himself were the proud father, the one responsible for the litter. Five had come out. Five of the tiniest, messiest, cutest, furry little dachshunds that had ever been born into the heart of Elliot Chamberfield. The mother was licking off the latest arrival and waiting patiently for the next.

"They're adorable," Rosalynann said. "You see, there's no problem."

"I guess we'll have to sleep on the floor tonight."

"I wasn't planning on staying tonight, Elliot."

"You're not going to leave me with all this, are you?"

"I didn't bring any clothes with me."

"So you'll go back to your place in the morning. Jesus, Rosalynann, don't you even care about our dog?"

But there were complications. Elliot had changed out of his suit and Rosalynann was on the living-room floor under the hairdryer (Elliot was afraid the humming of the machine might make the dogs uneasy), when Thumper began shrieking.

Elliot heard the commotion and rushed in to get his secretary. A newborn was coming out awkwardly. The shoulder was emerging first and the head was twisted back in the womb. Thumper was screaming her head off.

"Do something, quick! She might die!" Elliot had panicked again. "Easy, Thumper, take it easy, girl. Do something, Rosalynann, please!"

"Hold her. Don't let her squirm."

"I can't." He tried to hold her down.

"Be careful, she might snap. She's in a lot of pain."

Elliot finally secured hold of her mouth and squeezed his free hand down onto her chest. "My Thumper wouldn't snap at me. Would you, baby? Would you, Thump?"

As soon as Elliot had pinioned the animal down, Rosalynann tried to work the new puppy out. It took all the strength each of them could muster to keep Thumper from thrashing herself to death. The pain must have been excruciating. "Be awfully careful, Elliot. I once saw a cow come out like this on my uncle's farm and it moved around so much the calf kicked the cow's stomach out and the mother bled to death in minutes."

"Oh, my God!"

Rosalynann finally managed to push the shoulder back in and twist the tiny head into position so it would present itself to the world first.

Elliot kept turning his head so as not to have to watch

227

the details. Finally the little one was pulled out, but it was dead.

"Poor thing, I probably broke its neck."

"Oh, God!"

"Hold Thumper while I get this one away. I don't think she should be allowed to see it."

"What are you going to do?"

"I'm going to wrap it in newspaper and drop it down the incinerator."

He was shocked. "You're not! Rosalynann, that's hideous."

"Well, what would you like me to do with it. Bury it in the flowerpot?" She carted the stillborn away.

The seventh and final one came out an hour later with no problems whatever. Thumper licked clean the placenta as she had for the others born earlier. Elliot washed his hands repeatedly, though he had hardly come into contact with the messy part of the operation.

Rosalynann's annoyance turned to amusement when she saw he was serious about sleeping on the floor. She spread sheets and a clean blanket, since the air conditioner had a tendency to chill at night. They wrapped their arms around each other and lay together as lovers.

"Elliot, honey, when are we going to get married? You haven't brought the subject up for months."

He tried to pretend he was asleep. It was never a question he had much interest in answering.

But she poked him. "Elliot!"

"I don't know, Rosalynann. It's a hard decision for me to make. Aren't we practically married now?"

"No. I'm tied to you, but you're free to do whatever you want, and I'm almost thirty years old."

"You think I cut out on you?"

"How do I know what you do when I'm not here?" She released herself from his arms and turned away, letting him face her back.

Elliot propped his head on his hand and leaned sideways on his elbow. "After two years of being together, do you really think I'm sleeping with other girls?" It was actually a suggestion that flattered him.

"How do I know? Anyway, that's not all there is to it."

"You sure don't trust me very much, do you? I love you, Rosalynann, I really do."

228

"Then why do you refuse to marry me? I can't keep this sort of thing up forever."

"What sort of thing?"

"Being 'practically' married. If my father knew he'd come after you with a shotgun. Our family's very old-fashioned, you know."

"I know. I just need a little time, that's all. I've got so much other pressure on my head right now that to have to decide about something as important as marriage—it's just not the right time."

"Yes, and when will the right time be?"

"Soon. Okay, Rosalynann? Soon. I promise."

17.

There is a tendency among people in command situations to disengage themselves from their battles from time to time, to step back from the trees for a view of the forest, so to speak.

When Bill Peters rejoined the show, and as the various story lines initiated by Maude O'Keefe began to mesh with what could be considered a normal and acceptable level of soap-opera complexity, Phillip found himself doing just that. And basically what he saw was that a strong parallel had begun to develop between the roles the performers were playing and the machinations of their daily lives. The seduction game between Daphne and Charles appeared to have extended itself outside of the boundaries of the show. Whether Gaye and Bill were actually carrying on a romance was difficult to tell, but their whispered conversations and quick, meaningful glances indicated much more than a solid working relationship. They never left the studio together, of course, since Bill's wife generally called for him in the afternoons. Besides, Gaye hardly confined her attentions to the male actor. She had succeeded in making herself popular with most of the males and several of the females on the show, both in front and behind the cameras and in a much too obvious way for Phillip. She seemed to slither around the set like a delicious serpent, rubbing against every available body in sight, particularly when the producer was on hand to notice. Not that there was any jealousy on his part, try as she might to make him feel it. He was purely and simply annoyed at her lack of professional decorum, but he kept his thoughts to himself, since Gaye was doing so beautifully on screen.

Then there was Vanessa. As the cataracts that Maude had invented steadily clouded Valerie's vision, Vanessa became increasingly distraught. On-camera it could still appear like a brilliant piece of acting, but, unfortunately, much too powerful for soap opera. To Phillip, who was aware of the psychological torment the girl herself was going through, her appearance was devastating.

And it was no less so to Chamberfield, who phoned Phillip every other day to know what her decision would be. But Phillip kept his word, and refused to push her. He waited, certain she would talk to him in time.

* * *

It was late Friday afternoon, after Vanessa's husband was safely off to Woodstock for a weekend at his brother's cabin, that Vanessa checked into Mount Sinai Hospital on upper Fifth Avenue. She filled out some forms at the desk and was assigned to one of the basement rooms. Three other women were already bedded. They watched her slip out of her street clothes and into a hospital smock, but except for a soft "hello" from the black girl near the door, no one ventured any greetings. She crawled between the white institutional sheets.

A nurse's aide came in with a hospital questionnaire on a clipboard. "Vanessa Langley?" she asked.

"I'm Vanessa Langley."

"You're in for an abortion, aren't you?"

The woman's tone was so matter-of-fact it made Vanessa shiver. She nodded, eying the women in the other beds.

"Ain't no need to be ashamed in here, honey. Everybody in this room's in for an abortion." She checked her sheet. "I got a couple questions to ask you here. First of all, when were you born?"

231

After the aide left, the woman assigned to the bed next to Vanessa's caught her attention. Vanessa figured she was about forty. "Is this your first time?"

Vanessa nodded.

"Don't worry too much about it. I've had one before. We're lucky to be here."

"Lucky?"

"I had my first one in a motel room before the law was changed. It cost me seven hundred dollars and nearly killed me. The guy who did it wasn't even a practicing doctor." The heavy blonde woman wagged her head and got up to go to the toilet. She returned in a few minutes and sat on the edge of her bed, eager to pursue the conversation and oblivious of Vanessa's desire not to. "My husband and I just don't want children and somehow birth control doesn't work for me. How far gone are you?"

"What?" asked Vanessa.

"How many weeks?"

She shrugged. "About six or seven. I'm not sure."

"Oh, then they'll just do a suction job on you."

"A what?"

"Vacuum aspiration. It's nothing. They just suck it right out. You hardly feel a thing."

Vanessa pulled the sheets up around her chin tightly. "No, I'm having a D and C."

The woman lit a cigarette and continued. "I'm getting vacuumed." She pointed to the black woman near the door. "That woman over there's going to have a D and C too. She and her husband have three children and can't afford a fourth."

The woman who had been observing Vanessa from the far side of the room broke in. "Excuse me, aren't you on television?"

"Television!" exclaimed the blonde woman, looking surprised.

"You're on *Affair Of The Heart*, aren't you?" asked the woman from across the way.

"I thought I'd seen you before!" said the blonde. The black woman sat up too.

Vanessa thought to deny it, but decided they'd only press her until they got the truth. She admitted to playing Valerie, and bore the questioning stoically. It even helped. For a little while she managed to forget where she was—

232

the drabness of the room, the efficient politeness of the staff, and what was going to happen to her in the morning.

* * *

The phone was ringing. He took a towel, gave himself a quick rub, and padded into the bedroom. "Hello."

"Phillip?"

He recognized the voice instantly. "Yes. . . ."

"This is Jacqueline."

"Hang on a second. I just stepped out of the shower." He placed the receiver on the unmade bed and finished drying off. He slipped into a robe, lit cigarette number one, and retrieved the receiver. "There, sorry. What's on your mind, Jacqueline?"

"I thought I'd try you at home, since I haven't had much luck at your office." She attempted to make it come out offhand. "I'm in town with Papa."

"How is he?"

"That's one of the reasons I called."

"He's not ill, is he?"

"No, nothing like that. He wants me to talk to you about something." She paused. He waited. "Phillip, you know how much I hate talking on the phone. Could we meet some place for a late breakfast? That is, if you don't have company or plans."

There was something in her voice, something he hadn't heard in quite a while. An honest, direct, plaintiveness. "Well, I don't—"

"We could make it just coffee, if you'd prefer."

Didn't he owe her that much? "All right, are you at your father's now?"

"Yes."

"Okay, make it Martell's on—"

"I remember."

Of course she would. He had inadvertently picked one of their former haunts. Or had it been inadvertent? "Give me an hour."

"Thank you, Phillip."

The restaurant had not yet moved into its daytime busyness. Phillip took a table with a clear view of the window, so he could peer out over the Saturday-morning awakenings of the upper East Side. Coffee arrived just as the familiar gray Rolls-Royce glided up to the front door. The chauffeur, in matching livery, hopped out and circled around to open the curbside door. The long elegant legs preceded the body of his former wife. She was wearing a light-beige long-sleeved wraparound dress. Her face was hidden beneath a wide-brimmed hat and behind a pair of oversized sunglasses.

Inside, she spotted him immediately and wove her way through the narrow passages between the empty tables. Then she removed her glasses. Her eyes were bright and shiny. "Hello, Phillip." She offered a hand to be squeezed, a cheek to be kissed, and settled into the chair.

"You're looking well."

"You are, too. But then men grow older more gracefully than we do. Something I'll never become reconciled to, I'm afraid. I had my hair cut at Sassoon's. Do you like it?" She took off her hat and laid it on the windowsill.

"Yes, I do. Shorter, isn't it?"

"About four inches. I got tired of fooling with it in this heat."

"I've ordered coffee for you. Would you like anything else?"

"No, thanks. I'm still not much of a breakfast eater."

"How's Papa Goodhart? Still refusing to slow down?"

"I think he gets more done every year. I'm afraid he'll drop dead one day at the office and that'll be it."

"I hope you're not trying to talk him into retiring."

"Why not?" She checked the sharpness of her retort. "The company can run itself. He just doesn't want to let go of any control, that's all."

"If he does, he's dead. Retirement is not his style. Like my father . . . worked hard all of his life, retired, and he fell apart. Didn't know what to do with his free time and just gave up living."

The waitress brought Jacqueline's coffee, giving her time to push away the feelings of jealousy Phillip's relationship with her father always stirred in her. She sipped slowly and looked up over the rim. She waited until he had tasted his eggs and nodded his approval to the waitress. "So how's life on your soap opera?"

He shrugged noncommittally. "National Nielsens this week showed a slight upward swing."

"Bravo, another victory for the Searing biographers."

He chewed and swallowed before responding. "Could be."

"Papa wanted me to tell you that you could come back to Goodhart Soaps anytime you want to."

Phillip didn't look up.

"Of course, you know you could have your old executive producership back if you wanted. But there is something else he wants to talk with you about. Something new."

This time he did look up.

"You gave him a suggestion last year that he's decided to implement. He's planning to start a film-production division, films for the family market, perhaps even series for TV. He's willing to commit ten million dollars to it initially and he wants you to head it."

"Presidency?"

"I would think so. You'll have to discuss the details with him, but I was given to understand you'd have complete autonomy."

Phillip's mind raced. Why was Goodhart making the offer? Was it sincere? Or was it only to bring him back into the family?

Jacqueline checked the roughness on the tip of a fingernail with the tip of her tongue. "You can't be too happy about being dropped back to a mere producer. Are you interested?"

"I'll have to talk to him first."

She nodded and motioned to the waitress for more coffee.

There was something more than the offer, he felt. Something in the manner she presented it. "How's everything with Jacqueline, Jacqueline?"

It was her turn to shrug with that whisper of a smile she used to use so effectively. "I was out on the coast with Papa a few weeks ago, but most of the time I spend in Grosse Point." She gazed out of the window and revolved some grains of sugar on the soft tips of her fingers. "I miss you, Phillip. There are times I wake up in the morning and you're not there and I hate you for not being there. Then there are times when I hate myself for not having understood you more." Her voice dropped. She seemed shaken. "I want you back, Phillip. I need you."

So that was it, and an offer of a presidency to sweeten the package—not to twist arms, but to encourage him to think favorably. It wasn't Goodhart's fault. He would like Phillip back in the company as a son-in-law or not, but to allow his daughter to make the bid this way. Sorry, Papa, my personal life's not for sale—not for sale under any conditions.

They were so much alike, the Goodharts. Unable to deal with their personal lives on any other level but buying and selling. Why not? It had gotten them everything they had always wanted before. But now it was different. He was different, and even though he could argue with himself that perhaps he had been bought when he was a dewy-eyed kid from Stanford, he also knew that he had loved the girl then. But now things were different. What they'd had together was over for him.

But there was something else burning in the back of his mind. He would play fair with them both. But that didn't mean he couldn't use the offer to his own advantage.

Her monologue had run its course. She was struggling to regain her composure, and waiting for him to say something. He began slowly, treading carefully on the thin ice of her emotions. "Jacqueline . . . I understand. I understand your need. But we've both changed, grown, matured, or whatever you want to label it. We're each on a different path now and unless our paths happen to come together again naturally—not just because one of us wants them to—it can only lead to more frustration for both of us. We can't recapture what we had before and we can't go on hoping we can start again. I know it's painful. I know it's lonely."

"So you don't want me back."

"I'm sorry," he said as gently as he could.

"But you promise to speak to Papa about the offer? You will do that, won't you? Or has that path also veered in another direction?"

"I'll talk to Papa."

"It's just that he thinks so much of you. I don't want you to hurt him, too, Phillip."

"Jacqueline, I don't intentionally hurt anyone. But people shouldn't lay expectations on me. I can only do what I feel is right. I hope you understand."

236

The rustic interior of the restaurant was filling up with the lunch crowd.

"I guess that's it," she said. "No hopes for the future and all that rot?"

"Look dear. . . ."

She interrupted his attempt to mollify her. "Oh, don't coddle me, Phillip. For Christ's sake, damn it, don't coddle me."

She reached for her hat, pulled it low over the top half of her face, and turned to go.

"I'll speak with your father later, as I promised." But she was already hurrying through the aisles.

Phillip watched her step out into the harsh glare of the midday sun and walk briskly to the gray limousine. She opened the rear door by herself, slid in, and slammed it.

The Rolls pulled away and Phillip signaled for the check.

* * *

Vanessa closed the cab door and gingerly walked up the four steps into the building. Down the hall and up the one flight of stairs, stopping every second or third one and clutching the banister for support.

Her hand trembled as she wiggled the key into the lock. Something was wrong. It turned the opposite way. She found the silver-plated key to unlock the police bar. But that lock seemed jammed. She forced her weight against the door.

"Ness? That you?"

"Joey!" My god, he's home!

The door was yanked open and there he was, staring at her. "Jesus, Ness, what's happened to you, baby? Are you all right?" He bolted the door and led her down the hall. "It was raining up at Woodstock, so I came back to my woman. What's the matter? Sit down. You're pale as a sheet."

She dropped on the couch and closed her eyes.

"Can I get you something? Glass of water?"

"I lost the baby." She closed her eyes to avoid looking at him. "I started hemorrhaging Friday night and by the time I got to the hospital I'd lost it."

"Oh, my god, Ness. Why didn't you call me?"

"It happened so fast I—" But she was too weak and

237

sleepy from the lingering effects of the shot the nurse had given her to make up stories.

Joe put her to bed and brought in some warm milk. She drank half of it before settling back and falling into a deep, drugged sleep.

Night had fallen when the ringing of the phone beside the bed woke her and she groped for it in the darkness. Somewhere in the dreamy distance she could hear her husband's footsteps approaching.

"Hello, Vanessa. It's Phillip Searing."

"Phillip. . . ."

"I'm sorry to disturb you on Sunday but I wanted to tell you not to bother to learn scene four. Maude is changing it. You'll get new lines tomorrow morning. Don't worry. It won't be much. It's a hospital scene."

"Hospital," she repeated vaguely, the sleepiness muddling her perceptions. "It's over now. It's all over, Phillip."

"What do you—oh, I understand," he said. "You had the abortion."

"Yes." She let her head lean groggily on the receiver. "Abortion. . . ."

"You poor thing. You sound tired."

"I'm tired. I'm so tired. I have to hang up, Phillip."

"Yes, of course. Get some rest. I'll see you tomorrow."

"Good night, Phillip," she said slurringly. Then she hung up.

But before she could fall asleep again the ceiling light came on, shocking her out of the darkness. Joey stood over her anxiously. "What did you mean—*abortion?*"

"What?" she murmured, shielding her eyes from the glare.

"I heard what you said on the phone. What did you mean about an *abortion?* Did you have an abortion?" His eyes were strained with disbelief and he was trembling.

"No, I—"

"Did you have an abortion, Vanessa? Answer me!"

She tried to clear her mind, but it remained foggy and diffused. She let herself sink back down into the bed. "I'm so tired. Please let me sleep."

"You did, didn't you?" he cried. "It wasn't a miscarriage. You did it on purpose!"

"Please!"

"You killed it, Vanessa! Our baby!"

"Oh, God, I don't feel well."

She tried to twist toward the wall, but Joey sat on the edge of the bed and gripped her tightly. "Answer me! You did it on purpose, didn't you?"

"Yes," she moaned.

"Why? Why, Vanessa?"

She closed her eyes and tried to shrug him away. "I'm so tired, Phillip. Please, we'll talk about it later."

Joey stiffened. "Phillip! I'm not Phillip!" And all of a sudden her husband made the connection. He pulled away from her. "Oh, my God," he said, shuddering. "Oh, my God, Ness!"

But she was moving too fast toward sleep to hear.

* * *

Phillip replaced the receiver on the hook and wandered out onto the terrace. He was relieved that Vanessa's decision had been made, not only for the show but for her sake as well. Agonizing as it must have been to bring herself to it, at least now she could begin to live again.

And then there was Papa Goodhart. Why not? There was no harm in hearing out his proposal, especially if RBI got to know about it. It well might help him solidify his position there.

He placed his call. "Julian, this is Phillip Searing. May I speak to Mr. Goodhart?"

"One moment, sir, I'll see if he's in."

There was a short pause, a click, and then Franklin Goodhart came on the line. "Hello, Phillip, I've been waiting for your call."

"How are you, sir?"

"Fine, son, fine. I'm anxious as hell to talk to you. When can we get together?"

"You're referring to the proposition Jacqueline spoke of?"

"Yes, of course."

"There's something I'd like you to do before we meet, sir, if you don't mind. It's just a formality, but I think it's necessary. I'd like you to call Russell Keel and let him know we're opening discussions. It's something RBI asks of its executives, that we let them know when we're being approached from the outside. That way we'll be keeping everything aboveboard with them."

"Understood, Phillip. And a damn fine formality it is. I ought to initiate a code like that myself. I lose so damn many executives that way. They're gone before I even know they've been approached. I'll make the call to whomever you like. What's his name—Chamberfield is your superior, isn't he?"

"Technically yes, sir, but he's out on the West Coast until Wednesday. I suggest you call Russell Keel on Monday morning."

"Certainly. I know Russ well. I don't want him thinking I'm sneaking behind his back. We do a hell of a lot of business with RBI. Can't strain those relations."

"Good, he's usually reachable between ten and ten-thirty fairly comfortably. After that he's in staff meetings."

"Fine, I'll call you in the morning after I've spoken to him and we can set up our meeting."

They exchanged a few pleasantries and rang off. Phillip stretched out on a chaise. It was a little cooler now that the sun had gone.

The plan was in effect. Goodhart would inform Keel that he was going to try to talk Phillip into returning to his company. That call would be completed hopefully by about ten-thirty. Keel would say something like, "Of course we can't keep Phillip against his wishes, but we'd hate to lose such a man." Or some such nonsense. Then, as soon as he hung up, the network president would turn the whole affair over to Elliot.

Therein lay the danger. Were Chamberfield there, he might well tell Keel that the show was doing well and Barry Friedman working out as daytime head, so "in all good conscience it wouldn't be right to pressure Phillip into staying with RBI." Thereby relieving himself of his rival in one shot. But, and this was where the plan depended upon exact timing, since Chamberfield was on the coast, and the three-hour difference in time would make it only 7:30 A.M. in Hollywood, Keel would wait until at least noon, New York time, before calling. That left an hour and a half for Phillip to get through to Keel himself. He would tell him personally about the Goodhart offer and give him ample time to commit himself verbally to returning Phillip to his former position. Either that or Keel would wish him good luck with Goodhart, indicating he wouldn't mind being rid of Phillip himself. But Phillip was counting on the former, that Keel would go out on a limb to keep him. Elliot, in short, would be checkmated from firing Phillip on anything less than a monumental error.

The plan was complicated and depended upon all parties acting in their habitual manner. But that was his old game: know your opponent, find his weaknesses, and then attack.

He switched on the terrace lights and ripped into Thursday's script with relish.

18.

Shortly before 5:00 A.M., Vanessa woke up. She lay under the twisted sheet, listening to the clatter of garbage cans and the whine of the Sanitation Department's hydraulic trucks. She buried her head under two pillows to muffle the sounds and shut out the glare of the ceiling light that had been left burning.

And then she remembered. The sickening, tightening, knot of emptiness grew in her stomach until she felt she would vomit. "Joe," she called out. "Joey, are you there?" Her head throbbed with the drugged pounding of artificially induced sleep until she couldn't stand to stay in bed any longer.

She toured the apartment.

His guitar was leaning against the wall, next to the brushes he'd used to paint over JOEY'S HOUSE. A pair of socks was draped over the radiator cover and one tennis shoe peeked out from the floor apron of the couch.

The fluorescent light for the plants in the window came on automatically, providing instant daylight for the room. The plants needed watering.

In the kitchen, the sink still contained the plate of cookie crumbs, the pan he'd heated the milk in, and a former peanut-butter jar turned drinking glass with a thin milky detergent film inside. She put on the coffeepot to heat some water. She had two hours before she had to report for rehearsal. Two hours to fill.

Where was he? His brother's house? She should phone Woodstock and make sure. No, too early. She'd call just before leaving for the studio.

She'd call—and say what? Maybe Joey had had a right to that baby. What if she'd given up the baby to keep the job so Joe could continue with his analyst, when all the cure he would have needed was the baby itself. But suppose she had given up the job to keep the baby, and then sometime in the future, after he had grown to love it, care for it, need it, it turned out that it wasn't his, after all. What then? Wouldn't that destroy him totally?

Sure, it was painful for him. Of course he must be suffering, but how about her? Didn't her torment at having a baby-to-be scraped out of her womb, no matter whose it was, didn't that count for something?

But she called and there was no answer. NO AN-SWER! He should be there at six-thirty in the morning. All of them should. There had been no doubt in her mind that he would be there. And where was his brother? She hung up and redialed on the chance she'd made a mistake, but the second time around there was still no response. And then she became very frightened.

* * *

She dragged herself through the rehearsal, trying desperately to keep her mind on the directions, but lines breezed in and out of her memory and she had to be reminded twice where to stand for the teaser.

At every break she tried the Woodstock number and immediately after that her answering service. Nothing!

It was obvious to everyone that something was seriously wrong with her, but they all figured it was just an extension of the down she'd been on for the past few weeks.

Phillip approached her quietly during one break in the technical rehearsal and told her he would keep the reason for her behavior a secret from everyone but Chamberfield.

Later, there was a trifling spat with Gaye, when the director complained that the redhead wasn't giving enough intensity to her scene. "How the hell am I supposed to be intense when I'm fighting against tapioca pudding? Vanessa's been in orbit all morning."

"She's right, Pat, I'm sorry," said Vanessa. "I'll try to give her a little more to work with." But she didn't.

"Forgive me, Vanessa, I feel awful about cutting you down before." Gaye stayed in from lunch to be with her dressing-room mate. She looked at her in the mirror on the counter. "One day I'll have to stuff a gag in my mouth."

Vanessa nibbled on a sandwich and said it didn't matter.

"Listen," said the redhead, "I've been watching you lately and, well, I don't know what it's all about. It's certainly none of my business, but I thought that if you ever need somebody to talk to, you know, or feel you want a shoulder, or whatever, I'm here. You know what I mean? That is, if you don't find me too obnoxious. You can call me anytime at home, at night, anytime." She jotted her telephone number on a scrap of paper and shoved it over to Vanessa. "Here."

Vanessa watched the dazzling girl with a muted kind of amazement. She'd never shown her any warmth before.

Gaye uttered a short laugh. "I've been thinking about saying that for over a week now, but it's a little painful to be rejected, so I don't like to—" She stopped speaking and got up to leave the room. Vanessa hadn't said a word, but Gaye felt she had gotten the message.

The taping was lamentable. The producer and director discussed going for a second run, but Phillip killed the idea because of cost. After the Teague affair, expenses had to be watched much more closely. Besides, he doubted if much improvement could be expected.

"Do you know what it's all about, Phil?" The director asked, minutes before the afternoon story conference.

"Yes, but I don't want to go into it. We'll have to give

244

her a little more time to work it out. She'll be fine in a few days."

Despite the day's bad taping, Phillip's spirits were reasonably high. The Goodhart-Keel ploy worked nicely. Phillip had called Keel at eleven-fifteen, shortly after Papa had, on the pretext of informing the network's president of Papa's proposal. Phillip had pretended to be surprised that Goodhart himself had already been in touch. Russell seemed remarkably anxious to assure him that RBI had no intention of letting him go easily. In fact, he thanked him for personally taking over *Affair* and whipping it into shape. He intimated that Phillip should be in for a healthy raise when he regained his former position on the forty-third floor. Phillip would have that just as soon as they all agreed *Affair* could stand without him.

He continued the façade through the meeting with Papa G. that evening. The old man called for him at the studio. Phillip climbed into the back of the gray Rolls before Julian could open the door, and they glided off toward New Jersey.

"What do you say to shooting down a couple of skeets before dinner, son? I've got my shotguns in the back."

"Fine with me, sir."

"Good. I think family's allowed to mix business with a little pleasure. Will you have a drink? I waited for you."

"Happily, it's been a rough day."

The old man pulled open the bar and produced a bottle of Chivas and some ice in two glasses. "I see you can dispense with ties these days."

"Yes, sir, we're a little more informal at the studio."

"I sure wish I could get away without one, but the people I have to do business with would pee in their pants if they ever saw me try it. Then again, it's become a habit with me, too. I think I'd feel like a streaker in anything less than a three-piece suit."

They took Riverside Drive up toward the bridge, crossed it, and headed into New Jersey. Then they followed the Garden State Parkway into the country. An hour later, they turned into a narrow gravel road, lined by tall poplar trees and marked "private." Three quarters of a mile more and they arrived at a rustic building set into a clump of trees, facing a wide-open area. The area was marked with a semicircle of mounds. Some distance out, to the right and left, stood two small structures containing machinery to pitch skeets with. A man was shooting. He readied his shotgun, called for the pull, and an attendant activated the remote-control button that hurled the round plastic plate. The shooter fired and the skeet exploded in the air.

Goodhart exchanged a few pleasantries with some men in the clubhouse. Then he donned his shooting vest and they went out to the range. Julian prepared two shotguns and when their turn came they did a round. The old man had been an excellent shot in his day, but was out of practice. "I didn't even do any deer shooting last season. What do you think of that?"

"You know what I think of it, Papa. I wish you didn't do it at all."

"Oh, Christ! I forgot about your attitude on that."

"I never did like to see an animal shot for nothing."

"All right, you've got your vices too. Go on, blast those plastic things out of the air. You're a damn good shot, you know?"

"I used to spend my allowance at carnival shooting galleries," he said.

"Go on, shoot. It's your turn. And why don't you see if you can't miss a couple, too. You're showing me up too much. Carnival shooting galleries, indeed!"

When they were finished they had a drink in the clubhouse and carried a second one on a walk through a wooded field. The offer of the presidency was extended again, this time in complete detail. It was a tempting offer, but Phillip declined. "I've thought about it since the other day, Papa, when Jacqueline outlined it for me."

"No strings, Phillip. Remember, I don't want you to think I've got ulterior motives, much as Mother and I would like to see you back in the family."

"I know that, sir, but the thing is it's just too seductive. It's a way to fly out of the whole pressure cooker I'm in, but if I did that now, it would be like quitting. You see, except for the people whose livelihoods depend on the show, nobody really cares if it succeeds or not, not any more. But I've got a personal stake in it now and I shouldn't turn my back on it."

"And once that's accomplished?"

"Well, *if* that's accomplished, we'll see." They walked on in silence for a little while, watching the sun set behind a distant farm on a hill. "Papa, do you remember that talk we had many years ago, when I first left the company for television?"

"Yes."

"Well, sir, it's part of the same thing. You're probably the only person I know who would understand my feelings in the matter. I fell in love with television at that time. I thought that because of its immense audience it would be the perfect medium for someone like me. I wanted to use it to help enrich the lives of the people who watched. My background is not too different from theirs. I understand them, sympathize with them, I'm aware of many of their frustrations. I wanted to do something with television that would ease some of those frustrations, take their minds away from them. They need that. But at the same time I wanted to give them something solid, something they could build on and learn from, that would help them develop themselves a little more. A lot of those people out there would be content to watch *Looney Tunes* for the rest of their days and that's what men like Elliot Chamberfield feed them just to keep the ratings high and sponsor advertising costly, and to maintain their own positions. To me he's rather like Richard Nixon. He craves the power a certain position can give him, but he uses that power only for his own benefit and I think that's corrupt. When I was dropped down to producer of *Affair*, I was in the process of building every daytime show on our schedule, not only to draw ratings, but so it would be a full contribution to the lives of the women who watched. They deserve more than pap, sir. More than cotton candy for their meals."

"Do you *really* think it's possible to achieve your goal within the existing structure?"

"I'm not as sure now as I used to be, but I have to give it a serious try."

"Son, I respect you," he said. "Even though you played a little trick on me."

"What do you mean?"

"With the attitude you've just expressed, you didn't need to have me bother Russ Keel."

Phillip tried to cover the hint of a grin that spread onto

247

his face. And both of them burst into laughter. "Phillip, I guess I'm getting old, but then I'm kind of glad you did trick me, you scoundrel. That way I got a chance to see you for dinner."

"Thank you, Papa. I miss the times we used to chat together."

"I do too, son; I do too. Come on. Let's get back and scrounge us up some food. I'm so hungry I could eat a bear."

* * *

The phone rang just as she was getting into bed. Her brother-in-law was calling from Woodstock. "John! John! Where have you been? I've been trying to get you since this morning. Is Joey there?"

"Hey! Hold on, what's up? I got messages all over the place that you called."

"Is Joey there with you?"

"No, should he be?"

She sank into the chair. "Have you seen him in the last two days? Or heard from him?"

"No. I was up on a hilltop outside of Bearsville with some friends."

"John, listen to me. Joey's gone! He left Sunday night. He left very upset. I'm afraid, John. I'm really scared for him. I hurt him, John, and I'm afraid he's going to hurt himself."

"Want to tell me what happened?"

"I can't. I just can't. John," she said pathetically, "it's serious this time."

There was quiet on the other end and then: "Okay. I'll drive down now in the van. I'll get in pretty late, but I'll check some of the pads he might be crashin' in. I'll call you in the mornin' or as soon as I've found him."

"Thanks, John, I don't know what to do any more."

"Just try to sleep. I'll find him."

She hung onto the receiver long after the connection was cut.

248

19.

Tuesday sparked a flame of anguish in the upper echelons of RBI, also. It started when Rosalynann Patachoutz made a late-afternoon dentist appointment, since her boss was out of town.

Her teeth were found to be in excellent condition; she was brushing properly and her gums were healthy and pink. But as soon as the inspection was over, the doctor, a man she had only recently been referred to, suddenly hastened to the sink and washed his hands. He whispered a few words to the nurse who unhooked the dental bib and led Rosalynann into the consulting room of the office. After a few minutes, he came in and took a seat behind the desk. He seemed to find difficulty in bringing out what was on his mind. He pulled the venetian-blind cord next to him, shutting off the view. "Miss Patachoutz," he said eventually, "I've noticed something on your gums, just to the side of your left molars, that I think you should have checked into. Have you had a temperature this past week?"

"Well, yes, at the beginning of the week, but it was just

one of those summer colds you get running in and out of air-conditioned buildings all the time."

"Miss Patachoutz, I feel it necessary to suggest that you have a Wasserman test."

"A Wasserman?" She blanched. "You mean you think I have. . . ." She couldn't finish.

"I don't know, but I'd have it checked on if I were you. You have a chancre in your mouth that's just begun to open. If it is what I think it is, it can be treated immediately. And it's very good that we caught it now. It's possible that it's nothing, but—"

Rosalynann stood up abruptly. She gathered her purse and a few papers she had left on the office couch next to her and raced out of the room, mortified.

*   *   *

The flight had been miserable. The plane had hit turbulence that lasted over twenty minutes and caused Elliot to chuck up his dinner. He took a Bromo and drank a half a bottle of liquid Gelusil (the airport's drugstore had been out of tablets) and then he brooded.

Elliot had always had difficulty fitting into the golfing, swimming, barbecue style of life the West Coast entertainment industry did business in. It was a casual and chatty kind of atmosphere that he found abrasive. He did, however, enjoy a few days in L.A. every now and then, since no one on the West Coast of RBI carried as much rank as he, and they rolled the red carpet almost to the doors of his limousine. And this trip had been an easy one. He had looked over the two dozen or so on-the-air promos for the fall nighttime lineup and had met with the producers of the three new pilots he felt were ready to go into production. He had also gotten a little sun on his face, which Rosalynann had been telling him he needed. Then late in the afternoon of his last day, that goddamned call from Russell had spoiled the whole fucking trip.

So the son of a bitch was trying to box him into a corner, was he? Waiting until he was out of town before he had Goodhart call up. Clever move, Searing. One for you. The problem was what the hell to do about it. The only weak point in *Affair* was Vanessa Langley. Maybe he ought to lay off trying to pressure her out. But maybe if he lay on enough pressure, she'd fuck up so badly the ratings would begin to drop and he could fire Searing for not having fixed the show. It was ugly, but it was the only thing he had to work with.

He was tired when he got into the limo and it was raining. "Take me to Sixth Avenue, will you? I want to stop at the office. Then I'll go home and catch some sleep. But don't put the car away."

He tried Rosalynann's number from the car phone, but there was no answer. When he walked into the office, there she was, lying on his couch. Her face was blotchy, her eyes laced with fine red lines, and her hair disheveled. Elliot put down his briefcase. "Christ, I had a lousy trip. What's the matter with you? Are you sick?" He started over to her.

"Don't touch me!" She spat.

"What the hell——!"

"You son of a bitch!" She shouted.

"Rosalynann, keep your voice down. Everyone will hear you." He hurried back to close the door.

"I don't care. I hate you! I hate you!"

Elliot was aghast. "Look, Rosalynann, I don't know what the problem is, but my office is not the place for it. Please stop crying. I have a lot of work to get out of the way. And I'd like to go home first and get some rest."

"Oh, excuse me for interrupting your work schedule, Mr. Chamberfield!" She lashed out at him. "I'm so sorry to have bothered you at all, but you're the cause of it—you filthy pig!"

"What are you talking about?"

"I couldn't even look anyone in the face in the elevator. You've made me feel so dirty!"

"Rosalynann, what the hell are you talking about?"

"I'll tell you what I'm talking about. I've just gotten the results of a Wasserman test I had done last night. And I have VD! That's what, VD!"

Then he became angry. "And you're calling *me* names? I didn't give you that. If you have it, you got it with somebody else. So don't blame me. I guess that's how much I can trust you."

Her mouth fell open. "You dare say that? You *dare* say that! You stand there and tell me it's my fault?" She slapped him hard across the face. "I haven't slept with anyone but you for two years. Two years, Elliot! You lied

251

to me. You swore to me that you weren't sleeping with anyone else, and now I've got this—this disease! And don't tell me I picked it up from a toilet seat. You can't get it unless somebody else gives it to you—and *you* gave it to me. Boy, did you give it to me! I should tell my father. Maybe that's what I'll do. Let's see you talk yourself out of it with him, you bastard!"

His cheek had the bright-red imprint of her hand on it. He listened to her in amazement, at first ready to deny, but then it dawned on him. That one evening with Gaye Vulkner. Wilson Vulkner's daughter had given him the clap. The clap? No. He suddenly remembered that small sore on his penis. It was syphillis. She'd given him syphillis! That high-class slut probably had slept with everyone in town!

He stopped rubbing his cheek and sank into the chair. Rosalynann glared at him. Elliot realized that he had no choice. He would have to confess. If she leaked the news, it could cost him his job. Vulkner was a puritanical son of a bitch; his strict sense of morality was the burden of every officer in the company.

He looked at her as beseechingly as he could. "Rosalynann, I'm sorry. What can I say? I feel ashamed . . . and I forgot. That's all, I forgot about it. Yes, there *was* someone else. Just once. I swear to you, darling, just once." He wandered over to the window to try to get control of his thoughts. He turned and looked at the grief-stricken girl. And he confessed. He confessed like a small boy in front of his mother. "I had to try another woman, Rosalynann. I don't sleep around." He paused and then he made his decision. "Rosalynann, we've been going together for so long I *had* to try one more. Just once. Just one more time, before I could make up my mind about you. Before I could make up my mind about marriage."

"Marriage!" she exclaimed.

"You see, Rosalynann, it's been so good with you all this time, I thought. . . ." His brain spun feverishly. "I thought that maybe that it was good with you only because I'd forgotten what it was like with someone else. So I tried. Don't you see? Before I asked you to marry me, I had to experience one more time. I had to know for sure that you would be a choice I could live with the rest of my life. And I found out. Rosalyann, I found out."

"What?"

"I found that I was crazy to look for someone better. You're the best, Rosalynann, the best I could ever have." He paused and looked down at his hands. Sweat was forming in his palms. "I want to marry you, Rosalynann."

It hung in the room like a luminous sphere. Elliot Chamberfield had asked her to marry him! How long she had waited for this moment; she had almost given up hope. She wouldn't give him an answer now, of course. But she knew. Of course, she'd marry him. VD or no VD.

Elliot's thoughts were elsewhere. So Gaye Vulkner had given him a dose. That meant Searing would have one, too. He figured that guy was into that redhead's pants two minutes after he saw her. He chuckled out loud at the thought of Phillip with a dose. His secretary looked up at him with a radiant face. "Are you as happy as I am? Is that it?"

"Of course, that's it, darling. I'm ecstatic."

By the end of the afternoon, he had convinced himself being married wouldn't be so bad. He did love her, after all.

* * *

Gloria buzzed Phillip on Thursday morning at nine-thirty-five. "Colin's calling from the rehearsal hall. Line two."

Phillip picked up the receiver and punched the button with the end of his pen.

"Phillip, she just walked in."

"Send her up."

"With pleasure."

Phillip arranged a few papers under the horse statuette and cleaned his fingernails with a letter opener. Gloria knocked twice, and ushered in the stunning redhead. Gaye walked to the couch and stretched out full, her hand across her forehead, moaning melodramatically. "Okay, Dr. Searing, let me have it. I've been a naughty girl."

"Sit up!"

"I'm exhausted. I'd rather take it lying down."

"Sit up," he said sharply. "Now!"

She sat up slowly, crossing her legs and arms, and stared at him. "Well, I'm up. What other trick would you like to see me do?"

"This is serious, Gaye."

"Oh, everything with you is serious. Where is the man of late I loved?"

"Shut up!"

She snapped her mouth closed and glared at him. He dropped the letter opener back on his desk. "Your behavior is becoming more and more unprofessional, Gaye. You know it as well as I do."

"And what constitutes unprofessional behavior?"

"It means for one thing, showing up late for scheduled rehearsals. Pat tells me you've been late twice this week for the 7:00 A.M. call and three times for the afternoon read-through."

"And that's all you give a damn about!" she said, running the tips of her nails across her pouting lower lip.

"No, that's not all."

"You want to know something?" she said, cutting him off. "I know a reporter from *Inside-TV* who tells me they're getting twice as many inquiries about me from readers as about anybody else on any soap out of New York."

"That has nothing to do with it. You've been late too many times and I can't let you get away with it anymore than I would let anyone else get away with it. And another thing: I'd appreciate it if you'd keep your amours out of the studio. You're getting a little too open, Gaye."

"Oh, my, so that's what's worrying his'm's. The only time we're alone is when you want to talk about this fucking show. Well, I'll tell you something. I'm getting fed up with this little world of yours. It bores me silly, if you want to know. Getting up every morning at six; slaving all day, getting home at four-thirty to sit down and memorize a bunch of lines that would make anyone with half an ounce of brains retch over their stupidity. I'm getting sick of it, you understand. And now you want to start running my private life also? Well fuck you, buster!"

"You little rich bitch. You've never had to work a day in your life and now you're finding out suddenly that the rest of us suckers have more guts and determination than you and it pisses you off. Well, let me tell you once—and that's it. Either you shape up or shove off. Do you understand?"

She was furious. "Sure, I understand. Well, maybe I'd rather shove off, as you so cutely put it."

"You do and you'll never work again in the entertainment profession."

"I'm the daughter of Wilson Vulkner and I can work anytime I want."

"Listen to the child who disowns her stepdad, except when it comes to getting a job. Well, let me tell you a secret. Wilson Vulkner wouldn't hire you for one minute if he didn't think you could hack it. Anyone who knows him knows that he will not tolerate unprofessional behavior. Not even from his own stepdaughter. Just try him."

"I may just do that. I've been invited to his home for dinner next week."

"Terrific. I'll still fire you if you don't come around. I have that authority and he will back me up."

They sat glaring at each other. "Are you through with me or are you going to slap my hands with a ruler?"

"If I thought it would help, I would." A twinkle lodged in his eye. "But I'm a little afraid you'd enjoy it."

She tried to maintain her sense of annoyance, but the laugh trickled out and then she couldn't contain it because Phillip started laughing too. "Okay, producer, I'll try harder. But only because you've promised me that ruler." She stepped to the door and then turned. The smile had broadened into a seductive challenge. "By the way, I promised my old man you'd be bringing me to that dinner. He was delighted, and anxious to make your acquaintance."

"What!" he exclaimed.

But she slipped out and ran down the hall like a tickled little girl.

Phillip might have followed her to find out more about this dinner, but Gloria buzzed that Chamberfield was on the line. Phillip waited a silent count of ten, to prepare himself and to make Elliot uptight, and then he offered a courteous hello.

"What the fuck's happening to that Langley girl? She's falling all over the screen!"

"She's had your abortion, Elliot. But she's having some emotional aftereffects. I'm working on it."

"What the hell does that mean? She stinks and you're working on it."

"She doesn't stink, Elliot; she's a damn good actress."

"Not any more. Lately she's been revolting."

255

Phillip tensed. He wasn't going to get into a shouting match with the man. That was Chamberfield's pleasure. "We're not employing mechanical puppets," he said quietly. "These actors are people. They have good days and bad days, like you and me."

"I've never had a bad day in my life in the office. I'm not paid to have bad days."

"Well, that goes to show who's human and who's not."

There was a pause on the other end. And then: "But I'll tell you something, Searing. I'm not running a clinic for psychotics. If you can't solve the Langley problem by the middle of next week, I'll personally fire her."

"You insensitive son of a bitch!"

"And if you put up one iota of resistance, I'll fire you, too, and by the way, that little game you played—having Goodhart call Keel—won't help you a bit. I run my own department and you'd do yourself a favor to understand that." The phone crashed down.

A few moments passed before Phillip loosened his grip on the receiver and placed it carefully on the cradle. His hand was shaking.

The air show was on. He switched the volume down on the monitor and let the characters dance around silently in the little square box. The two female rivals were accentuated by the lack of sound. Gaye, smirking and voluptuous, rolled out of the screen more than when she verbalized. And Vanessa was the picture of someone about to have a breakdown. Her face was pinched and drawn, and Mary had tried to cover the dark circles under her eyes with makeup. Her hands fluttered like frightened birds— flicking back her hair, smoothing an eyebrow, rubbing her nose. It was as though her raw nerve ends had been laid open.

The cast was trying to make the best of the situation. But what came across the tube was chaos. Instead of being the traditional heroine, faced with adversity but attempting to overcome her shortcomings with strength and determination, Vanessa looked like an accident ready to happen. And those hands . . . if she could only still those hands.

Phillip couldn't watch any more. He switched the set into blackness and worried about how many viewers all across the country were doing the same thing, or, worse, switching to another channel.

20.

Ever since he had written Gaye Vulkner into his life, Brian Hocholtz had been battling the urge to tell Gus Shassty and his miserable magazine to go fuck themselves. The fact that he continued to grind out his blurbs week after week was due only to momentary economic consideration, because the future, he was certain, was becoming more rosy every time he spoke to Miss V. Of course, he hadn't done too much more than speak to her in the past two weeks. She'd been so busy, except for the other night, and that wasn't the pleasantest of encounters. But nonetheless, he was reasonably content. "See you later, Gus. I'm going over to the *Affair Of The Heart*. I've got a tentative with Gaye V."

"Yeah, bring something back this time, will ya? I'm getting sick of laying out bread and not getting nothing back. The garbage you've been writing wouldn't interest nobody."

He shot across Forty-Third Street to Eighth Avenue, ducked down into the Forty-Fourth Street subway station, and grabbed the fast local up to Fiftieth. He came out at Fifty-Second Street, near the front of the train, and hoofed it west to the studio. He hoped she wasn't still annoyed about the other night. She couldn't be. She had to realize that it was too much to ask him to go down on her in that taxicab. She couldn't have been serious. It wasn't even completely dark out. No, she was more rational than that. After all she had a public reputation to uphold. He had at least to give her the illusion that he was ready to protect her.

He went through the door, winking familiarly at the guard, and walked back to the dressing-room area. The place seemed deserted. He stepped into the men's john to wash off the grime of the day, took a comb to put his hair just right, sipped from the water fountain, and then went out and rapped brightly on dressing-room three.

Gaye herself opened the door. "Oh, shit, it's you again."

Brian deflated like a punctured inner tube.

Vanessa was sitting at the counter in front of the long wall mirror, removing her makeup. She remained silent.

"Can I talk with you a minute, Gaye?"

"I'm rushing to an appointment."

He ventured a slight, baby step into the room, letting his shoulder maintain the open crack of the door. "I'm sorry about the other night. That is, I'm not sorry, but I feel I should explain myself to you."

"There's nothing to explain, dumpling. I don't know what you're talking about." She turned away from him, reached behind her back, and unhooked her bra. She slipped out of it, exposing those mountainous breasts of hers for a few seconds before wiggling into a thin, revealing, summer sweater.

"Gaye, please won't you let me—"

"Listen, I'm busy!"

"Well, when can I see you?"

"Christ, man, I don't know. Never—how about that?"

"Why? What did I do? It was for your own good that I—"

Gaye saw that Vanessa was becoming nervous. "Nothing, honey. You didn't do a thing. Now, look, this little girl over here is not feeling too well, so why don't you let her enjoy a few moments of peace, okay? You come back some other time, hmm?"

"When?" he asked. He was becoming anxious. He could not believe that the world he was preparing to enter was putting up so many defenses so quickly.

"Brian, just *go*, will you? Don't be a pain in the ass. Go back to your friends on Staten Island. I'm tired of being a ladder for people to climb on." And with that she shoved the young reporter out of the door and closed it. "Miserable son of a bitch," she muttered. "They're all alike. They climb all over me for my name, but when it comes to giving out they just don't know how to do it. Simpletons. Professional fucks. That's all they are, and they can't even give good sex."

And just as Gaye was preparing to leave, Vanessa suddenly broke out of her silence and tore into the redhead with all the emotional force charging within her. "Is that all you ever think about? Sex? Is that the only thing on your simple mind? You don't do anything but wiggle your tail up and down the studio at every man who will look at it. It makes me sick. Don't you have any sense of privacy? Do you have to involve everybody in your sexual maneuvers? Jesus, Gaye!"

Had Gaye been in a different mood, the beautiful heiress might have answered back with the caustic wit she was known for. Her brain and tongue were fast enough to answer such an outburst, but she realized how easily Vanessa could be crushed. Besides, the outburst was over; Vanessa buried her head in her hands. Gaye watched her carefully for a frozen moment, then slipped quietly out the door.

She was crossing the studio when she spotted Phillip. "Is Vanessa still here?" he asked.

"Inside, but I'd watch myself if I were you," she said. "I think the little lady is ready to explode."

Phillip waited until Gaye left, rapped softly at the door, and, receiving no response, turned the handle and entered. Vanessa was in front of the mirror, her elbows planted on the counter and the heels of her hands pressed tightly to her temples. She gave no indication that she had heard him come in.

He studied her, so lovely and so frail. "Vanessa," he said as softly as he could. "I think it's time we had another talk."

She didn't move, didn't make a sound, but the hands

259

pressed harder at the temples, squeezing the anguish back into the brain. Even the muscles of her thighs stood out hard against the tightness of her levis.

Then without warning she screamed—a long, piercing tearing sound that loosed itself somewhere from the core of her agony. Phillip was riveted to his spot. And then words formed, incoherences pushed through the clutter of lips and tongue and saliva. "What more do you want from me? I let you force me to abort my baby. Are you happy? Does that make you happy now, Mr. Producer!"

She grabbed a chair and hit the mirror; it smashed, and with all the force of her body, she swung the chair back again in the direction of Phillip. It caught him off guard. One foot hit him in the solar plexis and knocked him down.

Phillip managed to catch hold of the girl by her wrist, but she slipped out of his grasp and raced from the studio.

21.

The first-floor rehearsal hall was littered with scripts, cigarette butts, and partially empty styrofoam coffee cups. Vanessa followed Judy's entrance into the room from her position at the far end of the conference table. The pretty production assistant whispered something to Pat, who glanced up in Vanessa's direction and made a sign that indicated a phone call for her outside.

She ran through the double doors and down the hall into the production office. The girl behind the desk told her she could take the call in the director's office.

The hollowness of his voice hit her like a cloud of cold, damp fog. "What is it, John? Tell me."

"I found him."

"Where is he? Can I speak to him?"

"No."

The breath caught in her throat. "What's happened?"

"He's in the emergency ward at Bellevue. He OD'ed."

"Oh, my God!"

"He ain't dead, but he's in a coma. They're pumpin' his stomach now."

"Is that where you're calling from? The emergency room?"

"Yeah."

"Tell me how to get to you."

John was leaning against the pale-green wall of the emergency waiting room when Vanessa arrived. "Where is he?"

"Inside. They told me to sit down and shut up."

"What do you think?"

He shrugged, and turned away from her. The nurse at the desk looked harried. She was trying to fill in an information form for a Puerto Rican woman with two young children, who didn't know any English. A black man was holding a bloody towel to his cheek and sitting forlornly on a long, oak bench. He was accompanied by two policemen who were busy filling out forms. There was an old man in a wheelchair who kept up a constant moan. Whoever had wheeled him in had pushed him to a corner facing a blank wall and had not thought to turn him around. Not that it mattered. His eyes were closed, anyhow. There was a steady call for doctors on the loud-speakers. The room smelled strongly of vomit and disinfectant.

Vanessa unzipped her shoulder bag and fished out a package of cigarettes. She offered one to the tall, taciturn young man who looked so much like her husband. He declined. "When did you take up smokin', Ness?"

"About a week ago."

"Bad for your health."

"I know." She tried to strike a match, but her hands were shaking too much. John took the match and lit it for her. The smoke seemed to quiet her nerves a bit. "How did you find him?"

"Didn't. Ran into a guy who said two buddies found him in a playground over on Avenue C. He was out cold, slumped over a bench. They figured he'd overdosed, so they took him to their pad, shot him up with salt water, and packed ice on his cock."

"What the hell did they do that for?"

"Street remedy for OD'ing."

"Who brought him here?"

"They did. Dropped him out of a car onto the sidewalk outside."

"They left him on the sidewalk?"

"They didn't want to get involved. Might have been arrested themselves."

"But how could they just leave him like that?"

"Listen, kiddo, if he pulls through, he'll probably owe it to those two freaks. Don't put them down—they did everything they could."

She looked back over the room, her eyes sweeping the suffering humanity. "When will they tell us something, John?"

"No news is good news, I guess."

She whirled. "What does that mean? You don't think . . . he's not going to die, is he?"

"I don't know. I just don't know."

Vanessa stared at the ceiling and the dismal light fixture with its accumulation of filth.

They sat in silence for nearly an hour. It was probably close to seven when an East Indian nurse came up to the desk and called out the name "John Langley." The two of them bolted up and hurried over to her.

"Are you John Langley?"

"Yes, ma'am."

"Come with me." She looked at Vanessa.

"I'm Vanessa Langley. The patient's wife."

They went through a swinging door into a long, dim corridor, and followed the nurse to a small cluttered office. She entered, laid a file on the desk, and indicated two metal folding chairs, "Just wait here. Dr. Gellens will be in to see you." She walked out.

The desk was piled with files and letters, some still in their envelopes. A large metal filing-cabinet desk took up most of one side of the room. The only respite from the drabness was a calendar with a color photo. It showed a lone skier, small and insignificant, against a cloudless expanse of blue sky and a gleaming white slope of snow.

John studied his hands. "I saw him, you know. I had to identify him since he didn't have his wallet on him. They took me back to see him."

She wanted to ask, but couldn't.

"He didn't look so good."

They looked up every time they heard footsteps in the hall. Twenty minutes passed. John went out into the hall for a drink of water and then came back, leaning his tall, bony frame against a doorjamb. Finally a doctor in a white coat that looked clean, but unironed, appeared and introduced himself. "I'm Dr. Gellens. Are you the brother?"

"Yeah. And this is his wife."

The doctor, almost as tall as John, with short hair and long sideburns, came into the office and settled in a swivel chair behind the desk. He opened the file the nurse had left, wrote a few words, and then closed it. John folded himself into the empty chair.

"We've done everything we can, Mrs. Langley. He was in very bad shape when we found him outside. Blood, urine, and gastric samples indicated that he had taken a large dose of fairly pure heroin. I think they call it 'brown dope' on the street. He could have shot thirty bags of garbage and he'd never have OD'ed. But it only takes one bag of brown to do the trick."

"Dr. Gellens, please, how is he?"

"Your husband's entire body has undergone a devastating shock. His vital systems are malfunctioning. Until they can repair themselves he's going to have to stay on what we call a life-support system. It's a series of machines connected by tubes to his own systems to carry on the necessary functions mechanically for him until his own organs are strong enough to take over again."

"How long will that take?"

"My guess is several weeks. Maybe more, maybe less. And it's going to be expensive, Mrs. Langley."

"I earn a good salary. Whatever he needs, just whatever he needs."

The young intern stared at her, probably wondering how such a healthy young woman could get mixed up with a junkie. "Yeah," he said finally, and rose.

Vanessa stood up slowly. "May we see him?"

"Not now. He's still in the emergency ward. As soon as he's regained consciousness, we'll move him and then you can visit."

"Thank you."

"You'll have to fill out the necessary forms before you go."

She nodded absently.

* * *

He eased the Jaguar off Pelham Parkway and under the ornate gate with its carved standing bears and reindeer. A parking spot presented itself on the far side of the circle of grass that surrounded the fountain. He killed the motor, settled back into the leather seat, and absorbed the sounds of the splashing water as it played over statues of plump nude children, riding on seahorses perched on half shells.

It was hot already and it wasn't even ten, but he could do quite well without the air conditioner. That luxury had been a concession to Jacqueline when the car was first purchased, but he rarely used it. Instead, he contented himself with a light breeze that escaped from the fountain and drifted through the car window.

The letter on the dashboard was from Katina. It had arrived as he was leaving the apartment and he hadn't yet had a chance to read it. He looked out over the rapidly filling lot, but did not see his rendezvous partner, so he tore open the envelope.

Dearest Phillip,

I'm sitting on a terrace covered by brilliantly purple bougainvillaea (the terrace, not me), gazing across the red-tiled rooftops of a tiny village, down, down, down to the azure blue of the Mediterranean Sea. The sun is already high, which is indicative of the fact that I'm being very lazy, since I've just started sipping my morning cappuccino. The village is Haut de Cagnes and it's not far from Cannes, and the plasticky world of the Riviera. The contrast is remarkable. Here it's another century; a lovely sixteenth-century church and browned smiling people—but mostly the foreigners—the French have been obnoxious this year. The smell of freshly baked bread from a bakery is at this precise moment wafting up to my perch on the lightest of breeze. WHAT THE HELL ARE YOU DOING IN STINKYTOWN?

So, you ask, how does one, Katina Wrens, fall into such a paradise? Remember our host in London? Belongs to a friend of his from the States and a bunch of us came down and have been sponging in this lap of luxury ever since. The villa is large, ten bedrooms, at last count. Revolting, revolting, revolting you might say. It has been absolutely mad. Since most of the others sleep in the mornings, I pop up and work on my poetry. So it isn't all a vacation. And guess what else? This host of ours is connected to a publishing house in New York, and he conned me into reading some of my scribblings to him. He loved them. (At least he said he did.) Anyway he wants me to let him send some back to NYC and see what happens. Now I'm really torn. Should I try that route? Publishers, reviews, critics, and talk shows—fame—fame and frustration? Or should I simply allow it to dwell in the house of Katina forever? It's been the only pure thing I've ever done and I'm terribly afraid of defiling it. Anyway, some of your friend Gaye's previous amours are slinking about the area, by the way, and my own special one, too. So you see, dear P—

"Well, are you done?" The familiar gravelly rumble broke into his concentration.

"Maude! I didn't see you come up." He punched the button on the glove compartment and tucked the letter in the box.

Maude stepped back from the car and gave forth with a low whistle. "Wow, is this some classy chassis! You never cease to astound me by your taste."

"Money, darling. It doesn't take taste for one of these. Just money."

"Ah, yes, money—that elusive dream. Come, let's go before the place is jammed." They strolled down a narrow path between several towering black maple trees. "Have you ever been here, Phillip?"

"Not for years."

"You're in for a treat. The Bronx Zoo's been my unwinder. I use it like Kennedy used the beach on Cape Cod. Whenever I start to tighten up on a script I put on my walking shoes and stroll through these grounds. I live just over there." She waved in the direction of the front gate. "I used to bring my sons here on Sundays. I don't know how much they enjoyed it but I did, I can tell you. That's for sure." They stopped to let a diminutive Chinese mother push a baby carriage past them.

"I've never liked the idea of zoos very much," said Maude. "Seeing animals in cages has never appealed to me, but here it's done so intelligently. Look at those bison." She pointed left to where a dozen or so brown American bison were grazing on a field. A stream of water ran along beside them and trees were in the background. The path that Maude and Phillip were walking on was so distant that the slow, plodding animals took no notice of them. Phillip followed her finger politely.

"Okay," she laughed, and squeezed his arm. "I know you didn't come up for a discourse on zoos." She stopped and asked seriously, "You don't mind meeting me here, do you? I thought it would be nicer than sitting in my apartment."

"No, not at all," he responded, "but we've got a lot to talk about. I received the Seventy—Market Nielsens yesterday afternoon."

"What's the matter? We dying?"

He lit a cigarette and let his attention wander to a field of elk. "No, we're not dying. We're holding an even level, but we're not going up, just holding."

"And that's not good enough, is it?"

"Not if we want the show to survive. *Affair* is two and a half points behind being even a marginal show. We've yet to pull our fair share of the viewing audience, and with four networks that's at least twenty-two and a half percent of the viewers in our time period. As of now, we're only pulling twenty. A marginal show has a chance to make it, but anything below means we're out."

Breaking away from what he was saying, Maude tugged on his arm again. "Let's get to our rallying point for this morning It's up ahead. Isn't it gorgeous?"

It stood on the crest of a hill like a futuristic castle. Its variegated concrete walls swooped in and out in a series of curvilinear wings. "Maude, we have a lot to talk about this morning."

"Right, and we'll talk about it in the most unimaginable place in New York City."

Phillip followed her chunky form up the hill and through a set of glass doors. Signs asked them to keep voices low and movements slow. As they wandered

267

through a maze of dimly lit walks, banked on either side by separated worlds, distinctive in flora, climate, and bird life of specific regions, Phillip explained the necessity for dealing with the matter quickly. "We have three weeks, just three weeks to raise our ratings to the level of even a marginal show. I'm not concerned about pushing it into a 'hit' area. That's too much of a fantasy now, but we do have to bring it up to an area where we at least have a chance."

It was a pep talk, but rooted in reality. What he didn't tell her was that even if they did advance to the marginal plateau, Elliot might still drop it just to rid himself of the producer. The only real safeguard against such an action would have been to have made it a hit, but thirteen weeks had been just too damn short to produce a miracle of that caliber. No, now all bets were off, but if they could boost that last two and one half points Elliot would be in the position of having to make a difficult choice. In terms of business it would be very foolish to dump a show that was moving up so fast. "The thing is," he continued, "there's only one way to get even those two and a half points. We're going to have to resort to a gimmick."

They edged through a group of people standing two deep in front of a glassless window protecting a display of New England birds. "We're going to have to put somebody's life in jeopardy and I think it'll have to be Valerie's."

"I thought you didn't want to do that sort of thing, Phillip."

"I didn't."

"In fact I remember a monologue you gave when I first came on the scene. You said we're not going to stoop to low soap-opera tricks; you wanted to deal with issues more pertinent to the lives of our lady watchers."

"That's true, but we're in trouble. Either we do something drastic like putting Valerie's life on the line or the life of the show will definitely run out in three weeks."

"You're talking about serious changes."

"I suppose I am."

"That means I'll have to throw away a whole batch of scripts and you're not going to be able to get ahead any on your taping schedule."

"We don't have much choice," said Phillip.

"Okay. Well," she said, sighing, "Valerie *is* going in for an eye operation, isn't she?"

"That's what I was thinking. Cataracts. But suppose she was found to have something besides cataracts at the last minute, something more serious."

"Like what? A tumor?"

"Could be. She could have a tumor on the brain affecting her eyesight. You'd have to check out the medical veracity of anything we chose, of course, but something to give her less than a fifty-fifty chance for survival."

"I see," she said thoughtfully. "I suspect we'll have to do it right away, won't she?"

"I think so, and it means a major reworking for you. Monday and Tuesday are out. We're already using them to deal with the subplot, but we can write in a scene for the doctor for Wednesday in which we can have him discuss the situation with Valerie's aunt."

"Umm. Well, okay, that also gives you an out if you decide to can Vanessa."

"Can Vanessa?" The thought seemed to shock him.

"Sure. Valerie's on the operating table with a brain-tumor operation underway, so if Vanessa's performances don't start to improve we can kill her off with no trouble at all."

"No."

"Don't tell me you haven't thought about it," she said, seeing he was a bit perplexed.

"I haven't, oddly enough. I haven't at all. I wasn't even considering the possibility of Vanessa's not improving."

"Come on, Phillip. You can level with me. I know how much of a problem she's been. I haven't been working till the wee hours of the morning trying to cut down on her scene load for nothing. This gives you a perfect out in case she doesn't improve, and you know it. In fact, it's a very logical move."

"She will improve. She's just going through a difficult time right now."

"Well, I wouldn't call that an overstatement." She winked at him, then rubbed her hands together, and sighed. "Oh, my, if I were as young and pretty as these birds of yours, maybe somebody'd fight for me too when

I fell off my perch. Look, do you see that strange-looking creature over there?"

"Where?"

"There." She pointed. "On that dead tree stump."

It was a weird creation with mottled gray feathers and an irregularly round body.

"Oh, yes."

"That's me," she said, "a tawny frogmouth. Sleeps all day and works all night, and its call is a bark, just like mine. We two are survivors—not flashy or pretty, like some of our friends, but survivors. We hang on."

They pushed open the swinging doors and walked up a steep ramp which shot out of one side of the building and curved sharply back, bringing them into the second floor.

"This is my jungle." And it was, three stories' worth. Palm trees, a waterfall cascading down the face of a cliff . . . it even smelled of the tropics. "Every afternoon at two they have a tropical storm in here. I've always wanted to come in with my umbrella." A bright-purple bird swooped suddenly over their heads to the other side of the narrow bridge on which they were standing. "That's a lilac breasted roller," proclaimed Maude profoundly. "It does loop-de-loops. See?" It was true. The small bird dove and climbed in remarkable vertical patterns, doing somersaults in the air.

But Phillip paid scant attention. The remark about Vanessa disturbed him. "What do you think, Maude? Should I fire Vanessa?"

"You're asking me?"

"What would you do in my place?"

"I'd never be in your place. People are more important to me than ratings."

"And you think people aren't important to me?"

"Well, it's a question of priorities. When a head is full of numbers, there's not much space left for people. I shift lives around on paper. You're the one who's got to do it in reality. I'd never be up to that kind of responsibility."

* * *

Phillip checked the answering service when he arrived home and found that Colin Dawes had left a message. "He said it was important, sir, and that you could call him back as late as you liked."

"Thank you." He scribbled the number on a pad of paper and tried it immediately. A well-rounded "hello" came across the wire. "Colin, this is Phillip Searing. My service said you called."

"Oh, yeah, hi," he said, losing the faint quality of seductiveness he'd started with. "How are you?"

"I'm fine. What's up?" Since he'd discovered the young man was feeding gossip to Elliot Chamberfield, Phillip had precious little inclination toward friendly chatting with him.

He began hesitantly. "Phillip, look, I'm not sure I should be getting into this. In fact, I was asked specifically not to discuss it with anybody, but, well, I've been thinking. Vanessa's in trouble."

"What do you mean she's in trouble?" he asked.

He cleared his throat. "She called me a little while ago from the hospital."

"What hospital?" he shouted.

"Her husband's in the hospital. The reason she's been so bad on the show the past couple of weeks is that they've been having some problems at home. He's a junkie, Phillip."

"I know about that, but I thought he was off the stuff."

"So did I, but I guess he went back on. Vanessa's been keeping it inside of her all this time. But a few nights ago he went away."

"He left her?"

"Yes, then he landed in the hospital. He took an overdose of heroin."

"Oh, Christ! How is she?"

"She's all right, I guess. She says *he's* in very bad shape, though. I was afraid you might fire her because of her lousy performances, and I wanted you to know that there were serious extenuating circumstances. I tried to call Elliot, but he wasn't back from Delaware yet. I think they went out to see Rosalynann's parents about something."

That's odd, Phillip thought. If he were playing spying games what was the purpose in talking about it? "I don't understand," he said. "Why would you want to call Elliot? What does he have to do with it?" He opened a carton of

Dunhills from the kitchen cabinet, cradling the phone in his shoulder while he lit up.

"Well, he asked me to some time ago. I wasn't supposed to tell you about it, but I guess it's out in the open now, anyway. He was worried about the show a while back and was concerned that you would have to bear the entire brunt of everything yourself. He knew you weren't the sort of person to go running for help, even if you needed it, so he asked me to kind of keep him abreast of what was happening so he could lend a hand from his end."

"Elliot was going to lend a hand?"

The young man's naiveté was beyond belief.

"You know, do whatever he could, I guess. I thought it was an awfully nice gesture on his part, so I told him I'd be glad to help."

"I see."

"He asked me not to tell you, but at this stage of the game, with all that's at stake—Vanessa's part, the show—I guess it wouldn't matter to him."

He didn't know. The kid simply didn't know. And now he'd have to be kept from knowing. "Uh, Colin, I think it might be better for you if you didn't let Elliot know you told me. He's kind of a stickler for keeping a promise and if he told you specifically not to say anything to me, I expect he'd be furious with you."

"Even in light of the situation?"

"Even in light of the situation. He's been known to fire people for the same sort of thing."

"Oh, my God! I thought I was helping—Jesus! Oh, Christ," he whined. "I didn't know. Honestly, I didn't!"

"All right, don't worry about it. I won't tell him, and don't you tell him, either. But thanks for telling me about Vanessa. I'd like to know anything that happens with her, for her sake."

He really had no notion what compelled him to do it, but after hanging up on Colin and staring into the kitchen sink long enough to watch an empty Scotch glass fill with the drippings from a leaky faucet, Phillip looked up Vanessa's address in the cast roster, changed into a pair of jeans, and left the apartment. Since he hadn't put the Jaguar into the garage yet, he drove it to the West Side. The vestibule of Vanessa's house was dimly lit by a flickering neon bulb. He pushed the Langley button and waited. Nothing. He tried again. Still nothing.

He was going to wait in the car, but the night was so pleasant—an early evening thunder shower had moved out the week's accumulation of pollution—that he decided to set up his lookout from a playground across the street. A group of ten or twelve teenagers were smashing bottles on the basketball court.

Phillip picked a swing to sit on and rocked back and forth gently, facing the house. A few people came and went, but no one resembling Vanessa. And the inevitable question arose. What the hell was he doing there? What did he hope to prove? He bounced his heels on the rubber coating cemented down to protect the little playgroundites. He wondered how many children actually used the place, anyway, in proportion to the amount of winos and junkies and muggers or other assorted members of New York's outer social community.

What was he doing there? What could he offer that would mean something to her? That could help alleviate the misery she must be feeling? In a selfish way he had been glad to hear about Joey. He knew that. He tried to shove the gladness away from his mind, but it wasn't possible. He had been terribly worried that the distress, the anxiety—all of the torment that had blended into the rotten performances Vanessa was giving—were caused by the abortion and for that, he had developed a considerable amount of guilt. Not that he had any reason to feel that way. He hadn't initiated the idea. He could have worked with her through her pregnancy with no trouble at all —dress her carefully, aim the cameras above the stomach, stay with beauty shots as much as possible. He could have worked her through nine months easily, and no one would have known any difference. No, he was only a messenger in the affair. Elliot was the one playing God-executioner, and the guilt should rest squarely on his shoulders, but nevertheless he felt it eating away at him, had been feeling it for some time, and the only relief had come when he learned about the husband. The thought that her problems might not stem from himself provided a feeling of considerable relief.

He twisted himself in the chains of the swing, then let it jerk straight again. All that was fine, but it didn't answer the question of why he had come . . . or what he would say to her when she arrived. The shocking sound of fire-engine sirens bore into the privacy of his thoughts. In a moment a hook-and-ladder truck blasted its way against the traffic on Horatio Street and another greeted it from Hudson. The new sounds of police cars appeared somewhere in the distance. The corner of Hudson and Horatio quickly filled up with a variety of emergency vehicles, but before the last arrival got there, the first was on its way out. Phillip stood on the swing seat and paid vague attention to the circus. Another false alarm, he assumed. He walked over to the bank of seesaws and tried to run up the down side to the middle. The first try landed him back on the rubberized ground, but he made it on the second. He set one foot on each side of the fulcrum and strained to keep the ends from tapping the rubber.

She was certainly worried about her job. He could assure her that she wasn't in danger of losing it—that he would ride out the troubled time with her for as long as it took, put himself on the line no matter what happened. But could he? Was he really prepared to sacrifice the entire show for this girl? The jobs of everyone on it as well as his own career? And why? He hardly knew her. Maude's right, he thought. Numbers do get in the way of people.

A cab pulled up to number twenty-eight. He bounced down on one side of the seesaw and ran off the board to see who was paying the fare. It was a white-faced old man with a hat and long coat despite the summer heat. He was assisted by an old lady, probably his wife.

The bottle breakers took off down Little West Twelfth Street. Two bearded young men came out of the building with a medium-sized black dog, and crossed over to the park. The dog defecated in the glare of the street lamp, just in the jump position of the closest basket. Phillip coughed, which reminded him to light another cigarette. It tasted foul and bitter. Why couldn't he smoke only at the good times?

Vanessa appeared around midnight. The moment was a trifle awkward because Phillip had to shout out her name from behind the playground fence, and then run around the gate to reach her. She was apprehensive, of course, hearing her name called from a darkened playground at midnight, but as she recognized her producer crossing between the parked cars, her apprehension changed to puzzlement.

"Forgive me," he began, looking up the stoop at her from the level of the pavement. "I didn't want to scare you by ringing the bell after you'd already gone in. Vanessa, I heard about your husband. Colin told me. Vanessa, I just want you to know that anything, anything I can do for you, please ask. If you need money, if you need medical help, whatever you need, I'll get it for you."

He looked a trifle sheepish. "I just came to tell you that."

She watched him for a long while, and when she felt the sorrow begin to rush to her eyes, she turned and pushed her way into the vestibule. Phillip waited until he heard the inner door close, then left.

22.

June King filed the last of the eight-by-tens from the Young Character Males group and stretched a bare arm across the desk to catch the fifth ring of the phone. She worked her long lithe frame around to the chair again and plopped down before saying "Claire Pappas's line," her soft Alabama accent sweetening the tone.

"Hello, magnolia blossom, how's the most feminine dyke at RBI?"

"Now, Brian, you hush your mouth. I am not a dyke and one of these days I'm going to come over there and prove it to you."

"I'm waiting, honeysuckle. In fact, I've got my cock in my hand right now if you'd care to slip over and slide around on it."

"Oh, you do talk dirty," she said, her titillation showing in her voice. "I ought to put a tape recorder on this phone and play it back to my husband. I'm sure he'd just love to hear some of the things you've been saying."

"Yeah, he could take it down to his precinct and give the boys in blue a charge."

"He'd be as likely to come over and beat you silly."

"Oh, well, in that case, don't do it. I'm a devout coward and I can't stand brutality, especially when it's directed toward me. I guess the old douchebag's not in," said the reporter. "Otherwise, you wouldn't be keeping me on the phone like this."

"I'm keeping you!" she exclaimed. "You have your nerve. Claire's on the other line. She'll be off in a minute, if you'd care to wait."

"If I'd care to wait, she says, in her best southern accent. Just listen to the honey drip out of that gorgeous mouth. You know I have fantasies about that mouth of yours."

"What. . . ."

"Do you get more pleasure out of sucking cocks or pussy?"

"What?" It was the loudest whispered shout one could imagine.

"You swing both ways. I know you do."

"How do you know that?"

"I can't believe you can work for Claire Pappas without going down on her every once in a while, or letting her go down on you."

The military toughness of Claire cut into the wire with, "Is that so, you prick! What's all this talk about?"

"I'm getting off this line," said June, flustered and flushed.

"Talk," said Brian, after he heard the secretary click down, "that's about all I can do these days, if I want to be a halfway decent guy. Guess what I came down with?"

"A new job."

"I wish. No, a lovely case of syphilis."

"Really?" exclaimed the feisty little casting director, "Join the party. So have I, and so do three technicians on *Affair Of The Heart*. But that, my dear, I tell you as a friend. It ain't for publication."

"You're kidding!"

"Wish I were. I just found out about my dose the other day. In fact, I'm on my way over to see my doctor now. I've never had syphilis before. There's something creepy about it. But seriously. Don't you dare even allude to it in your magazine. I mean about the guys from the show having it."

"Come on, Claire, do you think I'd do that sort of thing? I've never, ever, used a story I didn't clear with you. I'm surprised you'd even think such a thing of me."

"Well, I just wanted to make the point with this one. It could be a little tricky. I wish I knew who was causing it. I wouldn't even be surprised if you didn't introduce it to us."

"Me? Screw you. How do I know it wasn't you?"

"You see the problem? Nobody's going to come out and say it, and who knows how many others are involved. Well, anyway, I've got to run. What did you call about? Anything important?"

"Not really. I'm home this afternoon and I was just sitting here trying to dream up a new angle on a story —or rather an angle for a new story. I wanted to ask you some details about the power structure at RBI. But that can wait, if you've got to run."

"I do," she said, "but call me tomorrow. Actually, these days it's very simple in the programing department. Elliot Chamberfield controls everything. Everybody else is a puppet."

"Uh-huh. Elliot Chamberfield. I wouldn't mind at all doing a story on him. Do you think I could get to him?"

"Hard to say. That's not something I personally could help you with, but I'll see who I know who could. Meanwhile, let me get out of here."

"Okay," he said, "Bye. Talk at you tomorrow, love. Thanks."

"Ciao!"

Brian replaced the receiver on the wall phone he'd swiped from the office and hooked up as a kitchen extension. Still thinking about the new information he'd heard. What a gold mine, he thought, a syphilitic show. He padded over to the refrigerator and hung on the door. He spruced up some cottage cheese with a tablespoonful of sour cream, and went into the living room, eating out of the container. Crummy apartment . . . plaster breaking off the walls, paint peeling, a corner drip where an upstairs shower pipe leaked. How he hated the squalor. How he'd like to be rid of it. Staten Island to West Forty-Eighth Street, but the next move'll be up to something important. And maybe that little bit of information can help. A syphilitic soap opera . . . no, he wouldn't publish it. But maybe there's another way to use it. He licked the cottage cheese off the spoon and let the lump roll around the inside of his mouth. But it wasn't only the cottage cheese he was tasting. There was something else. He was going to make a move, and this time he would cross the line, the line that separates the losers in New York—who live in West Forty-Eighth Street tenements, and have to squeeze past garbage cans on the way to reeking subways, and the winners—who live in doorman-tended buildings, take cabs to steel and glass offices, and let the company pick up tabs at the Four Seasons.

The cards would have to be played very carefully. Very, very carefully, indeed. The right person at the right time. It was a shot in a lifetime and he knew it. Brian smoothed his mustache down against the corners of his mouth, and thought about which suit he would wear.

* * *

The enormity of the executive conference room on the forty-fourth floor dwarfed the three men at the far end. They were framed in pools of light from recessed ceiling fixtures. While the white-jacketed butler (who'd been with RBI longer than any of them) cleared the silver and crystal, the remains of the veal with lemon sauce, the creamed cauliflower and salad, Messrs. Keel and Chamberfield leaned back in cushioned chairs and watched Barry Friedman labor through the end of his delivery.

He was standing in front of a large metal board, shuffling magnetically backed nameplates bearing the titles of all daytime television programs. The huge board looked like a gigantic railroad schedule, each of the networks having its own color column divided into half-hour time periods from 8:00 A.M. to 4:00 P.M., and filled with the names of shows to be presented. In the case of the other three networks, the information was the fruit of an espionage system of spies and gossipmongers from the ad agencies who sold them; the rumors were checked and cross-checked for the utmost in accuracy. RBI could hardly afford a Bay of Pigs fiasco. It had American stockholders to answer to.

Friedman reached for the last title plate for the RBI afternoon schedule. "This brings us to the toughest decision we'll have to make sometime in the next three weeks," he said *"Affair Of The Heart."* Elliot dropped two sugar cubes into his second cup of coffee and nodded

279

encouragingly at his friend. "This time slot is our only doubtful position on the whole lineup."

The bespectacled young man moved to an easel on one side of the immense board. The servant came in from the kitchen with a second silver pot of coffee. Barry continued. "Russ, if you'll notice this ratings graph here. The blue line represents *Affair*. As you can see it was running consistently below its competition at the beginning of the six months, but gradually, and here and there"—he pointed—"by leaps and upward bounds—its been moving closer and closer to eliminating the gap. It's only two or three below holding its own now, but it hasn't yet reached a marginal footing."

Elliot loosened his belt two notches and unbuttoned his middle jacket button. Good boy, Barry! You're doing a respectable goddamn job. Nice frontal delivery, letting the facts speak for themselves. Russell's reaction could only be negative. Since *Affair* was failing to hold its own it would, a priori, have to be dropped from the schedule. And its producer, Mr. Searing, along with it.

Barry worked around to his closing. "So that's it. We have two choices for recommendation to Mr. Vulkner next week. Either pick up *Affair* for another thirteen weeks, gambling that it'll continue to strengthen, or drop it in favor of the new game show Vern Tuttle's been working on until we can develop a more solid soap to replace it."

"What's that called again, Barry? That new game show Tuttle's been on?"

"*The Winning Hand*. It's a cross between *Gambit* and the *Joker's Wild* with a little bit of show biz thrown in."

"He's testing it on the coast, isn't he?"

"Yes, sir."

"How's it doing?"

Barry nudged his glasses back up on his nose and gave a quick glance to Elliot. "Well, n-n-not too well, actually. It's, uh—"

Chamberfield broke in. "It has a few kinks still to come out of it, Russ, but Tuttle and I discussed it in detail and we feel the new version which tapes this coming Thursday irons them all out."

"Any ratings projections on it yet?" Keel ran a hand over his bald head and massaged the back of his neck.

"I can answer that for you, Barry." Elliot fumbled

through a stack of papers on the large round table in front of him, fished one out, and slid it across to the president of the network. "They figure that with the proper on-the-air promotion, advertising, and a decent kickoff, it should open with a twenty-five percent share."

Keel scrutinized the paper in his hand. "Just twenty-five, that's all?"

"Course it could build rapidly, once it's on. It's a fun game with a nice twist." He didn't want to look like he was pushing the matter too hard.

"Your man Searing is doing such a terrific job; *Affair* is moving up so well. Don't you think with another thirteen he could develop it into a solid position on the board?" He flipped the paper back to Elliot.

"Yeah," Elliot said thoughtfully. "It could make it, but it may not happen for another thirteen weeks and by then the opportunity to recharge the afternoon may have passed."

"It's going to cost a hell of a lot more to put a new show in its place, isn't it?"

Barry took the fore on that one. "Yes, sir, that's true, but the sales department thinks they can make up the difference in increased revenue with the new game show." The scrawny young man took the opportunity to slide into one of the richly padded chairs. The waiter poured him a cup of coffee and he helped himself generously to the cream.

Good boy, Barry, thought Elliot.

Keel swung around. "Look, I know this show is your baby, Elliot. It was your creation and you've managed it beautifully. You took a few lumps at the beginning, but then you threw Searing in and he's whipped it in shape for you. I hate to blow the damn thing out of the water just when it seems to be ready to pay off."

"Russ"—Elliot carefully lit a cigarette and decided how he would respond—"I just can't play favorites any more. Sure this show was my baby, and I worked my ass off to get it on the right track. But we have to think of the whole afternoon schedule now and I have to do what's right for the company. That's all there is to it."

Russell nodded religiously. "Well, we all do, don't we, Barry?"

"Yes, sir." And he reddened considerably.

"All right," said Keel, "let's leave it at this. Since we have three weeks from today to notify the show if we are going to renew the contract or not, let's wait and see how *The Winning Hand* tests out. If it looks good I'll recommend to Vulkner we gamble on it. If not, we'll give Searing another thirteen."

"What will I tell Mr. Vulkner at our presentation next week?" asked Barry.

"You'll tell him exactly what Russ said. We'll know after the game show's taping which way we go." Elliot's curt reply brought more red to the young man's cheeks.

"Fine," said Keel, "you want to ring down to the attendants and have them lock up the board. I wouldn't want our new changes to be broadcast to the street before we want them to."

Barry started for the white phone.

"Just a minute, Barry. I want you and Russ to hear something first. It's personal, that is, I. . . ." It was Elliot's turn to be flustered. "I just want you two to know first, I'm going to marry Rosalynann."

"Hey, congratulations! Nice going, fella!" Russell shook Elliot's hand with vigor. Barry, on the other hand, was not so pleasantly shocked. Why hadn't Elliot told him before anyone else? Why was he telling his business superior at the same time as his friend?

"I'd like to keep it pretty much between us until her parents make the announcement."

"Sure, we understand, don't we, Barry?"

He nodded sadly. "Yeah, sure. That's really a surprise, Elliot. I had no idea you two were that serious."

"Well," he said, laughing self-consciously, "you know how these things happen. One minute you're a swinging bachelor and the next you're caught like a fish."

"Marriage is a grand institution, Elliot," Keel said expansively. "I highly recommend it and the board will be pleased, too. Vulkner likes to see his key men in settled, family positions." He patted him on the back while Barry called the attendant. "You two will have to come up for a party or something before the big date. Georgette'd love to throw you a shindig."

"That'd be swell, Russ. It won't be for a while yet. Rosalynann's mother is talking about a big church sort of affair sometime in November."

"Well, when you're ready, you let me know, and I'll make sure *Variety* gets a story up on it. After all, you're a hell of an important broadcaster these days."

They walked through the darkened portion of the room, past the three soft couches in front of the color TV monitors, and the curtained-off windows of the projection booth. Keel patted Barry on the shoulder. "That was a very nice presentation, Barry. Vulkner should be impressed with our new daytime director." And he ambled down the hall to the men's room.

The not-so-future Mrs. Chamberfield looked up radiantly at her intended. "That Brian what's-his-face listed there is a reporter from *Inside-TV*. He wants to do a story and picture layout on you."

"Why?"

"I don't know, but I gave him some time tomorrow morning. If you want to cancel it I can call his office."

"No, that's all right. Leave it. I could probably use a little publicity." And he sauntered into his office without giving it another thought.

The only chance left was the game show. If that proved out he could force it in. Otherwise, with the attitude Keel showed it would be awkward to try to force *Affair* out. It would be peculiar and suspect, and that was the last thing he wanted. Of course he could order Searing to fire Vanessa Langley, but at this stage of the game what would that accomplish? Besides she'd already had the abortion, or so Searing said. Too bad, for her, anyway. Well, TV's a tough business. We all have to take our knocks. If she continues doing as badly as she has been maybe she'll even cause the show to lose a couple of points—then in comparison to whatever the game show does, it should look worse. No, he wouldn't fire her now, but he wouldn't tell Searing, either. Let him twist slowly . . . slowly in the wind.

* * *

Since the appointment was for ten-fifteen there wasn't much point in going over to *Inside-TV* first, so Brian phoned in and said he was running a fever. "I'll be in in the afternoon if I'm feeling better." The haircut Jason had given him yesterday evening for twelve fucking dollars looked terrific. He took his new suit out of the plastic bag. A nice conservatively sporty blue serge from the Gentleman's Resale Shop, and after a moment of careful deliberation, decided on a maroon tie with stripes.

He felt right as he swung down the Avenue of the Americas and entered the RBI building. Snappy as he clicked past the security man, poor slob. Guys like that will never make it, he thought. Uniforms and yes, sirs all their lives. They just don't have the guts to put themselves on the line.

He stepped into the elevator and pushed the button that would launch the rocket of his career.

"I'm Brian Hocholtz from *Inside-TV*. I've got a ten-fifteen appointment with Mr. Chamberfield." The frosted receptionist was perfect for the plastic elegance of the floor.

"Won't you sit down, please, Mr. Hocholtz. I'll inform his secretary that you're here."

"Thank you."

No sooner had he seated himself in the modernistic reception room than a very attractive young secretary came to fetch him. "Won't you come with me, please. It's more comfortable to wait back here." She led him down a carpeted corridor to the small VP reception couch beside her desk.

His goddamn secretary's got more room here than I do at *Inside*. "Coffee?" she asked.

"Yes, please." Why not? If she offered it must be for drinking, right?

When the girl got up to make the coffee, Brian sauntered over to the window. Jesus, what a view! Straight up Sixth Avenue past CBS and ABC to the park, and the ritzy apartments of the wealthy. And to the opposite side, the magnificence of Rockefeller Center, gigantic towers rooted firmly in a foundation of fine, hard money.

"Mr. Hocholtz, your coffee."

He spun and faced the secretary. Pretty girl, but nothing special. A man as powerful as Elliot Chamberfield should have a dynamic secretary, but this little girl's just attractive. Maybe he'll mentioin it to him. He's a busy executive. Maybe he misses little things like that. He received the coffee from her hand, not failing to notice it was served in a fine cup and saucer, and not a styrofoam container, and threw her his best, most nonchalant, executive smile.

"And Mr. Chamberfield will see you now. You can take that in with you."

Shit! He didn't like that at all. It was awkward to walk in to a meeting as important as this one juggling a coffee cup. "Oh," he said. "Well. . . ." And he held out the cup.

"It's perfectly all right," she said.

It wasn't, he thought, but what could he do? He didn't want to just leave it there, did he? He put the cup down for a moment, straightened his tie and suit jacket.

Rosalynann watched him go through the motions as she'd watched so many before him. He took up the coffee cup, tucked his new attaché case under his arm—in which he was carrying solely the *Daily News,* and entered the chambers of one of the most powerful men in television.

"Well, Mr. Chamberfield, I'll be candid with you," said the reporter, after the opening trivialities were dispensed with. "I'm not here to interview you at all. I just used that ploy to get past your secretary."

Elliot's jaw tightened noticeably, but he held his temper in check.

Brian paused to give him time to say something, but when he saw he wasn't going to he continued. "I'm sorry for that, Mr. Chamberfield," he continued. "I don't generally like to deceive people, but a man in your position is so well guarded, and what I have to say is for your ears only." He paused again, thinking the executive would cut in.

Elliot sat back in his chair, stone-faced, mutely studying the brash son of a bitch.

Brian attacked all at once. "I know about the syphilis outbreak on *Affair Of The Heart.*"

Elliot leaned forward slowly, placing his hands palms down on the desk. His small eyes squinted a little tighter. "I don't know what the hell you're talking about."

"You should," said the reporter, nervous but holding control. "It's the kind of story that could cost you a lot if it ever got out to the public."

"You're telling me there's an outbreak of syphilis on one of our shows?"

"*Affair Of The Heart.* Shocking, no?"

285

"I think you're lying."

"Do you want a list of names? You can verify it yourself."

"You have a list?"

"I'll be happy to show it to you."

Elliot filled his lungs with what was for him an unusual amount of air. His fingers slipped over to unbutton his suit jacket. But outwardly he offered no indication of the fear within him. "All right," he said, as he straightened a pile of show proposals on the corner of his desk slab. "If there were such a situation, why come to me? Why not just publish it? Or are you not a reporter, either?"

"Oh, I'm a reporter, all right. And a damned good one. I'd have to be to get hold of a story like that, wouldn't I? The point is, Mr. Chamberfield, I'm interested in something different. I'm not interested in hurting RBI or you or anybody on that show. Whether this story breaks is immaterial to me. It would be another piece of gossip in the daily papers and in my lousy show business rag. I do work for *Inside-TV*. If I broke it the only thing I could come out with would be a hearty pat on the back from a cigar-chewing editor whose guts I despise. Mr. Chamberfield, I want you to get me a job on Republic Broadcasting International's news team."

"You want me to what? But how can I do something like that?" Elliot suddenly became very congenial. He had found the weakness. The kid didn't know the first thing about how a network operates, for all his shrewd-assed maneuvers. "Look, Mr."—he looked at his appointment calendar—"Hocholtz. What's your first name?"

"Brian."

"Brian. Brian, I should explain to you how we work here. You see, I'm not in any position to hire you for news no matter how high a regard I may have for your investigative skills. And I want to tell you," he said, maintaining as flattering a tone as he could, "if it's in any way true what you say I'll be seriously in your debt. As far as your working for RBI, you'd have to see the news department. But let me say this," he expanded. "I'd be more than happy to put in a call to show my appreciation, and set up an interview of some kind for you over there."

"In other words, you're giving me an executive brush-off."

"Not at all. They'll give you an open and fair interview. They certainly wouldn't slight you coming from me."

"Mr. Chamberfield," said Hocholtz, studying the shine on his new shoes, "I may not have made myself perfectly clear. I'll be delighted to have such an interview and very grateful to you for arranging it. But if for some reason it doesn't bear fruit, and I don't get a solid offer of a job I'll probably go to one of the other networks with my story. They might well be interested in my talents, and the benefits of the reportage I've done."

"But I tell you I don't have any pull in the news department."

"Yes, well, I'm sure if you tried you could find a way."

"What you're saying amounts to blackmail, you know that, don't you?"

Brian thought for a moment. "No, it doesn't. It's just a different creative kind of salesmanship. If you don't want to buy my product somebody else will. But I do know one thing. Wilson Vulkner, your chairman of the board, is one of the most image-conscious leaders in the industry. I think if I were to deal directly with such a man he'd find a way to use my abilities, and not allow them to be turned against his company."

They stared at each other like two male dogs deciding how threatening each other's smell was. Then Brian rose and picked up his case. "It was a pleasure meeting you," he said. "Think it over. I'll call you on Thursday to see what you've decided."

Elliot watched the man leave. The bastard was right. Vulkner wouldn't take well to a syphilis outbreak.

Elliot had a lousy taste in his mouth and a burning sensation in his upper stomach. He popped a Mylanta onto his tongue. Filthy bitch! Daughter of the C of the B! She should have had the decency to let him know before screwing him. There was always the chance that in some sinister way the whole affair could creep back to envelope him.

No, he had no choice but to squelch the story, squelch it as quickly as possible. But how? He had no leverage with the news guys—or did he?

He kept his ten-thirty and ten-forty-five appointments waiting in the reception area while he stared out across the East River, mulling over possible avenues of operation. He was loathe to ask for a personal favor with nothing in hand to pay it off with. You could never tell what would be demanded in return. Eventually one line of attack did emerge that might just work, though it was costly. He returned to the desk and hit the intercom button on the phone. "Get me Paul Gash on the line, Rosalynann."

"Who?"

"Gash, VP of news, and snap it up."

"Yes, sir!" Jesus, she thought as she got him the call, what do I want to marry him for? "Line two, Elliot," she pouted.

"Hello, Paul, how's your end holding up?"

"Just sniffing around for scandals," he said. "What can I do for you?"

"Paul, I have in my hand your proposal request for a nighttime special time slot."

"Don't tell me. Let me guess," he said sourly. "You just can't manage to find a slot that wouldn't destroy your schedule."

"No. Surprise, surprise. I think we might get it on, but I have a favor to ask of you."

"That's a switch. What can I do for you?"

"Well, first of all, Paul, I hope you realize that the difficulty you've been having in securing prime-time slots hasn't been coming out of this office. It's the sales department that's been fucking you up. I'm all for news shows. I think they present the right image for us."

"Yeah," said the newsman, believing not a word. "So what's the favor, Elliot?"

"I know a young man, very bright, quick, with a pretty good background in rags, and a hell of a nose for a story. You find a spot for him, and I'll throw some muscle behind your strip-mining exposé."

"You want to load me with dead wood, is that it?"

"Not at all. He's a bright young guy. I think he'd be an asset to you."

"So why doesn't he come up through the front door?"

"I don't know. I didn't get into that with him. Look,

do what you can. Place him somewhere, and, believe me, I'll be in your debt."

"What is he? The son of a friend of your mother's or something?"

"Something like that, yeah. Will you do it?"

"I'll try."

"Thanks. I have to know for sure by Wednesday."

He laughed. "I'll call you back. By the way, I have two more proposals for time slots."

"Jesus, Gash!" he exploded. "You've already had two nighttime specials in addition to your regular periods!"

"Two in three months, Elliot. Two in three months," he chided. "See what you can do for me, and I'll see what I can do for you."

"All right, Paul, you drive a hard bargain. Wednesday, don't forget."

"I'll get back to you before noon."

23.

Phillip squinted through the rainwashed windshield and found the opening in a clump of trees. He nosed the Jaguar into the entrance and through the line of foliage to the house. It was a brightly lit, ultramodern structure, designed by someone obviously influenced by Greek architecture. "Either we're early or we're the only guests."

"You can leave your car under the portico. Ramon'll park it for you."

Phillip came around and opened Gaye's door, offering his hand to steady her out. There was something special about this lady tonight, he thought, something deeply beautiful compared with her usual brassiness and flash. Perhaps it was the dress, a high-necked, long sleeved gown that fell gracefully in soft folds of forest-green silk. Or maybe it was her hair, swept up like a Degas dancer. In any case, Phillip was glad he had worn his dinner jacket.

They were admitted to the entrance hall by a butler. "Good evening, Miss Vulkner. A pleasure to see you again."

"Thank you, Ramon; this is Mr. Searing."

"How do you do?"

"Ramon."

The servant helped Gaye off with her wrap and showed them through a set of double doors to the living room. It stretched out before their feet, just short of forever, and ended in a sheer wall of glass. "On a clear night, you can see across the bay to the lights of the mainland," she said.

"May we offer you something to drink?"

"Yes, please, Ramon, a gin collins and—?" She turned to Phillip.

"Scotch please, with a dash of soda."

"Very good, sir."

When the drinks arrived they wandered through a few of the rooms with their cathedral ceilings and pure white walls, walls that provided an ideal setting for an astonishing collection of modern art. And what Phillip found even more astonishing than the collection was the degree of knowledge that Gaye seemed to have about it. She was not only versed on the pieces in the house, but on the backgrounds of the artists as well. There were Rauschenbergs, Oldenbergs, Miros, even a gigantic Stella in a special place all its own, and several Picassos and a Dali. "I read a lot," she explained, "after he and my mother were married. I had little else to do. They were involved with themselves and left me alone much of the time. I decided I wanted to learn as much about art as he knew so I could trip him up from time to time."

"Did you?" He smiled.

"Learn as much as he knew?"

"Yes."

She laughed. "I never got much of a chance to make a comparison. By the time I thought I was beginning to learn something I was shunted off to boarding school. Anyway, I doubt it very much. Anybody who trades art pieces with Nelson Rockefeller's collection is nobody to sneeze at."

"But you certainly know modern art. I always thought I did and you put me to shame."

She smiled. "I suppose—for whatever it's worth." She took another sip of the collins.

He found himself following her as she drifted from room to room. She was like a princess in a dream, gliding through a castle where everything was related to her, but nothing was her own.

There was no attempt to impress him in any way, to startle him, to use any of the devices that had become such an integral part of her repertoire. No caustic comments, no sexual thrusts, nothing. She just let herself be, and what emerged was a simple, lonely girl.

Returning to the living room she selected a cigarette from a crystal box on a glass coffee table near an armchair. "Would you like another drink before dinner?" she asked.

"No, I don't think so."

"My father won't be here until later," she added. "So we can begin whenever we like."

"He won't be here until later?" Phillip asked, startled, as she knew he would be.

"Not until later. Something's come up." She wondered how much he minded.

"And there are no other guests?"

"No. It was to be just us three, but now—"

"It's just us two."

"Yes."

He said nothing, but followed when she turned and walked across the plush white carpet to the dining room.

The main table had been set against the wall and a smaller one placed in the center of the room. Ramon held one of the leather-backed chairs for Gaye and Phillip helped himself into the other. They started with cold Scottish salmon, sliced paper thin, with capers and lemon. Phillip tested the Pouilly Fouissé and Ramon filled their glasses.

"You seem a bit ill at ease," noted Gaye when the salmon plates were exchanged for cups of vichyssoise. "Are you nervous because you're in my father's house?"

"I'm not nervous," he replied. "Just a little puzzled. Tell me something about him."

"I thought you'd met."

"Only officially. A hearty handshake at a couple of formal programing presentations."

"You probably know him better than I do," she quipped cynically. "Anyway, he's not totally different from you, I guess. A man of ambition who's dropped his soul into a career. The career part's over for him, so now he collects things . . . objects. He's driven, but I don't know really what drives him any more than I'd pretend to know what drives you. I think he's mellowed now, a little bit. He's gotten much older these past few years."

"I thought you hadn't seen him since you came back."

"Did you really think that was possible?" She smiled. "I just told you that. I like to keep up the pretense for some reason or other. I've seen him several times since I got back, and you know I've even gotten to like him a little."

The butler cleared the soup service and rolled the main course in on a wagon. He presented them with a rack of lamb for two with mint sauce and buttered French beans. The wine with the course was a Chateau Haut Brion, 1959, a numbered bottle with an extraordinary aftertaste.

"My mother fell in love with Vulkner when I was eleven or so. They met at a social function when my father was on one of his trips. He was an explorer of sorts, my real father, always getting involved in technical projects for foreign governments. He used to take us with him, until my mother decided she'd had enough of that kind of life and insisted on staying in America. That was when I was about eight or nine; I can't remember. I never saw him again. He was so angry with Mother for not going with him he never came to see me, either. And then a few years later we got word he'd died in some kind of mining accident in Alaska. It didn't affect me very much. I'd locked him out of my mind by then." Gaye finished her wine and ran her fingertip around and around the rim of the glass, creating a soft hum. "Do you know you can shatter good crystal if you do this long enough?" she asked.

"Yes, but you have to reach the right pitch," he said.

"You know everything, don't you?"

"No, but I know that."

"My mother knew a lot of things, too, little things— useless, inconsequential things that never meant anything but were always fun to hear about. She was the most beautiful woman I have ever seen. I'm beautiful, I know that, but she was something else again. God, how men used to chase after her, but she just ignored them. And I used to be so jealous of her. . . ."

Phillip watched her float away with her thoughts.

Ramon served dessert in the living room: poached peaches with raspberry purée, accompanied by a light burgundy. He set it on a low table in front of one of three couches facing a fireplace. Since there was a chill in the air, a fire had been started and lit the room romantically with its changing golden light. Gaye leaned back comfortably against the corner of the couch. Phillip found her sad, a mood he'd never seen her in before. A few strands of dark-red hair fell charmingly out of place on her swanlike neck. "Do you know I was expelled from five schools after they sent me away? I managed to do something to embarrass and frustrate him every chance I ever got." She stopped talking and turned to look at Phillip. "I was a blossoming Lolita at thirteen . . . really blossoming. I was lonely, I was jealous of my mother, and couldn't decide whether I loved her handsome new husband or hated him. So one night when he came to kiss me good night before going into the city to meet my mother, I made a pass at him."

She stopped for a time before going on. "It was the only time I've ever seen Wilson Vulkner lose control of himself. I think he might have wanted me and that fact terrified the hell out of him."

"What about you?" asked Phillip softly.

"I wasn't ashamed if that's what you're asking. I was furious. First, because he rejected me, and, second, because I saw a man who had become something of a model almost disintegrate before my eyes. Nothing he could say erased the fear I saw in him, the fear I had made him feel. It made me realize the power I had over men."

There was a decanter of brandy on the table. Phillip poured a finger into each of the two snifters that accompanied it. He presented one to Gaye and then rose to stand in front of the fireplace with his back to her. "Do you think that's a reason to hate a man? Because he didn't satisfy the whim of a thirteen-year-old girl?" he asked.

"What was so devastating was that he did absolutely nothing except have me sent away. He didn't take me and he didn't punish me. He just sent me away to school—talked my mother into it. He was always distant with me after that. Even when my mother died six years ago he kept away from me, except in public. I never saw him alone until I came back to work for you. I've gotten to know him a little this time. I think he's still afraid of me but he's my stepfather again. I think he felt as much cheated out of a daughter as I felt cheated out of a father."

Phillip turned around and looked at her. She sat primly on the couch, her eyes cast down, her hands folded around the brandy glass. "He won't be here tonight, will he?"

"No. He flew to St. Croix yesterday morning."

Only the crackling of the burning wood disturbed the stillness of the giant room. Gaye looked down into her glass. "The party I originally invited you to was to be tonight, but it was changed to three days ago. My father went down to the island for the meeting of the corporation board."

The board meeting . . . Christ! thought Phillip. Shows how much out of things I've become. It would have been of prime concern had I still been up on forty-three. I would have been busy for weeks with presentational matter.

"I decided not to tell you because I wanted to be alone with you. I have the use of the house again." And then she added in a very small voice: "Don't be angry with me. Please don't be angry."

Phillip was flattered, but as desirable as Gaye was, sitting there open and willing, he was unwilling to take advantage of her. He sensed she was beyond being toyed with now and he didn't want to hurt her by indulging himself.

They left, at his suggestion, shortly before eleven. He'd managed to hold his distance—and kept the good night at her apartment door to a double kiss on the cheek. It required uncommon will power.

The only interesting mail waiting for Phillip when he arrived at his apartment was an express letter from Paris. It was from Katina, saying she would be coming to New York sometime in the next week:

The guy I wrote you about who liked the poems I showed him actually has a publisher who's interested. Can you imagine? But I got something else out of that happy-time villa down there in the So. of France. I, my dear, have picked up my own personal, first-class dose of the lowest-class disease known in the hollows of man and woman. Not clap, not crabs, but the real goddamn thing—syphilis. And surprise of surprises—we think we traced it to Jacques, that friend of your friend Gaye Vulkner, so if he ever comes over and hanky-panks with her you'd better keep your own little dipper out until you're sure what's what. I went in for shots today. Jesus, it makes me feel crummy!

Phillip stuffed the letter back into the envelope and waited for the doors to open. Syphilis, Christ! Well, Gaye didn't have it. She couldn't or he would have gotten it through her in London. He was just inserting the key in the lock when a voice from the shadows at the end of the hall stopped him. "Phillip Searing?"

Phillip turned quickly, instinctively, unlocking the door as a precautionary measure. "Yes?"

A tall, lanky kid with a head of bushy brown hair stepped into the light. "I'm John Langley. Vanessa's husband's brother."

Phillip was perplexed. How did he get past the security guard? He'd have to speak to the building superintendent. "Yes."

"I've got somethin' important to talk to you about. Would ya mind if I came in?"

There was something about the way in which the question was put that made Phillip a bit wary, but he said, "All right, come in."

It wasn't until he flipped the interior light on and the boy passed into the vestibule that Phillip caught his first glimpse of John Langley's eyes. There was something in them that Phillip didn't care for—a panic, perhaps, a strain of violence that belied his easy hayseed look.

They went up the little steps into the living room.

"I heard about your brother, John," Phillip said as casually as possible. "Vanessa told me he's in the hospital. How's he doing? Will he be out soon?"

"That's what I come here for. That's what I come to see you 'bout."

"Yes?"

"They had him in a life-support system. That was so they could keep his body systems functionin', even if he didn't want 'em to be."

"Didn't want them to be?"

The broad-shouldered boy wiped his hand across his nose. "Yeah, they had him in straps, tied down like a hog so he couldn't do no damage to himself, no more, that is, than he already done. Well, he broke outa them straps this afternoon, and he fuckin' yanked all them tubes and shit outa his arms, and you know what that done to him, Mr. Searing? Lemme tell you what that done to him. It threw him into a coma. My brother's in a coma right now, Searing. He's in a coma."

Phillip was startled. But why was John here with this news at this time of night? It meant something to Phillip; of course it did. It meant Vanessa would have that much more weight on her shoulders, but why the hell was this kid telling him? He wanted to ask, but didn't dare. Phillip had seen other people balancing themselves on the same tightwire of violence as this boy. . . .

The boy didn't say any more. He stood there glaring at the producer, or perhaps glaring through him. His fists clenched and unclenched nervously and every so often he rubbed one of them across his chin.

"John," Phillip said finally, measuring him carefully. "It is John, isn't it?"

The boy nodded with a short chop of his disheveled head.

"John, I know you must be upset about your brother. I would be, . . . I'm somewhat at a loss to understand what I can do about it. I mean, why have you come to me? Is there something I can do?"

John snorted out a short bitter laugh. "Do? You? You've done more than enough!"

"I don't know what you're—"

John cut him off. "Joe's not just in a coma, pal. He had them needles'n tubes outa himself too long. His brain was without oxygen for so long that even if he comes out of it he'll be a vegetable for the rest of his life!" His face was contorted.

The news was chilling to Phillip, and more so since the trembling mountain of a boy seemed to blame him in some way. "I . . . I'm awfully sorry to—"

"You can drop the phony executive shit, Mr. Searing. I know you couldn't give a pig's fuck about my brother. You're probably goddamn pleased, ain't ya? Ain't ya?" he screamed. "You cocksucker!"

He took a step toward Phillip, but Phillip stood his ground. "Look, fella, I don't know what you're talking about. I'm sorry to hear about your brother, but I didn't have anything to do with putting him in the hospital and I don't like being called names in my own house. So I think it's time you took off."

"I'll take off, all right, but not until I tell you the rest—so you know! Right? So you know and you can't go around sayin' you don't know! Right? It is your goddamn fault my brother's where he is, you son of a bitch! Your goddamn fault and you know it." The rage was spilling out of his mouth in waves. "You don't understand! Are you playin' dumb with me or what?"

"No, I don't. I really don't know what you're talking about."

"I'm talkin' about why my brother wanted to die! Why he pulled them tubes outa his body! You stupid fuck—what do you think I'm talkin' about! He knew all about you and his wife!"

"What!"

"Does that surprise you? Yeah, that does, doesn't it? Don't be so surprised, Mr. Hotshot. Joey knew that kid she was carryin' wasn't his! He knew all about you two and it ate him up inside. How do you think that feels, Searing? Being married to a broad who says she had a miscarriage and then findin' out it weren't no miscarriage after all, but she had an abortion 'cause the kid wasn't his? Well, that's my brother, pal. That's him! It wasn't his kid—it was yours!"

Phillip was dumbstruck. Vanessa's baby his? Could it be? Was it possible? They had only slept together once. Just once. She must have been with her husband hundreds of times. How could it be his kid? There was no affair, nothing for her husband to know "all about." He spoke haltingly, unsure of his ground. "I think you don't have your facts right. Have you . . . talked to Vanessa about—"

"I don't have to talk to Vanessa about nothin'. It's yours all right. See, my brother ain't been able to make it with his wife for a long time now. He couldn't get it up, poor bastard. You talk to Vanessa. You ask her next time you're snugglin' down in bed with her." His voice finished raucously and his face turned a murderous red.

Phillip rubbed his forehead, trying to massage a semblance of coherence into his thoughts. If what this boy says is true, no wonder Vanessa was on the verge of a breakdown. No wonder she had avoided him. A wave of self-revulsion swept over him.

Suddenly, John let out a muffled cry and lunged forward with a long hunting knife that he pulled from his boot. Phillip looked up just in time to see the shiny steel blade catch the light. He turned, but it struck him anyway, jamming into the soft flesh of his shoulder. The knife came out, but before it could be used again he seized John's hand at the wrist and twisted it with all his might. John raised his knee and just missed Phillip's groin. They fell against the end table, knocking over a lamp which crashed down to the floor. The room was plunged into semi-darkness.

Phillip still had a grip on the knife arm, but John wrenched it free and swung back to strike again. Phillip lashed out with his foot, catching the boy in the chest sending him reeling backward against the window. The weight of his body tugging the draperies tore them, bringing down the rods and valance as well. The knife, too, bit into the material. Phillip leapt up and kicked out at the arm while the knife was snared in a drapery. His toe hit the nerve just under the bicep and John let go with a squeal. The knife clattered to the floor and Phillip kicked it under the couch, but John managed to rise and slam a hard fist into the side of his head, sending shooting stars into his vision.

He heard John scramble to his feet, felt him coming up behind, but he didn't make a move to ward off the hammer blow that crashed down on his neck. And when he fell to his knees he just stayed there, even when the thick-soled hiking boot swung forward and crunched into his ribs.

John stood above him, breathing heavily. Phillip was conscious, but he didn't move. Let the kid do what he

299

would. He was spent. He didn't want to fight Vanessa's brother-in-law any more. But fortunately John was finished, too. He'd made his point. Slowly he turned and walked toward the door. He opened it and went out, leaving it ajar.

Phillip lay in pain at the foot of the couch, pain from the knife, from the fists, from the knowledge he now possessed. He rolled over on his back. The room swam before his eyes. Sleep . . . sleep. . . . Close your eyes and sleep. It'll be over in the morning. It'll all be gone in the morning. No. No, that wasn't possible. He needed to know.

"Vanessa, this is Phillip. I . . . I'm coming to see you. Right now. Please, let me in when I ring your bell."

24.

He had enough sense to put on another jacket, since no cabdriver in his right mind would pick him up with blood running down his arm and he was in no condition to drive. Under the jacket, he'd pressed a cold wet towel.

He stumbled over to Union Square and hailed a southbound cab. The shoulder hurt badly, so did the ribs where he'd been kicked. He felt with his fingers to tell if there was a crack, but it was too agonizing to touch.

He hadn't taken the time to think about anything. He just made the phone call, left, and plodded west. What the hell was happening to him? It was all so bizarre. What was he, Phillip Searing, tennis player extraordinaire, powerful purveyor of entertainment for the masses, cool and proper gentleman, doing slumped in the back of a taxi at one in the morning, bruised and bleeding, heading toward the apartment of a man who was dying in a hospital from an overdose of heroin? No answer came to mind —only the face of the wife of the man.

The taxi came to a stop and the interior lights flicked on. "We're here, buddy," said the cabbie. Phillip pushed a couple of bills into his hands. He climbed out and stood for a moment in the drizzle, his hand on the throbbing shoulder. Then he mounted the stairs. Langley was number seven. He pushed the bell. There was no intercom, but after a moment or so the buzzer sounded and he leaned against the door, nudging it open. The hallway was dark; two circular neon bulbs set in the ceiling at either end gave feeble illumination. When he reached the stairs, he heard a bar being shifted and an apartment door opened a crack. He assumed it was Vanessa's, so he went on up.

When she saw the condition he was in, her jaw dropped in surprise. She pushed the door open wide. He rested at the top of the landing for a second, steadying himself from the exertion of the climb. They looked at each other, through the prism of their individual misery.

"John Langley came to see me a little while ago," Phillip managed to get out. "He said . . . he told me something about your baby. He said . . . it was mine."

Vanessa just stared at him, clutching the top of her robe, her eyes wide with shock. Her body was rigid.

Then he asked the question directly. "Is it true, Vanessa? Was the baby you were carrying mine?"

Her breath came out; her muscles fell limp.

Yes, he thought, it's true. Just to look at her was to know it was true. She said nothing, but led the way into the apartment.

They sat in their individual islands of darkness and thought about each other.

Sometime later, maybe half an hour or an hour, Vanessa got up and put some water on to boil in the kitchen. She made a pot of tea and served it silently. It was only then that she noticed the blood running down Phillip's arm. "Did John do this?" Phillip nodded. She made him remove his jacket and bathed the wound in a basin of hot water. "You're not . . . going to go to the police, are you?" He shook his head. "The wound's deep, Phillip," she said, concerned. "You have to see a doctor in the morning."

Normally Phillip didn't like to be fussed over by women, but at the moment he had neither the strength nor the desire to resist her attentions. In fact there was something very soft, soothing, and comforting about her hands binding the wound in a clean, white dishtowel; he secretly wished they would continue forever. He didn't mention the ribs.

Vanessa insisted on taking his dress shirt and washing the blood stains out of it, then hung it in front of the open oven door to dry. She gave him a skivvy of Joe's to wear in which Phillip felt uneasy.

"He wouldn't even let me visit him when he regained consciousness," murmured Vanessa. "He didn't even want to see me."

Phillip could think of nothing to say. Why hadn't she told him? he wondered. Why hadn't she asked for help? Why? Why should she have? What could he have done for her? Nothing, he reasoned. Once it happened there was nothing any of them could have done . . . and Joe's way of handling it for himself? Well, thought Phillip. That probably couldn't have been prevented, either. It wasn't like Joe hadn't shot dope before, and he was still alive—or was he?

Phillip could not remember ever feeling so helpless before, so lost. All he could think of was this disturbingly lovely girl, who sat so resolutely now at the window. A hard glare from the street light outlined her silhouette on the sheer white curtains. It caused an artificial glow to highlight the curve of her neck. Should he go to her? Should he put his arms around her? Or bury his face in her lap and ask for comfort himself? Nothing . . . he could do nothing. For once in his life, he could do nothing.

And yet he wanted to—he desperately wanted to.

An alarm clock went off in the bedroom at five-thirty and Vanessa went in to silence it. She came out a few moments later carrying a blouse, a pair of slacks, and some underthings. She was about to pass into the bathroom to prepare herself for the call at the studio, when Phillip looked up from his seat on the couch. Something in his look stopped her. Such a wounded lion, she thought. She put her things on the stereo set and came around the coffee table and sat next to him. She circled her arms around him, kissed his forehead, and pulled it gently down until it rested on her breast. She held him tightly, letting their pain and strengths merge, until he drew back himself.

"It's so unreal," he said at length.

"No," she answered. "It's pathetically real."

"What will you do?"

"What can I do? Just wait and see what happens. But

303

you won't have to fire me now. I'm past that point. As of today I expect to be getting much better."

"I wasn't going to fire you, Vanessa," he said.

"Yes, you were, and you would have been right."

* * *

Phillip didn't go into the studio that morning—the first morning of work he'd missed all summer. He called Colin and told him to handle it. It wasn't scheduled to be too difficult, anyway. After Vanessa left, he took a cab back to his apartment on Irving Place.

Dr. Wolfe saw him at nine-thirty. He sewed up the knife wound. "It's going to throb for a week or so since it's so deep, but you're lucky it didn't chop into any nerves." He rebandaged it with medical expertise. He also gave Phillip a tetanus shot.

As for the ribs, the X-rays showed they were only bruised. Painful as hell, but no cracks. Phillip didn't volunteer any information as to the cause of the injuries and the doctor, whom he'd known for several years, didn't ask. He taped the rib cage tightly, so that no undue strain would be placed on it and suggested that the knife wound be reported to the police. Phillip declined, however, and hoped aloud that the good doctor wouldn't report it, either. "Otherwise I'll be forced to say I inflicted it on myself and that could cause me a lot of trouble. Seriously, Doc, treat it as an accident."

It was ten-thirty when he got out and thought there was really no reason why he shouldn't go into the studio. Christ knows, there were enough things that needed attending to, not the least of which was a meeting with Maude on the changes she'd made in the story line. But first he stopped for coffee and a Danish; he hadn't put anything into his stomach since dinner at Vulkner's.

Gloria knew instantly that something had happened. It wasn't so much the bruise on the side of his head (which he passed off as a "walk into a cupboard door"), but the general manner in which he carried himself. There was no power in his step, no immediacy in his stride. He moved slowly and sat with far too much lassitude behind his desk. And, of course, she couldn't help but notice his eyes when he thanked her for the coffee she brought him.

There was a vacantness there, something she'd never seen in him before.

Maude appeared for a read-through of the newly revised tumor scenes. He listened quietly as she laid them out and gave her the go-ahead to lock them in. And that seemed to surprise her, too. She peered at him over the tops of her bifocals. "This is the first story conference we've ever had where you didn't give me at least a dozen corrections."

"It doesn't need it. Relax, it's good work," he said.

Never one to add unnecessary weight to her load, Maude shrugged and stuffed her notes back into her case. "I'll give them to Gloria to type and have distributed." She waited for him to speak, but when he didn't even look in her direction, she mumbled a brief "see you" and went out, closing the door behind her.

Phillip received a rundown on the morning's activities from Colin, who assured him that all had gone well. "Just lounge in bed, boss, anytime you want. I'll take care of things just fine." So enthused was he to have been given the responsibility for handling the show (or at least the morning's work) that he hardly noticed anything was wrong with Phillip.

Phillip was pleased that Gaye wasn't scheduled into the show that day. The awkwardness of having to face her in the condition he was in was one thing he'd be able to avoid. How long ago last night seemed, and the comfort of that roaring fire.

Ten minutes before the taping he slipped down to the studio floor. He'd spot-checked the camera rehearsal and saw that Vanessa had indeed improved. A certain determination was making itself felt in her performance. He caught her in the hallway as she was coming out of her new dressing room. "I came to see how you were."

"I'm all right," she said, "and you?"

He nodded. "Have you heard from the hospital?"

"He's still the same . . . no change one way or the other." She gave him a look reflecting the feeling she'd left with at the apartment: whatever was to be, would be, but she had enough of wallowing in misery.

He watched the taping on the office monitor, keeping himself safe from the control-room tensions. Gloria had ordered him a sandwich and left it on the coffee table with a fresh cup of coffee. He nibbled on it during the half hour, but in the end left more than he'd eaten. When it was over he asked the young secretary to hold all but the most important incoming calls, and to keep visitors at bay as well. He sat down and tried to prop his feet on the desk, but was stopped by a symphony of pains. He assumed a more appropriate position. His little horse statue had fingerprints on it. He wiped them off and studied it.

The question that plagued him more than all others was why he hadn't realized, hadn't suspected! CHRIST! The baby Vanessa was carrying had been his! Was he so arrogant? So removed from the fate of others? All right, he didn't think that a married woman would have protected herself, and of course he hadn't known about her husband's impotence. But not even to think of the possibility once? What kind of hide had he built around himself?

He looked at the statue in his hands, a small golden racehorse galloping at full stride. It was probably the only personal memento he'd ever kept. Betsy had given it to him . . . tiny Betsy from college, who used to hang around the tennis courts watching him play, until Jacqueline started showing up regularly. She'd sent it to him on the eve of their graduation with a note he'd memorized instantly. "Get on this horse, Phillip Searing, and ride it till the gold sweats blood, because you have the potential to set paces of lightning and you owe it to the world to do so." He was so naively touched. It embodied all of the grandeur he had ever hoped he could achieve.

The statue had stood on every desk he occupied, through the early advertising days all the way to the present. But now for the first time he began to wonder about the horse, to fear that instead of climbing on gold, he'd climbed on a gold-painted horse. A wooden horse on a merry-go-round. Around and around in circles went his job, his life. What's next?

25.

Friday dawned upon the city with a brilliance generally reserved for mornings in spring. The rain had washed the air clean and the sky was a radiant blue. Sun bounced off the sides of buildings, bringing apartment dwellers to the point of thinking about giving their windows a good scrubbing. It was a good morning to buy a green-potted plant to hang in one's window. It was an exquisite morning and it gleamed in the faces of those on the streets, who were forced to lose sight of it by eight or nine o'clock, to coop themselves up in square office boxes and live by the light of fluorescence.

Elliot Chamberfield had been out early himself. But not in wonderment at nature's excessess. He was in his office near the top of the RBI tower at 8:00 A.M. The building was silent. He waited, in shirt sleeves, behind his desk, his back turned to the monitor cabinet. The RBI set was being tuned to the closed-circuit channel by a special attendant. The game show had been rushed in by overnight courier from Los Angeles, but the attendant was having trouble getting the man on the tape machine across town to pick up the phone next to him. Elliot held his temper.

"Hello? Hello?" The soft-spoken electrical technician tried to raise the errant machine man. "Will? I got him. That you, Will?" He covered the mouthpiece and leaned toward the back of Elliot's chair. "He's on, sir. Should I give him the cue?"

"Of course." Elliot whirled around and stared down at the blank screen in the formica cabinet.

"Roll 'em, Will."

The color bars and tone at the top of the tape flickered on and held. The technician bent over and twisted some knobs. A slate with the name of the show, director's name, and tape-segment number appeared briefly with a stage manager's voice reading the information in the background. *The Winning Hand*. Opening. Take Two." The set faded to black. Music came in. The title faded up, surrounded by a band of twinkling lights and the announcer's voice punched out: "Straight from Las Vegas! The game which tests your luck against the house! *The Winning Hand!*"

"Jesus, this better be good," Elliot mumbled to no one in particular.

The technician adjusted the sound and then backed away to a chair in the far corner, his eyes glued to the set, watching vigilantly for any signs of machine dropout.

Elliot leaned back to study his winning hand.

Twenty-eight and a half minutes later the credits rolled over the announcer's voice. By then Elliot knew precisely where he stood. "Shut the damn thing off!" he blurted, and then waved him out of the room.

That show stunk from here to California. Not a damn sight better than the previous tapings. They'd taken all his suggestions and reworked the basic game, adding a little bit of overall suspense, but it didn't work. It wasn't enough. The show was a bomb and that was it. He didn't have to wait for any audience-testing results to know it on this one. Even Barry, who was scheduled to look at the tape at ten, would pressure him to bury it.

He punched the button and rang for the operator.

"Get me Vern Tuttle in Hollywood." He read off the private number of Vern's hotel.

"It's only five-thirty in California now, sir," she said, trying to be helpful.

"I can tell time, Operator. Wake the bastard up." The show smelled like shit and he should know about it. Serves him right. He promised me a winner. Fucking no-talent shmuck. Should have known better than to put that spineless wonder in to develop a game show. The guy's had no experience, no track record in the field. He jammed a cigarette into his mouth.

The operator interrupted his anger. "I'll ring you back when he's on the line, sir."

"I'll hang on."

"We're having a little trouble with the tie line this morning, sir."

"Well, make it snappy, will ya?" He let the receiver fall into its cradle. Now what the hell could he do? The failure blew his strategy all to shit. He couldn't force *Affair* out without a replacement. And it was too late to come up with a second show. *Affair* could have been canceled in two weeks if this goddamn show had been halfway decent, but this one would be laughed off the air and they'd end up by canning him, too.

He found himself breathing hard. Instinctively he reached his hand under his left breast. The heart couldn't take much strain like this. He dug into his pants' pocket and slipped out the small vial of pills his doctor had given him for just these trying moments. Popping one into his mouth, he rose to wash it down with a glass of water left in the decanter from the previous day. The phone stopped him. He swallowed the pill with a dry gulp and reached for the receiver, cursing because Rosalynann had not yet deigned to show up for work when she knew he was coming in early. "Yeah?"

But it wasn't the long-distance operator. "Elliot? This is Brian Hocholtz. Sorry to be disturbing you so early this morning. But I wanted to catch you before you got jammed up."

"What's on your mind, Hocholtz?" This was the last guy he wanted to talk with.

"I just wanted to tell you that I met with Paul Gash

309

yesterday afternoon and I'm hired. Start work Monday. Of course, it isn't an on-camera job but. . . ."

The shmuck. Wants to start as a newscaster! He ought to be grateful for wielding a broom.

". . . I guess I can't start at the top. Paul was very considerate and promised that I'd soon be moved up to the editorial department."

"Yeah? Well, that's good. I hope this puts an end to any ideas you had."

"You can count on that, Elliot. And I really want to thank you for arranging the interview."

"Yeah, don't mention it." While Brian had been talking, Elliot glanced down at the pad in front of him with Tuttle's phone number on it. He was down to his last plan of attack and he needed to make certain it wouldn't fail. Someway, he had to strengthen his own hand. "Yes, uh, Hocholtz. . . ." Elliot searched for the right words. "You mentioned you had a list of people on *Affair* that were affected by this outbreak. I'm curious. Just between me and you, is Phillip Searing's name on that list?"

"Searing? No. He's one of the few who isn't, though."

"And the Langley girl? Vanessa Langley. Is she?"

Brian laughed self-consciously. "I think you picked the only two people who didn't catch it. But then, from what I've heard, there's a reason for that."

"Why?"

Brian snorted. "Well, from what I hear, they didn't get it because they've only been into each other."

"What?" Elliot's heart pounded excitedly. "You mean the two of them are having an affair?"

"I'm not positive, but the way I heard it is they've been kind of together for a long time. I can't absolutely verify it, but I think they probably are, if you ask me."

Searing making it with Langley? Of course. That explained why he won't fire her. Fucking Colin Dawes, Elliot raged inwardly. That fruit! Why didn't he get me that information? He congratulated the kid on his new job and rung off.

So Searing was sleeping with Vanessa, and the little whore was a married woman! That made it all so much easier.

Two other things came up before the day ended that made Elliot realize he had to deal with his rival quickly, if he were going to be successful. First, an advance copy of *TV Guide* appeared, as it usually did on Fridays. It was always sent by the publishers a few days before it hit the news and supermarket stands. There was an article that didn't delight him at all, an interview on the set of *Affair* with that has-been old fart, Justin Teague. Elliot skimmed it dispassionately until one particular paragraph leapt off the page. The old bastard had the nerve to be quoted as saying that "Phillip Searing is the hottest young producer in television today and the industry needs more just like him in order to survive and grow." Jesus, Elliot didn't need that! The only good thing about its appearing now was the fact that the entire board was with Vulkner and Keel down in St. Croix. The issue would be a week old by the time they returned. It was just conceivable that they'd miss it altogether.

The second thing that Elliot noticed upset him even more. Toward the end of his day, Rosalyann brought in the story projections Barry's daytime staff had prepared showing the directions in which the soaps on the web were heading. Elliot hadn't caught *Affair Of The Heart* the last couple of days; he had more important things to do than waste a half hour watching a show he knew exactly what was wrong with. So he caught up on the plot developments by reading an outline of the goals Searing had recently installed. The new twist involving Vanessa Langley's character didn't sit well on his lunch-stuffed stomach. So Valerie's cataracts had now become a tumor and she was to have an operation which would put her life in jeopardy. The son of a bitch was preparing an exit for her. He was already outmaneuvering him. With that kind of setup, he could kill off Valerie anytime he wanted. Elliot didn't like that one bit. Now that *The Winning Hand* had turned up nothing but jokers, the only way Elliot could possibly get Searing out was by forcing him to countermand a direct order—refuse absolutely to undertake a responsibility he was given—and the only order *that* could be was the firing of Vanessa Langley. It was all he had to work with. And he had supportable reason to give Phillip the order: Vanessa was ruining the show. But if Phillip was planning to knock her off while she was on the operating table, if that was what he was building into, then the clever bastard had him against the wall.

Elliot pulled a bottle of Jack Daniels out of his desk drawer and poured a stiff double shot into the water glass on the decanter tray. He chugged down half of it on the first try, and then thinned out the rest a little bit.

But maybe that wasn't what Phillip was planning at all. If that pimp who called in the morning was right, and Searing and Langley were having an affair, then Phillip wouldn't be planning to dump her so easily. He might just be planning to keep her juggling back and forth between life and death—the hospital bed and a series of operations in order to build up the audience. What he was really doing was developing the show around his girlfriend. Since she was having problems, he was giving her character problems, and when the problems got too bad he'd just put her onto the operating table so she wouldn't have to deal with dialogue, acting, or any of the other things she's drawing a fucking-good salary for. Yeah, he's putting the broad on ice.

Elliot paced nervously around the room, waving off Roslynann who slipped in for a quick good-bye kiss before going down to Delaware to do some work on the wedding with her mother.

Yeah, he thought to himself, that's what the bastard's going to do . . . put Vanessa on ice and let her hover near death for as long as he can milk tears out of the audience—and as long as the actress is fucking up. In that case, there was no problem at all, because Phillip would certainly balk at letting her go. There'd be a certain amount of questioning, but nobody would dare question his moves under such conditions. After all, to refuse a direct superior order? How could you run an operation with such disobedience?

Okay, fine. The anticipation excited him. The confrontation would have to take place as soon as possible because it should be dead as an issue by the time Russell got back from the meeting in St. Croix.

The numbers on the digital clock on the cabinet read five-forty-nine—much too late to get hold of Searing now. It would have to hold for Monday morning. He sat down at his desk, nervously fidgeting with a pencil. Then he put a yellow legal pad in front of him and wrote a note for Rosalynann. "First thing, Rosalynann, send a memo to Phillip Searing on the *Affair* set. I want to send just two words. *Fire Her!* and sign my name." He was about to add, "I'll call you at your mother's this weekend," but then he remembered Rosalynann wouldn't be receiving the note until after the weekend had passed.

26.

Phillip arrived at the office at his usual hour and attempted to shake off the malaise he had fallen into. Gloria noticed he was trying, but it made her all the more aware that something was troubling him deeply. They chatted briefly about a private screening of a new Warner Brothers' film she had attended on his pass and then he closeted himself in the office for an industrious hour, tallying up cost sheets and budgeting out the remainder of the month's operations.

After the camera run-through he stopped down to talk to Pat, who happened to remark that Vanessa looked like she might be starting to pull out of whatever it was that had been ailing her. He also got hold of Colin and had him start nudging the set department for the elaborate operating-room pieces they were now in a rush for, and he saw Gaye for the first time since the night at her father's house. She seemed much more subdued than before. There certainly wasn't the open antagonism that had punctured their working relationship.

He climbed back up to the office to watch the taping. Gaye had two nice bits on the show today, and Phillip observed her work with a growing respect. It was comforting to be reminded that his decision to hire her had begun to pay dividends. Yes, she was filling out admirably as an actress. There was a new depth, a new sensitivity.

There was a wide shot which covered the whole of Daphne's chic apartment. She and Charles were having their morning coffee in the breakfast nook.

CHARLES.
(*Miserable. Puts down his coffee cup firmly.*) We can't go on like this. I should have never stayed the night. It isn't fair to Valerie.

DAPHNE.
(*Coyly*) Is it fair to you?

CHARLES.
(*Rising, takes cup to kitchen counter for refill*) That isn't the point.

DAPHNE.
Then what is?

CHARLES.
(*Whirls to face her*) Can't you tell something is wrong with her? She's hiding something. She's not acting herself. I just know it.

DAPHNE.
(*Tears forming*) And what about me? Don't you care what I feel?

CHARLES.
(*Comes to her, but doesn't touch her*) Of course I do ... but ...

DAPHNE.
Well, then . . . (*She rises and puts her arms around him. Over his shoulder we see her begin to smile.*).

The camera moved in to a closeup of her. How extraordinarily beautiful she was, thought Phillip. But then he saw something that disturbed him. It was on her lip, at the corner of her mouth, out of range of the lipstick . . . a small sore, like a cold sore. Mary's pancake hadn't hid it very well. It must be new. He hadn't noticed it before.

Suddenly his mind made a jolting connection so forcefully that his body lurched forward in his seat. The letter from Katina! He'd forgotten all about it. It had disappeared into the confusion of the Langley attack and the long night's vigil with Vanessa. It must still be in the pocket of the slashed tuxedo jacket. Katina wrote that she'd contracted syphilis from a friend of Gaye's. Did Gaye have a dose of it, too? And if she did, why didn't he? Or did he? But he hadn't noticed anything.

He was forced to wait until the end of the taping, but as soon as the last act ended, he burst through the door and shot past Gloria. She was delighted to see he'd retrieved some of his old vigor. But Phillip had to pause at the staircase, for the quick movements had caused his shoulder and the pain in his side to throb again.

He barged into her dressing room without knocking. Before Gaye could get a word out he took her roughly by the chin and brought her close to examine the lip. "Do you have syphilis?"

"What?" she exclaimed, jerking her head back.

"Syphilis, Gaye, do you have a dose?"

She thought he was kidding. "Phillip," she said, laughing, "you are a man of surprises. Is that any kind of accusation to make to a lady?"

"I'm not joking. What's that sore on your mouth?"

Her hand flew up to it as if to cover her only physical flaw. "A fever blister, I guess. I don't know." She was perplexed. "It's only recently come out."

"I think we'd better check it with a doctor."

"Now hold on a minute, Mr. Boss-man!" Her anger didn't waste much time in reaching the surface. "Don't you come charging into my dressing room making wild insinuations. I'm over twenty-one and I can take care of myself. It's my business if I do or not. And if it's anybody else's it's certainly not yours!" She dropped petulantly down into her makeup chair.

Phillip calmed himself a little. "All right, look, I'm not playing moralist. It *is* your private affair. And I personally don't care if you have leprosy—well, that's not true. I do care, because I care about you. But I care about the others, too. You've been a very active young lady. If you do have it, and you just well might, you've got to do something about it immediately. And if you do, I'm going to want to know how many others connected with this soap opera have it too." She seemed too frightened by the prospect to be faking surprise. He rested his hand on her shoulder. "I think we'd better go see a doctor, don't you?"

316

He called Dr. Wolfe again and arranged an appointment right away for the two of them, but asked the doctor not to mention his own injuries in front of the girl.

Gaye was subdued, if somewhat pouty, when she finished and came out to the reception area. Then Phillip went in and had his test. "I would really appreciate anything you could do to rush it through, Bob," he said. "Is there any chance you can get me the results tonight?"

"There's a chance. But get out of here quick, and let me have this sent over to the lab. Call me at home tonight. I'll see what I can get for you by then."

"Thanks, Bob, very much."

"If it's positive you'll come in tomorrow morning and I'll start sticking needles in your ass. Bring your friend along, too. I wouldn't mind sticking something in hers, when she's cured, of course."

"Filthy-minded bastard! I thought you medical guys weren't turned on by that stuff any more."

"Are you kidding? What do you think we dream about at night? Dissected cadavers? And speaking of cadavers, how's the shoulder?"

"Sore."

"Ribs?"

"Sore."

He took a quick look and released him. "Try me around five. I ought to be home by then."

Phillip took Gaye's hand as they walked south toward the giant Pan Am tower that straddled the wide avenue, blocking the view. They walked in silence for several minutes, occasionally finding themselves scrutinized by passers-by, who must have been struck by the physical handsomeness of the pair. After what Phillip felt was an appropriate amount of time, he brought up the subject as diplomatically as possible. "I know this will be embarrassing for you," he said. "But if the Wasserman is positive—and from examining your chancre Dr. Wolfe seems to think it will be—I'm going to need something from you for the sake of everyone else. I'll need a list, Gaye, a complete list of everybody you've had contact with sexually since you got to New York."

"Impossible," she blurted out. "You've got to be out of your mind."

"Of course it's possible."

317

"Well, you aren't on it for sure, are you?" she said cynically, releasing his hand.

"Look, I'm not concerned about myself. I'm concerned about the others, especially those on *Affair*. If the results are positive, we have to move immediately to stop the spread. If you give me a list, I'll personally contact all the names you've remembered and have each of them get shots. They can contact their own friends themselves."

"Wonderful," she muttered. "Just ducky."

"Don't worry. I won't mention your name. We'll go back to the studio and I'll give you an *Affair* personnel roster, so you can refresh your memory."

"Oh, don't be such a fucking puritan. What do you think I was into—paganistic orgies? They're not that many!" But her face was almost as red as her hair.

Gaye drew up her list in the privacy of her dressing room. She came upstairs half an hour later, looking like a naughty child who'd been spanked for playing doctor and nurse, which indeed was fairly close to what had happened. Suppressing a grin, she avoided looking at Phillip and took a seat primly on the couch.

Phillip turned the paper face down on his desk. "I don't have to look at it, until we get the results of the Wasserman."

"Oh, go ahead. I know you're dying to," Gaye blurted out, and sank back into the cushions.

Phillip hesitated, then grinned and turned the sheet over with mock tremulousness. He wasn't surprised at the length of the list, only the diversity. Gaye had been a perfect revolutionary in her tastes . . . liberty, equality, and open legs for all. But he screwed up his face when he came to Elliot Chamberfield's name. The son of a bitch hadn't wasted any time trying to use her to get to her stepfather. There was only one of the thirteen names that was unfamiliar. "Who's Brian Hocholtz?"

"Reporter for *Inside-TV*. A friend of Claire Pappas's. Oh, better put her down too. I forgot."

He tried the doctor as soon as he hit home. Positive for Gaye, negative for himself. "How can that be, Bob? From what I figure she must have picked it up about the same time I met her. I think I know the guy she caught it from and he hasn't been in the country since then."

"Have you been having intercourse with her regularly?"

"No, in fact only once."

"Maybe she was in the first development stage herself at the time. It doesn't get too contagious until the chancre opens up. And maybe she developed it after you were with her."

"That's possible. Okay, look, thanks a lot. I don't want to hold you up. How's Gilda?"

"She's all right."

"Give her my love. It's been a hell of a couple of months, but as soon as the pressure eases up a little, I'd like to take you both out to dinner."

"When's your pressure ever eased up? Just call and come over when you've got a spare hour. If we waited for you to get free before eating, we'd starve to death."

"Soon, I promise."

Phillip called Gaye and gave her the news first and then he tried Claire at home.

"You're a little late, Phillip, I've known for two weeks. What's the matter? You just get a dose?"

"No, I didn't. Surprised?" And he hung up.

It took him until late Saturday afternoon before he could finish the list. Two of the victims were married men with children. He asked them to call him back when their wives weren't nearby. At least that would give them time to get over the first shock, if they didn't know about it already. He'd reached everybody except the Hocholtz character; neither Gaye nor Claire had been home all day to give him the number. But he tried again about six o'clock and did manage to get an answer. "Claire, this is Phillip Searing again. I forgot to ask you when I called last night if you had Brian Hocholtz's home phone number. I understand he's a friend of yours and *Inside-TV*'s closed today."

She laughed her low, guttural growl. "My, aren't you the thorough one? How did you happen to get his name?"

"Never mind that. Do you have his number or not?"

She thumbed through her personal address book and gave it to him. "But if he's not there you can reach him through the switchboard on Monday."

"The switchboard? RBI's switchboard?"

"Yeah, he just got a job with the news department. In fact," she added, just to show her ears were open, "your old pal, Elliot Chamberfield got it for him." She waited for a response, but he only thanked her and said good-bye.

He had a cigarette before dialing the number. Strange, he thought. Chamberfield getting a news job for a rag-magazine reporter. . . . The phone was answered on the first ring. "Brian Hocholtz?"

"Yes?"

"My name is Phillip Searing. I'm the producer for—"

"I know who you are, Phillip. What can I do for you?"

Phillip didn't like the guy's tone of voice. Too cocky. Too quick with the first name. "I just wanted to inform you that your name was given to me as having had sex-ual contact with someone who is known to have syphilis."

There wasn't even a pause for breath. "Too late, Phil. Thanks, anyway, but I'm getting my shots already."

"Fine, good-bye." And Phillip hung up. He'd always imagined that if Elliot had any friends they would come out of a mold just like Hocholtz . . . which brought him around to the King of the Mountain himself. Elliot was also on the list. Subconsciously, he supposed, he'd saved the best for last. Well, how shall we put it to old Elliot. Most of the others had known about their infections for some time, but Chamberfield probably wouldn't. It was highly doubtful the man would know what a syphilitic chancre looked like. He should call him, but no—why not wait until Monday after taping when he could go over to Sixth Avenue and tell him personally, then enjoy the shock that would spread all over the big man's face? God knows he'd had few enough pleasures of late. He'd tell him. Of course, he'd tell him. It would be inhuman not to, but waiting two more days would not hurt him.

He finished the cigarette before moving from the Eames chair. He shouldn't have sat there. The relaxed curve the easy chair put his body in was killing his ribs. He should have sat in the Voltaire, but one of the legs was broken. There had been more damage than he'd thought at first. One pair of draperies was shredded beyond repair; two lamps had been smashed, an ashtray knocked over, its contents crushed into the carpet, and there was a large bloodstain on the beige sofa. He stood there, an addition to the general collection of disaster items. He hadn't been out of the apartment all day. He was still wearing the Levis and tee shirt he'd dropped into when he awoke at ten o'clock. His hair was rumpled and he still hadn't shaved. He felt in perfect harmony with the present state of his immediate environment: wretched. He extracted another cigarette from the pack and tossed the empty container away. It was the second one he'd finished since the morning. Fortunately there was another half a carton upstairs in the dresser, so he wouldn't have to go out before it was time to buy the Sunday *Times*. He was smoking a lot. He should think about doing something about that.

It was the kind of evening that made him want to be with somebody, and talk about anything at all, but it had to be the right sort of person, not someone involved in any of the anguish of the moment.

Phillip dragged himself upstairs and flipped the television on. He dialed through the channels to see if something could catch his interest. There wasn't much to choose from: the ends of a couple of lousy forties gangster pictures, a panel show in which a member of the state legislature was lauding the progress of his committee in dealing forthrightly with administrative corruption, a cooking program, and a talk show with former Vice President Agnew, who was discussing his recent life as a martyr. Phillip wheeled the set over to the door of the bathroom. He dropped the rubber plug into the tub drain and turned on the water, leaving it running while he went back out to remove his clothes.

He was just about to step into the bath, the first relaxation he'd offered himself all day, when the buzzer from the guard at the front door sounded downstairs in the entrance hall. Now what the hell does he want? He snatched up his robe draped across the unmade bed and padded down the carpeted steps as quickly as his wounds allowed him to. The doorman kept his finger on the button the whole time, "YES!" Phillip shouted into the box. "Dammit, do you have to keep ringing like that?"

"Sorry, Mr. Searing, didn't think you heard. You got a visitor comin' up."

"What?"

"Yeah, he said he was a friend of yours. I seen him before, so I just let 'em go."

"Look, what the hell are you there for?" Phillip exploded. "I didn't want any visitors today. Certainly not unannounced."

"Sorry, sir," he said jauntily. "It won't happen the next time." But it would. It had been happening since he was hired.

There wasn't even time to wonder who the visitor might be before the front door chimed. Just in case it was John Langley again, he wanted some time to prepare; he was in no condition for another match. He hooked the chain across the door before opening it. "Barry!" he exclaimed when he saw the young man. "What are you doing here?"

"I've been trying to reach you off and on, all last night and today. Your line was busy. I thought it might be off the hook."

"No, I've been on the phone. What's up?"

He looked a bit awkward, standing in the hall with his shirt opened farther down than he had the chest for and a man's duffle bag slung over his shoulder.

"I've just got something quick to tell you. Are you going to make me stand out here?"

Phillip realized the chain was still on the door. He unhooked it and Barry stepped in. "Holy Mary, mother of Yussel, what happened?"

"You wouldn't believe it if I told you."

"I probably wouldn't!" Phillip was amused at the shock he displayed. "You don't want to tell me?"

"Not really." But he felt he had to say something. If he didn't, Barry would blab the first chance he got. He was a well-intentioned guy, but he had a big mouth. "I was robbed two nights ago," he lied.

"No!"

"Umm, but I caught him as he was getting away."

"You caught him? So he didn't get anything?"

"No, but the fight caused a lot of damage."

"You're telling me! Are you all right?"

"Yes."

"Did the police get the guy?"

"No."

"Wow!" He treaded lightly around the large room, peering wide-eyed at the results of the holocaust. "Blood! Christ, there's blood on the couch—did you see that? Maybe you wounded him."

"No, it's mine." Barry jerked his head up to look at Phillip. Phillip found it hard to keep from smiling. "He nicked me with a knife he had; it's not bad, looks a lot worse than it is." Suddenly, he remembered the bath and hurried upstairs.

Barry followed him, afraid the burglar was still around. He was considerably relieved when he saw the bathwater had caused the alarm.

"I think I'm going to get away from you," Barry said. "Your stars are obviously in clashing orbits these days. You don't need any help cleaning up downstairs, do you?" he asked, clearly hoping that he wouldn't.

"No, the cleaning woman will be in on Monday. She'll take care of everything then."

"Good. Listen—what I came to tell you—I had a couple of drinks with Elliot after work yesterday, and, just between you and me, *Affair*'s in for another thirteen. We both saw the pilot Vern Tuttle's been working on. You know about that, don't you?"

"I'd heard rumors."

"Yeah, well an interview with a Fuller Brush salesman would draw more audience. *Affair*'s going to stay—it'll even have Keel's backing—but I think Elliot's going to make you fire the Langley girl. And I guess I see his point. She's really been screwing up, hasn't she?"

"What do you mean he's going to *make* me fire her?"

"That's what he said. He was pretty drunk, though. He doesn't take care of himself at all, even after that heart-attack scare he had. Weird guy, Elliot, I guess I'll never understand what makes him tick."

"Power, Barry, that's what makes him tick. There's never been any secret about that."

"I'm supposed to be a good friend, and you know something? He's getting married, you know."

"No, to whom?"

"His secretary."

"I'll send her my condolences," he said cynically.

"No kidding—and you want to know when he broke the news to me? The same time he broke it to Russell Keel. Can you imagine? He didn't even tell me first." Barry shrugged. "That hurt me. It really made me feel left out. I think he should at least have told his friends before he announced it to the company people."

"Well, that's your friend, Elliot."

Phillip killed the television set after Barry left. He'd

take a long hot bath, but he wouldn't blitz his mind with trivia. There was now a more vital question to be dealt with. So *Affair* would stay. He'd won the first round without even getting up to the bell. After sliding into the tub and adjusting to the temperature, Phillip wiped his hands dry on a towel and reached into a small green cabinet by his head for a pre-rolled joint. He always kept a few there expressly for such times.

The question, he realized intuitively, had little to do with Vanessa. Elliot was locked into a corner, since Tuttle's show hadn't worked out, and to his regret he'd have to keep *Affair* sailing with its producer at the helm. Next best thing to do was to pick on Vanessa. He probably sensed she was a weak point with him, or was it because—? Yes, that must be it. Elliot wasn't going to pick on Vanessa because she was doing poorly. That wasn't his logic at all. He was after her because he was afraid she would do too well. He knew her malaise was only temporary. He must have figured that by the time she came out of it, that is, by the time Valerie came out of the hospital, Vanessa would be back in shape, giving it all she had, and the combination of the hospital situation and some stunning performances would draw a hell of an audience, putting the show way up in ratings by the end —not of this thirteen-week period, but the next one. And then it would be impossible to fire anybody. What a clever, clever guy he really was! He had a long-range plan to weaken the show—by firing the best actress the show has. Vanessa was just a patsy.

He took a long pull on the joint and lay back in the bath, taking care not to wet his shoulder bandage. The rib taping would probably hold and if not it didn't matter much anyway. It could always be done up again, and the warm water felt so good. The marijuana was starting its climb to his head.

How could he stand by and let the girl be fired? But then what else was there to do? If he put up a fight he'd be fired himself and it is tough to help anybody from street level.

But there were cards to be played from his side of the table, too. Keel liked his work. He'd told Papa Goodhart as much and there was every indication Russell was for bringing him back to the forty-third floor as soon as possible. He most likely also knew that Elliot had given him a free hand to handle things the way he saw fit. A free hand was a free hand. If Elliot tried to force him to fire Vanessa against his will, he was breaching that agreement. By rights Keel should back him up. Well . . . time to see. Time to put the question to the test.

27.

The memo arrived about ten-thirty, delivered by a pimply faced RBI mailroom boy in a striped shirt and extra wide tie. "Fire her, the bastard writes. Just like that. Fire her!" Phillip crumpled it up and tossed it in the wastebasket. "Barry, do me a favor," he said, when he got him on the line. "Try to find out when Elliot will be alone today, will you? Anytime after two. Could you do that for me? Don't let on that I want to know."

"All right, I'll see if I can."

Barry called back in forty-five minutes. He said it looked like after four would be the best time.

The taping checked out well. It was a good show. Both Vanessa and Gaye did nicely, and Bill Peters, who had a breakdown scene when he found out about Valerie's tumor, was superb. The ladies of the afternoon would wring out their housewifely hearts with him. Phillip took his time leaving—a quick talk with Pat, some scheduling problems to settle in the set shop, Maude O'Keefe on some end-of-the-week dialogue, then out, walking the distance across town to let his strategy crystallize in his mind.

"Congratulations, Rosalynann. I hear you're getting married."

"Yes, thank you, Mr. Searing."

There was no reason not to be pleasant to the girl, even if she had the abysmal taste to be linking herself in matrimony with Elliot Chamberfield. "I'd like to see Elliot —is he in?"

"I'll find out."

He'd see him, all right. Elliot would not want to postpone a confrontation in which he had the upper hand. Phillip took a seat, and fifteen minutes later he was summoned.

"So what do you want? Did you fire her?" Elliot asked as Phillip walked into the room. Elliot did not take his eyes from the copy of *Variety* he was supposedly reading.

Phillip sat on the couch on the far side of the office. "No, I didn't fire her, Elliot. I have no intention of firing her. The girl's gone through too much to be kicked out now."

"She's ruining the show," he said, minus conviction.

"No, she's not. If you'd looked at it today or Friday, you'd know she's started to make a comeback."

Elliot examined his cuticles, ostensibly unconcerned with the gist of the conversation, but beneath the flat slab of a desk Phillip noticed his right leg twitching involuntarily. "The girl's out, Searing. That's all there is to it." And he looked him coolly in the eye.

"I'm not going to fire her."

"Really? Then I guess I'll have to fire you so I can do the job myself. You're countermanding a direct order."

"Elliot, you made a promise to me when I first took over your show: I was to run things my way."

"You have, haven't you?"

"Up to now, yes."

"So what are you bitching about? I just want to help the show, Phil. Since you don't seem to have the guts to cut out the cancer, I'll have to do it."

"Vanessa's not a cancer. She's the best performer on the show. She's been down for a while. It happens to all of us at times."

"Not to me!"

"But she's coming back now. If anybody'll help shoot those ratings up, it'll be Vanessa."

"Sorry."

Phillip sat silently for a time. They both knew the truth of the situation, and Elliot knew that Phillip knew, not being one to underestimate an enemy, so there was no point in Phillip's bringing it up. Elliot would only deny it. And he wanted to avoid bringing Keel into the picture as long as possible. Nobody liked arbitration by a higher-up, least of all *the* higher-up. It wasn't the sort of test of strength Phillip would relish.

Elliot watched him closely, enjoying seeing him squirm. He hated self-confidence like Phillip's. He had no right to be holier than thou. Change places, he'd fight just as dirty.

"All right, Elliot, why don't we get down to facts? You don't give a damn about Vanessa Langley. Why don't you leave her out of it and concentrate on me."

"I don't know what you're talking about."

"Yes, you do."

"Do I?"

"You want to get rid of me, not her."

"I can't say I'd miss you if you decided to depart."

"But I'm not planning to leave, so why play games with Vanessa? She's had enough trouble as it is."

"I'm telling you to fire her. That's an order—pure and simple. You still work for me, remember?"

"I'm not a line producer, Elliot." His tone toughened. "I'm the vice president of daytime programing who's rolled his sleeves up in a pinch to help the company."

"Right now you're the producer of *Affair Of The Heart*, and you either follow orders or get the fuck out."

"No, I don't accept that. You made a promise that you're backing out of." He leaned forward on the couch and put every bit of frigidity he could into his words. "Elliot, let me tell you something. I'm not about to be eased out of RBI, not without putting up a hell of a squabble. I refuse to fire Vanessa and I don't accept being fired myself. I hate to do it, but I'm going to have to take the matter over your head and let Keel straighten it out."

Elliot couldn't help smiling. "Russell's out of town, Phil. I'm sorry to have to tell you. Probably throws a monkey wrench into your tactics. He's on a yacht, somewhere off the coast of St. Croix. Didn't you know? He always takes a vacation after the annual meeting of the board."

Phillip was stunned. It was the one thing he hadn't

328

counted on, and it must have shown on his face because Elliot seemed unusually pleased. But Elliot also realized that if the son of a bitch was thinking about going to Keel, he would definitely be planning on boiling up some trouble. Elliot had no doubt he would win in the end, but to get embroiled in an open intracompany hassle could tarnish his reputation as well. "I was thinking. Maybe you have a point about the Langley girl. You know, if, for example, you were to leave—if, for argument's sake, the offer your friend Goodhart made you a few weeks ago suddenly sounded more attractive and you decided to bid our little family farewell nicely—I doubt that I could afford to fire Vanessa." He spoke with slow deliberation, letting the bribe dribble from his mouth like honey. "You see, it would be bad enough for *Affair* to lose its most popular and dynamic producer, but to lose its star as well? I suppose I'd be obliged to keep her on. I wouldn't want to inflict pandemonium on the other members of the show." They stared at each other, two poker players putting up someone else for their ante.

Phillip refused to respond to the blackmail, so Elliot sweetened the pot. "Actually," he said, lighting a cigar, "I suppose I'd even have to guarantee that I wouldn't fire her, if you left RBI, that is. And if she did improve, as you say she's started to do, I might even be tempted to give her a run-of-the-show contract. I wouldn't want to lose such a fine—"

Phillip cut him off. "Forget it!"

"Think about it."

"Forget it!"

"Now, where is all that sanctimonious bullshit about doing the poor girl dirt? It all ends when your *own* job is at stake, doesn't it? Here you have an ideal opportunity to keep her working and you're going to blow it by putting up a silly fight. Searing, you're out, because I want you out. I hired you, and now I'm going to fire you. You get out like a gentleman and you can help your girlfriend. But if you put up a stink I'll have you both thrown out on your asses. And that, my friend, is a promise I won't back down on."

"When's Keel coming back?"

"You're going to push it, are you? Okay. I expect he'll be back in a week or two, but you'll be replaced by tomorrow morning." He sat back in his chair and lifted his feet up onto the desk, showing Phillip the soles of his dirty shoes. "Of course, if you want to call him up next week and come see him as a visitor I couldn't stop you, but it might be awkward for you. On the other hand, there's always the ship-to-shore telephone. Maybe he's got one on board. It shouldn't take you more than a couple of days to get the number and I'm sure Russell will be delighted to be interrupted in the middle of the only vacation he's had all year."

He was right. He couldn't interrupt Keel, and if he allowed himself to be kicked out now the whole ballgame would have changed by the time Keel got back. He wouldn't be thought of in the same way. Even one week's distance would put him on the outside looking in, and that was no position to plead a case from. The shrewd bastard had shoved him into a corner. He had only one direction he could turn in. He reflected for a moment: the odds were against him, but there didn't seem any choice. He looked up at Elliot. "I'm taking the matter to Vulkner."

The two thick legs dropped off the desk and thudded heavily to the carpet. Elliot bolted forward in his chair. "Vulkner? You want to take this thing to Vulkner?"

"You don't leave me any choice."

"Searing, you must have lost your mind! Vulkner's not going to bother with a fucking producer."

"I'm not just a producer, Elliot, you keep forgetting."

"Well, pal, the party's all yours, but if you don't think that the chairman of the board—even if he does consent to see you—is going to back up the highest in command, then you're a hell of a lot dumber than I thought! If I were you, I'd take my offer and keep your girlfriend working."

"She's not my girlfriend!"

He grinned. "That's not what I heard. But I guess she's not if you turn your back on her at a time like this, particularly, as you said, after all she's been through."

"How do I know you'd even keep her on?"

"I'd guarantee it," he said seriously.

"It seems to me I'm experiencing the crumbling of one of your guarantees right now."

"It's a different situation."

"Yeah, until it changes. No, I can't trust you. I'll take my chances with Vulkner. We'll straighten this thing out once and for all. Will you set up the appointment, since you're closest to him?"

"Not me, pal. I wouldn't bother him with a thing like this. As far as I'm concerned you and the broad are off the payroll. She's out in two more weeks when her contract ends and you're out as of now. If you want to call Wilson Vulkner, you go right ahead. But use another phone, if you don't mind—I've got to line up a replacement for you."

Vulkner would see them in an hour, since the request was so urgent. That gave Phillip time to wash up and have a cup of coffee in the thirtieth-floor cafeteria. He sat at a table in the corner and hoped no one recognized him. He needed the time to plan.

28.

Wilson Vulkner may have sheathed the exterior of his building in white Vermont marble to indicate publicly the strength, moral uprightness, and pristinely functional image of his corporation, but the forty-fifth floor, reserved for himself and ten other executives, who had successfully weathered the climb up the mountain, was anything but utilitarian.

Phillip stepped off the elevator and headed for the open space at the far end of the hall. It wasn't just the luxuriant deep blue-velvet pile carpet under his feet, nor the enormous area dwarfing the matronly receptionist who served the ten division presidents and the corporation's chairman of the board. Nor was it the intimidating silence on the floor, so distinctly different from the bustle on the forty-four floors below. It was the generating of power behind the oaken doors. The RBI complex grossed half a billion dollars a year, and this floor constituted its brain. With the singular exception of Chamberfield's office, all points below were manned by drones, operatives who carried out orders, edicts, sent down from this floor.

The receptionist smiled when he was exactly six paces away from her. "May I help you?"

"Phillip Searing to see Wilson Vulkner."

She glanced at a leather-bound appointment book, the only object on her desk other than a phone.

She looked up again, smiling with slightly more grace. "Yes, Mr. Searing, you're expected. Mr. Chamberfield has already arrived."

Phillip glanced at his watch. It was precisely 5:30 P.M. Leave it to Elliot to get in earlier; he's probably sowing a mine field.

The receptionist pressed a button on her phone and spoke quietly into the receiver. "Mr. Searing for Mr. Vulkner." She listened for a second and then hung up. "His appointments secretary will be right out. Would you be seated?" Behind a large, black, early Henry Moore statue representing a family group, there were several couches.

"Thank you, I'll stand." He sauntered over to the floor-length windows that pointed west toward the Hudson and the Palisades of New Jersey. Funny, he thought, one floor up doesn't change the view much—only the perspective. He decided against having a cigarette. He didn't need one. He was calm, breathing easily. He knew just what he was going to say.

The swishing sound of nylon-encased thighs rubbing together signaled the approach of the appointments secretary. He turned when he caught a faint whiff of her perfume. She was tall, expensively dressed, and looked more like a top executive's young wife than a secretary. Vulkner liked to surround himself with beauty.

"Mr. Searing? If you'll follow me, please. Mr. Vulkner's expecting you." She turned and he followed her down a corridor paneled with rosewood and hung with more originals. When she reached her own door, she stood aside, allowing him to enter first. Only a typewriter on one of the two desks indicated the use of the room; otherwise it could have been an expensive law office with glass-fronted cabinets and a low, modern couch. She shut the door softly behind him and crossed to a set of double doors. She knocked softly, but without waiting for a reply opened it and announced, "Mr. Searing."

Phillip walked in.

At the far end of a room that looked like a private art

333

gallery an enormous eighteenth-century Florentine desk sat in a pool of light. The figure in a guest chair turned his head. It was Elliot Chamberfield, looking like he'd swallowed a flock of canaries. The second figure stood as Phillip came nearer and extended his hand across the desk; Wilson Vulkner, king of the mountain, framed by a gigantic Matisse in white and two shades of blue. The man belonged to the room as Caesar belonged to Rome. He was tall and lean, sixty-four or -five, according to official RBI biographies, but looking more fit than Elliot after three tough months as programing chief. He was dressed in a blue pin-striped suit with one concession to modernity: his tie was wide, a dark maroon. He had a tanned, unlined face set off by peppered gray-and-white hair, close-cropped to his distinguished-looking head. There was no indication of age in his face, no weakness in his handshake. The gesture lasted only a shade longer than what one would call perfunctory. He indicated an empty leather chair in front of the desk and sat back down, folding his hands church-steeple fashion.

Phillip nodded to Elliot as he sat and Elliot was confident enough to smile.

Vulkner began to speak in a modulated voice suited to the elegance of the room. "Elliot has been filling me in on the background of this situation—from his point of view, of course." Elliot's face fell a bit. Vulkner turned his patriarchal profile to Phillip. "Would you care to outline your position?"

"Thank you." He glanced at Elliot and began. "When I agreed to assume the producership of this serial—"

Vulkner interrupted him. "Excuse me. You say, 'agreed to assume.' I was under the impression you had personally volunteered to man the helm?"

"No, sir, I did not. But I was willing to perform a needed task for the good of the afternoon schedule. However, when I undertook to do so, I was promised carte blanche—to do as I saw fit, make any changes necessary with no interference in order to raise the ratings. Since that point in time, those ratings have improved by 4.7 points."

Vulkner nodded. "The board is aware of that increase."

Elliot shifted uncomfortably. His collar seemed a bit tight.

Phillip brushed a piece of lint off one knee and continued. "The problem involves an actress, Vanessa Langley, who plays the part of Valerie. She became pregnant some weeks ago and for some reason, yet unknown to me, Elliot saw fit to pressure me into forcing her to have an abortion."

Vulkner frowned and looked over at Elliot, as Phillip continued. "It was either that, he told me, or fire her. I relayed the ultimatum to Mrs. Langley and, after much personal torment, she did decide to abort. That set off a chain of unforeseen and devastating circumstances for her: her husband left her, took an overdose of heroin; he is now in a coma at Bellevue Hospital."

Both Elliot and Vulkner's eyebrows rose as they received this information. Phillip paused, allowing the news to sink in and then proceeded with deliberate coolness. He was reporting facts; he could be just as correct as Vulkner. "Because of what she has had to contend with, Mrs. Langley has been understandably distraught and her performances on the show have been affected. However, it is my opinion, and may I say those also of my colleagues on the show, that she is one of the finest young actresses on daytime today and that despite a temporary falling off in quality, she has still maintained high professional standards, fulfilling the terms of her contract, and has shown every sign of coping with the enormous emotional pressures put upon her. In short, she'll improve—I have no doubt about it. So for this reason, I don't wish to fire her. And Elliot has ordered my dismissal because of it. I feel the young woman has been treated unfairly and RBI owes it to her to keep her on, until such time as she is clearly detrimental to the show."

Vulkner swung his high-backed leather chair toward the bank of windows to his left. "Your support of this actress is commendable, Phillip."

Elliot broke in eagerly. "Excuse me, but I think we should mention *why* he's supporting her so much." He shot a venomous look at Phillip. "I'm sorry to bring up such a personal matter, but I think it only fair that Wilson know you've been having an affair with her. It might help explain your devotion."

Phillip felt a slight tensing in his thigh muscles, but the

expression on his face remained unchanged. Vulkner watched closely. "Is that true, Phillip?"

"My personal relationship to Mrs. Langley has nothing to do with my professional judgment. I can assure you of that. I won't deny we had a very brief relationship some months ago, but that in no way has affected the execution of my responsibilities. If I felt she were hurting the show, I would not hesitate to fire her even if she were my wife." He stared back at the older man.

"But she's not. She's somebody else's wife," Elliot added.

"Phillip, you must admit that your relationship does add a new color to the discussion."

"No, sir. My interests have been and are to produce the best soap opera on all four networks. I am asking for the freedom to do just that."

Elliot lit a cigar. "Freedom is relative; you still work under me."

Vulkner stood and walked from behind his desk to some paintings grouped near the windows. The afternoon sun shone on them and he tugged at a cord, closing the draperies. He turned back to the two at the desk. He was angered. He spoke much more crisply. "I do not make it a practice of getting involved in intraoffice disagreements. Generally these matters are handled by the next in command. But as Russell is out of town, I received you both this afternoon because I respect you as professional members of the RBI team."

Gaye was right. He *was* a cold fish. His consuming passion was for his team to function as smoothly as possible.

The old man wouldn't make waves. His obligation was to the next highest authority in the chain of command that ended with himself. Elliot had guessed that. Phillip was on his way out. A sinking sensation filled his gut. His gamble had failed. He knew it and so did Elliot. Phillip Searing was being canned and Elliot Chamberfield had won . . . never mind how.

Vulkner paused and came toward them, standing beside his leather-backed throne. "I have no choice but to support Elliot's position, right or wrong. He's your superior and he's given you his viewpoint."

So that's the way it's played, no question of morals

whatever. No right or wrong. No fairness or justice. You play as hard as you can, and if you can't win fair you kick balls. The only way to beat Chamberfield was to fight with no holds barred, go for the jugular. A shot of adrenalin raced through his body. Phillip took a deep breath and plunged in. "There's something you should know—this is an ugly affair, but it'll demonstrate my attitude against Elliot's." He looked at Chamberfield when he said it. "There is a little matter of syphilis."

Elliot almost choked on a lungful of cigarette smoke. Vulkner quickly sat down and leaned forward. "Syphilis? I don't understand."

It was Phillip's turn to take the floor. "There has been a rather extensive outbreak of the disease on the show. It was only recently brought to my attention and I moved quickly to find the source and check its spread. Not only because it's a filthy disease, but because if the news leaked out it would sully the image of RBI."

Vulkner didn't miss a word. Phillip paused, reached for a cigarette, lit it, and continued. "Elliot, on the other hand, has known about the outbreak for some time; rather than instigate an investigation, he has tried to cover it up."

"That's a lie!" Elliot's face was beet red. Veins stood out on his forehead.

Phillip proceeded with his attack. "I have proof, Mr. Vulkner, that Elliot swept the whole affair under the carpet in the crudest and most obvious way. It was bound to come to light; in fact, as you can see, it did."

"Proof? What proof? You're lying, Searing, through your teeth."

Vulkner raised his hand like a judge. "Gentlemen, please." He, too, studied Phillip. "This is a serious accusation, Phillip. If it's true, it's. . . ." He didn't finish. "The image before the public of this corporation is of prime importance to myself and the board. We're dependent upon the public's respect."

Elliot swung toward the desk. "He can't have any proof. He's just trying to save his own neck." He stubbed out his cigar in the crystal ashtray before him.

"Yes, I'm interested in saving my job. But I do have proof. I've got proof that Elliot took no action whatsoever to stem the tide of this epidemic."

"Name it." Elliot was breathing harder now.

Phillip's pulse raced and he tried to collect his thoughts. All he had was a wild hypothesis, no proof at all, but he had gone this far and couldn't back down now. Besides by the look on Elliot's face, Phillip knew that there must be some proof somewhere. Gaye's list of sexual conquests flashed before his eyes. The names—two outside of *Affair* —Elliot Chamberfield and Brian Hocholtz. Hocholtz had to be it. He had no choice. He had to try.

Vulkner was waiting. "Elliot asked for substantiation of your charge."

Phillip began slowly: "It is not easy for me, and I don't undertake the accusation lightly, and I'm well aware of its consequences. But if you check with the news department you'll find that a young man by the name of Brian Hocholtz has just been hired there."

The look on Elliot's face was proof enough for Phillip. In desperation he had stumbled onto the truth. "Hocholtz was a reporter for a gossip rag called *Inside-TV*. I'm still waiting for certain details, but I do know that Elliot arranged for him to be hired and I understand it was to shut him up. But that, Mr. Vulkner, is all he did. Fourteen RBI people have been contaminated by syphilis in the past two months. You don't clear that up by sweeping it under a rug."

Elliot sputtered. Vulkner turned to him, and the stony cast on his face demanded to know whether the story was true. Elliot cleared his throat. "Okay. Okay, part of what he says is true. Hocholtz did come to me, and I did arrange for an interview with Paul Gash. But I did it to protect you, Wilson."

"Protect me!" exclaimed Vulkner in astonishment.

"It involved your stepdaughter. I believe she started the whole thing." He turned to Phillip in a rage. "Don't you have any more decency than to bring this up in this office! Didn't you know Gaye's name would be mentioned?"

The old man's backbone seemed to stiffen. "You wanted to protect me, Elliot?"

"Yes, sir. I knew how upset you'd be if you found out your stepdaughter was involved. That's why I tried to hush it up."

There was a flash in Vulkner's eyes. "You failed to realize, Elliot, that regardless of who started this filthy business, it should have been disinfected, not covered up to fester."

"I just wanted to spare you the—"

"I know what you wanted to spare me. And just what made you think I would be spared if I had to read in the newspaper one morning that RBI is a sewer of venereal disease? Whatever tarnishes the name of this company tarnishes my name as well." He took a moment to calm himself, then asked Phillip to detail everything he knew about the outbreak, including the steps he'd taken to remedy it.

Vulkner listened as Phillip recounted the moves he'd made since Friday. Elliot squirmed. The tables were turned and he knew it. It was he who was now fighting for *his* position.

Phillip came to the end of his remarks. "I contacted everyone on the list Gaye gave me, all but one. Elliot Chamberfield." Phillip turned and looked at the rotund figure in the next chair. "I'm sorry I didn't call you sooner, Elliot. I was going to mention it today, but this other business came up."

Elliot glared back. "And what about you, Searing? Did you get your shots yet?"

Phillip reached for the ashtray. "I don't have syphilis, Elliot. That can be proved easily."

Vulkner's tone froze Phillip's spine.

"The behavior of my stepdaughter long ago ceased to surprise me. The issue, Elliot, is not who started this revolting business, but who moved to correct and eliminate it. This thing could have ignited like a tinderbox. I'm shocked and appalled at your inaction!"

Vulkner turned to Phillip. "Would you mind waiting in Mr. Keel's office downstairs? I'd like to speak to Elliot privately."

It was not until Phillip reached the forty-fourth floor that he became conscious again of his own self. He was drained emotionally and physically. His shoulder throbbed and he felt lightheaded. He knew he had won. But there was no sense of elation.

On forty-four, he turned toward the men's room, pushing open the swinging door and entering the cool white-tiled silence. It was empty. He ran cold water in the washbasin and bathed his face. In reaching for the towel, he glimpsed his mirrored face. He stared back at himself coldly and unemotionally. That was Phillip Searing. And Phillip Searing had won his match. But he felt dirty. He wanted a shower. And there was a look in his eyes he didn't like.

29.

Jacqueline Goodhart Searing pulled the draperies on the double French doors leading to the garden terrace and the morning sun flooded into the drawing room. She stood for a moment, letting it warm her face before unlocking the doors and stepping out on the tree-shaded terrace. She was still groggy from her flight to New York and the pills she had felt obliged to consume in order to compensate for the time difference. She called into the house that she'd prefer breakfast on the terrace, then sat down, pulling her long, light, pink dressing gown around her bare legs.

In a short time, a tray with freshly squeezed orange juice, coffee, toasted English muffins, marmalade, and a soft boiled egg in the shell under a silver cup were set before her on the white, wrought-iron table.

The maid disappeared for a moment, returning quickly with *The New York Times*. She placed it beside the breakfast tray. Jacqueline nodded unconsciously, glancing at the headlines before buttering the muffin. It wasn't even eleven yet and she was already bored. A phone rang somewhere inside the house. After a few seconds the same maid brought a white extension out to the terrace. "Your father is calling, Mrs. Searing."

"Martha, my sunglasses. On my bureau. Bring them out, please." Jacqueline picked up the receiver. "Papa? What makes you call so soon? I just got up."

"I've been up for hours. Have you read the *Times* this morning?"

She glanced at the paper on the tray. "It just arrived."

"You haven't come across the article yet?"

"What article?" She picked the newspaper up.

"I just got a call from Fitzsimmons in New York; he read me something about Phillip."

"Phillip? What about Phillip?" She cradled the receiver under one ear and used both hands to thumb through the pages. "What'd it say?"

"It must be on the television page. It has a picture."

She turned to the last page of the second section and there it was, a photo of Phillip taken at least three years ago. It was under a headline. "PHILLIP SEARING NAMED VICE PRESIDENT OF RBI WEB REPLACING CHAMBERFIELD." His ex-wife looked anything but pleased.

The article was brief with a short biography of Phillip's professional history, but the body of the story added little information beyond the headline.

Papa G. could tell that his daughter was greatly disappointed. His voice came back with a forced cheerfulness. "Well, it looks like he's made it. Vice president of network programming. It's a big step up for him. Fitzsimmons said it was quite a surprise to everyone in the business. Evidently happened overnight. Lot of strange rumors as to the gist of the whole move, but it seems this Chamberfield guy has been kicked upstairs to some paper-shuffling position and Phillip'll be announced as the new cheese this afternoon. Vulkner's doing it himself."

"Isn't that just terrific for Phillip?" The bitterness oozed into the phone. "Just terrific."

"Well, I guess we both lose out. I doubt he'll even consider my offer now."

"Why should he? He's got exactly what he's been pushing for." Martha stepped onto the terrace and handed her the sunglasses. Jacqueline snatched them from her.

342

"I sent him a congratulatory telegram as soon as I heard."

"I'm sure he'll have hundreds."

"It would be a nice gesture if you wrote him a short note."

"Yes, I suppose it would be, but I'm not quite up to nice gestures at the moment."

"Jacqueline, don't be disheartened. Please."

"Me? Disheartened? Whatever gave you that idea? You think I'm upset because Phillip has gotten what he wants? It doesn't make any difference, Papa. We were finished long before this."

She sat for a long time, sipping her coffee and smoking; she felt hollowed out. Why on earth had she come back to New York? To see Phillip again . . . but too late. He didn't need her or her father, not any more. He'd made it all on his own.

* * *

That same morning Phillip had his last meeting with the production staff of the show. Only Gloria was absent. She was cleaning out his files, sorting what would be moved across town.

The faces were grouped around the conference table. They reflected a mixture of exuberance at the news that *Affair* would be picked up and sadness at losing their producer. Tough old Maude sniffled into a handkerchief. Pat rubbed her hand and kidded her. "It's rough to lose your father figure."

"Father figure?" she snorted, stuffing her handkerchief back into her purse. "I'm old enough to be his grandmother!"

Colin was wild with the excitement of having been named acting producer. "Maude, we'll manage somehow; I'll be your new father figure."

"You? You're younger than my youngest son!"

"Just call me Oedipus, baby."

"It won't be the same *Affair* without you, Phillip. We'll miss ya," Pat said fondly.

Phillip poured him a glass of champagne. "Drink up, Pat. You've got a show to do. And remember, all of you, I'm just across town. You'll be getting memos if you screw up."

343

Maude kissed him tenderly on the cheek. "Thanks, Phillip, for resurrecting an old broad."

"Thank you, Maude, for everything."

Colin reached out to shake his hand. "Don't worry, Phillip. I'm just going to follow your ideas."

"You've got a good team, Colin. We'll talk in about a week, or whenever you feel you need to." They left and he walked briskly back to his office.

Gloria was bent over a large cardboard packing box. Brushing a stray lock of hair from her forehead, she said, "The phone hasn't stopped ringing all morning."

Phillip picked up the list of incoming calls. "Half of these people I haven't heard from in three months. Now I'm suddenly popular." Vanessa's name wasn't on the list. She was off for the day and he hadn't heard from her. He tossed the clipboard back on the desk and looked around the office. "I'm glad you're coming with me. I'd hate to break in a new secretary now."

"I hope I can handle the job."

"Would you like to know something? I feel the same about myself." He checked his watch. "Gotta run. If anything comes up I'll be at the Plaza. If not, I'll see you on the forty-fourth floor. Okay?"

"Yes, sir. I'll make sure you're set up by the time you get back for the press conference."

"Thank you, Gloria."

She smiled at him until he was out of the office. Then she started packing the personal things. The horse statuette was the first to go in.

Phillip entered the fashionable restaurant in the Plaza Hotel. Katina was already at a table. She'd flown in from Paris the night before, the night of his promotion. She was sitting near a collection of society matrons, who were resting themselves from the ordeals of their pilgrimage from Saks to Tiffany's. She hugged him joyfully. "God, it's good to see you! I picked this table because it offered a little privacy." There was a palm leaf brushing her hair.

"I thought you were hiding under there."

She squeezed his hand. They ordered drinks and brunch. bloody marys and eggs benedict. After the waitress left, Katina leaned forward and looked into his eyes. "Well, you don't look much different. How do you feel?"

He shrugged and lit a cigarette, then looked at her apologetically. "Sorry, I'll blow the smoke away from you."

"What difference does it make? Just breathing this air in this stale old city is smoking three packs a day."

"Well, you're certainly in good spirits. Your publishing meeting must have been successful."

"For me it was."

The drinks arrived and they lifted them toward each other in mutual congratulations. Their eyes held and they sipped silently. She looked lovely—relaxed, fresh, tanned and ebullient.

"You look like a Scandinavian peasant."

"My new image. Like it?"

"If you do, yes."

"Then you love it."

"So tell me when it's coming out."

"What?"

"Your poetry."

She shook her head and smiled warmly. "It's not."

"What do you mean?"

"The guy isn't going to publish them."

"He brought you all the way over here, put you up at the Plaza, to tell you he's not going to publish them?"

"Nope. He wants to publish them, but I don't want him to."

"You?"

"Right, *me*."

"What happened?"

"The guy wanted some changes, rewrites, to capitalize on some new market he said there was. He called me a happy Sylvia Plath! And wanted me to alter my work to a more thoughtful, introspective, liberated kind of approach. So I thought, and introspected for a minute and decided I was already liberated. I refused to change a word. A happy Sylvia Plath! Can you beat that? I guess to sell something you are required to sell out first."

"That's an idiotic remark. Just because the guy wanted you to write for a specific market doesn't mean you're selling out."

"Doesn't it? Well, then tell me, Phillip. What does selling out mean to you?"

He paused. "Selling out is completely subjugating yourself and talents in order to make a buck."

"Right. I don't want to sell out. Not yet, anyway. My poetry is for me. It would have been super if the guy said he'd publish them as is, but to rewrite—to gear them for this new audience he kept talking about. Bullshit! I could just as well go back to RBI and get my old job back."

"It's your life."

"And it's yours, too." She stopped long enough for the plates of food to be placed before them. "Tell me, Phillip, are you happy now you're vice president and king of the whole circus?"

He picked up his fork and examined it. "What does happy mean? I've worked hard to get where I am."

"In other words, you deserve this promotion?"

"You're goddamn right I do." He didn't even bother to temper his tone.

She dug into her eggs. "You sound a little like the man you've just replaced." She raised the fork to her mouth, and then put it down. "I'm sorry. Well, then, if you've worked so hard to get there, you should be ecstatic now. Are you?"

"Katina, I'm in no mood for one of your peace-and-love sermons. I'm a professional man; my life is my career."

"Then you ought to be deliriously happy right now."

"Yes!" he shot out like a bullet. "I'm happy!"

"Good!" She grinned. "That's all I wanted to know."

They finished their brunch in silence. Phillip was angry. He had expected them to have a victory brunch. Instead he felt uptight and guilty. It wasn't until they were having their second cup of coffee that she spoke again.

She held his eyes. "When the game you choose to play makes you wear a mask in order to win, there's a great danger that you'll become that mask eventually. And then you're trapped."

That was the problem with Katina, always telling you how to run your own life.

She reached across the table and took one of his hands. "I could tell when you walked in you were miserable. If you're not happy, be aware of it. Don't hide it and don't think it'll change—you can't legislate that change. It has to come from within."

346

30.

Strange woman, Katina. We seem to have grown so far apart and once we were so close. Did she change so much in such a short period of time? He was the same as he'd always been, maybe a little the worse for wear. The shoulder still hurt like a bitch.

He had less than forty-five minutes to the press conference, and a truckload of responsibilities to prepare for. Forty-five minutes and Vulkner himself would be introducing him as the new chief of RBI programing, the most powerful job in the network. The afternoon should be the most glittering moment of a great career.

He was one floor up from where his game plan aimed him. Not forty-three at all—forty-four! If he played his cards right from here on in, he could probably be the next division president. There was absolutely nothing in his way.

He paused in front of the Episcopalian Church on the corner of Fifty-Third Street to watch a weaving band of Hare Krishnaites dance and bang their drums, chanting their bizarre liturgy with glassy-eyed abandon. He dropped a quarter in the box of one of the shaven-headed priests.

He was dreading the afternoon. He felt in no mood to celebrate his victory with a public press conference. He knew what was bugging him, had known it the moment he looked into the washroom mirror after the showdown with Elliot. Yes, he had won. But how had he done it? The same as Elliot. He had played the corporate game according to corporate rules, dragging in the whole syphilis affair, dragging Vanessa's life up for Vulkner's scrutiny, dragging Gaye's name before her stepfather. Yes, even Chamberfield had been right. He cared about Vanessa, and deeply. Yet he had not taken Elliot's offer, had gambled her job and livelihood.

He turned down Fiftieth, past the sunken outdoor garden restaurant at Rockefeller Plaza, toward the white RBI tower over on the west side of Sixth. The normal masses of tourists lined the walls, looking down onto the people seated below. Jacqueline used to bring him ice skating there. The duck pond up at Grosse Point came back to mind, the evening he told Papa Goodhart he was leaving advertising for television. What was he then, no more than a kid, a kid with grandiose dreams of changing television! Well, now he was in the position to do just that, but he knew better. Not much change would come. The system wasn't built to withstand much change. He'd come a long way since that evening at Grosse Point. Why the hell was he feeling so low?

He crossed Sixth Avenue and looked up the sheer white walls of the building. There, forty-four floors up, so far up that the stories blended together in indistinguishable perspective, a new office of power awaited him. So what the hell if he had let his ends justify his means. Katina can call it selling out as much as she damn well pleased, but to him, at that moment, as he entered the revolving door, it was merely taking a shortcut. Eventually he would have made it anyway. If not now, then in a few months or years. The showdown yesterday wouldn't change him. He was the same inside, the same idealistic kid, wasn't he?

The elevator whisked him to his floor. He was on his way to join them. He was one of them now. After three long months, a winner again.

The receptionist smiled broadly and wished him a good afternoon. Heads buried over papers in the small cubbyhole offices suddenly shot up as he passed. He was the new king of the floor now, and they knew who buttered their bread.

The corner office, Elliot's old room, was now his. Gloria was on her smudged hands and knees, pushing files into the interior office section. She looked tired but happy as she bounced up. "Look at your desk."

It was covered with telegrams in neat little piles. "Not to mention the phone calls. I got a girl from the office pool just to answer your line." Her enthusiasm bubbled over as she watched him read through a couple of the cables before dropping them back with the rest. "How was lunch?"

"Fine, thank you." He walked to the window and looked down. Tiny toy figures scurried along the sidewalks. They could probably be obliterated by one big gob of spit.

"Mr. Vulkner's office called. They want you to call back right away."

"Are they all set up in the conference room?"

"They said they'd yell when they were. I've never seen a news conference before."

"It won't be very special, but you can come if you like."

"Oh, yes." She left him standing by his desk, picking out a random telegram to read. There was one from Papa Goodhart. He'd love to call the old man, just to talk. Well, there wasn't time for that now. His phone buzzed. It took a moment to register. He leaned over to pick it up.

"It's Vanessa Langley on line two," said Gloria. "She says it's urgent. Shall I put her on?"

"Vanessa calling? Yes, yes I'll take it." He hit the appropriate button and sat down. "Hello, Vanessa, how are you?"

"Phillip, I . . . I just wanted to. . . ."

"What's wrong, dear? What's the matter?" There was silence on the other end. He could hear her struggle to control her breathing. "Vanessa?"

"Joe died during the night."

Phillip's head sank to the back of the chair. The receiver slipped a little in his hand.

The small broken voice on the opposite end continued. "I just called Colin. He told me about your promotion. Congratulations. I've . . . I've quit the show."

Joe's dead, and Vanessa quit the show. The facts slowly seeped into his brain. Automatically, as if it had been programed, the shooting schedule of *Affair Of The Heart* leapt before his eyes. Valerie was already in the hospital. The operation was planned for tomorrow's episode. Something will have to go wrong and Maude can kill her off while she's under surgery. JESUS CHRIST ALMIGHTY!

His eyes snapped open and he yanked himself forward. The machinery in his brain had worked instinctively. It had focused on the problems of the show. He hadn't even thought of the girl on the phone. The waste, the horror of it all. His own involvement. Revulsion swept over him. "Vanessa . . . Vanessa, I can't tell—"

"Please, Phillip, don't. I didn't call you for that. I just wanted to tell you I'm leaving—tonight."

"Where?"

"I have to get away. We buried Joey this afternoon. I can't sit in this apartment any longer. I just wanted to tell you good-bye . . . and good luck. That's all." She was struggling hard with her tears.

"Vanessa, where are you going?"

"I don't know. I'm just going to buy a ticket to somewhere. Somewhere where there's a beach and some sun."

She was leaving. He couldn't let her do that. "I want to see you before you go. I'd like to. . . ."

He rubbed his hand across his forehead, trying to clear the cobwebs that entrapped his mind and tongue. "Vanessa, I'm tied up here until half past five. Please let me see you after that. I want to say—oh, shit! Vanessa I don't know what to say."

"No, there's no time, and it's better left as it is. I wish you success with your new position. I'm sure you'll do well. Good-bye, Phillip." She hung up.

He remained seated, the phone receiver pressed against his face. A man had died. He was implicated. A baby was lost, a marriage ruined, and he was at fault. And Vanessa, the woman he had sold out to keep his own job. Who was he kidding? He sold her out in a gamble. He was exactly like the others. Out for Number One. To play is to win. To win is to destroy. We become the bloody masks we project. His eyes . . . he had seen his eyes in the mirror after he'd won: steel hard and vicious, capable of destroying anyone.

He shoved open his door and walked past Gloria. The conference room on her left bustled with newsmen, reporters, columnists, and photographers. The white arc lamps were already warming up. Barry jostled his way to the doorway and grabbed Phillip's arm. "Hi, Phil, they're about set up. The old man should be on his way down." Phillip nodded and left him standing in the hall.

The executive washroom was once again empty. Everyone was waiting for his appearance in the conference room. He walked over to the mirror and turned on the cold-water tap. And again he examined his eyes. The confidence was gone. He looked older, more tired. He could see only defeat. On his day of victory he saw defeat.

Phillip wasn't aware of the exact moment he made his decision. It could have been when he was drying off his face, or after he returned to his new office, detouring by a rear hallway around the conference room. He closed the blinds and buzzed for Gloria. He dictated two letters for her to type. One was to Vulkner, and the other was for herself. Then he opened his briefcase as she sat stunned into silence, watching him load things, a few letters, some books, and a framed painting a friend had given him in memory of a pleasant afternoon. He took the statue of the horse from his desk. He held it out to Gloria and told her he'd like her to have it. "I don't think I'll be needing it any more."

He came out from behind his desk, leaned over, and kissed the girl's tear-stained cheek.

By the time he reached the elevator his back was straighter, and when he reached the revolving door in the lobby he sensed some of the old jauntiness back in his stride. By the corner he felt better than he had in years and he entered the phone booth in a mood that one could almost describe as a high.

She picked up the phone on the third ring.

31.

She stood alone at the base of the stairs leading to the ticket booths, a large and a small bag beside her, her eyes shaded by a pair of dark glasses. She stood solemnly waiting, a silent island in a busy sea washing across the marble floor of the modernistic terminal.

He watched her, studied her, and tried to understand the why of it all. Where were they heading? What would they do? Were they to be together or apart?

Times and numbers and distant lands were announced on the speakers overhead. Faces changed and lights glittered . . . taxis pulled in and out, the glass window reflecting the images of their charges. Which place would they choose.

Where would they go? Perhaps it didn't matter. This would be the first uncharted course of his life. The first unscheduled stop. They would start together, maybe they'd finish together.

Something made Vanessa turn and she caught sight of him standing beside the pillar. And when their eyes met, they began to move. Blurs of heads and other faces passed between them as they came closer and closer together, and when they reached one another he kissed her face, and they held as tightly as they could.